**An excerpt from *Making a Marriage Deal* by Sophia Singh Sasson**

# "During the parties, there may be an expectation for us to kiss...

"Our first time shouldn't be in front of a crowd." They were going to build a life together. It was only natural that there would be physical affection between them. "If we look awkward, it might raise questions."

"I guess we better get on with it then."

Vivek reached out and traced his finger across her forehead and down her cheek, then tucked a wayward lock of hair behind her ear. She was glad for the towel still wrapped around her shoulders to hide the goose bumps that prickled her arms.

He leaned in. "Just because our marriage will be without love does not mean it needs to be without pleasure." His breath caressed her ear, and a sweet warmth spread through her. Pleasure? She had not thought about pleasure. They had not talked about pleasure.

He bent his head, and she closed her eyes, her entire body warming, anticipating, *wanting*...

An excerpt from *Her Best Kept Secret* by **Naima Simone**

# That voice. She knew that voice.

And if she hadn't immediately recognized it, the shiver skipping its way down her spine would've notified her of the person's identity.

Deliberately, she turned away from the partying guests and met a piercing pair of such light gray eyes they almost appeared silver. The intensity and beauty matched the voice. Hell, it matched everything about Joaquin Iverson.

He shifted, an infinitesimal amount forward, but it was enough to nearly dwarf her. Because goddamn, the man was huge.

From across the length of the wide room, she couldn't have gauged the breadth of shoulders and chest that any Seahawks linebacker would envy. Couldn't have guessed the looming height that had her suddenly feeling tiny and delicate, a feat that had never occurred before. Couldn't have surmised the power that emanated from his thick muscled arms and thighs, with a simple white dress shirt and dark dress pants clinging to them like shameless groupies. And at some point, he'd rolled back the sleeves, revealing corded forearms liberally covered in tattoos, and even more crept up toward the base of his throat.

Once more, her breath did that curious and irritating phenomenon where it evaporated into nothingness.

# SOPHIA SINGH SASSON

## &

### *USA TODAY* BESTSELLING AUTHOR
# NAIMA SIMONE

———

## MAKING A MARRIAGE DEAL
## &
## HER BEST KEPT SECRET

Recycling programs
for this product may
not exist in your area.

ISBN-13: 978-1-335-45754-7

Making a Marriage Deal & Her Best Kept Secret

Copyright © 2023 by Harlequin Enterprises ULC

Making a Marriage Deal
Copyright © 2023 by Sophia Singh Sasson

Her Best Kept Secret
Copyright © 2023 by Naima Simone

For questions and comments about the quality of this book, please contact us at CustomerService@Harlequin.com.

Harlequin Enterprises ULC
22 Adelaide St. West, 41st Floor
Toronto, Ontario M5H 4E3, Canada
www.Harlequin.com

**Printed in U.S.A.**

# CONTENTS

**Sophia Singh Sasson** puts her childhood habit of daydreaming to good use by writing stories she wishes will give you hope, make you laugh, cry, and possibly snort tea from your nose. She was born in Bombay, India, has lived in Canada and currently resides in Washington, DC. She loves to read, travel, bake, scuba dive, make candles and hear from readers. Visit her at sophiasasson.com.

Visit the Author Profile page at Harlequin.com for more titles.

You can also find Sophia Singh Sasson on Facebook, along with other Harlequin Desire authors, at Facebook.com/HarlequinDesireAuthors!

Dear Reader,

Thank you for taking the time to read my book. Arranged marriages have been a part of many cultures for centuries and still exist in India today. They are often seen as forced marriages, but that is not true. Just as online dating is used as a way to meet people who understand what you are looking for, marriage arrangements are a way to get set up with others who are ready to settle down. Think of it as a global dating service run by parents and relatives.

I'm excited to share Vivek and Hema's journey with you. If you've read the previous books in the series, you'll remember Vivek as the fiancé who was left at the wedding mandap in *Running Away with the Bride*. His parents had an arranged marriage and have been happy for decades. That's what he wants, too, but after his last experience, he's convinced he can't open his heart again. Hema has also been hurt, not just in love, but by a dark family secret that ruined her trust in marriage.

I hope you enjoy their story. Hearing from readers makes my day, so please email me at Sophia@SophiaSasson.com, tag me on Twitter @sophiasasson, Instagram @sophia_singh_sasson, Facebook/authorsophiasasson, or find me on Goodreads, BookBub @sophiasinghsasson or my website, www.sophiasasson.com.

Love,

*Sophia*

# MAKING A MARRIAGE DEAL

## Sophia Singh Sasson

This book is dedicated to all those who feel
that love will never happen for them.
It will. Keep your heart open.

## Acknowledgments

Thank you to the awesome Harlequin Desire
editorial team, in particular Stephanie Doig.

It's lonely being an author,
but the amazing community of South Asian
romance writers always keeps me going.

Last and most important,
I wouldn't be an author without the
love and support of my husband.
Love you, Tom!

# One

It wasn't at all like the movies. Hema peered over the railing as the ship pulled away from the dock. There were no crowds of people waving goodbye, no balloons or streamers wishing bon voyage. Just a few bored-looking dock workers watching the ship's bowlines get winched into the hull. The spa deck where she stood was empty. Blue-and-white loungers were aligned in perfect rows waiting for bodies to lie in the sun. They'd be empty for most of the cruise. Indians were loath to tan in the sun. The hot tub bubbled, sloshing a little water over the edge. The sounds of the city dulled as the cruise ship moved gracefully away from the Manhattan dock and eased its way into the Hudson River.

Where were all the aunties and uncles? They'd

been all over her when they boarded. *Such a beautiful bride you will make.* They must be getting dressed for the night's festivities. She'd left her friends enjoying the open bar in the lounge downstairs in search of fresh air and solitude.

It was mid-June, and while the sun beamed warm, the breeze had a bite to it. She wished she'd brought a shawl; the cotton yellow-and-cream sundress gave her little warmth. Seven nights, eight days. When the ship returned to New York, she'd have a new life, living a world away from her home in India, and married to a man she hardly knew. *Am I doing the right thing? Is it really worth it?* She stared at the skyscrapers and imagined her new life as a doctor, and as the wife of a prominent New York businessman. It was easy to imagine being a doctor. It was what she'd been dreaming of for a long time. Being a wife? Could she play the part?

The cruise terminal shrank from view as the ship gained speed. What if things didn't work out? What if she was wrong about everything? Her chest tightened and she leaned forward on the deck, sucking in the fishy smell of the Hudson River. She shook the self-doubt away. If she could get into the most competitive residency in the world, she could do anything.

"Don't jump now. The river is filthy. Wait till we get to the open water."

She startled as the man she was about to marry came up behind her. Vivek was dressed casually in board shorts and an untucked white polo shirt that set off his deep brown skin. His feet were bare like hers. He leaned forward and rested his forearms on the polished wood railing, close to hers. As he stared out at the passing Manhattan skyline, she studied his profile. Thick black eyelashes fanned across his dark eyes, his profile perfectly angular with high cheekbones, a straight nose and a slightly rounded chin. He had shaved. There was a tiny dot of red where he'd cut himself on the jawline. He was a good-looking man. Hot, even. Had she met him socially, she'd have been attracted to him.

"Jumping wouldn't help," she said. "I'm an excellent swimmer."

"One more thing I didn't know about you."

"There's a lot we don't know about each other."

"Having second thoughts?" He was trying too hard to keep his voice light.

*Yes!* The shoreline was still in sight. Thirty-minute swim, tops.

"No," she said, injecting as much certainty in her voice as she could muster.

He turned towards her, and she met his gaze. His eyes were the rich brown of an old sandalwood tree. A flutter resonated deep in her belly and made its way through her body. *It's nerves.*

"If you've changed your mind, now's the time."

She almost laughed. *It's much too late for that.* One thousand, three hundred sixty-nine of their relatives and friends had flown in from various corners of the world and were on board this ship. She doubted there was a single corner of the eighteen hundred cabins for her to hide in if she called off the wedding. Plus, she could never do that to Vivek. Not after what had happened to him the last time he was at the wedding *mandap*.

She began shaking her head, but he placed his hand on hers. The warmth of his touch reached up her arm and spread through her chest. *He's a good man. A kind man. The type of man to marry.* "You will have all the things I promised you. Financial support to pursue your medical residency, freedom to do what you want… There is only one thing I need you to promise. That you will never, ever lie or embarrass me."

She nodded. He wasn't asking for much, not compared to what she was getting in the bargain.

"I need you to be sure."

She placed her other hand on top of his. "I'm going into this with my eyes wide open. You're not asking anything of me that I haven't carefully considered. We made a deal, one that benefits both of us. You get a wife, and I get to pursue my dream of training in robotic surgery. We're starting our marriage with honesty and friendship. That's a lot more than most relationships."

*What about love?* She tamped down on the annoying voice in her heart that still thought she could love again after what had happened with Arun.

The waves broke across the ship as they eased into the waters of Sandy hook bay. The wind picked up and she shivered. Vivek walked over to the hot tub area and grabbed one of the rolls of blue and white towels that were neatly stacked on a shelf. He

wrapped it around her shoulders. She smiled gratefully at him. His chivalry was one of the first things
she'd noticed about him when they met a month ago
in New Delhi. He unfailingly opened doors, pulled
out her chair, and stood when she left the table. *The
type of man to marry.*

She turned to see Vivek staring at her intently as
though he could see right into her soul.

"I was just thinking about what it'll be like to live
in New York. I've travelled around the world, but
India has always been my home."

He put his hands on her shoulders and she was
a little surprised at how comforting his touch felt.
"Don't worry, you'll hardly notice you're in New
York. My neighbors are just as nosy as they are in
India, my parents live one floor down and will con-
stantly interfere, and our chef makes the best *rajma
chawal.*"

She smiled. The kidney beans and rice dish was
her favorite.

"And you're welcome to take my private jet to
India any time you miss your family."

"I appreciate that, though I doubt I'll have much
time once residency starts. The first year is intern-
ship, and they work us pretty hard." So hard, in fact,
that at least one resident failed out each year. Would
she be one of those? What if she couldn't cut it? She'd
still be married and would've given up her life for
nothing.

"See, you won't have time to be homesick."

He straightened, and she had to look up to meet

his gaze. "Actually, I came looking for you because there's something I want to bring up." He cleared his throat. "During the parties, there may be an expectation for us to kiss. Our first time shouldn't be in front of a crowd."

That was thoughtful of him. While they weren't planning on a traditional marriage, they were going to build a life together, and it was only natural that there would be physical affection between them. It was nice that he wanted their first time to be special.

"If we look awkward, it might raise questions."

*Not so thoughtful after all.*

"I guess we better get on with it then." She resisted the urge to close her eyes and pucker her lips like a cartoon character.

He reached out and traced his finger across her forehead and down her cheek, then tucked a wayward lock of hair behind her ear. She was glad for the towel still wrapped around her shoulders to hide the goose bumps that prickled her arms. He leaned in. "Just because our marriage will be without love does not mean it needs to be without pleasure." His breath caressed her ear, and a sweet warmth spread through her. *Pleasure?* She had not thought about pleasure. They had not talked about pleasure.

He bent his head, and her eyes closed instinctively, her entire body warming, anticipating, wanting. He touched his lips to hers so lightly that she wasn't sure if it was him or a kiss of the wind. She leaned in closer, but he was already backing away.

"*Aare*, there will be plenty of time for that." Hema's

eyes flew open, and she turned to see her mother approach, her aunt trailing behind her. She stepped away from Vivek as if she was a teenage girl caught with her boyfriend. The two sisters were dressed in perfectly tied sarees and teetered on heels that weren't meant to be worn on the twelfth floor of a cruise ship sailing into the wind.

"The engagement party starts in thirty minutes, and look at you two. Only six days to your wedding. You can wait that long, can't you?" Her aunt Reshma's voice was teasing as she took Hema's hand.

Hema shook her head. "*Maasi*, come on, I'm not a kid anymore."

But Reshma wasn't having it. She wagged a finger at Vivek. "I suggest you also go get dressed. Your brother is looking for you." Tugging on Hema's arm, she led her towards the elevator banks. Hema turned to look over her shoulder. Vivek stood grinning at her and another pulse zinged through her chest. The decision has seemed so simple a month ago but now she wasn't so sure. *What have I gotten myself into?*

"Tell me again how this plan makes any sense."

Vivek looked through the tags on the neatly hung sherwanis squished together in the closet. You'd think as the groom he'd be entitled to one of the suites, but his parents decided there were too many VIPs and not enough suites to go around, so he had a regular room that barely fit a queen bed and a little side table. At least it had a balcony, which was where his brother

Vikram now stood, leaning against the door, creating a wind tunnel into his room.

While the two brothers were often mistaken for twins, Vikram was his exact opposite in personality. Where he preferred to operate from the shadows, Vikram loved being the center of attention.

"It's simple. Hema's parents will not financially support her medical residency in the US unless she gets married. She's tired of being set up with men who don't understand her career aspirations. She's happy to have an arrangement where she gets to pursue her dreams." He checked the tags on the clothes that his assistant had clearly labeled with the date and event name. He selected the correct one.

"That part I know. What's in it for you?"

"Our parents off my back. A respectable wife for society. She's an intelligent, beautiful woman who understands what I can and cannot give her and accepts it."

"She's not your type."

"I didn't know I had a type."

"She's vivacious and fun, and you're a hall monitor."

Vivek threw a pillow at his brother. They were only two years apart and had always been close. Vikram caught the pillow and threw it back.

"Seriously, you've met her, what, twice?"

"Three times counting today."

Vikram snorted.

"Look, we may have only physically met twice before today, but we've video chatted, emailed, texted.

Neither of us took this decision lightly. We discussed it, slept on it, then discussed it again."

"This is not the way to get over Divya."

A chill went down his spine. "I'm over Divya." He slipped into his sherwani and looked in the mirror. He was tired of being reminded that the love of his life had run away from the wedding *mandap* with a complete stranger. To add salt to the wound, she was now married to that stranger.

"This is not about Divya. It's about getting on with my life."

"You hardly know this girl. How do you know she won't jump into a lifeboat and hightail it out of here?"

Vivek rolled his eyes and slipped on the traditional *jutti*. It was a beautiful gold shoe with a pointy toe, but the leather was stiff as cardboard.

"Hema is not going to run. She knows what betrayal is like. She wouldn't do that to me."

"I was kidding, Vivek." Vikram said solemnly.

Vivek put his laundry in the closet and slammed the door shut. He was tired of reliving his last wedding. The story was the butt of social media memes for weeks. Just when it had died down, Divya became a singing sensation, and the story stuck like a stubborn stain on a white carpet. He couldn't take a business meeting or attend a social gathering without Divya's name coming up. *Did she really run away during the wedding? You had no idea? Is it true she didn't know the guy she ran away with? How come she married him?* The same questions circulated through business dinners, cocktail parties, and hallway conversations during boardroom meeting breaks. The worst one was, *Are you okay?* Every time Divya released a new record: *Are you okay?* As if that's all his life was about. He was done with it.

Marrying Hema would change the narrative. Not only was she okay with the idea of a pragmatic marriage, she was the daughter of a prominent industrialist. In the Indian social circles, he'd won the marriage match lottery. Hema elevated his social and business standing. Since the wedding cards had been sent, questions about Divya had stopped.

"I'm just saying that it's not too late to rethink this insane plan. You can't marry someone you hardly know. Have you thought through all the things that could go wrong? We're talking about a lifetime commitment here."

He had thought about it, and he'd set up three simple rules for his life once Divya left:

Rule 1: Don't develop feelings for another woman.

Rule 2: Don't get in a romantic situation where you're not in control.

Rule 3: Set rules for the relationship and stick to them.

Vivek smirked at Vikram. "I know what I'm doing. Nothing is going to go wrong."

# Two

"Hema, if you don't know how to tie a saree, then why choose one?" Her maasi rolled her eyes as she draped the saree *pallu* across Hema's chest, pinning the delicate material to her shoulder so it stayed it place.

"Because I knew I had you to tie it for me," she said cheekily, blowing an air kiss towards her aunt. When she was a child, she'd often wished her maasi was her real mother. The two sisters couldn't be more different. Where her mother was cold and stiff, her maasi was warm, fun, and loving.

Reshma bent down and adjusted the pleats that formed the skirt of the saree, making sure each fold was the same size and creased along the seam. "All this happened so fast. I didn't even have time to buy you a present."

"Your coming is the only present I want." Hema said sincerely.

Reshma stood and put her hand under Hema's chin. "Is this marriage what you truly want? Do you love Vivek?"

Hema blinked. *Love*. How could she talk to her aunt about love? Her maasi had rebelled against her family for love. She had eloped with the love of her life, not caring that she'd been disowned by her parents and lost her sizable inheritance. Her husband died of cancer just a few years after their marriage. Though it had been over a decade, she hadn't remarried, despite the fact that she was only forty-five.

Hema had an answer ready. She'd known that her maasi would ask, and she'd practiced the words to say. *He's a kind man, the type of man you marry. He understands me, wants to support me. What more can I ask for? The words soured in her mouth. How many people would she keep lying to?*

"Vivek and I have an understanding. He's going to support me financially so I can do my medical residency in New York."

Reshma gasped. "You are marrying him so you can do a medical residency? Come on, Hema. There has to be a better way. If it's money you need, I can help you out."

Hema hugged her aunt. The woman worked as a kindergarten teacher and was still paying off the exorbitant medical bills from her husband's illness. Yet she knew without a doubt that her aunt would sell a kidney to support her if Hema asked.

"It's not just about the medical residency. I have to get married at some point, and Vivek is a good guy. The type of guy you marry."

"You sound like your mother. There is no *type* of man you marry. You marry the person you love."

Her aunt couldn't understand. She was of the same generation as her mother, where marriage defined a woman's life. For Hema, her career was going to be what gave her purpose and meaning.

"My career is the love of my life." The tears she'd been holding back escaped her eyes. There was a time when she'd been naive, believing that her life could be a Bollywood movie: that she could have love, marriage and her career. Now she was focused on dreams that were within her power to make come true.

"No, no my child. You can't settle. You are so young; you don't know what it's like to live a life alone. Your soul mate will come along."

"Maasi, I don't need or want a man to make me happy. I've thought through this very carefully." Hema lifted her head. "I get along very well with Vivek, and he will support my career. It's a good decision."

"Don't mind my saying so, dear, but you can be very impulsive. You don't always think through the long-term consequences of your actions."

Hema rolled her eyes. "I've been planning my medical career since secondary school. How is that impulsive?"

"When you were a little girl, you wanted a dog, but your mother wasn't going to let you have one. Most children would have begged, pleaded and bargained with their parents. But not you. What you did was get a dog from a neighbor who had puppies and paid your maid from your pocket money to keep him in the servants' quarters."

Hema smiled at the memory. She'd gotten away with it for a whole month before her mother found out. At that point, her father had intervened and allowed Hema to keep the dog as long he didn't come into the house. He'd even paid for a doghouse to be built on the property.

"Darling child, when you want something really badly, you'll do whatever it takes to get it. Make sure you aren't making the wrong decision because you want this residency so much."

Her heart clenched. *So what if I am?* No one understood that becoming a surgeon wasn't just a career ambition. It was her purpose in life. It wasn't just that she'd worked hard to get this residency. It was an achievement, one that was hers alone. Her father hadn't made a donation to the program. No favors had been called in. She had done this on her own. When she'd gotten the email letting her know that the school was offering her a spot, it was the moment she'd known that she had finally gotten control of her life. Once she did this residency and became a practicing physician, she would dictate the terms of her life. A man, whether it was her father or her husband, wouldn't decide the next steps in her life.

"Maasi, it's not just about the residency. This marriage is going to give me my freedom."

"How is that?"

"Have you forgotten what it's like to be a woman born in India? Even a privileged one?" Reshma focused on lining up the pleats on Hema's skirt, and refused to look at her. If anything, her maasi should understand her position. "Despite that fact that I'm educated, I have no way to support myself financially, and therefore I have no control over the major decisions in my life. I love Dad with all my heart, but he's very old-fashioned in his thinking. He insisted on seeing me married." She took a breath. Hema was close to her father; he had always been her ally. Except when it had come to her having an independent career without the protection of a respectable marriage. Without her father's financial support, not only couldn't Hema afford to live in New York on a resident's meager salary, she wouldn't have been able to get the necessary visa for her residency. She needed to show financial means to support herself and without her father's signature and bank balance assuring her financial needs, she wouldn't have gotten her work papers. It was the one point of contention in the otherwise great relationship she had with her father. He'd supported her in everything she'd ever wanted to do, except this time he'd insisted she get married first. She had argued, screamed, cried but he remained unmovable, and she had to come to terms with the fact that she had to get married. "Vivek has my Indian values, but he's a modern man. He wants a partner in life, someone who understands him. Once I train in the US, I'll have options. I can practice almost anywhere I want, make my own decisions, live my life the way I want. Of all people, you should understand why it's important for me to get my independence."

Reshma was silent as she finished tying the saree and Hema considered her reflection in the mirror. The soft pink chiffon saree embroidered with delicate silver thread and tiny diamond-like beads shimmered on her body. The blouse ended right below her bra line and was backless, held together in the back with tiny beaded strings. The skirt started right below her belly button, and the slightly see-through material showed off her waist perfectly. "Nice job, Maasi."

"Just remember one thing, Hema." She turned towards her aunt, bracing for another admonition. "If you need a getaway car or boat, I'll drive."

Hema was trying to focus on what Maasi was saying, but her attention was drawn to Vivek walking towards her. The engagement party was in full swing. The lido deck's indoor and outdoor space had been transformed with twinkling lights, yards of fabric draped artfully, and buffet tables lined with little plates of samosas, chaat and mini glasses of mango lassi.

As he approached, she found it hard to pull her eyes away from him. How had she not noticed how handsome he was? He looked swoon-worthy in an understated sherwani. She'd noticed him earlier, but for the last hour, he'd been surrounded by wedding guests. Likewise, she'd been accosted by various aunties and uncles who she didn't recognize but pretended to, grateful that Indian culture dictated that all elders, regardless of actual relationship, be referred to as aunty or uncle.

"Reshma Aunty, you look sensational." Vivek remarked.

"Of course I do. Where do you think Hema gets her good looks from? But please, call me Maasi from now. Aunty is for those oldies whose names you can't remember."

Both Hema and Vivek laughed and Reshma quietly excused herself.

"How many people do you actually recognize at this party?" Vivek grinned.

"Aside from you, my parents and my maasi? Maybe one. I saw a few of my medical school friends earlier, and I strongly suspect that they're in the casino, having fun."

"You look amazing, by the way." The way his voice dropped sent a little shiver through her.

"Nisha designed this for me. I met her at that party in New York where you and I first met. Remember how awkward that was…" *Why am I babbling?* "Actually, Nisha recently married Sameer, Divya's brother." The look that crossed his face immediately made her regret her words. *Why did I have to bring up Divya?*

"So, how many times has someone made a joke about how my previous bride ran away?"

Hema relaxed at the amusement in his voice. "I've lost count. How many times has someone mentioned that my parents had originally arranged my marriage to Arjun, Divya's older brother?"

He pretended to count on his fingers, then flipped his hand, grinning. "Just about every person who I've talked to."

"They talk as if they're sharing some big secret with us." She lowered her voice and leaned in close. "Did you know that…"

"…quite a story, don't you think?" he finished for her, imitating the deep baritone of an older man.

They both laughed.

"Arjun and Rani are here, you know," he said quietly.

She nodded. "I know."

"Doesn't that bother you?"

She shook her head. "I didn't want to marry Arjun any more than he wanted to marry me. I was so glad when he fell in love with Rani. I'm happy they're here. I always thought of Arjun as a brother of sorts, and Rani is amazing."

Vivek frowned. "But I thought you said you'd been betrayed by the man you loved."

"I was talking about Arun. I was dating him at the time that Arjun and I were supposed to get engaged. That's why I was so glad that Arjun broke it off. At the time, I wanted to marry Arun."

A lump formed in her throat. What she was too embarrassed to tell Vivek was that she'd been stupid enough to fall for Arun. He'd turned out to be a con man. There would be no such problems with Vivek. Not only had he agreed to an airtight pre-nup without so much as a question, but he had also been honest with her from the beginning that he couldn't love her and didn't expect her to love him. There was no pretense between them.

*There is also no love.*

"Well, you don't have to worry. Divya declined the invitation to this wedding."

She hadn't been worried. In fact, she and Divya were close friends, and she'd been upset that Divya hadn't come to the wedding. She hadn't wanted to steal Hema's thunder by being there and having people rehash the disastrous wedding with Vivek.

"Have you seen her since…"

"Since she ran off with another man?" He shook his head. "I've talked to her, and I had my assistant send a wedding gift."

Were things still unresolved between Vivek and Divya? Hema had confronted Arun after seeing the pictures her friend sent of him kissing the other girl. He'd woven a convincing tale about how she was an ex-girlfriend who was trying to reconcile. Hema had been dumb enough to believe him. The second time he'd been unfaithful to her, she hadn't had the strength for an in-person showdown.

"Are you ready for this type of life?" Vivek gestured vaguely towards the party. "Business in New York is conducted at cocktail parties and fancy dinners."

"It's no different in Delhi. My earliest memory is watching my mother get ready for a dinner party. It's a life I'm used to." But was it a life she wanted? She shook the thought away. The only time her mother seemed happy was when she was getting dressed and looking forward to a social event. The parties were a highlight of her parents' otherwise miserable marriage. "I imagine the New York scene is not much different than Delhi: wives competing to see who has the bigger diamonds, husbands comparing the size of their…their…"

"Airplanes?" He grinned at her. "It does get tedious after a while, but eventually it becomes routine. Show up, have a cocktail, smile, write a check if it's a charity event, and leave as soon as dessert is served."

"What about the dancing?"

His eyes crinkled at the corners. "You like to dance?"

She tilted her head. "With the right partner."

He held out his hand. She hesitated, then placed her hand in his. They locked eyes, and little flutters danced deep in her belly. He twirled her, then pulled her into the middle of the floor. It was supposed to be the pool and casual deck, but the loungers and outdoor tables and chairs had been cleared, and a live band was playing soft music. He pulled her close and placed his hand on the cool skin of her back. His hand clasped around hers. The heat of his body warmed hers. They were an inch apart, and she was too warm, her skin too sensitive.

The band was playing the instrumental version of a Bollywood love melody. He knew how to lead. He put slight pressure on her back and tugged gently on her hand. His movements were slight and well-timed.

His thumb moved across the bare skin on her back, and she inhaled sharply.

He leaned in so his breath caressed her ear. "How am I as a dance partner?"

*Freaking amazing.*

"You could use some practice."

He grinned and twirled her again. This time he pulled her close enough that her breasts skimmed his chest. She was grateful for the built-in padded bra so her hardened nipples didn't betray the heat coursing through her. *It is just a slow dance!* She looked up at him and put some distance between their bodies. He bent his head. Their noses were almost touching. If she tilted her face ever so slightly and leaned forward, she could kiss him. Her every cell was aware of him. The woodsy smell of his cologne, the heat of his body, the touch of his hand on her back, the whisper of his breath across her lips. Just when she thought he was about to lean in the last centimeter and kiss her, he pulled back and dipped her. A bunch of people clapped.

She caught her breath. Did she really want a physical relationship with Vivek? When they'd discussed it during a video chat, they'd decided that having sex would be a mutual decision. She hadn't been intimate with anyone since Arun. What if Vivek was terrible in bed? What if he was fantastic? Their relationship was already so complicated. They'd talked every day for the last month. She thought they'd discussed everything there was to negotiate for their unusual relationship, but there was so much more.

"Warning. Incoming."

She followed his eye movement to see both their mothers barreling down on them.

"You two are just too sweet." Hema's mother gestured to Vivek to lower his head. He rolled his eyes, then complied. She waved some bills across their heads. The money would be given to the staff working the event. It was an old tradition to ward off the evil eye or anyone who might wish them harm.

Hema liked Vivek's mother. Unlike her own mother who was proper and stiff, Vivek's mother, Seema aunty, as she used to call her, was effusive and affectionate. She put an arm around Hema now. "Come, *beti*. It's time for the ceremony."

She led Hema to the indoor/outdoor patio area. The dining tables and chairs had been cleared from the outdoor dining area. A large silver tray sat on a pedestal. Two ring boxes sat on the tray along with a lit *diya*, marigold flowers, and sweets. Gold-and-maroon cloth was draped across the windows and fluttered in the wind. The ship was somewhere off the coast of Virginia as it moved south towards the Caribbean, and the temperature had risen. The breeze was pleasantly cool, tempering the hot sun that hung just above the horizon in a blaze of red and orange.

Guests had already gathered, and Hema and Vivek took their place in front of the tray. Hema's father was given a microphone, which he tapped a little too loudly, then gave a nervous laugh. "Ladies and gents, thank you for gracing us with your auspicious presence on this occasion of my daughter's wedding."

her head and he bent his. His lips parted, but then he pulled back. *Enough of this.* She grabbed a fistful of his sherwani and jerked his head down, lifting herself up on tiptoe to meet his lips. His surprise lasted barely a second. Then his mouth was hot on hers, exploring, pushing, tasting. His hand pressed on the bare section of her back as she deepened the kiss. He slid his hand under the saree blouse, and she pressed her body against his. *Does he want me as much as I want him?*

His hand was warm against her back and his body hard against hers. A breeze wisped its way across their hot faces, and he broke the kiss. He stared at her, and for a second, she was sure he was going to grab her and kiss her senseless. Then he turned away from her and tugged on his sherwani. "Well, I'm glad we got that over with."

*Over with?* The kiss was a checkbox for him?

"I guess I better get going."

He was almost to the door when she found her voice. "Can I ask you something?"

He turned towards her.

"What happens if you end up wanting more?"

"What do you mean?"

"What if—ten years down the line—you meet someone and fall in love?"

"I won't."

"How can you be so sure?"

"Because I've already been in love, and fallen hard. It sucks. I'm not going to put myself on the line like that again." He opened the door then turned around again. "But even if that happens, I need you to know that once we take those seven circles around the sacred fire, we're tied for life."

She should have been reassured, but her stomach coiled into a hard knot.

# Three

Vivek woke up with a start when he realized what he'd missed last night, and slapped his head. He hadn't asked her what happened if *she* wanted more. He knew his own heart, but not hers. He got out of bed and hopped into the shower. There were a lot of things he didn't know about Hema. Like her ability to turn him on with just a kiss. He had been seconds away from ripping the saree off her last night and taking her right on the deck of her cabin. He had no doubt that she would've let him. The only thing stopping him was the realization that he'd wanted her bad. Too bad. There was only one other time in his life when he hadn't had control over his emotions, and he didn't intend to go back to that place.

He turned the water colder, hoping the temperature would clear his thoughts. A physical relation-ship would make their marriage a lot more real than he intended.

He dressed in shorts and a T-shirt and made his way to the lido deck. The decorations from the night before were gone, and the deck was back to an in-door and outdoor dining area. A scrumptious buffet of fruits, pancakes, waffles, bacon, sausages, eggs, oatmeal, cereals and potatoes was laid out. He loaded his plate with fruits and waffles and walked to the outside seating section.

Only one table was occupied.

"Avoiding the crowds or feeling lonely?"

Hema smiled and waved him to the chair be-side her. She was wearing a loose cotton T-shirt and shorts. Her hair was scraped back into a ponytail, and her face was clean of makeup. He'd noticed how beautiful she was before, but how had he missed the way his pulse kicked up when he looked at her?

"The crowd is dining in the restaurant, so I came up here. I'm trying to pace myself with the aunties."

"Let me guess. They want to know when we'll have kids."

She grinned. "Worse. They want to know which of my friends is single so they can try to set them up."

"I warned my mom that seven days in close quar-ters was a bad idea. Bored aunties and uncles are bound to get up to mischief."

She leaned forward conspiratorially. "The key is to make sure we're not the target of their boredom."

"Have any suggestions?"

She pretended to think. "We need to sacrifice someone."

"Vikram's being a real pain in the ass."

"He's going to be my brother-in-law; I wouldn't feel right about it."

"Then we're going to have to hide."

She smiled, and his heart gave a kick. It was so easy to be with her.

"What do you plan to do today? she asked.

"I am going to hide in my cabin and take care of some business."

She nodded, but he hated the way her smile dropped. He almost wanted to change his mind and ask what she wanted to do but stopped himself. He wasn't courting Hema, wasn't trying to make her fall in love with him. Once they were married, they'd be living together but leading separate lives. It was best to start that dynamic right from the beginning.

"There's the honorary couple."

He groaned as Sameer and his new bride, Nisha, approached the table. He had avoided talking to Divya's brother since the night that he'd shown up to their New York hotel to beg Divya to come back to him. She hadn't been there, and Sameer had called security to escort him from the hotel after he refused to leave. The humiliation of that moment burned his soul. Yet another reminder of why he couldn't let anyone burrow into his heart so deeply that he lost control over himself.

He stood to shake Sameer's hand, and Hema gave

Nisha a hug. "I got so many compliments on the saree yesterday. I told everyone you designed it."

Vivek wanted nothing more than for the couple to walk away, but his Indian sensibilities made him invite them to sit. He hoped they would decline in favor of getting breakfast, but it was his bad luck that they'd already eaten.

Nisha and Hema began talking about Nisha's fashion label and upcoming shows. Sameer turned to Vivek. "Divya sends her regards. She didn't think it was appropriate to come to the wedding."

Vivek looked away. He'd fought with his mother about sending Divya an invitation, but there was no way to invite the entire family and exclude her without looking petty.

"I hope she's happy."

Sameer nodded. "Look, I'm now New York based—running the Mahal Hotel. I'm sure we're going to run into each other in social circles, so I want to clear the air. That night at the hotel..."

Vivek slapped him on the back. "It's forgotten. We're both on to a new chapter of our lives, the past is irrelevant."

Sameer stared at him a beat. Vivek wondered whether Nisha knew about the incident, and his chest burned. He never wanted Hema to find out about that moment. If he'd had his way, he'd have cut Divya and her family out of his life entirely. Unfortunately, that's now how it worked. The South Asian community was tight-knit, especially those who ran global businesses. Their social and business lives were connected like an electrical grid. Cutting off one connection could reverberate through their business deals and personal relationships.

Nisha and Sameer took their leave after extracting a promise that they'd have a meal or drink together later.

He caught Hema staring at him. "What was that intense discussion between you and Sameer?"

Vivek shrugged. "Just some old business." Aside from Sameer, only hotel security had witnessed his shame, and he planned to keep it that way.

He returned to his cabin and sat down in the balcony chair with this laptop. After completing his MBA at Harvard, he had worked for a prominent financial company before taking over his father's business. He'd grown the company nearly 25 percent in the first two years as CEO. But that success came at the price of a high profile in New York society. His missed the days when he was a nobody and his life was his own, when his business didn't get affected by his personal life. Many of their shareholders and business partners had been at his last wedding. It had been over a year, and he still saw pity in their eyes. His business relied on people giving him millions of dollars of their hard-earned money to invest. He'd had a hard time getting them to trust his instincts when all they saw was a groom who couldn't even keep his bride by his side. Investments had gone down more than 40 percent in the last year. But all that was already turning around. Since the invitations to the wedding had gone out, he'd been getting calls and emails. A number of the wedding guests had asked him for meetings. He was going to get back on top, and this time he wouldn't let his heart get in the way of his success.

He worked through the day. The evening festivity was a live music and dance show in the theater followed by an around-the-world dinner buffet. He dressed in chinos and a light blue shirt, open collar, and paired it with a khaki jacket. Both he and Hema were caught up with wedding guests throughout the evening. He caught sight of her every once in a while. She wore a royal-blue cocktail dress that was held up by thin shoulder straps and barely skimmed her knees. She moved with an easy grace, and his breath stuck in his chest every time she passed close enough for him to catch a whiff of her intoxicating perfume.

He finally caught up with her at the end of the evening. He'd come to think of the top deck as their spot. The sun had set, but the last rays clung to the sky in hues of pink, purple and orange. Feeling the warmth and humidity in the air, Vivek guessed that they were off the coast of Georgia. The deck was empty. The lounge chairs had been stacked and tied down. Below them, the lido deck was a hive of activity as staff went about setting up buffet tables. Vivek had lost count of the number of cuisines his mother had planned for the night. His mother had gone to extremes, as desperate as him to make people forget about the previous over-the-top wedding she'd planned.

"Glad to see you're still in one piece," he said.

"Only physically." She put a hand on her head dramatically. "Up here, I've suffered greatly today since you abandoned me."

"You know what they say, what doesn't kill you…"

"…makes you insane."

He touched her bare arm. "Was it really that bad?"

She shook her head. "Not at all. I enjoyed the day, actually. Your mother organized spa appointments, card games, jewelry shopping at the ship stores."

He'd forgotten about the spa and shopping on the ship. As much as he'd justified it to himself, he had wondered whether Hema had spent the day alone.

"Everyone was busy, so I was able to sneak away and spent the day in the library."

"You spent the day alone? What about your friends?"

"Are you kidding? Free spa? They were elbowing the aunties out of the way for appointments. I actually liked having the free time to catch up on my reading."

"Read anything good?"

"The different cell types in a squamous ovarian tumor."

"Light reading, then." He'd dated some pretty impressive women, but Hema was in a league of her own. He had learned that less than 1 percent of people who applied to the robotic surgery program in New York actually got in. It was a new and highly competitive program that required a background in surgery and engineering. Most medical students who wanted to do the program didn't even qualify to apply, let alone get in.

Hema grew quiet, staring at the deck below. He

followed her gaze and caught sight of Hema's parents. From the vigorous hand gesturing, it was pretty clear they were arguing.

"What is your parents' marriage like?" she asked after a few minutes.

"Nauseatingly loving. They had an arranged marriage, fell in love after the wedding and have been happily married. My father adores my mother, and she worships him. They have their little issues. She thinks my dad is too hard on me and doesn't really care for her mother-in-law, my *dadi*. My dad wishes she wouldn't spoil me and Vikram. Even their disagreements are cute." He had hoped to find the same thing when his parents set him up with Divya. His friends called him old-fashioned for believing in arranged marriage, but it wasn't as if he hadn't given traditional dating a chance. His first serious girlfriend had balked at the idea of living down the hall from his parents. *What adult man wants to be in proximity to his parents?* The kind whose parents had always supported him, who enjoyed talking stocks with his father and cricket with his mother. The second relationship to last more than a few months ended when he learned that his girlfriend was more interested in his credit card than him. That's when he realized why arranged marriages worked in his parents' generation. There was a pre-vetting of expectations, an assurance that the couple's interests were aligned. It cut out 80 percent of the work of figuring out if the person was with you for the right reasons. Or at least, that's what he'd thought. Divya had checked all the boxes, except the one that mattered the most. She didn't want him.

Hema sighed. "I wish I knew what that kind of marriage was like. I don't remember a single time when Ma's been happy. It always seems that she wants to be anywhere but in our house. I think my dad loved her once. I remember when I was young, he'd bring her imported chocolates and little trinkets from wherever he traveled for work. She would end up giving them to the servants. I've often wondered whether she was ever capable of love." She stopped abruptly as if she didn't want to say more. He placed a hand on her back.

She turned towards him. "Do you regret falling in love with Divya?"

He stared at the deck below. Hema's parents had moved out of sight. "Yes. Divya is the only thing I've failed at in my entire life. I was a straight A student in school, I got into an Ivy League university, and I've done well running my father's business. I had never failed at anything. Except love." Not only had he failed, he'd made a spectacle of himself and his family.

"Love is not a pass or fail. You don't get marks for doing it well or poorly."

"Don't we?" He leaned forward, looking down at the inky water below. "If I asked you to rate your parents' marriage, you'd give them an F. I'd give mine an A. Every single phase of our life is measured. How well we do in school, how good the college is that we get into, whether we marry up or down, and then it all repeats with our children."

"That's a really cynical way to look at life."

"It's reality."

"So, if Divya had married you, but you were both miserable in the marriage, would it still be a ten out of ten?"

He rolled his eyes. Hema was still a little naive. While accomplished, she'd lived a sheltered life under her parents' protection. She didn't have to deal with the sharks in the business world who were always circling, ready to move in as soon as they smelled blood. There had been an attempt at a hostile take-over of his family company right after the wedding scandal. A bunch of wealthy NRIs—nonresident Indians—had banded together to see if they could buy enough shares to have a controlling interest in his company. They thought that he'd be too busy licking his wounds and dealing with the scandal to notice. And it had almost worked. His company was still in jeapordy, at risk for a hostile takeover. Most of the major shareholders were invited to the wedding. It was a nice excuse to corner them and shore up their support.

"If Divya and I had gotten married, I would've kept her happy."

"You seem really sure of that."

"I am. My parents had an arranged marriage. They hardly knew each other, but they've been happy."

"Because they fell in love."

"Because they respect each other, they had shared

goals, and they wanted to build a life with each other. That's where I went wrong with Divya. I was so blind; I never bothered to stop and ask whether she wanted the same things I did."

"If she loved you back, but wanted different things, would you have still married her?"

The question punched him in the solar plexus. Divya had never shared her dreams of wanting to be a singer with him. He'd assumed that she was content with running her family business. They'd talked at length about business strategy and global markets. Would his feelings have changed if he knew that she wanted her life to take a different direction? He stared at the lifeboats on the deck below. During their safety briefing, the captain had proudly declared that he had never needed to use the lifeboats on any ship he piloted. It was a good goal in life, to never have to jump off a sinking ship.

"Let's not talk about Divya. She's history, and we have our life in front of us. I plan to make our marriage an A-plus."

She smiled, and his heart kicked. Hema had one of those smiles that reached up into her eyes and crinkled her nose just a little.

"Can I ask you a question?" He'd been waiting all day to ask her. She nodded, and he swallowed against his dry throat.

"You asked me last night what would happen if I wanted more. What if *you* want more than what this marriage can give you? If you want more than what *I* can give you?"

She looked down at her feet. The silence stretched between them, and his throat grew tighter.

"There is only one thing that is nonnegotiable for me. My medical career. As long as I have that, I will be fine."

"And what if you can't have that? I know you're marrying me so you can accept that residency at the New York hospital. But what happens if they cancel the program? Or…"

"…or this boat gets hit by an iceberg."

"We're in warm waters, no iceberg."

"Fine, a hurricane then. My point is that there is only so much that can be planned in life. We can't see the future, so we have to go with what feels right at the moment."

"I have the next twenty years planned out."

"I know." She chewed on her lip, then held out her hand. "What are you doing tomorrow?"

It was a port day. The ship was docking at George Town in the Cayman Islands. He had meetings scheduled at a couple of banks that his company used, and then he'd planned to come back to the boat and spend the day meeting with some shareholders and reviewing the latest earnings report with them. He was still doing damage control. Hema looked at him expectantly.

"What do you have in mind?"

"Trust me?"

"I don't like surprises."

"I know."

There was a mischievous look in her eyes that was

too tempting to resist. "I want to take you on a shore excursion tomorrow when we dock."

He raised an eyebrow. "What kind of trip?"

She leaned forward, and he caught a whiff of her perfume. It was a clean, sweet smell that made him lose his train of thought. "It's a surprise. Sometimes it's good to loosen up, be spontaneous. It's good for stress relief."

"There are other ways to relieve stress, you know." The words were out of his mouth before he could stop them. Between the heady scent of her perfume and the mischief in her eyes, all he wanted to do was to drag her to his cabin and show her what his idea of letting loose was.

She cleared her throat. "C'mon, be impulsive. See what it feels like to live a little, to let go of your plans."

He placed a hand on his heart and mocked shock. "You talk as if you think I can't be spontaneous."

"Prove me wrong."

"You're on. Let's see what you can cook up for tomorrow."

# Four

She glanced at her watch again. Barely a minute had passed. She looked again towards the tenders coming from the cruise ship. Because of the reefs close to shore in the Cayman Islands, the cruise ships had to dock in deep waters. Little boats carried ten to twelve passengers at a time from the ship to the main dock in George Town. The turquoise-blue waters shimmered in the morning sun. The water was so clear that she could see the schools of fish dancing over the rocks of the riprap.

"Hema, we'll miss the tour. Let's go." She looked with irritation at Aunty Neema, her mother's cousin with a gratingly nasal voice. She turned towards the tender that was approaching the dock. Her heart fell. *Guess he isn't coming.*

Hema sighed and followed her aunt to the waiting minibus, which would take them to the boat tour location. She could text him, but what was the point? The bus was already loaded. He wouldn't make it.

What had she been thinking? He'd made it clear yesterday that he planned on keeping her at arm's length. They'd always gotten along since the day they met, but the last couple of days had been different. Was it just the physical attraction? She was feeling a closeness to Vivek that she hadn't anticipated. The wedding, the constant chatter among the guests about love, and the honeymoon-like setting were playing with her mind. She'd gotten caught up in the moment and forgotten that they weren't a real couple.

The driver opened the bus doors with a whoosh, and a blast of air-conditioning hit her in the face. She climbed into the little bus after her aunt, who was complaining about everything from the heat to the size of the steps on the bus. She stepped into the cramped aisle after her aunt. While her aunt fussed over finding a seat, she found Vikram sitting alone in the first-row aisle seat, so she tapped him to move over. He shook his head. "My dear, *Bhabhi,* brother dearest has been saving you a seat for the last half an hour." She looked down the aisle to see Vivek grinning at her from the back row. Her heart gave a little jolt. Why was he having this effect on her?

Shaking her head, she took the seat next to him and set the beach bag at her feet. The bus lurched forward, and Vivek placed an arm in front of her to keep her from hitting the seat in front of them.

"Nice of you to make it. I was worried you'd backed out."

"Never."

"I didn't see you at breakfast. When did you leave the ship?"

"I took the first tender this morning. I had some errands to run."

She leaned in and whispered so no one else could hear. "What's the situation here?"

He leaned closer, and she caught a whiff of clean soap and spicy aftershave. She breathed him in, enjoying the masculine scent. "Ten aunties, four uncles. I had to force Vikram to come just so we'd have some backup."

"What? Where are all our friends?"

"Sitting on a beach in a resort lounger with piña coladas in their hands."

"Traitors."

"Don't worry, I have a plan for revenge." He bent his head, and his lips grazed her ear as he spoke. A delicious shiver went down her spine. "When we get back to the boat, I'm telling the purser to cut off their Wi-Fi access."

She laughed. "That is truly evil."

The bus dropped them off at a dock where a boat waited. The captain was a young man who looked like a California surfer. His two crewmates included a young girl who couldn't have been more than fifteen and a big, tall man who looked like he should be a bouncer at a seedy nightclub. The crew sized everyone for fins and snorkels and gave them a safety briefing as the captain piloted the boat out into the clear waters. The water in this area was an unreal turquoise that she'd only seen in paintings, with waves so gentle, the boat glided through the water.

The bouncer showed them how to don their snorkels and fins and talked about the stingrays using a stuffed one as an example. "Now remember, they are called stingrays because they can sting. Stay away from their tails."

One of the uncles raised his hand, then spoke without waiting to be acknowledged. "What happens if we get stung?"

"Don't," came the dry reply.

"But what do we do if it happens?"

"You get stung, it is not our problem. You all signed the release papers."

"But you have some medical treatment here, right?"

"Do I look like a doctor?"

Hema looked at Vivek and saw that he was also suppressing a laugh. The uncle, who Hema vaguely recognized as one of her father's business associates, looked like he wanted to jump out of his life vest and strangle the man. "Uncle, don't worry, I'm a doctor. I'll take care of you if something happens," Hema said soothingly.

As the boat approached stingray city, their guide leaned overboard and threw some food. It was only a few seconds before a dozen stingrays appeared, their gray-black-brown flat bodies gliding beside the ship, their spine-like tails causing whispers among the guests.

Once the boat was tied off to a mooring ball and a ladder dropped, their bouncer guide instructed them to put on their gear and get in the water. The guests began shedding their swim cover-ups. Hema had debated her choice of swimsuit, torn between a sexy bikini and a matronly one-piece. She'd finally chosen the one-piece knowing that she wouldn't feel comfortable wearing the bikini in front of her uncles and aunts. She caught Vivek staring, and her face warmed. After dinner last night, he'd walked her back to the cabin and given her a chaste kiss on the cheek. She hadn't invited him in.

More stingrays appeared as bouncer man floated in the water, throwing out food. An aunty shrieked as she made her way down the ladder, then promptly climbed back up to the boat. "Those things come right up to you."

Hema stood at the top of the ladder and eyed the creatures, fear snaking its way through her veins. Despite her assurances to the other guests, there really was no treatment for a sting, and it hurt quite a bit. She'd booked the excursion because it was *the* experience to have in the Cayman Islands. Surely it was safe?

Bouncer man swam to the bottom of the ladder and held his hand out. "Don't worry, they are very friendly."

"C'mon, it'll be fun." She glared at Vivek for using her words from last night.

"I'll go first," Vivek offered. He climbed down the ladder awkwardly as his fins got in the way. She giggled. Just before the waterline, he looked up at her. "If I die, tell my parents I love them. And make sure Vikram doesn't get my car."

"I heard that," Vikram shouted from behind her. "Not only am I taking your Tesla Cybertruck, I'm spray-painting red flames on it."

Vivek splashed unceremoniously into the water as the fin caught the last rung of the ladder. He came up choking on a mouthful of water. Hema laughed. Every time she'd seen him, he was so put together, perfectly poised. She even had trouble picturing him farting. Seeing him splash inelegantly in the water made her want to hug him tight.

"Oh yeah, you think you can do better?" he challenged his brother, still sputtering water.

She sat on the side of the boat and put on her fins. Once done, she flipped backwards and slipped into the warm water. She swam underwater and came up behind Vivek, running her fingers up his back.

He froze for a second, then turned around and touched her arm. She tried to swim away from him, but he caught her within seconds, wrapping his arms around her. He was grinning, but she was suddenly aware that her breasts were crushed against his bare chest. The swimsuit she thought was matronly suddenly seemed skimpy.

A stingray flapped its slimy body as it swam past her legs. She yelped and instinctively wrapped her legs around Vivek. He tightened his grip on her, his hands moving down her back to steady her. The water was about ten feet deep but the fins gave him both of them some natural buoyancy. "Don't worry, my love. While there is breath in my chest, I will protect you." He'd said the words in Hindi, quoting a Bollywood movie they'd agreed had been both sappy and entertaining.

Another school of stingrays swam past, and she clung to him, the feel of their rubbery wet bodies making her cringe. She closed her eyes tightly. The slimy feeling was worse than nails on a chalkboard.

"You can open your eyes now."

She noticed that Vivek had moved them away from the boat. The stingrays were still swarming the area where bouncer guy continued to entice them with food. A couple of brave aunties had made their way to the water, and bouncer guy was holding up a stingray for them to pet. She shuddered at the thought of voluntarily touching them.

Then she realized that her legs were still wrapped around Vivek, her arms holding on tight. Despite the bright sun, his eyes were dark. She pointed her chin up, and he brought his mouth down on hers. The kiss was not polite. His mouth was hot and wet, and she returned his fire with heat of her own. She shifted her legs higher, pressing against his groin. He grew hard, and her own body responded with a rush of heat to her core. He groaned and moved his hands to her butt. He lifted her higher, and she gasped as she felt him between her legs. She ground against him, desperate to ease the pressure building inside her. He pushed his tongue into her mouth. She sucked fervently, and ground her body hard against his.

He moved his hand between them, separating their bodies. A protest escaped her lips, but it was only for a second. Then his fingers reached beneath the swimsuit and slipped inside her. She clenched against him, and used the natural waves of the water to rock against his finger. "More," she breathed into his mouth and he slid another finger inside her. His tongue matched the thrusts of his fingers, and pressure built inside her.

"Hey, you know you guys have a perfectly good room back on the boat."

She gasped as Vikram swam towards them. Vivek extracted his fingers, and she loosened her grip on him. She couldn't bear to look at her future brother-in-law. Vivek kicked away from her, putting distance between them.

"Didn't you hear the horn?" Vikram shouted.

"What horn?" Vivek said, his voice thick.

"It's time to go back to the boat. The guide sent me to get you. Everyone else is already onboard."

That's when she noticed that they'd swum a little distance from the boat. The stingrays had swarmed to another boat, following the promise of food.

They swam quickly to the boat, the fins speeding them up. When they got to the ladder, Vivek reached down, took off Hema's fins and handed them up, then followed suit with his own.

Hema couldn't bring herself to look at Vivek, her body still recovering from his touch, craving it with an intensity that surprised and scared her. *It's probably not the end of the world to be turned on by my fiancé.* The thought brought a smile to her face. While she had mentally prepared herself for a life of vibrator pleasure, the new development in their relationship was much more desirable.

She sensed Vivek looking at her, and she turned to see him frowning. "What's wrong?" she asked.

"I'm sorry about…" He swallowed. "That was really inappropriate. It won't happen again. I'll keep my distance from you."

# Five

Hema seethed as she slipped on a strappy white sundress for the beach party scheduled for the evening. She hadn't had a chance to talk to Vivek after their stingray city excursion. When they returned to the dock, Vivek dashed off for some meeting while she was left to deal with the teasing from the aunties and uncles who'd apparently enjoyed their "smooch show" from the boat. She'd begged Vikram for help, but he was the worst of them all.

"Bhabhi," he drawled, "What *jadoo,* magic, have you done on my robotic brother to show his human side?"

She'd endured it good-naturedly, but Vivek's disappearance bothered her. He turned hot and cold in seconds. She never knew where she stood with him.

Did he want a physical relationship with her or not? For that matter, what type of relationship did he want? A few days ago, she'd been clear on where they stood. Friendship, respect, honesty. That was the mantra for their life together. She'd met him twice, once in New York and once in India, before she agreed to the wedding. They'd talked about everything she could think of. What their life would be like, what she expected from him, what he was willing to give. She'd been on even footing when she arrived. Now she was standing on shifting sand, solid one minute and sinking the next. Was this how life would be with him?

She met her parents on deck one, where they boarded the tender that would take them to the beach. Her father put his arm around her as the boat revved its engine. It picked up speed as they floated away from the ship. "How is my little girl? Are you happy?"

She leaned over and gave her father a kiss. "Very happy. The wedding is beautiful." It wasn't a complete lie. She was very happy thinking about her residency, about all that she would do once she finished her training. The wedding *was* beautiful, and all the guests were enjoying themselves.

"All your mother's doing."

She looked at her mother, who was staring out at the water. Her mother had taken care of a lot of the wedding details. It was the most she'd done for any major event of Hema's life.

"She's trying," her father whispered so quietly that Hema wasn't sure if he'd said the words or if they'd come from her head. Her mother had been trying for the last few years. The woman who regularly forgot her birthdays and never came to her school events had a sudden change of heart a few years ago when her engagement to Arjun was broken. It was as if she'd suddenly woken up and realized that she was a mother. Hema could forgive her mother for the way she'd treated her, but couldn't excuse the way she'd hurt her father.

The beach party was held at the Royal Cayman Resort. White pergolas with twinkling lights strung across the ceilings dotted the beachfront. Underneath were long rectangular tables covered with white cloth and bursting with fresh flowers. Several of the guests had already arrived.

She mingled among them, exchanging pleasantries, listening as they recapped their days, and trying not to look for Vivek. When she finally got a break, she headed to the beachside bar to get a drink. She ordered a piña colada and had just taken the first sip of the sweet frozen cocktail when Vivek appeared beside her.

"What percentage of aunties showed up here in sarees and heels, and how many uncles in suits?"

She turned to see him wearing an untucked white linen shirt and khaki shorts. His feet were in sandals. His skin was tanned and slightly red from being out in the sun all day. His hand was wrapped around a tumbler of whiskey, and her eyes dropped to his fingers.

He cleared his throat, waiting for an answer to his question. She brought her thoughts back to the conversation. What were they talking about? Aunties, dressing inappropriately.

"I'd say at least 50 percent."

"And what percent read the invitation instructions that specifically encouraged them not to do that?"

"Oh, 100 percent." She tossed her head dramatically and put a hand on her chest. "What nonsense. Who tells you to wear casual and comfortable clothes for a wedding event?"

Vivek grinned and mimicked her over-the-top gestures. "T-shirt and shorts! Rubbish, this must be for the Americans."

She laughed. They took their drinks to the table assigned to them. Vikram soon joined them along with Nisha, Sameer, Arjun, Rani and several of their friends. Hema gestured to Nisha to come sit next to her. Vivek was on her other side, and she felt him tense. Was it because of Sameer? Vivek had assured her that he was over Divya. She was happily married, and he wished her well. Then why did he tense every time her family was in the vicinity?

"Where are you guys planning to honeymoon?" Nisha asked.

Hema looked at Vivek. They hadn't discussed a honeymoon, not even a fake one.

"We'll have to postpone the honeymoon a bit. Hema starts her residency, and I'm launching a new product."

Sameer clicked his tongue. "Bad move, dude. Trust me, make time for it. Once you get back to the daily grind, it's hard to find minutes in the day." He looked fondly at Nisha, and Hema's chest tightened. The way Sameer looked at Nisha, it was clear that he was madly in love with her. Hema had known Sameer since she was a child. Their families had been friends for years. He was the troublemaker in the family. The guy who broke hearts and never looked back. Until she saw him take the seven circles around the fire with Nisha, she would've never believed that he would settle down and marry.

"We're treating this trip as a second honeymoon." Sameer said.

"Well, that explains why we haven't seen much of you two," Rani said teasingly.

Nisha smiled shyly, and Hema's chest constricted even more. She would never have that. A man who looked at her like she was his entire world. A man who longed to spend every second with her.

"Well, if you'd seen these two at the stingray excursion, you'd swear they'd already started the honeymoon," Vikram quipped.

Hema's face grew warm. How much had people seen?

"Well, we had to give those old aunties and uncles some inspiration," Vivek said laughingly, and Hema put a hand to her mouth, shaking her head.

The table laughed, too. Nisha elbowed Hema teasingly, then leaned over and whispered, "It's a good sign that you can't keep your hands off each other."

Vivek's arm went around her, and the warmth in her face spread throughout her body. His thumb stroked her bare shoulder, and a mix of desire and irritation coursed through her. Was he putting on a show for their friends?

The first course was shrimp cocktail with a pineapple relish. Hema wasn't a big fan of seafood, but it was deliciously flavored. Andy, Vivek's college roommate, regaled them with stories of pranks he played on Vivek. Of all the people at their table, Hema wouldn't have pegged Andy, a sandy-haired guy with an easy smile, as one of Vivek's closest friends. He was outgoing and boisterous and completely the opposite of Vivek's poise and reserve. She liked the way Vivek's shoulders shook as Andy entertained the table.

"You know, I thought hiding ten different alarms to go off every hour was funny, but replacing all the Oreo fillings with toothpaste, that was just cruel." Vivek's words said he was annoyed, but there was clear laughter in his voice.

Hema liked seeing this new side of Vivek. She'd never pictured him as the type of guy to rush a fraternity or drink beer from a hat.

"Now, this is not fair. We've spent all dinner making fun of my younger and dumber days. How about someone spill some of Hema's secrets?" He looked down the table at Aashni, Hema's medical school friend who had come from India for the wedding.

Aashni shook her head. "Your wife-to-be is very straitlaced. She did nothing but study."

"Oh, she wasn't always that way." Karishma, Arjun and Sameer's sister, spoke up. She was a couple of years younger than Hema, but the two of them had spent time together as children. Karishma was beautiful just like her sister Divya. Large almond-shaped eyes, long dark hair, and a generous mouth with a wide smile. Hema shook her head at Karishma, which just encouraged her more.

Karishma leaned forward over the table so she could make eye contact with everyone. "This was before she became all serious. Our families went on holiday together in Goa, and we were sharing a room in this fabulous resort. Hema tells me that one of the waiters told her that a guest had found a snake in their room. I am terrified of snakes. The next night, she put one of those toy snakes in my bed, the ones made of rubber that feel cold, and she put Vaseline all over it so it was slimy. I screamed so loudly that half the hotel came to our door."

Hema waved at her. "Hey, you forgot the first part of the story, when you changed my phone language to Chinese. It took me a whole day to figure out how to change it back."

"It hardly compares." Karishma said cheekily.

Hema plucked a flower from the arrangement in front of her and threw it at Karishma. It missed and fell into Karishma's plate. She promptly returned it. Vivek reached out and caught it before it landed on Hema's head. He opened his palm and presented the crushed flower to her. It was a throwaway gesture, something he did without thinking, so why did it reach into her chest and touch her heart?

Dessert included cheese plates, fruit trays, sorbets and petits fours. They were all full, but the food looked too decadent to pass up. By the time they were done eating, everyone was ready to pass out from food coma.

The tenders began arriving, and guests lined up to go back to the ship.

"It's going to be a while before they get everyone on the boats. Want to take a walk?" Vivek asked.

They walked along the shoreline, letting the warm water lap at their feet. They watched the tenders going back and forth to the ship, full of guests bloated with food and alcohol. Hema felt light, the two piña coladas she'd drunk relaxing her muscles and her mind. They walked in companionable silence, their arms brushing against each other. At one point he found her hand and grabbed it.

Hema stopped, turned towards him and stepped so her chest was crushed against his. He ran his hands softly down her arms. "Your skin is so soft," he murmured. She closed her eyes, enjoying the feel of his hands. The breeze whispered around them, the setting sun bathing them in a soft orange glow.

His breath quickened; her heart thumped a little louder. He bent his head, and just before his lips touched hers, she stepped back.

He frowned, the confusion clear in his eyes.

"Am I overstepping?" he asked.

"That depends," she said, feeling bold.

His lips twitched. "On?"

"On whether you can be straight with me about what's happening between us."

He ran his fingers through his hair and took a breath. "Honestly, I wish I knew."

She raised her brows. "Are you or are you not attracted to me?"

He laughed. "Are you kidding?" He tugged on her arm and she went to him. He kissed her hard, and she matched his fervor, the spicy taste of whiskey on his lips spurring her on. He put his hand on her back and pressed himself against her. "Do you have any doubt about how attracted I am to you? He pressed his lips to her neck, just under her ear. "Every time I leave you, I vow to behave myself, but then, I want to throw you on the nearest bed and pleasure you until neither of us can think straight."

*Then do it. Do it right now.* Her entire body was on fire, lit by a fuse that burned fast and furious through her.

"What's stopping you?" she whispered, unsure of whether her vocal cords were capable of any more.

He pulled away from her, stepping back. He rubbed the back of his neck. "We're going to be married."

"Right. Married couples having sex? How scandalous!"

He rolled his eyes. "Things are already so complicated between us, I'm afraid of what might happen if…if…"

"…if I'm disappointed in your performance." She smirked at him.

He leaned forward. "In that regard, I don't disappoint. But what if…"

"…what if I like it so much that I fall in love with you?"

His smile dropped, and she shook her head, then walked towards the dock. "I'm going back to the ship," she yelled behind her. "I'll try not to fall in love with you on the way."

# Six

Vivek lay back on his cabin bed, wondering what he said or didn't say that pissed Hema off so much. It's not that he expected her to fall in love with him, but it was only natural that she might develop feelings for him. If they became intimate, would she still be content with their arrangement? What if Hema wanted more from him than he could give?

He tugged on his hair in frustration. It was largely his fault. He was the one who couldn't keep his hands off her. Every time she was near him, all he could think about was the smoothness of her skin, the sweetness of her mouth, the goose bumps on her arms when he touched her, the way she moaned against his lips when he put his fingers inside her at stingray city. Just thinking of that moment made his body long for her.

Had it just been too long since he'd been with someone? Divya hadn't wanted to have sex before they were married, and he'd respected her wishes. Since their breakup, he hadn't been with anyone. Before Divya, he'd been casually dating. *That's what it is.* He was just horny because it had been a while. It had nothing to do with Hema. Besides, how long could they both keep denying the chemistry between them? Soon enough they'd be sharing a bed. He was just delaying the inevitable. He stood and ran his fingers through his hair to tame the locks that were protesting the abuse he'd put them through. He thought about texting Hema, but what would he say? *I need you. I want you. I really need to know what's happening between us. I can't sleep without you.*

A knock on his cabin door caught his attention, and he groaned, hoping it wasn't Vikram or Andy. He'd refused a bachelor party. His brother had thrown him an outrageous one before his previous wedding, and he had no desire to replicate that night. As a result, his brother and friend had dragged him out the previous two nights to drink until all hours, shamelessly flirting with the ship's crew. They had threatened to do the same tonight, and he wasn't in the mood. There was only one person he wanted to see, but she was two decks up on the other side of the ship.

He sighed, got out of bed, and opened the door, prepared to make excuses. He stopped short. Hema stood there in the same strappy white dress she'd worn to the beach. The dress that hugged her body in just the right ways and bared her skin in just the right places. The dress he longed to rip off her.

"Have you ever fallen in love with someone because you had great sex with them?" she asked.

He blinked, trying to process her harsh tone. "What…" She brushed past him and entered his room. He closed the door behind him and turned to face her.

"Do you think you're going to fall in love with me if we have sex?" She put her hands on her hips.

"Of course not."

"Then you have a really high opinion of yourself if you think you're so good that one romp with you will have me tumbling head over heels in love."

He stared at her, his pulse racing. *What's she saying?*

She sighed. "Look, I know our deal. You're in love with someone else…" He began to protest, but she held up a hand. "Don't deny it. It's clearly written across your face every time someone mentions her name or you see her brothers and sisters." She reached out and put a hand on his chest. "You were honest with me from the beginning, and I with you. This isn't a love marriage, and it never will be."

He rubbed the back of his neck. This was exactly what he wanted, what he needed to hear. So why wasn't he relieved?

She stepped closer to him. "But as you said, there's no reason we can't have pleasure."

The last vestiges of control vaporized as she tipped her face up and parted her lips. She stood on her toes and met his mouth, kissing him with the same desperation with which he wanted her. He moved his hand from her back down to her butt, lifting her up as he crossed the two steps it took to get to the bed. He set her down and gently pushed her to lie back. He moved down her body, lifted her dress, and kissed her through her panties. She moaned, and he pulled the panties off, needing to taste her. She curled her fingers in his hair as he put his whole mouth on her, and pushed his tongue into her, enjoying the way she writhed and moaned with pleasure.

"I want you inside me," she said breathlessly, and he needed no further encouragement. He unbuckled his belt and dropped his shorts. Hema sat up and touched him through his boxer briefs. Her touch was light and gentle. Too light. Too gentle. He grabbed her hand and pressed it into him. She got the hint and stroked him harder. It felt so good. Too good. The pressure inside him was intense. Too intense. He took a breath to slow himself. It was their first time together. He wanted to make sure she enjoyed it. He couldn't go too fast.

Suddenly the balcony door flew open and a horn blared. Something wet and stringy hit him. Hema stood quickly, pulling her dress down, and he turned to see Andy in the balcony with two cans of Silly String in his hands, spraying all over the room. Vivek moved towards his friend, fully intending to throttle him, when he caught a face full of Silly String. He cursed as he felt his way towards the bathroom to get a towel, stubbing his toes several times along the way in the tiny room.

He grabbed a towel and cleared his face, then handed one to Hema, who had smartly moved towards the cabin door, as far away as she could get. At least her dress was still on. He was wearing nothing but a shirt and underwear.

Andy finally ran out of Silly String, then seemed to notice Hema in the room and Vivek's state of dress. He put a hand to his mouth, failing to hide his laughter. "Sorry guys, didn't know you were in the middle of… I thought he'd be alone. I had to get this guy."

"Were you standing on the balcony the whole time?" The thought of Andy seeing Hema partially undressed filled him with an unexpected rage.

Andy seemed to sense the change in his voice and held up his hands. "I got here about one second before I opened the door. I swear I didn't see anything."

"How did you get there?"

"The balcony next door. It's Karishma's room, so she let me in, and I climbed over the railing." He stepped forward and slapped Vivek on the arm. "Just for old time's sake, man. I thought you'd be alone." He looked apologetically at Hema, who was grinning.

"Seeing his face was worth it," she said cheekily, and he glared at her, ignoring how pretty she looked with that smile on her face.

"Out!" he yelled at Andy, who held up his hands in surrender and moved towards the cabin door.

"Oh no, you get to go back the way you came."

"You want me to put my life in danger a second time?"

"I couldn't be so lucky as to watch you fall into the ocean. Out!"

Andy waved goodbye to Hema, who waved back, then went out the balcony door. He swung one leg over the balcony and easily slipped onto the other balcony. There was a glass partition between balconies that left just enough room for someone to grab the railing and climb over with ease. Vivek banged the door shut, locked it, and then pulled the curtains across.

"I am going to have some words with Karishma," he muttered.

"They were just having fun. All that talk of pranks at dinner must have inspired them."

He looked at the room and groaned. It was covered in Silly String. The gooey, sticky substance stuck to the mirrors, spread on the bed and clung to the lamps.

"Let's get out of here," he said, desperate to get her back to bed, and in the mood they'd both been enjoying before Andy had ruined it.

She shook her head. "We can't leave this for the poor room steward. We have to clean it up." He kicked himself for ousting Andy. He should have left him here to clean up the mess while he took Hema to her room and finished what they started.

It took more than an hour to strip the beds and pluck the string off the surfaces. At some point, the room steward showed up and began helping. When they were done, he asked Vivek to leave for a few minutes so he could remake the beds and vacuum. Vivek made a note to leave the man a tip. A big tip.

"Your room?" he asked hopefully.

She shook her head. "Maasi's sleeping there. My mother had a fight with my dad and moved in with her. After a few hours, Maasi couldn't stand my mother and moved in with me."

There was a catch in her voice, one he didn't like.

"Let's go to the café and get some coffee," he suggested softly. As it turned out, the café was closed, but they found a quiet bar, and the bartender made them Irish coffees. He generally found most of the ship's indoor spaces a bit over-the-top in terms of decor, but he liked this lounge. The polished dark wood top bar, high-backed leather stools, and backlit glass shelves were reminiscent of a high-end British pub.

"Why are your parents fighting?"

She stared into her drink and licked a dollop of whipped cream from the top of the cup. The sight of her tongue flicking out stirred the fire that he was trying hard to tamp down.

After a long pause, she finally spoke in a small voice. "They've never gotten along. It's always something between them. I had hoped they could put their differences aside this week."

The bitterness in her voice pinched at his heart. *She knows.* His parents had made inquiries about Hema's family when Divya's parents, the Singhs, had first suggested the *rishta*. It was standard procedure. With Vivek's family's wealth and profile, they had to be careful. Their law firm's private eye had informed them that Hema's mother had been having an affair for years, and Hema, as well as her father knew about it. Affairs were pretty common among his generation but rarer in his parents' generation, where societal reputation was too important to risk. An affair that had gone on for so many years and was still a secret was highly unusual. It had taken some digging for the private eye to find.

He put a hand on her shoulder. "Weddings can be stressful for parents. I know my parents have been quibbling all week, about silly things like whether to serve dinner at eight or at eight thirty."

"I wish my parents fought about the little things. I'm afraid their issues are much more serious and not as easily solved."

He placed his hand on hers, and she gave him a small smile. "It's okay. You can tell me, whatever it is."

He let the silence settle between them. Their friendship was still new, but there were a lot of things they'd talked about that were deeply personal. He'd shared how Divya had broken his heart, what it had done to his entire outlook on marriage.

Finally, she shook her head. "It's nothing dire. Just their usual squabbles. As you said, wedding decisions just put added stress on everything."

His jaw clenched. She wasn't going to share her family secret, unload her burden on him. Sharp, bitter disappointment seeped into his chest. *She doesn't owe me her deep, dark secrets.* He knew that type of trust came with time, but he'd bared his soul to her, told her how the real pain of Divya's betrayal had been that she hadn't thought him worthy of sharing her dreams and doubts. There had been plenty of opportunities for Divya to tell him that she'd changed her mind about marrying him, that she didn't love him, that she wanted something different for her life. Divya running away from their wedding had stung. But what broke his heart was that the woman he loved hadn't even given him a chance to give her what she wanted.

Divya hadn't trusted him enough. He hoped things would be different with Hema.

# Seven

Hema stared at the passing hills as the jitney bumped its way across the impossibly steep road. The island of St. Thomas stretched out in all directions. The jitney was the local bus on the island. It was a large open-air jeep. The main cabin had been modified with brightly painted row seats. The roads were narrow, pockmarked and steep, curving up and down on the hills of the island. As they rounded certain corners, she'd catch a glimpse of the perfectly blue water sparkling in the sun.

"Hema, please explain why you didn't rent an air-conditioned van like the one that's on our bumper." Her mother held on to the bars crisscrossing the top of the jeep as she grumbled from the row behind them. Hema shared a smile with her father, who was seated beside her.

"Ma, this is no worse than riding a Delhi scooter."

"Your mother does not ride in Delhi scooters, dear," her father quipped, earning himself a glare from her mother.

Hema sighed. Her parents' marriage was mercurial at best. She had spent her childhood wondering whether she was the reason for the stress in their marriage. Her mother seemed to resent Hema's presence in her life. It was only a few years ago that she'd finally found out the cause of their marital strife. It was around the time that Hema's engagement to Arjun broke. Hema was in love with Arun at the time and was purposely eavesdropping on her parents to find out the status of the negotiations between the two families. She had encouraged Arjun to break the engagement, but her parents had put pressure on Arjun's family until she had come up with the gumption to tell them the truth: that she didn't want to marry Arjun.

That's when she overheard a conversation between her parents where her father gave her mother an ultimatum that she either end the affair she'd been having for years or their marriage would be over. Her mother had chosen to end the affair. She had never confronted her parents with the fact that she knew the truth. Since then, every fight that simmered between them had the stink of the affair. She'd spent her childhood thinking her mother didn't love her, but she now understood the truth. Hema was the ball that had chained her mother to a marriage she didn't want. Divorce in her parents' generation was rare, especially for a couple with a daughter. No one would marry a girl with divorced parents, the theory being that if her parents couldn't respect the sanctity of marriage then the girl wouldn't either. Thankfully times had changed, but perhaps too late to help her mother.

With Hema out of the house, she hoped her parents would get clarity on their own marriage.

"I have to go shopping with the ladies after this. How will it look, me showing up all sweaty?" her mother asked.

"It's hot out, I'm sure they'll all be sweaty," her father said irritably.

"I'll put you in an air-conditioned cab early so you can go freshen up on the ship before you have to meet everyone in Charlotte Amalie." Hema said quickly, trying to avoid another blowup between them. Yesterday they'd fought over how long they planned to stay in New York after the cruise. The argument had devolved to such a shouting match that her mother had to move into Maasi's room.

She'd wanted to tell Vivek about it last night, share with him the burden she carried of knowing the secret about her parents' marriage. But she couldn't. Her father didn't know that she knew about the affair. He worked so hard to pretend that her mother loved and cared for both of them that it would devastate and embarrass him to find out that she knew the truth. That's why she'd decided not to tell Vivek. She couldn't bear the thought of her father finding out that Vivek knew. There was one thing her father valued more than her, and that was his reputation and respect. To learn that his daughter and son-in-law knew his darkest secret would tear him apart.

Could Vivek tell that she was hiding something?

"Why didn't Vivek come?" her mother asked.

"He doesn't have to be with me 24/7," Hema said with more frustration than she intended. Hema had planned this trip to include Vivek, thinking it would be a good opportunity for him to get to know her parents. But he'd texted her in the morning to say that he had some business in St. Thomas and wouldn't be able to join her. She didn't try to hide her annoyance as she texted back to let him know that she wouldn't be making any more plans to include him. He was blowing cold again, and she was sick of it. What was his deal? He hadn't asked her back to his room last night after their Irish coffees. She'd assumed that he'd been just as tired as her but after this morning's curt text, it was clear that he was freezing her out. Again. Was he having second thoughts?

They arrived at Blackbeard's castle. Hema hoped that visiting the historical site with furnishings and restored buildings dating back to the 1800s would give her parents something enjoyable to talk about. They were both history buffs and enjoyed comparing British Colonial architecture. It was one of the last days that she'd have her parents to herself before the wedding festivities took over in full swing.

She tucked her arm into her father's and signed up for a tour. Just as it was about to start, Nisha and Sameer arrived. Hema greeted them enthusiastically and invited them to join their tour. Nisha refused. Initially Hema thought that she didn't want to intrude on Hema's family time, but then she noticed the way that her mother stared at Nisha.

"Has something happened between you and Nisha?" Hema asked her mother once they were out of earshot.

Her mother shrugged. "I don't know what you mean."

"I saw the look that passed between you two. Why wouldn't Nisha and Sameer join us on the tour? They are literally a few minutes behind us."

"How should I know why Nisha said no?" her mother said irritably. Hema recognized when her mother was being evasive. The woman had spent Hema's lifetime lying to her daughter and husband. Hema had confronted her mother about the affair the day after things ended with Arun. Hema was burning in anger, and facing another cheater gave her an outlet for her rage. Her mother hadn't denied or explained it. She'd just apologized and said that she was trying to make amends. Whatever that meant.

Her parents were silent through the tour. Her mother was clearly glad when Hema called her a car to take her back to the cruise ship. Her father offered to stay with Hema, but she sent him off. She was going to go to Coki Beach to spend time snorkeling and relaxing on the beach. But first, she was going to find out what her mother was hiding.

Hema didn't have to wait long before Nisha and Sameer appeared. Nisha's eyes searched the area, and if

Hema had any doubt that Nisha and her mother were keeping something from her, she didn't anymore.

"My mother left to go back to the ship." Hema volunteered. Nisha tried to hide it but it was clear from the slight drop of her shoulders that she was relieved. "So, how about you tell me what's going on between you and my mother?"

Nisha exchanged a glace with Sameer, and Hema took a step closer to them. "Please don't insult me by saying it's nothing. I consider you my friends, and as such, the least you can do is tell me the truth."

Nisha sighed. "You're right. But let's not do it here. Let's sit down somewhere."

Hema heard a jitney barreling down the road, and she hailed it. There was no public transport system on the island. The privately operated jitneys were the means for the locals who didn't have cars to get around. The jitney looped around the main road of the island, picking up passengers who hailed them and dropping them off wherever they asked. During cruise days, the jitneys were busy, and this one was nearly full, but everyone crushed themselves closer together to make room. One local even gave Sameer his seat, opting to hold a pole and stand on the running board on the side.

Sameer chatted with a local woman sitting next to him, and based on her recommendation, they got off at a local coffee shop.

The shop roasted its own coffee, which was delicious. The only place to sit was a couple of plastic tables set up in the parking spots immediately outside the café. They all took a seat, Hema on one side and Sameer and Nisha on the other. She looked at them expectantly.

"I was really hoping that your mom would have told you…"

"My mother is particularly good at keeping secrets and sharing only what she must."

Nisha swallowed visibly. "You know that your mother was having an affair."

Hema froze. How did Nisha know? Nisha was waiting for a response, so Hema nodded, her mouth too dry to speak.

"There's no easy way to say this… Your mother was having an affair with my father."

The table, the parking lot, Nisha and Sameer blurred in front of her. She blinked several times trying to dislodge the lump in her throat. She stared at Nisha, hoping that she had misheard, that her brain was playing tricks on her. Nisha reached out and grabbed her hand. "I know how you're feeling right now. When I found out that the woman my father blew up his marriage for was your mother, I felt gutted. I confronted her about it. She told me that you knew."

Hema couldn't talk. Her mouth was too dry, her throat too tight. The hot air and silence pressed against them. Finally, Hema found some words. "I knew about the affair. I didn't know who it was with."

Nisha bit her lip. "I know this can be a shock to you."

"Does your mother know about the affair?" Hema finally asked.

Nisha nodded. "She's known for years and put up with it. But she's finally had it. She's divorcing my father. In fact, their divorce hearing is this month."

That was another punch to her gut. Hema had known the affair was with another married man and had assumed that the secrecy and ending of the affair was to preserve their families. But if Nisha's parents were getting divorced, did that mean her mother would continue the affair? Or did she plan to leave her father?

As if reading her mind, Nisha spoke up. "Don't worry, your mother assured me that the affair is over and she doesn't plan to rekindle it."

"I think I'll go back to the ship. The sun is really hot and I'm not feeling well." Hema stood and immediately grabbed the table to steady herself.

Sameer and Nisha both stood, too. "We'll come back with you."

Hema refused. She needed to be alone. Sameer called her a proper taxi and instructed the driver to take her to the pier where their ship was docked, giving him several bills to make sure he dropped her as close to the ship as possible.

When she arrived at the pier, she barely had the wherewithal to find her cruise card and put her beach bag through the ship's security. As she walked through the metal detector, Vivek appeared. Where had he come from?

"Sameer called and asked me to meet you."

As if she needed another person to witness her humiliation. Her mother had an affair with someone in their social circle. Not an unknown man. It was with someone her father knew. Probably someone her father had done business with. Nisha's parents had been invited to her wedding. Her mother had managed the guest list. If Nisha's father had agreed to come to the wedding, would her mother have stood by?

Vivek picked up her beach bag and led her to the elevators. The cool air of the ship's air-conditioning blasted onto her, and she took a deep breath, instinctively leaning into Vivek.

When they arrived at her room, he didn't wait to be invited in. She dropped onto the couch. Without asking, he ordered water, cold drinks, and sandwiches from room service.

"You don't have to stay. I'm fine."

He shook his head. "You are not fine, and I'm staying until I'm sure you are."

"Don't you have better things to do?" She didn't bother to hide the hostility in her voice.

He stared at her. "You are going to be my wife. There is no place else I want to be."

"Then why did you cancel on me today?" If he'd been there with her, then she wouldn't have been alone to hear yet another one of her mother's shameful secrets.

He shifted on the couch. "Remember when we talked about what we both wanted from this marriage? We agreed that we would always be honest with each other. While we may not share the traditional love between a man and a woman, we said we would be friends. We would lean on each other. I was angry that you didn't want to share what was really going on with your parents."

Her eyes widened. "You know?" Had Sameer told him? How many people knew? Did Vivek's entire family know? She couldn't imagine what her father would go through if he found out that both Vivek and Sameer's family knew their family's dirty secret.

Vivek nodded. "When the Singhs first proposed your rishta to my family, my dad hired a private investigator to research your family." She turned away from him, but he placed a gentle hand on her chin and made her meet his eyes. He looked worried. Contrite, even. "You have to understand that the Singhs don't have a great reputation with us after what Divya did. We knew about your family from social circles, but my parents are always worried about gold diggers."

A sound escaped her throat. The idea was preposterous. "Don't worry, I know you're not marrying me for my money. In fact, I'm marrying you for yours." She couldn't help the smile that twitched at her lips. "But the private investigator we hired noted your mother's travel patterns and found the affair."

A new anger unfurled in her chest. How careless had her mother been? "How many people know?" she asked in a hoarse whisper.

"Sameer knows from Nisha. His mother knows because Nisha's mother confided in her. I don't think Arjun, Rani or the rest of the siblings know. It's none of their business. My parents and I know, but that's it."

She sank back into the couch. "I need to tell Papa. He can't find out from anyone else that the secret is no longer between him and Ma. But he doesn't know that I know, and if I tell him, it'll devastate him."

"Why didn't you say something last night if you knew I wasn't telling you the whole story?"

He shrugged. "It was for you to tell me. If you don't trust me enough to tell me things like this, then we aren't at the place in our friendship that I thought we were."

Her chest tightened. *Is that what he thinks? That I didn't want to tell him because I don't trust him?* She shook her head. "I didn't tell you because I didn't want to embarrass my father. He would die if he knew that you know. Respect and social standing mean a lot to him."

Vivek nodded. "I get that. But that's all the more reason you should've told me. So I can protect you, and your family."

She was about to tell him that it wasn't his job to protect her, but stopped. "That's what Papa has done all his life. Protect me."

He placed an arm around her. "I should've been there with you today."

Her eyes welled, and before she could stop them, teardrops fell down her cheeks. Vivek pulled her into his arms, and she rested her head against his strong chest, letting the sobs escape from her soul. "Why did she have to choose someone from our social circle? If she had to have an affair, it could have been anyone. You know how tight-knit the Indian community is. What must people say about him behind his back?"

Vivek rubbed her back. "Every family has its secrets. We all understand that. And while the aunties relish good gossip, there are some things that no one talks about. This is one of them."

She'd never talked with anyone about the secret that had weighed down her soul for years. Now the words wouldn't stop coming. "Papa has never disparaged my mother. Ever. He's always told me that a mother gives life, and deserves a child's unconditional love and understanding. Not one bad thing. Even when she missed my dance performance at school, or the year she extended one of her travel trips and missed my birthday, he had a ready excuse for her. He never let me miss her love. He knew about the affair for years, but he kept their marriage together for my sake. He didn't want my mother's reputation to tarnish mine. He finally gave her an ultimatum a few years ago."

"Why did he let it go on so long? Why didn't he give her an ultimatum sooner?"

She shrugged. "Maybe he suspected but didn't know?"

Vivek shook his head. "Our investigator wasn't digging into your parents' private lives. He was just looking at their finances, and it wasn't hard to find your mother's unusual travel patterns. Your father is an intelligent man. Have you considered that maybe he was okay with her having the affair? Or maybe they had an agreement?"

Hema stared at him in horror. *An agreement?* The idea was preposterous. "Who in their right mind would agree to an arrangement like that? I don't see my father doing that. He's pretty traditional. He refused to let me move to the US alone. There is no way he would be willing to share my mother with another man. How would you feel about sharing your wife with another man? I mean, if you were getting a real wife."

His face darkened. "You are going to be my real wife, Hema. We will share our lives, support each other, and build a family together. In all the ways that matter, our marriage is real."

*What about love? What about intimacy?* She wanted to scream the question. Shake an answer out of Vivek. Were things still the same for him? How could he still look at their relationship with the same clinical detachment?

"Why didn't you invite me back to your room after drinks last night?" He wanted her to be completely open with him. It was time for him to do the same.

There was a knock on the door. Vivek let the steward setup the small coffee table with food and drinks. He handed Hema a bottle of water. "Drink. It was hot out there."

He was right, but he was also stalling. She gulped down the bottle, then looked at him expectantly.

"Last night, it was obvious you weren't telling me everything about why your parents were fighting and why you were upset. You didn't feel comfortable sharing with me. It reminded me of how Divya wouldn't talk to me. She kept everything inside and then let it explode on our wedding day. Later on, she told me that I never made space for us to have these conversations, that I barreled on with our plans without giving her the opportunity to stop and process things."

Hema swallowed against her tight throat.

"I'm trying not to make the same mistakes I did with Divya, so I thought it best not to rush you."

*Is Divya going to be between us for the rest of our lives?* "I didn't give you the whole story because I don't feel it's my secret to share. I'm not even supposed to know about it. It wasn't about you and me. It was about respecting my father."

She placed a hand on his chest. "I'm not like Divya. I will speak up when I need to, and I won't abandon you."

He nodded, but his eyes gave him away. He'd been hurt by betrayal, just as she had, and that was hard to let go.

She stood. "I want to rest for a bit before I have to start getting ready for the *sangeet* tonight."

He left, and she sank back onto the couch, wondering whether she'd made a promise she couldn't keep.

# Eight

It wasn't like Hema to be late. Had he missed her somehow? The damn dining room where they were holding the *sangeet* was two levels. The event was a night of dancing and music to celebrate the upcoming nuptials. He didn't like leaving her earlier, but it was clear she wanted to be alone.

"Looking for your all-too-real fake fiancé?"

He turned and gave Vikram an irritated look. "Must you?"

Vikram grinned. "All I'm saying, *bhai*, is just a couple of days ago you were telling me all about how this is going to be an arrangement, but every time I see you guys together, you can't seem to keep your hands off each other."

"What can I say? I'm irresistible."

Vikram rolled his eyes. "So, how does this marriage work? Is it like friends with benefits or do you guys keep separate beds?"

Vivek smacked his younger brother on the arm. "Our love life is none of your business."

Not that he didn't want a love life with her. It scared him just how badly he wanted it. The taste and smell of her permeated his senses, toyed with his self-control and clouded his judgment. This marriage was never supposed to be more than an agreement, a promise of friendship and respect. Intimacy was not part of his equation. He'd assumed that his flat physical response to Hema at their first meeting and phone conversations would continue.

But now just looking at her turned him on. He felt a jab at his side and he looked at Vikram in irritation, who gestured with his eyes towards the top level, where Hema had entered.

As if sensing his eyes on her, she looked down. His breath hitched as he took in whatever that sexy outfit was that she was wearing. The strappy blue blouse was nothing more than lines of fabric on her shoulders and back and a strip of cloth to cover her breasts. The skirt was the same royal blue as the blouse with gold embroidery, and the *pallu* was a delicate gold-colored cloth with shimmery threadwork. It hugged her in the right places and left just enough bare skin to be modest yet sexy. He mouthed *Are you okay?* and she gave him a nod and a small smile.

She didn't get very far before she was accosted by a gaggle of aunties.

"So, when are y'all going to bust out into a co-ordinated dance like in the movies?" Andy slapped him on the back.

"We only do that when the White people aren't watching," Vivek replied.

Andy laughed and handed Vivek a tumbler of whiskey. "So, tell me again what this shindig is and why I'm wearing the most uncomfortable shoes in the world."

Andy had asked to dress in traditional Indian clothes, so Vivek had arranged for a kurta-pyjama, a traditional long tunic with leggings like pants, for him. The shoes were the traditional *jutti* that were clearly meant to test a man's tolerance for pain.

"The sangeet is meant to bond the two families by giving them a night to let loose, and..."

His voice was drowned out by a loud beat as a man dressed in a turban, bright yellow shirt, and shiny red *dhoti*—pleated pants—walked in wearing a large *dhol*—a double-sided drum. The beat started slow, then intensified in tempo as he walked around the dining room, attracting people on the second floor down to the first and onto an area where a makeshift stage had been set up. He stood on the stage and beat faster on the drums peppering his strikes with loud shouts of "hai" and "ho."

Someone pulled Hema onto the floor, and she began to dance, raising her hands in the air and moving her feet to the rhythm of the drums. Andy pushed him towards the floor. He shook his head and tried to resist, but the crowd parted to let him through, encouraging him with hoots and slaps on the back. He reluctantly joined Hema on the floor, doing his best to match her rhythm. He was much better at slow dancing, a skill acquired through private lessons when he was in middle school so he could impress his date. Bhangra was a little out of his league, especially when all eyes were on him.

Hema grabbed his hand and shook her hips. She gave him a big smile and pulled his eyes away from the crowd and onto her. She moved sinuously with the beats, her movements fluid. She looked pointedly at his feet, and he understood. He mimicked her foot movements. She waived with her other arm, inviting the crowd onto the floor. They didn't need any encouragement. Within minutes the floor was full of guests stomping their feet and shaking their shoulders. The man with the dhol was replaced with a DJ, who began mixing the latest Bollywood hits.

Hema pulled him off the floor. "Thanks for the rescue," he muttered as she dragged him out of the dining room and down the hall. Clearly there was something on her mind. She opened a door, and they entered the top floor of the dark and deserted theater. There was floor lighting to make sure some drunk guests didn't go hurling down the four-level theater.

She let go of his hand and turned to face him. His heart thumped wildly. He wanted to pull her into his arms and press his lips to her bare shoulder, work his way up her neck and to the delicate area on the corner of her mouth.

"Are you okay?" His voice was thick.

She nodded. "I don't want to talk about my parents. I want to focus on us."

They were standing inches apart, but she felt too far away. He burned with the need to hold her, to feel her against his body.

She blinked, and with every ounce of restraint he had, he ran a finger down her cheek and to her mouth. Her lips parted, and he bent his head, kissing her lightly, then moved his mouth to that spot under her earlobe and whispered, "I haven't stopped thinking about you all day." The sharp intake of her breath and the goose bumps on her arms took the last vestiges of his self-control. He pulled her into his arms, pressed his lips against hers and plunged his tongue into her mouth. She met his fervor with an intensity of her own, grinding her body against his.

He turned her so her back was against a wall and lifted the skirt of her dress. She wrapped a leg around him, her core rubbing up against his groin, torturing him. He ran his hand up her leg and to her panties. He rubbed her through the silky cloth, and she moaned sinfully. He slipped a finger inside her. She was hot and wet, and he couldn't take it anymore.

She lifted the long tunic of his kurta and pushed his pants and boxers down. She stroked him. The damn dress crowded around her legs but there was a piece of fabric that was pinned to her, so he couldn't take the thing off.

"I swear these clothes are designed to be chastity belts," he muttered as he gathered up the cloth of her skirt and bunched it at her waist.

She slid her panties off, and he put his hands underneath her butt and lifted her. She reached between them and grabbed him, pulling him towards her. She placed his tip inside her. He wanted to take it slower, give her more, but the feel of her tightening around him was too much for him to handle. He plunged inside. "Yes, yes, this is what I want," she screamed and his body responded, matching the movements of her hips as she thrust them forward to pull him deeper. Her fingers dug into his shoulders, and she tightened around him to the point that he could barely move. She held him in a vise and shuddered into him, her moans igniting him. As soon as he felt her tremble around him, he let himself give in to the pressure imploding in his body.

She rested her head against his chest. "About damn time. I've been waiting for you to push me against the wall and take me."

He smiled. "And I've been waiting for you to throw me on the bed and have your way with me."

She slid her legs down, and he let go of her. "Are you sure you can handle that?" Her eyes twinkled mischievously.

He leaned forward and gave her a soft kiss. "Try me."

He put his clothes back on and found her panties on the floor. He held them up. "Can I keep these as a souvenir?"

She snatched them from him and slipped them on. "Souvenirs are for places you want to remember; I expect you to return over and over again."

*Hot damn.* He pulled her into his arms. "I'm ready for a second visit." He kissed her bare shoulder and licked his way down her arm. She moaned, and the sound swelled inside him.

"We need to get back to the party or someone will come looking," she said half-heartedly.

"Screw the party. We can go back to my room. I'll lock the balcony door, draw the shades and tip the steward to stand guard."

He knew he had her by the way she sighed and let her body relax into him. Grabbing her hand, he led her out.

"Wait, let me make sure I'm presentable. If anyone sees us…" She looked at her image in a decorative mirror by the theater door and groaned.

"I can't go out like this. My lipstick is all smudged, and the pallu is hanging all wrong. I'm a mess."

"You look great to me."

She gave him an exasperated look "There is a good chance we're going to run into somebody, and we can't look like we just…we just…"

"Had a happy ending?"

She smacked him playfully. "For a guy who doesn't like public embarrassment, you are awfully blasé about this."

He put his arm around her possessively. "You're going to be my wife. I don't mind people knowing I put that glow on your face."

"Don't you have a high opinion of yourself. I'll have you know that the glow is thanks to my makeup artist's perfect bronzer."

"Now, that sounds like a challenge to me."

He hugged her close, and she pushed him away. "Go find Nisha or my maasi and tell them to come help me."

"Does that mean we're not going back to my room?" He put a hand to his chest and stumbled backwards.

"It means that the night is young, and anticipation will make the prize all that much sweeter."

# Nine

*I'm done anticipating.*

Hema smiled as she read the text from Vivek while her feet soaked in a bubble bath that smelled like coconut and lime. The sangeet had become an all-night party with free-flowing alcohol, a midnight buffet, and a bunch of aunties who were convinced they could sing. By the time the party ended, Maasi was really tipsy, and Hema had to drag her back to their room and stay with her. Vivek did a poor job of hiding his disappointment that she wouldn't go back to his cabin with him.

She'd feigned nonchalance, but she had been unable to get Vivek out of her mind. The feel of him inside her, the way he filled her, the heat that coursed through her body kept her tossing and turning all night. She'd hoped to get him alone at breakfast, but the dining room was closed to clean up after the party, so breakfast was only offered on the lido deck, which meant Hema and Vivek were not alone at their table. As soon as breakfast was finished, Hema's friends dragged her to the spa. It was a sea day, and her friends had planned a girls' day. She'd already had a bachelorette party in India. It was a raucous affair in Mumbai with a party bus, private clubs and way too much drinking. As much as she wanted to be with Vivek, she'd been looking forward to the day with her friends.

Today is not your day. At spa now, then ladies' luncheon, then I have to sit for the mehndi. Wedding tomorrow. U can wait.

She could almost hear the groan on the other end of the phone. The henna ceremony was tonight, and while all the other ladies would get henna applied to their hands at the party in the evening, Hema had to sit for the bridal mehndi, which included intricate designs on her hands and feet and took hours. She would have hers done before the party to allow the mehndi adequate time to be applied and to dry.

Tomorrow night is 36 hours away. Can't you sneak out for a little bit?

She couldn't help herself.

I know how quick you can be but I'm the guest of honor. My absence will be noted.

No dots. He wasn't typing. Had she gone too far? Finally. Dots.

Challenge accepted.

She shifted in her seat. The room was suddenly too warm, her body too antsy. Had it been like this with Arun? Their relationship had been very different. He preferred professions of love over witty repertoire like Vivek. He sent her heart and flower emojis and told her he loved her five times a day. Sex had been good, but he'd never turned her on with a text.

And that's when it hit her. The ache in her heart that stabbed at her every time she thought about Arun had disappeared. For the first time since their breakup, her chest didn't contract when she thought of him. She was analyzing their relationship with clinical detachment rather than soul-crushing pain.

"I know that secret smile."

She looked up to see Nisha grinning at her. Nisha had come by to help Hema get dressed the night before, and they'd talked about the situation with their parents. Hema felt closer to Nisha. In a twisted way, she and Nisha were bonded by the illicit relationship between their parents. But even beyond that, she felt a familiarity, a comfort with Nisha. They'd had a connection since the moment they met.

"Thanks again for helping me last night."

Nisha smiled and leaned forward so the other women couldn't hear. "This feeling you have, the need to be with him every second. Hold on to it. Cherish it. Never let it go."

"Is it still there for you and Sameer? You know, now that you're settled into married life?"

Nisha smiled. "We had a history. I knew him in college. Yet when I saw him years later, nothing had changed. Even after being married for several months, it still feels like it did when we were dating."

Hema raised her brows. After a few months of being together with Arun, it had become routine. Had they ever had the fire she and Vivek had last night? She had wanted him with a ferocity that scared her. She hadn't thought about protection. While they'd both been health-tested, she had been a little lax with her birth control shots. She had been due to get her three-month dose a couple of days ago. She'd planned to get it in New York, but in the chaos of their arrival and immediate departure for the cruise, she'd let it slip. They had talked about having children, and she definitely wanted two, but after her residency. She had even talked about freezing her eggs to buy more time if they needed it. Thanks to modern medicine, women didn't have the same biological clock they used to. She made a mental note to look at the data on the birth control shot to make sure a few days wouldn't be a major issue.

Nisha leaned forward. "I can see the chemistry between you and Vivek. Next time I design your clothes, I'll make sure they can withstand being crushed against the wall." She winked as Hema colored.

Hema spent a pleasant morning in the company of

her friends. They drank champagne, got manicures, pedicures, facials and eyebrow threading. Nisha regaled them with fashion show stories, and Hema relived the crazy days of medical school. She was glad for the time with her friends. After the cruise, she'd be in New York, and all her medical school friends were going back to India. It felt bittersweet; they'd been together as group so long, spending night and day together, and now all of them were going to be in different cities and probably wouldn't see each other for a while. Two of her friends made plans to see each other over the Diwali holidays, and Hema felt another pang in her chest. She'd be so far away from everyone, there was no popping over to see a friend on the rare day off. Even Nisha, who was New York based, was going to be spending a lot of time in Europe for her fashion label.

It hit her like a cold blast of wind. She'd only have Vivek. Yes, there was video chatting, but they'd all be running in different directions. Would Vivek be enough for her?

The final spa treatment was a private massage. She had the first appointment so she could get to her mehndi sitting. A slight woman with a British accent showed her into a room with floor-to-ceiling windows overlooking the ocean. The room smelled of lavender, and classical music played from the overhead speakers. Hema was asked to take off her spa robe and lie between the sheets. She found herself sinking into the warmed bed, eager to spend an hour relaxing before the afternoon and evening festivities.

She lay facedown and closed her eyes, enjoying the feel of the soft sheets against her naked skin. Nisha had taught all of them some yoga breathing in preparation for the massage. She'd instructed her to take a breath and direct it deep into her core, then to breathe out in a slow measured way to clear her mind. Nisha had been in a bad accident, and she used the yoga breathing as a natural way to relax and ease physical pain. It seemed simple enough, but it wasn't working for Hema. Every breath brought her mind back to Vivek. The feel of his mouth on her skin, the way he filled her and exploded every pleasure center inside her. The sweetness with which he wrapped a towel around her when she was cold, or knew when she needed to talk. It wasn't what she'd expected. Their video chats had been academic at best. She'd felt comfortable with him, even-keeled. That's what she needed, a no-drama relationship so her sole focus could be on her medical career. She didn't want to get on another emotional roller coaster.

The masseuse knocked on the door, and Hema asked her to enter. She heard the footfalls of the masseuse, and then the sheet was gently lifted off her back. The hands on her back felt much rougher and bigger than the petite woman she'd met. Whoever it was, the hands ground into her back, finding the exact knots at the base of her neck and between her shoulder blades. She let her body sink further into the bed. The person kneaded her back, smoothing out the tension that she didn't even know she'd been holding.

"Oh my God, that feels so good," she moaned

gratefully when the masseuse pressed out a stubborn knot in the middle of her back.

"If I'd known this was your pleasure center, I'd have taken a different approach last night."

She turned, instinctively pulling the sheet over her. "Vivek!"

He grinned.

"What are you doing here?" she asked unnecessarily, her heart going from zero to sixty in seconds.

"Hoping to seduce you."

*Mission accomplished.*

He was dressed in jeans and a plain white polo, looking effortlessly handsome. She pulled the sheet up further, suddenly conscious of just how naked she was in the sunlit room.

"You're beautiful," he said in a thick voice. He ran a finger across her forehead and down her cheek. It was the briefest of touches, yet her nipples hardened and her core throbbed for his touch. His lips twitched as if he could see the desire written all over her face.

"Lie back down. Let me finish the massage."

That's the last thing she wanted. What she needed was for him to rip the sheet off her and devour her.

He gently pushed her shoulder down and she sighed and turned over, her body burning with need. He worked down her back, but she could no longer relax. Her core ached, throbbed and longed. His hands moved to her foot. His lips touched the inside of her ankle, and she couldn't restrain herself anymore. Flipping over, she slid down the table. Before he had a chance to react, she grabbed a fistful of his shirt and pulled his head down. Their lips crashed together. She looped her fingers into his belt and wrapped her legs around him. His hands roamed her body, cupping her breasts, running his fingers over her taut nipples. She stroked him through his jeans, enjoying the sound that rumbled from deep in his throat.

She unbuckled his belt and pushed down his jeans and boxer briefs. The massage table was the perfect height and she grabbed him, but he put a hand on top of hers. "This time, we do it my way. Slowly."

She shook her head, but he gently pushed her shoulders down until she was lying back on the bed. He lifted her knees then bent his head between her legs. Her back arched as his tongue flicked across her core, sending waves of heat raging through her body. She wanted him inside her, hard and fast, rubbing that pulsing need. "Please," she begged, "I need you inside me."

He put one finger inside her, then another. She rocked against him, the need for him driving her mad. Just when she didn't think she could take it anymore, he slid into her. She was already on fire. It didn't take her long to explode around him. Her nails bit into his back. Every cell in her body tightened around him.

They held each other for a while, their breaths heavy, their bodies sweaty and spent. Afterwards, she hopped off the table and grabbed the robe she'd hung on the hook of the closed door.

He pulled his jeans back on. "Next time, we take it even slower."

"It wasn't good for you?"

He smiled slowly. "I like to take my time."

She didn't want him to take it slow. It was already getting hard to remember that their marriage wasn't real. That he didn't love her. She didn't need him to make love to her like she meant something to him. "Slow is overrated," she said dismissively. He raised a brow, and she turned away from him.

It needed to be just sex between them. Amazing, mind-blowing sex, but just sex. Lust was something she could deal with, understand, and enjoy. Any more than that and their relationship risked getting too real. She couldn't risk developing feelings for another man who loved someone else.

# Ten

Of all the Indian traditions, the *mehndi* had always been Hema's favorite. Ladies sitting around talking and laughing as the paste was applied to their hands, then waiting patiently while it dried. It was a forced pause in the day. With your hands out of commission, there was nothing to do other than sit and take in the moment. No swiping on the phone, tapping on a laptop or taking care of errands.

Experiencing it as a bride was something else. She was dressed in a traditional lehenga with a gold-and-pink cap-sleeve blouse and a pink-and-blue skirt. She was seated on a leather couch, her skirt lifted to her knees. One lady sat at her feet using a cone-shaped henna applicator to draw fine mandala type designs on her feet, ankles and up her shins. Another two ladies sat on either side, one applying henna to each of her hands and arms. The designs wove from her fingers to her elbows.

Hema marveled at the artistry of these women, who worked without any stencils or designs. Their fingers applied just enough pressure to squeeze the right amount of the henna paste from the cone as their hands and arms moved to create the intricate patterns that rivalled the best mandala art to be found on Pinterest. They'd been working steadily for three hours.

"How long have you been a *mehndi wali*?" she asked the henna artist to her right. The lady's name was Shruti. She was a petite woman with bright eyes and a ready smile.

"Maam, I've been doing this since I was little. My mother was a mehndi wali and taught me." Hema smiled at the pride in her voice.

"It must be hard to have your hands working nonstop for so many hours."

Shruti shook her head. "I'm used to it, maam. Yours is easy. Normally I do both hands and the feet by myself, and it takes eight or nine hours."

"Do you like this work?"

Shruti shrugged. "What else to do, maam? My mother, she has the arthritis in her hands. My father is dead. I have to earn money to take care of my mother and two brothers. My mother was known as the best mehndi wali. She did the weddings of all the politicians in India." She gestured with her hands. "Until her hands stopped working."

"Have you taken her to a doctor?"

Shruti nodded. "I worked for six months on cruise ship, I saved all my American dollar tips and took her to a doctor in Mumbai. He says maybe surgery help, but best doctor is in America. My mother doesn't get visa for America. One doctor in Mumbai but he says he's booked for years."

Hema leaned forward. "I'm going to be a surgeon in six years. I'm going to learn how to do surgeries with robots so that a doctor can sit in America and do surgery in India."

Shruti's eyes widened, and she let loose a torrent of questions. The other henna ladies also paused their work to listen to Hema explain how telemedicine technology allowed physicians to manipulate machines to do specialized surgeries and that it was only a matter of time when even the rural villages in India could get the best medical and surgical care.

As Hema talked, her body filled with the energy that had fueled her for the last few years. After the disaster with Arun, she'd fallen apart, turned into a sobbing mess of self-indulgence. Then she found a more meaningful purpose in life.

"When I am finished with my training, I'm going to start clinics in India."

"Maybe you will be doing my mother's hand surgery?" Shruti asked hopefully.

Hema shook her head. "It's going to take too long for me to complete my training. Your mother can't wait that long. Her hands will get worse and then surgery might not help." Shruti's face fell. "Your mother will get her surgery now. I know lots of doctors."

Hema gestured towards her phone, which was beside her. "You put your number in my phone, and I will call you."

Shruti looked at her disbelievingly. "Really?"

Hema nodded, the hope in Shruti's eyes rubbing out the doubt she had about whether her residency was worth the sacrifices she'd made. It was. Once she was trained, there were so many more people like Shruti she could help with her money and connections.

"Is there any way I can get close to my bride?" How long had Vivek been standing within earshot? He looked resplendent in a deep maroon sherwani, a white stole around his neck.

"I'm told that I should be feeding the bride since your hands are occupied." He held up a plate of food.

The mehndi ladies clicked their approval, and Shruti stood. "I have finished. You sit here while I go make more lemon and sugar water." The mehndi that had been applied first had started to dry on Hema's skin. The mehndi walis had been dabbing it with cotton balls soaked with lemon and sugar water to keep it moist and help deepen the color that would imprint on her skin.

Vivek took a seat next to her and held out a *pakora*. He fed it to her, his eyes glinting as she took a bite.

"That was a really nice thing you did for Shruti."

Hema shrugged. "That's why I started a foundation before I left India. It's there to help people like Shruti. Hopefully we can find a doctor in India that can do the surgery. If not, maybe one of the attendings in the residency program would be willing to help. That's the beauty of robotic surgery. The surgeon does not have to be physically where the patient is. Only the equipment needs to be there. With my father's manufacturing plants, we can look towards mass-producing the specialized medical equipment."

Vivek smiled.

"Sorry, I know I've already chewed your ear off about my plans."

"Keep talking. You've never told me when you first knew that you wanted to be a doctor."

A fist formed in her chest. This was the part that she never talked about. Vivek put a hand on her shoulder. "What is it? You can tell me."

How could he read her so well? She took a breath. "How often do you go to India?"

He shrugged. "Not very. Maybe once a year for business."

"Have you ever visited a slum?"

He shook his head.

"I had a friend in college who lived in one. Her mother worked for a wealthy family, and they had agreed to pay her tuition for the college. Every day she spent two hours on buses, trains and walking to get to college. We were paired up in chemistry lab. If we hadn't, I'm ashamed to say that I'd never have gotten to know her. I took so much for granted, including the fact that I regularly skipped classes to go see my boyfriend. Even going to medical school had been a whim for me. I was good at biology and chemistry, and nothing else interested me. Meanwhile, Aashni suffered every day for the privilege to attend those same classes."

Her throat went dry, and she asked Vivek for the water sitting on the side table. He held it out for her, and she took a sip through the straw.

"Even after Aashni and I became good friends, she refused to let me pick her up or drop her home. I knew she was embarrassed about her living situation, so I didn't press. But one day she was violently sick at school. I insisted on taking her home. I had to nearly carry her to the little tin hut she shared with her mother and brother. That place was awful. There was open sewage running in canals, she and her family slept on threadbare *charpoy*s. They cooked on a charcoal stove in the same room. The air was so stifling, I could barely breathe. I ended up taking Aashni to my house, despite her family's protests, but that's the day I realized just how much I was wasting my life."

She took another sip of water, the memory burning her throat. "Aashni's brother had been doing some odd jobs for her mother's employer after school, gardening, running errands, cleaning. He was only ten, but he needed to work to help with the household expenses. One day he was helping move some furniture when a bookshelf fell on him. He was alone, and it was hours before someone found him. By then, the weight of the bookcase had crushed his legs. They took him to a government hospital, and the doctors there decided it was best to amputate. These hospitals are overwhelmed, and rarely do they have well-trained doctors. Had he gone to the private hospital, they probably could have saved his legs. On top of that, he was given ill-fitting prosthetics that were so painful that he didn't wear them. The employer finally felt guilty enough to pay Aashni's college tuition after they saw the boy in a broken-down wheelchair. That's why Aashni is studying to become a doctor."

Vivek held the water glass to her lips even though she hadn't asked for it.

"It was an eye-opening moment for me."

What she couldn't bring herself to tell Vivek was that Arun had refused to walk into the slum with her and Aashni. He'd turned his nose up and suggested that they dump Aashni and leave. He'd even gone as far as to insist that she stay away from Aashni. There was a lot that she'd overlooked about Arun, but his behavior with Aashni was shameful. She hadn't stopped being friends with Aashni, but she had lied about it to Arun.

It wasn't long afterwards that everything had blown up. She had to tell her parents that she didn't want to marry Arjun, that she was in love with Arun. In a classic third-rate Bollywood movie plot, her parents were convinced that Arun was using her for her money. They'd threatened to disown her, stop paying her college tuition. She had risked it all and planned to elope with Arun. It was sheer luck that she'd shown up at Arun's apartment unannounced and caught him with his ex-girlfriend. The very woman he had claimed he wasn't seeing. While Arun never admitted it, Hema later found out that he'd planned to marry her, then extort a ransom from her father for divorcing her.

After that, she couldn't trust any man she met. When Vivek came along, it seemed like the right choice. He hadn't even blinked at the idea of signing a pre-nup.

"Thank you for sharing this story with me. I would've never guessed looking at Aashni that she'd gone through so much in life."

Hema nodded. "I had to practically force her to accept the ticket from India. I tried to give her a Visa card for spending money, and she refused."

Vivek smiled. "Don't worry about it. I'll make sure Vikram takes care of her when we arrive in New York."

Hema looked at him gratefully, once again marveling at how different Vivek was from Arun.

The mehndi ladies had finished their work and were applying the final dabs of lemon and sugar water on the drying henna.

"How long do you lose the use of your arms and legs?" He asked as he fed her a bite of food.

"Wondering how long you need to take care of me?"

He leaned in to whisper, "Wondering how I can take advantage of the situation."

Her face warmed. He studied the designs on her right hand, and Shruti returned with a bowl. "*Sahib*, I have written your name in these patterns. You must find it on the wedding night," she said, giggling.

Vivek grinned. "What do I get if I find it?"

"It is said that if the groom can find his name before the wedding night is over, then he will be in charge of the marriage. If not, then the wife will dominate." Shruti dabbed the lemon and sugar mixture on her arm.

"Well then…" Vivek made a show of peering at her arm.

Hema smirked. "I had her write it in Hindi."

"Really?"

During one of their many conversations, she'd discovered that he didn't know how to read Hindi. The Devanagari script melted into the swirly designs.

"In that case, how about we make it more interesting?"

"What do you suggest?"

He leaned forward and whispered in her ear. "I want you for more than a few stolen moments. If I find my name before this night is over, you let me make love to you the way I want. Slowly." His lips brushed against her earlobe. "Very slowly." An electric current made its way through her body, curling her toes.

"And what do I get if you don't find your name?"

"What do you want?"

*Something you can't give.* The unbidden thought wound around her heart, squeezing it painfully.

"You should ask for a gold necklace," Shruti suggested.

Hema's face grew hot as she realized the ladies had been listening all along.

"Gold, no no. Diamond necklace. What do the

Amreekans say? 'Diamonds are girl's best friend,'"
One of the other henna ladies chimed in.

"I have more than enough jewelry. How about something you can't buy?"

He gave her a rakish smile. "What do you have in mind?"

"An IOU. I get to ask you for anything I want, at any point I want."

He stilled. "Anything?"

"Anything." She leaned forward, her lips inches from his. "Do you dare?"

They looked at each other. The room melted around them. The sound of the giggling mehndi walis faded away.

"Okay."

"Okay?"

She couldn't ask for what she wanted. Not right now. But one day, the time would come. Their moment would come and she'd wait until then. When he was ready.

# Eleven

"Look at the colors of his mehndi," Vivek's mom exclaimed as she examined Hema's hands. The color had seeped deep into her skin and settled into dark maroon patterns that perfectly complemented her light brown skin. "You know what it means when a bride's mehndi colors are deep like this? It means that her mother-in-law will love her."

The ladies seated around Hema laughed. They were in the lounge on the third deck. The party had spanned most of the deck, with multiple henna stations at the various bars for the guests. It was well past midnight, and most of the guests had made their way back to their cabins. Vivek's mother, her maasi, Nisha, and a few of her friends stuck around to see the final finish on Hema's henna, which had dried into black scab-like flakes. The mehndi walis had carefully scraped off the dried mehndi, then rubbed her arms and legs with a jasmine-and-rose oil to seal in the color and hydrate her skin. The mehndi would last three to six weeks—the honeymoon period.

"What does the color say about how much her husband will love her?" Hema asked.

Vivek had spent a good portion of the night with her, still trying unsuccessfully to find his name in the intricate patterns.

"How much a husband loves his wife doesn't matter so much as the mother-in-law." Shruti said wisely. Hema stifled a laugh. Shruti wasn't even married.

"Those are the old ways," Vivek's mother chimed in. "It used to be that Indian sons were mama's boys, and if your *saas* didn't like you, she could make your life miserable. My own *saas*…" She looked around surreptitiously for Vivek's father. "My first night in their house, she made me cook dinner for all the gathered guests. It was a tradition in their family that a new daughter-in-law makes dinner on her first night. I was so nervous that I mixed up all the spices. I put *hing* in the *chole* and *jeera* in the fish. It was a disaster."

Shruti put a hand to her chest. "Oh no, what happened? Your in-laws must have been so mad."

"My saas was furious, but my husband, he began eating and told everyone that the food had so much love in it that it was the best thing he'd ever eaten. He ate two platefuls as everyone watched." She dabbed at her eyes. "That's the moment I fell in love with him."

Now it was Hema's turn to reach for a tissue. Her eyes moved to Vivek. She could picture the scene his mother had described, and she could see him in it, doing the exact same thing his father had done. And she could picture herself standing there like his mother had, falling for him.

The room was too hot, the air too humid, her chest too tight. "I need to use the bathroom," she said, and fled the room. She hadn't said goodbye, and it was rude to run away from her party like that, but she couldn't go back. She stabbed the button on the elevator.

"Are you okay?" Nisha came up behind her.

Hema nodded, then shook her head. "I need to get all these clothes and jewelry off."

Nisha took her arm. "Let's go to your cabin, I'll help you."

As soon as she was in the cabin, Hema began pulling off her skirt. Nisha helped her undo the back buttons of her blouse and unhook her necklace. Hema pulled at her hair, meticulously pinned by a team of hairdressers. Nisha rifled through her drawers and came up with a sleep shirt that she handed her. "Hema, what's wrong?"

Hema wanted to tell her that everything was fine. Perhaps she'd just had too much sun, or too little water, or not enough to eat. Something to explain why her stomach was knotted so tightly that it threatened to come up through her throat.

Hema sank into the couch. Nisha took a seat next to her. "It might help to talk about it."

Hema buried her face in her hands. She hadn't talked about her deal with Vivek with anyone. None of her friends knew. The closest she'd come was to tell her maasi, but even with her, she'd stopped herself. She didn't want to explain why, justify her decision, assure people that it would all be okay.

"Vivek and I aren't going to have a real marriage. We made a deal." Without warning, a sob escaped her throat, and the whole story came spilling out of her. Nisha hugged her close and let her talk and cry.

"Have you changed your mind? Nisha asked once Hema's sobs subsided.

She found herself shaking her head even before her brain had fully processed the question. "There are other ways to sponsor your medical residency if your father won't support you" Nisha said. "I can take care of your expenses."

Hema frowned at Nisha. "I must look really desperate for you to make that offer; we hardly know each other."

A look crossed Nisha's face that Hema couldn't read. "We're friends. I'd be happy to help."

Hema shook her head. "I appreciate the offer, but it's not about that…it not that I'm feeling trapped… it's that…it's that…" She couldn't get the words out through the sobs choking her.

"It's that you're starting to fall for Vivek."

A fresh batch of tears welled in her eyes. When had this happened? How had she managed to do the one thing he'd asked her not to do? The one thing she'd promised herself she would never do again.

"You have to tell him."

Hema shook her head. "I can't. He's been very clear on what he can and cannot give me. I can't burden him with this."

"You're talking about your future, your entire life."

"What will change by me telling him?"

*Just don't fall in love with me, Hema. I never want to hurt you the way Divya hurt me.*

*Vivek had been very clear during their initial discussions regarding their marriage arrangement.*

"Have you thought about the fact that he might have developed feelings for you? I've seen you two together. Any idiot can see there's something there."

"That's just attraction, chemistry. His heart still belongs to Divya."

"You don't know that."

She did. She saw it on his face every time Divya's name came up. If she told him how she felt, he'd go running. She'd be the one left sitting in the mandap.

She smiled thinly. "I'm going to marry him no matter what. I've always known what I was signing up for."

Nisha grabbed her shoulders. "Are you really going to be okay married to someone you love who doesn't love you back?"

*Like my father is.* Hema's heart sank to her toes. Could she be content being with someone day in and day out who didn't love her back, as her father was? It was one thing when they were on equal footing, when her own heart was firmly closed as well, but could she go on with her life, yearning and pining for him?

*I'll always be faithful to you. Vivek had been clear on that point as well during their long talks about how things would work.*

It wouldn't be like her parents' marriage. Yes, their love might be one-sided, but he'd be faithful to her. *Will he?* Arun supposedly loved her. He maintained that even when they broke up, he'd loved her, and yet he never loved her enough to be faithful to her. What if Vivek fell in love with someone else? What if he wanted more? She'd thought of that possibility but figured she wouldn't be bothered by that. That was when she didn't have feelings for him.

Someone knocked on the door, startling her.

"It's probably Maasi. She's still bunking with me."

Nisha nodded and stood to open the door. Hema went into the bathroom. She needed to compose herself. This was not a conversation she wanted to have with Maasi. Her aunt would push her into a lifeboat in the middle of the night if she found out that Hema was having second thoughts. She'd seen the judgment on Maasi's face every time they talked about Vivek. The disappointment that Hema would settle, the pity that she would live a loveless life. She couldn't bear to face that. Not tonight.

Her mascara had run all over her face. She stepped into the shower. The mehndi walis had discouraged her from using soap on her mehndi tonight. The harsh chemicals would prevent the henna from soaking further into her skin. She took a washcloth and scrubbed her face until it was pink and raw. Then she scrubbed her arms and legs. The bridal mehndi she had loved just a few hours ago taunted her now. She ran her fingers over Vivek's name, artistically woven into the heart drawn on her wrist. He hadn't found it, and never would.

Once the water ran cold, she dried herself, put on the sleep shirt Nisha had given her earlier, and exited the bathroom. She stopped short to see Vivek sitting on the couch.

He stood. "You didn't come back. I got worried."

*Of course he did.* How was it possible that Divya hadn't fallen head over heels for him?

"Hema, what is it?" He stepped towards her and pulled her into his arms. She breathed into his chest, desperately forcing down the words she wanted to say. The wedding was tomorrow. It was too late. She couldn't do this to him. Not now. Her throat closed; her chest so tight that it hurt to breathe.

"I want this marriage to be real," she choked out, stepping away from him.

His face was inscrutable.

"What do you mean?"

"I mean that I don't want our marriage to be a deal, an arrangement. I want it to be real. I want us to have what your parents have. I want to fall in love with you, and I want you to fall in love with me."

"Hema...you know I can't..."

She put a finger to his lips. "I am going to marry you tomorrow. No matter what you say or how you feel, I will be there at the mandap. But you asked me for honesty, so I'm giving it to you. I want more. I want it all. I want your heart, and if you can't give it to me, then I want you to walk away tomorrow."

"We're at sea tomorrow."

"Take a lifeboat."

"Hema." He let out a long breath. "I can't."

"What is it that you can't give me?" She stepped back some more, putting distance between them.

He ran his fingers through his hair. "I can't love you."

She gave him a hard look. "Why not?"

"Because I'm not capable of it. I can lie to you and tell you that I'll try, but I can't. I care for you, but I can't love you the way you want." He paced the room, then turned to face her. "I know things have changed between us. We weren't prepared for the attraction between us, but beyond our physical relationship, nothing else has changed."

"Then walk away tomorrow."

# Twelve

Vivek pounded the running track on the spa deck. It was the middle of the night; the wind was strong, and the ship was moving fast. His head spun. Hema wanted a real marriage. *How am I going to deal with this?*

Hema was right. He had to walk away. If he didn't, he was setting himself up for a lifetime of pain.

He rounded the track and increased his pace. How could this happen? He'd vetted Hema very carefully. She had been the perfect combination of an intelligent woman who was focused on her career, and in the frame of mind to understand where he was coming from. There had been no doubt that she was just as incapable of love as he was. What had changed? Even as he asked himself the question, his body remembered the feel of her on the massage table and the darkened theater. Things had changed for him too.

His legs burned; his chest tightened, but he pounded the track even harder. It wasn't fair to her. It was one thing to be on equal footing in a relationship, it was another to be in one where one person's feelings overshadowed the others. To some extent he'd known that Divya wasn't as crazy about him as he was about her. But he'd foolishly believed that their love would grow after marriage. Did Hema think that way now? And if she did, was it fair of him to condemn her to a marriage where she'd be left wanting something he couldn't give her?

*I will be there at the mandap.*

She'd asked him to be the one to walk away.

"Slow down, man, you're going to run off the ship." Vivek stopped short, huffing as his lungs hungrily sucked in air, when he saw Vikram. His brother was wearing a Hooters T-shirt and basketball shorts and carried a soft-serve ice-cream cone in his hand. He saw Vivek eyeing it. "There's a machine in the corner. They change the flavors every day. It's chocolate and pineapple today. It's vile." He offered the cone to Vivek, who shook his head. Vikram shrugged and threw it in a nearby trash can.

"Having second thoughts?" Vikram wiggled his eyebrows and slapped him on the back as he coughed.

"What? Why would you say that?"

"You have that look."

"What look is that?"

"The one you had in high school when I told you

that Ma found your weed. The look that says, *Shit! How much trouble am I in?*"

He hated how well Vikram knew him.

"Just pre-wedding jitters."

"Is that all it is?"

"What else would it be?"

"Maybe you've come to your senses and realized that you live in the twenty-first century, where getting married is not the only way to get laid."

Vivek flipped him the finger and restarted his run. He'd gotten through one lap when he ran into Vikram standing in the middle of the track.

He sighed and tried to get past his brother, but Vikram grabbed his arm. "You need a drink. I know a bar that's still open."

Vivek shook his head. He didn't need alcohol, but Vikram wasn't to be deterred. They ended up at a bar in the same lounge where the mehndi had been held. He ordered a glass of water. Vikram did the same.

Vivek let the silence settle between them. Only Vikram knew about the arrangement he'd made with Hema. He didn't want any doubt cast on their marriage. Even his parents assumed that he'd instantly fallen in love with Hema.

"I don't know if I can love her."

"Why not?"

"Because I can't love anyone. Not after Divya."

"That's placing a lot of power in the hands of a woman who ran off on your wedding day."

"I loved her."

"Past tense."

"You've never been in love," Vivek said sullenly.

"I've been head over heels in lust enough times to know that it fades over time."

How did he explain to his brother that it wasn't the same thing? While the love faded over time, the wound stayed open as a ready warning system for the next time.

"I don't understand what's changed. I thought Hema was okay with the idea of a business marriage."

"She was. But now she has feelings for me, and she wants us to make this marriage real."

"Fantastic. So you get a wife who loves you. This is a problem, how?"

"I can't return her love."

"Again, that is a problem because..."

"It's not fair to her."

Vikram sighed. "For a man who doesn't love his wife-to-be, you seem awfully worried about her feelings."

Vikram's words stabbed into his chest. Vivek stood. "I need to go."

The lifeboats are on deck 3.

It only took a second before the message said *Read*. She waited for the three dots to appear. He was going to respond with something witty like, *Vikram's figuring out where the start button is*. She waited. No three dots. She set the phone down.

"Are you okay?" Maasi put a hand on her shoulder. They were in the spa, which had become the dressing headquarters for the bridal team. Everyone else was ready and out on the lido deck, where the wedding mandap was set up.

Hema forced a smile. "Of course. Just a big moment, you know." Her white-and-maroon wedding lehenga shimmered in the bright sunlight filtering through the floor-to-ceiling windows. Vivek was supposed to wear a white sherwani with maroon embroidery that matched the color of her outfit. Nisha had designed it to match Hema's lehenga. The entire family had color-coordinated clothes. Her maasi and mother were wearing white sarees with a maroon border and blouse. Nisha had brilliantly designed each piece so it was individual but elegantly harmonized. Today was supposed to be picture-perfect.

*It's not about being perfectly matched but well-complemented,* Nisha had said.

Her mother bustled into the room. "I don't know what's taking Vivek so long. We have to get this wedding started. The ship's captain is having a heart attack about the fire in the mandap. After all the money we paid, they only allowed a small one, and now they're giving us a hard time about that too."

"Well, fire is pretty dangerous on a ship."

Her mother gave her an exasperated look. "Do you have any idea how much planning went into this? Vivek was supposed to be seated twenty minutes ago."

"Then let's go." Hema stood, her bangles jangling, her anklets tinkling. Nisha had thoughtfully designed the lehenga with lightweight fabric, knowing the wedding would be outside in the heat and Hema would be seated in front of a fire. Still, between the long skirt, the *dupatta* that served as her veil, the bangles, anklets and jewelry, Hema was weighed down.

"Don't be silly. The groom has to be seated first," Her mother, Aparna, adjusted Hema's necklace, which was slightly askew. It was an heirloom diamond necklace that belonged to her father's mother. Set in darkened silver, it had round and baguette diamonds in a fringed dark design with pendant drops. Her father had commissioned their family jeweler to make matching earrings.

"We're going." Without waiting for permission, she made her way to the elevators. *Let's get this over with.* There wasn't going to be a wedding today, and the faster everyone figured that out, the sooner the charade could be over. There was no reason to keep the wedding fire going any longer than necessary.

Her mother and Maasi protested, but Hema wasn't listening. The plan had been for her parents to walk her to the mandap after Vivek was seated. She didn't know where her father was, but he didn't need to walk her to the mandap.

"Hema, this is not how it's done." Her mother trailed behind her as she exited the elevator. If she was going to be dumped, she was going to do it with her head held high this time. She wasn't going to slink away like she had with Arun, ghosting her friends, shuttering herself from the world. This time she had done the right thing. She had stood up for herself, demanded what she deserved.

The wedding festivities were underway. The wind carried the sounds of the nasally *shehnai* music as she stepped into the outdoor area of the lido deck.

"Hema, look at you. How beautiful."

"Wow, gorgeous, Hema!"

She ignored the guests who began to close in on her as she made her way to the mandap. Like the night of the engagement party, the dining tables were gone, replaced by chairs in neat rows and columns, all looking toward a raised pergola decorated with maroon and white roses. A pundit in loose orange clothes sat in front of a small firepit. The floor was filled with marigolds. There had been an hour-long conversation to decide what flowers would go on the wedding mandap. The traditional marigolds were orange and yellow and didn't fit the maroon, white and silver colors of the wedding. At the time, it seemed like such an important decision—how to incorporate the traditional flowers without ruining the color palette. Vivek's mother had come up with the idea of putting the marigolds on the floor. *That way, you can start your new life walking on flowers.* There was a time when Hema'd pictured her wedding day with the fairy-tale innocence of a girl who believed that love conquered all. After Arun, she thought she'd lost that girl.

As she approached the mandap, she debated what to do. She hadn't quite thought through how to do this. Should she stand in front of the mandap and make an announcement? Should she ask the pundit to say something? Should she take her seat on the low-level regal chairs that had been set up for the bride and groom and just wait for everyone to come to the inevitable conclusion that the groom had jumped overboard?

"Wow, when the bride is late, everyone waits. But when the groom is late, the bride takes over."

She froze. Vivek came up beside her. Her heart pounded in her ears. She turned to him, her eyes stinging. *Don't cry, don't cry.*

"You snooze, you lose...the bride," she said, her voice cracking.

He put a hand on her back, and she met his gaze. "Have I...lost the bride?"

The worry in his eyes and the plea in his voice made her knees go weak. He wasn't here to help her make the announcement like a gentleman. He was here to marry her.

She shook her head, unable to speak. He took her hand. "Then shall we make our way to the mandap?"

He led her up the stage to cheers and hooting from the guests who crowded into the space, taking their seats. The pundit directed them to their seats, and both sets of parents appeared on either side of them. Hema finally found her voice. "Are you sure?"

He nodded. "I want to give it a try. I want to see if we can make this real."

It's wasn't exactly a declaration of undying love, but she would take it. The pundit began his chanting. Hema barely followed the ceremony. Her mind was a running a mile a minute, her heart a jumble of emotions. Vivek had shown up!

When the time came for *kanyadaan*, her father

stepped up. The word meant "giving away the girl," and her father took her hand and placed it in Vivek's hand. With their hands joined, her mother poured holy water over her father's palm, letting it trickle through his fingers and down through Vivek's and Hema's joined hands. "Vivek, this girl is my life. I am entrusting you to her." Tears stung her eyes as he turned to her, his voice catching. "I wish you a lifetime of love and happiness." He kissed her on the forehead, and she let the tears stream down her face. Makeup be damned.

The fire, which had been a few measly flames, suddenly roared as the pundit put ghee in it. Vivek nudged her and gestured with his head. She nearly laughed when she saw two crew officers standing with massive fire extinguishers in a running-ready stance. Clearly they'd drawn the short straw that morning.

Soon they were at the *saat phere* part of the ceremony. This was the point of no return. These were the seven circles around the fire with vows that would cement their union. As they stood, she caught Vivek's eye. "Last chance. If you need a distraction, I'll throw the pot of ghee in the fire, get you cover."

He smiled and held out his hand. "I want us to circle the fire together. I want us to be partners in this marriage." Her parents gasped. The tradition was for the man to lead the bride around the fire; he was the one who was supposed to lead the marriage. His mother patted him on the back. Hema's heart filled to the brim with love for him. Who was she kidding?

There was no protecting herself? She was head over heels in love with this man. Her husband.

They walked around the fire together with the guests clutching their chests and dabbing at their eyes. The vows covered love, respect, physical and mental strength, trust, loyalty, understanding, companionship and friendship. When they were done, they touched the feet of each of their parents in turn, a tradition of respect to get blessed by their elders.

Her father stopped her from touching his feet and hugged her close. "This happiness on your face is what I have lived for all these years, my girl." Then he turned to Vivek. "Her love is going to change your life. Take care of her."

Vivek nodded and joined his hands in front of his chest, bowing his head. Her father placed his hand on Vivek's head, and Hema's heart nearly burst with love for both men.

The guests threw flower petals at them, and Hema soaked up the sunshine, love and joy in the air. It was the fairy-tale day she'd pictured as a young girl.

The wedding festivities lasted all day. After the wedding ceremony, Hema and Vivek were whisked off to take pictures around the ship. There were poses by the sea, formal portraits on a grand staircase, family pictures, photos with friends. It was endless.

The ship docked at a private island in the Bahamas owned by the cruise line. There were more pictures on the island. Then Hema was whisked back to the spa to get ready for the reception. Her hair was teased and redone. Her makeup was washed off, then reapplied. Her reception outfit was a royal-blue-and-silver anarkali, a long dress that was tight on the top and then flared at the waist, ending at her ankles.

The reception was an indoor-and-outdoor affair at a beachside resort. If the rest of the wedding events had been over-the-top, this was in a new stratosphere. The entire island was theirs. Helicopters and small yachts brought in guests who hadn't been invited to the cruise. Each section of the resort held a different party, themed for the different states in India. The Rajasthani section included traditional *Ghoomar* dancers dressed in brightly colored lehngas with dupattas that covered their faces. They clapped and twirled dizzyingly to folk music. The South Indian section served dosas, large crepes the size of a coffee table. Classical kathak dancers entertained the crowds. The Mumbai section was the most popular, with street foods like gol gappa, spicy puffed balls with chick peas and mint coriander water.

The dancing lasted well into the night, moving from indoors to barefoot on the beach. Vivek and Hema had to wait until a respectable number of guests went back to the ship before they were able to stumble back to her cabin. *Their cabin.* From now on her bed would not be her own.

She collapsed into the couch and reached down to pull off her silver high heels. "I don't think I could've stood for another second."

He sat on the floor beside her and grabbed her foot, rubbing it. She sighed as he traced the mehndi patterns with his fingers, and then trailed his lips along the red lines as he made his way up her calf. She began un-pinning the saree pallu from her blouse, her body eager for him. He stood, and she reached for his pants. He stilled her hands.

"We're going to do this my way. Slowly. Very slowly."

"You didn't find your name."

"I still have the night."

His voice was low, and it wrapped around her, filling her with fiery desire. He made love to her that night, taking his time to kiss her and lick her and let her explode with pleasure. Then he did it all over again until she was mad with the need for him. When he finally entered her, the pressure, the anticipation was so intense that she let him have her entirely, heart and soul. She exploded with pleasure and imploded with love for him.

The sun was coming up over the horizon by the time they were both spent and exhausted. She lay on his chest, savoring the feel of his arms around her, listening to the steady beat of his heart, letting his tenderness envelop her.

Her husband. She let the thought gather in her heart and banked the love that filled her soul. Everything she'd thought she knew about love was a mere fraction of what she felt ow.

"I love you," she murmured as exhaustion and sleep overtook her.

It was only when she woke up hours later that she realized he never said it back.

# Thirteen

*One month later*

Hema collapsed on the pillowy cream-colored bed. It was her first day off since she started residency two weeks ago. The floor-to-ceiling windows shimmered with the heat and haze of New York City. She stared at the tops of buildings and the Hudson River in the distance. It had only been a month since the wedding, and it seemed that their lives were moving in fast forward. Vivek had been busy following up on several business leads he had cultivated during the wedding. Hema's time had been sucked up in post-wedding social events and residency orientation. The day after orientation, she was thrown into her clinical program. Though her shifts were only supposed to be twelve hours because of some rule to limit the number of hours physicians spent treating patients to reduce medical errors, no one followed the time limits. Even after they clocked out, she and her fellow residents stayed at the hospital to watch surgeries or practice in the lab. During orientation, one of the second-year residents had warned them that the program was brutal and they had to spend a lot of time reading, practicing and watching if they wanted to keep up. Tonight, though, she was exhausted and left the hospital an hour after her shift ended. She had exactly twenty-two hours off before another week of fourteen-hour days. Vivek had texted that he'd be home in an hour, and she was looking forward to spending an evening, and a night, with him.

She sat on the bed and studied his bedroom. His penthouse was decorated in Vivek's style. Modern, elegant and minimal. He'd given her carte blanche to redecorate, but she had neither the time nor the inclination beyond some minor changes. Two dressing rooms off the master held dressers and custom closets. Hema's closet had already been filled with the clothes she'd brought from India when they returned from the wedding cruise. Her Indian clothes on one side, Western clothes on another. Shoes and jewelry were similarly organized. Vivek had the smaller closet on the other side of the room. The housekeeper, Marta, had said that Vivek had all his clothes in the bigger closet but had donated a bunch and moved into the smaller space to make room for her.

The chef not only knew her favorite dishes, but the

exact spice levels she liked. Marta made sure her favorite flowers, lilies, were on her nightstand and in the front foyer. Vivek never failed to text and ask her how her day was going.

It was the perfect life. On paper. She'd hardly seen him in the last couple of weeks. In the mornings, they were both in a mad rush to get out the door, and he was often asleep by the time she returned home on the day shift. On the night shift, he was already gone by the time she arrived home. They were still hot for each other and took every opportunity when she wasn't exhausted and he was home to find new ways to explore each other. But the missing piece of their relationship was ever-present, shading each happy moment like a dark cloud brooding in the distance.

She dozed off and stirred when Vivek walked through the door. He bent down and dropped a kiss on her head. "Wake up, sleepyhead, we're going to be late."

Rubbing the sleep from her eyes, she looked at him in confusion. "Late for what?"

"Did you forget? Today is the Singh charity event."

Hema groaned. "I thought that was next week." She laid her head back. "I am so tired; can we skip it?"

Vivek shook his head. "This is to benefit the refugees from Ukraine. I am the first major donor. They need me there with my big fat check to shame the rest of the tightwads to open their wallets." She almost asked if he could go without her. The idea of getting dressed and spending the evening on her feet in high heels held about as much appeal as giving a patient with diarrhea an enema. But she swung her legs over the bed. Divya was scheduled to perform at this event. Marta had made it a point to tell her that when she'd gone over the month's events.

She took a quick shower and studied the collection of gowns that she'd purchased in Paris for her post-wedding social life. Marta had offered to organize the gowns by event, but Hema hadn't had time to select and organize her clothes. It had just been two weeks since the start of residency, but already the idea of wearing anything other than clogs and scrubs seemed strange. She selected a Naeem Khan backless silver gown with royal-blue embroidery and a high leg split. She paired it with diamond hoop earrings, a diamond-and-sapphire tennis bracelet and silver ankle-strap sandals. There wasn't much to do with her hair, so she put it up in a messy bun. She sat at the dresser and yawned as she dabbed concealer below her eyes.

It was already Sunday morning in India, but had her mother gotten dressed up last night to go out? There was always a party on Saturday nights in Delhi. Were these the events where her mother met up with Nisha's father? Is that why she seemed so happy when she was getting dressed? Hema hadn't had the chance to confront her mother about the rev-elations from Nisha. What would be the point? The identity of the man, the way the affair ended hardly mattered. What was important was whether her par-ents would continue their marriage now that Hema was out of their daily lives. They would be back in two weeks for a social event. This date was marked in red on her calendar. She had to do a three-way shift trade to make sure she had the night off. Both Vivek and Nisha were getting young entrepreneur awards. She didn't know for sure but suspected that Nisha's father would be there.

Hema tried to talk to her father every few days. The ten-hour time difference and her schedule didn't allow them to connect consistently. He pretended to be in high spirits but couldn't hide his loneliness.

Vivek knocked on the door and entered when she called out to him. He came up behind her and kissed the back of her neck, making her even more frustrated that they had to go out. "I came to hurry you along, but seeing you in that dress, I'm debating whether we have time to take it off you."

She smiled seductively at him. "Are you sure your father can't step in for you? I was hoping we could've spent a not-so-quiet evening in bed." She held out her arms. The mehndi was fading, the deep maroon color now very light orange. "I'll give you a last chance to find your name."

He groaned and pulled her into his embrace, nuzzling her neck.

Vivek held his wife, enjoying the feel of her soft body against his. He glanced at his watch. They were already late. He hated being late. Hema began to turn away from him, and he caught sight of her naked back. *To hell with it.*

He ran his finger down her spine, and all thoughts

of time vanished from his brain when he saw the goose bumps on her arms. Trailing kisses down her back, he tugged on the zipper, letting the dress fall to the floor.

She stepped out of the dress, and his breath caught. All she had on was black lace panties. He shrugged off his suit jacket and undid his tie as she unbuttoned his shirt, kissing his chest as she went. The feel of her lips on his chest sent fire through his veins. She reached his belt and made quick work of pulling down his pants and boxers. He moaned as she took him in her hand first, and then in her mouth.

Their lovemaking on the ship had been hot and satisfying, but since their wedding, things had changed between them. The ferocity and passion was still there, but Hema was different, and he was different. They took time to enjoy each other's bodies, feel each other's breaths, hear each other's heartbeats. For the first time since Divya, he wanted to let himself fall in love again, to give Hema everything she wanted.

He gently pulled her away from him, then picked her up and took her to their bed. He laid her down and kissed her breasts, flicking his tongue across her nipples the way she liked. He touched her core and knew that she was ready for him, but he kissed and licked her some more. She moaned and bucked underneath him, begging for him to enter her. As much as he wanted to, he resisted. She was close, and he knew it. He used his finger until she moaned sinfully and clenched, shuddering as her orgasm ripped through her. Then he rubbed himself against her core, enjoying how she lifted her thighs, inviting him in. When he slid into her, she was tight and wet, and clung to him, rocking her body to his rhythm.

When they were both spent, he held her, enjoying the feel of her naked body against his. At the end of a long day, holding her was what he looked forward to most.

The buzzing of his phone finally caught his attention. He looked at his watch and jolted out of bed. *Shit.*

# Fourteen

Traffic was a mess, and by the time Vivek's driver pulled the town car up to the Mahal Hotel where the event was being held, they were very late. The hotel was owned by the Singh family and was the most elegant blend of New York style and Indian hospitality Hema had ever seen. They made their way to the grand ballroom. Silver-clothed tables with matching silver chairs perfectly complemented the royal-blue carpet and crystal chandeliers. The cocktail hour was long over, and guests were seated at their tables. Tuxedo-clad waitstaff served little plates of frisée salad to the glittering crowd.

Before they entered the room, Hema stopped Vivek. "I know this is the first time you'll be seeing Divya since…"

"…since she left me."

Hema nodded, swallowing. "I just want you to know that I'm okay with you needing to…to do whatever it is you need to do."

The words were not coming out the way she'd practiced them in her head, or in the sentiment that bloomed in her heart. *I know she was the love of your life, but I want you to say goodbye to her. I want you to excise her from your heart and make room for me. Think you can do that?*

He cupped her face and dropped a kiss on her forehead. "Divya is my past. You are my present and future. I don't have any unfinished business with her."

The breath she hadn't known she was holding released, easing the tightness in her chest. Their wedding night was the only time she'd dared to tell him she loved him, and he hadn't said it back. The thought stung her whenever they were together. Perhaps tonight could be the night he finally let go of whatever he was holding on to that kept his heart closed.

They arrived backstage as instructed. A harried event coordinator dressed in a black skirt suit rushed towards them. "I'm sorry sir, you are so late, we had to skip your part of the program."

"Excuse me?" Vivek's body stiffened beside her.

"We expected you nearly an hour ago," the coordinator said breathlessly. "I'm sorry, but we're on to the next part of our program. Your donation is listed in the program."

"That won't do," Vivek said woodenly. "Look, I'm

sorry we're late. Could we do the check ceremony and my speech at the end of the program?"

The coordinator looked uncertain. "I'll have to check with my boss."

"You do that, and please remind him or her that the funds haven't been transferred yet."

Hema flinched at the coldness in Vivek's voice. Once the coordinator was out of earshot, she turned to him. "You wouldn't really retract your donation just because we can't make a public show of it, would you?" Her voice was harsher than she meant it to be.

"The pageantry is important. That room is filled with the business vultures of New York. Seeing me on stage making this big donation sends the message that we are financially stable. That I'm in charge and everything is okay. Especially since my speech was listed in the program. If we don't do it, there'll be rumors." He turned away from her. "Dammit, we should've been on time."

She'd never seen him this antsy, and it left her feeling unsettled. He didn't often talk about the specifics of his work, and she hadn't realized the stress he was under. Why hadn't he shared that with her?

The event coordinator returned. "We will have you do the check ceremony and speech at the end of the program," she said curtly. She issued a few more instructions, but Hema wasn't listening. She followed Vivek's gaze to the curtain wings, where Divya shimmered in a strapless gold gown that seemed to be painted on her perfect body. Her long black hair hung loose down her back. Divya turned around, and the bright lights reflected off her, making her face glow with the type of angelic beauty that made Hema want to retreat back into the shadows.

Vivek walked towards her, seemingly forgetting that Hema was standing next to him. She stood back, telling herself that he deserved to have some privacy to talk to his former lover, but the truth was that she didn't trust her legs to move. Divya's face broke into a smile as Vivek approached. Hema couldn't see his face but could feel the sudden energy in his body, see the lift of his shoulders and the bounce in his step. She rubbed her arms, her body cold despite the warmth of the lights.

There was a second of awkwardness as Vivek approached Divya. Then he bent down and gave her a kiss on the cheek. It was a platonic gesture, but Hema's stomach churned and a bitter taste filled her mouth. She turned and fled.

Vivek had prepared himself for this moment. He was going to stand tall, paste a big smile on his face and show Divya that he had moved on, just as she had. Divya would never know how she'd wrecked his heart.

"Congratulations on your wedding." She looked over his shoulder. "Where is Hema? I thought I just saw her."

Vivek turned. "She was here just a second ago. She must have gotten pulled away by someone." He swiveled back to Divya.

"Hema is amazing. I'm so glad it worked out between you two."

"How's Ethan?"

Her face brightened at her husband's name. How had he missed the fact that she'd never looked at him the way she now looked across the room at Ethan? He'd been so blinded by his love for her that he hadn't seen what was right in front of him.

"There is something I want to say, Vivek, while we have a second alone." She shifted on her feet. "I'm sorry for the way things ended between us."

"You've already apologized." And she had, several times over email and text.

She nodded. "I owe you an explanation for why I ran that day. I know I said that I was running from the wedding, but clearly that isn't true."

*Of course not. Barely a year after you picked up your skirt and ran away from our wedding mandap, you married another man. You were running from me.*

"I wasn't running away as much as I was running towards something. All my life I followed the path that my parents laid out for me. I needed my freedom, a chance to take a breath and think about what I wanted to do with my life, pursue my dreams."

"Well, you certainly succeeded." He hadn't meant to sound patronizing but he'd stopped himself from adding *at my expense.*

She reached out and touched his hand. "I wasn't fair to you, and for that I'm sorry."

"Why didn't you just tell me you were having second thoughts?"

She looked away, then sighed. "I should have. But you were so focused on the plans you'd made; you were so sure that it was the right way to proceed. Things moved so quickly after you talked to my parents that I didn't have time to think, to process everything that was happening. There was no space for me to hit the pause button and take the time to figure out what I wanted."

"We spent months together. Surely there was a moment where we could have discussed things."

She glanced away for several seconds then looked him in the eyes. "Vivek, you are a venture capitalist. Your business requires you to process large amounts of data and make decisions in a matter of seconds. That's how you approach your life decisions too, but the rest of us are not like that. We need time to think, to experience, to feel. You were so focused on the next steps that you weren't really listening when I tried to talk to you. I could have been a little more direct, but I was honestly trying to figure things out. You are a good guy, the type of guy any woman would be lucky to marry. I needed time with the decision. I was torn between doing what was right for my family and what was right for me, and…"

"…and I rushed you along."

She took a breath. "Let's not dwell on the past. Clearly it all ended up for the best. If we had gotten married, we would have eventually realized that we didn't truly love each other. From everything Sameer, Nisha, Arjun and Rani have said about your wedding, you and Hema are clearly in love. You found the woman you were supposed to be with."

He was glad that he and Hema had put on a good show. Divya's name was called, and she was visibly relieved. She gave him a small smile and walked onto the stage.

He stared after her. What did she mean that he hadn't given her space to figure out what was wrong? Things hadn't moved that quickly. Certainly not as fast as his wedding to Hema. He would have listened if Divya had concerns. How had he allowed himself to get so sucked up in his relationship that he'd been blind to everything going on around him?

He watched Divya's performance, an uneasy feeling settling into his stomach. A slap on the back jarred him. He turned to see the chairman of his company's board, Rakesh Multani. "You finally decided to show up. You know James DeSouza is here as well. He actually had the nerve to ask me whether you didn't show because the company check bounced."

Vivek gritted his teeth. James DeSouza was the guy who had orchestrated the failed hostile takeover of his company.

"I got caught up with something. Don't worry, it's straightened out now," Vivek said.

Rakesh raised his eyebrows. "I would get caught up too if I had a wife like that." He raised a brow towards Hema, who stood in the shadows, and Vivek fisted his hand.

"Sir, I'll ask you to speak with respect when it comes to my wife."

Rakesh held up his hands. "Don't be so sensitive, son. Now, make sure nothing else goes wrong. The vultures are circling." He whistled and gestured above his head, then moved away.

Vivek took a breath. He knew how important tonight was. He'd worked on his speech for hours. This was the first major social event since the takeover attempt. How had he allowed himself to get so swept up with Hema that he'd forgotten what was important? That was the whole reason for marrying someone like Hema. To be with a woman with whom he could control his emotions, so he could keep his eyes on the ball. He was going down the same path he had with Divya, letting his emotions cloud his judgment, something he couldn't afford to do.

Hema stood in the shadows and watched Vivek as Divya performed on stage. Her stomach was twisted in so many knots that it threated to come up her throat and choke her. Vivek couldn't take his eyes off Divya. From Hema's vantage point, she could only see the side of his face, but the pain etched on his features was unmistakable.

She swallowed against her tight throat. He still loved Divya. Could she blame him? Hema and Divya had been good friends for years. Their families were close and often spent time together. Divya had always been a force: smart, capable, lively and beautiful. She was Vivek's first love, and Hema knew only too well what he felt. It wasn't his fault that the way he treated her, the way he listened to her, the way he made love to her, the way he reached into her heart and tugged at her strings had made her fall head over heels in love with him.

But his heart didn't belong to her. She'd have to live with the knowledge that no matter how perfect things seemed between them, he would never love her the way she loved him. He would look at her as a responsibility, as a contract that he had to fulfill. Their physical relationship was great right now, but without love, it would eventually grow stale. Could she live a life like that? The same life her father had lived, in love with someone who didn't love him back?

Her mouth soured and she resisted the urge to turn and leave. There was no place to run to, nowhere to hide. This was the deal she'd made, to be the trophy wife so she could become the kind of doctor she wanted to be, so she could make a difference in the world, provide medical care to people in the rural parts of the world that were largely forgotten by modern medicine.

Divya finished her song and exited the stage, smiling at Vivek. His eyes followed her, and he stepped forward and enveloped her in a hug. He finally pulled his eyes away from Divya when his name was called on stage. Had Hema not stepped out of the shadows and up to him, he might have walked onto the stage without her.

They presented the big cardboard check to the charity that was helping Ukrainian refugees. Vivek stepped to the podium and made an impassioned speech about how the world had forgotten that the innocent residents of Ukraine still didn't have homes to live in, had lost all their belongings and struggled to get basic food for their families while the New York elite would leave enough food on their dinner plates to feed most of Kharkiv. It wasn't the words he was saying, but the heart with which he said them. He really believed in what he was saying, and she was reminded about what drew her to him in the very beginning.

*"Why is it so important to do your residency in the US?"*

*"Because it's the best robotics program in the world. I need to understand that technology so I can bring it back to rural India. To the places where other well-trained physicians won't go, so people can get the care they need."*

*"I love that. Would you let me invest in your future clinic?"*

*"I don't need your money; Dad has already started a foundation. He supports my career; he just doesn't want me moving to America all alone without the protection of marriage. He's old fashioned that way."*

*"It's not about the money. I want to be part of something that makes a real difference in people's lives. I can't tell you how many charities I give money to where I have no idea what actually happens. The last one that my accountant looked into spends 80 percent of their money on administrative costs. Can you imagine? I want to be there when you build the first clinic. I want to see the look on people's faces when they get that surgery they need."*

In that first meeting, he'd understood exactly what

she wanted to do and why. Maybe it had been that moment when she'd started falling in love with him. Maybe that's why she'd been so quick to agree to the wedding. Looking back, how hadn't she seen it?

Vivek said a few more words, getting a standing ovation from the crowd. Hema sincerely hoped that meant more donations. She'd never seen him in action like this. As if it were even possible, her heart swelled even more with love for him. Maybe she could live with whatever it was that he could give her. Vivek had never lied to her. He'd never promised her his heart. He would treat her well, make sure she lived a happy life. What more could she ask for? Her father had spent over thirty years in a marriage with so much less.

Once they were off stage, Hema longed to sit and rest her feet, but they had to make the rounds and talk to some of Vivek's investors. It was all for a good cause, but Hema was exhausted. She'd lost count of the number of dinner invitations they'd received that Vivek had enthusiastically accepted. Just the thought of more social engagements made her long for their soft, comfortable bed and sleep.

At the end of the night, she collapsed on their bed when they returned home. Sleep was numbing her mind, but she had to talk to Vivek.

"How did it go with Divya?"

He shrugged as he took off his bow tie and began unbuttoning his shirt. "It went fine. Just pleasantries."

He was lying. She could tell by the too-casual tone of his voice and the way he wouldn't meet her eyes.

"It looked like a lot more than pleasantries," she said dryly.

He met her eyes and sighed. "It's the first time I've actually seen her since our wedding. I wanted to look her in the eyes and ask her why she didn't just talk to me, tell me that she didn't want to marry me. Why she ran away like she did."

"What did she say?"

"She said that I never gave her a chance. That once I make a decision, I'm too focused on executing it to stop and reconsider whether it's the right decision."

*She's right.* But that's not what Vivek needed to hear right now.

"I have to do the same thing. While we plan surgical procedures, rarely does everything go the way a textbook teaches us. We have to make split-second decisions that could literally mean the patient's life or death. There is nothing wrong with making quick decisions."

"There is if you don't learn from your mistakes."

*So, am I a mistake?* It was a question she desperately wanted to ask, but she would never bring herself to do so. She didn't want to know the answer.

# Fifteen

It was a blistering day, and the heat reflected off the black tarmac. She noticed the dark circles under her father's eyes as he came close. She hugged him tightly. "Are you okay?" Hema whispered in his ear.

He nodded then pulled away. "Why wouldn't I be okay? Just jet-lagged. I'm getting too old for these long flights."

Her mother made her way down the steps of their jet. "Where's Vivek?" she asked, hugging Hema.

"He had to work." Hema said evasively. Truthfully, she had no idea where Vivek was. In the short week since they'd seen Divya at the Ukraine charity event, he'd been distant. She tried to tell herself if was only her imagination. She'd been putting in sixteen-hour days at the hospital to make up for the day and a half that she was taking off to spend with her parents. She came home so tired that she hardly noticed or remembered what he was doing. Yet she had texted him earlier in the afternoon to remind him that her parents were arriving. While he was under no obligation to meet them at the airport, it would've been the courteous thing to do since it was their first time visiting Hema and Vivek as a married couple. Had seeing Divya finally made him realize that he'd made a mistake marrying Hema?

She forced a smile on her face when she saw the concern in her father's eyes. No matter what he said, the dark circles under his eyes were not from jet lag. He wasn't sleeping well. She knew that from the fact that he often sent her texts during the middle of her day, which was the middle of the night in India.

"I am going to melt in his heat," she said to break the silence.

"Oh, come on, this is nothing compared to Delhi."

"Yes, but the Delhi heat is dry. This humidity takes some getting used to."

They got into the air-conditioned town car that Hema had arranged to take them back to Midtown Manhattan from the private aviation terminal at JFK. After much argument, her parents had booked a room at the Mahal Hotel. It's not as if Vivek's penthouse didn't have room. They had five bedrooms, four of which were essentially guest rooms. Her father had an old-fashioned notion that an Indian girl's parents didn't stay in her house after marriage. *There's a reason for such traditions. When a girl's parents stay with her, it can become a source of friction in her marriage,"* her father had explained. What she suspected is that her parents had been fighting again, and her father didn't want her and Vivek to know. Her parents' hotel accommodations were a two-bedroom suite, and she would bet money they were sleeping in separate rooms again.

At the hotel, her mother left to go meet up with some friends for dinner. "Ma, I only have this evening and tomorrow off." Hema complained.

Her mother brushed her off. "I won't be long, and we can have dessert and chai together. Plus, if I see my friends tonight, then I am free all day to be with you tomorrow."

Hema didn't say anything, noting the firm line of her father's lips. She wasn't that upset; her mother's absence gave her an excuse to spend time alone with her father. They chose to eat at the hotel restaurant. Her father was tired, and neither of them wanted to sit in New York traffic. The Mahal Hotel had recently hired a Michelin-starred chef who specialized in fusion food. She'd been meaning to try it.

The restaurant was busy, but they were seated right away once Sameer caught sight of them. He and Nisha lived in a penthouse apartment at the top of the hotel. It was where Hema had first met Vivek. "If you have a minute, stop by the penthouse. I know Nisha will want to see you."

Hema promised to do so after dinner. Sameer gave her a code to the private elevator. "If you punch this code, you'll get straight to the penthouse. I'll text Nisha and let her know so she expects you."

Hema had a feeling her father would turn in early, and she had no doubt that her mother wouldn't be home until late, despite her promise to the contrary. It would be nice to see Nisha.

The restaurant looked like the dining room of a Rajasthani palace. Gold-and-maroon embroidered upholstery complemented dark wood tables. The walls were adorned with dark wood statues of gods and goddesses, some embracing, some in battle. Hema and her father were shown to a cozy banquette in the corner. A waiter filled gold-colored tumblers with water.

They studied the menu for a few minutes, then finally settled on a spinach chaat and salmon tikka for appetizers, and asked the waiter to bring the chef's surprise plates for their main meal. Her mother was a very selective eater, but both Hema and her father enjoyed experimenting with their food and liked tasting menus. Her father ordered a flight of whiskeys to go with the food, and Hema opted for the sommelier-recommended wine pairings.

They chatted about Hema's residency and his business. Their surprise entrée was a traditional thali, a plate with several compartments filled with an assortment of dishes. Chicken tikka masala, saffron rice, naan stuffed with nuts and raisins, lamb braised with garam masala, and watermelon mint chutney. It was all delicious, and they enjoyed the food.

When they couldn't eat another bite, Hema finally asked him, "How are things with you and Ma?"

He shrugged. "They are the way they have always been, my dear."

"Why do you put up with it, Dad?"

"What would you have me do? Divorce your mother? People would just assume that I am in the wrong. It'll be embarrassing for the family."

"Dad, that is old-fashioned thinking. Times have changed. Divorce doesn't have the stigma that it used to."

He took several sips of his whiskey. "Let's not talk of these things."

That's how he always ended any conversation about her mother. "How have you spent all these years knowing Ma doesn't love you like you love her?"

Her father stared at her. "Is this about that boy Arun? Are you still thinking about him?"

Hema shook her head. "You were right about him all along. That was a mistake that I'm glad I didn't make." Her father only knew a part of the story. She was glad that he didn't know the full extent of everything that had happened with Arun. "I just want to understand what it was like for you."

Once again, her father stared at her for a long time, then took a big gulp of his whiskey. "When you love someone with all your heart, there is a lot that you'll tolerate."

"Do you still love her?"

"I love what she has given me." He put a hand on her head in a fatherly gesture. "You! Every time

I look at you, I remember the gift that your mother has given me."

"You had a little something to do with my creation," she said teasingly, but her father looked away.

"You will learn, Hema, that marriage is rarely equal. There is always one person who is more invested than the other. And the person who is more vested is the one who has to compromise, to make things work. That's how you make sure to have a fulfilled and successful life. I know that the solution these days is to get divorced, but that is the coward's way out. If you love someone, you find a way to make it work with them."

*But how do you love someone who loves someone else?* She longed to tell her father that he had given too much to her mother. She wanted to ask him how he continued loving her when she shared herself with another, but she couldn't bring it upon herself to tell him that she knew about the affair. There was already so much pain in his eyes. She couldn't inflict more. If he still hadn't told her about it, then there was clearly a reason he didn't want her to know. She wouldn't take away that little bit of control from him. Plus, it wouldn't change anything in her father's life. He loved her mother too much to divorce her. He would suffer with her for the rest of his life. The question Hema kept asking herself is whether she loved Vivek enough to do the same.

As expected, her father wanted to turn in after dinner. He could barely keep his eyes open through coffee and a *ras malai* tres leches trifle. The chef had taken the traditional Indian cheese dessert smothered in cardamom milk and elevated it with additional flavors of rum and chocolate. She wished Vivek would have come. He would've loved the food. Before he made an excuse not to come to dinner, she had texted to let him know that she wanted to have dinner alone with her father.

Her mother had texted to say that she was caught up with her friends and would see Hema for breakfast. *No surprise there.* Hema dropped her father at his room, then made her way to the private elevator that Sameer had shown her. Her phone was dead. She wondered if she should look for a house phone to call Nisha, but she didn't see one immediately. Sameer had assured her that he would be working late that night, so the penthouse was empty.

Lost in her thoughts, she exited the elevator as it arrived at the penthouse suite. She stepped onto the marble floor and took in the fragrance of the peonies arranged on the foyer table. The foyer opened into the great room. She was about to call out to Nisha when a familiar voice stopped her. What was her mother doing here?

She should announce herself, but the few words that floated her way made her go cold. She took off her shoes and tiptoed into the room. The great room included a generous living room with couches set together in a square and a dining table that seated sixteen. The focal point was the floor-to-ceiling windows that gave a bird's-eye view of Manhattan. Nisha and her mother were standing by the kitchen island. A coffee cup sat on the stone counter in front of them. Their chairs were pushed back. By their posture and the angry expressions on their faces, it was clear that they were arguing.

"It is my decision whether or not to tell Hema," Her mother was saying.

"Aunty, I've tried to respect your wishes, but I can't lie to Hema anymore. We are friends, and I'd like to have a relationship with her. How long do you plan to keep this from her?"

"Until your father is ready to claim her as his own."

Hema couldn't help it. A gasp escaped her throat, and the two women looked towards her. Her mother's eyes widened, and Nisha came towards her. "Hema, what are you doing here?"

Bile rose in her throat. "Sameer gave me a code to the elevator. He said he would text you." The words sounded like they were coming from somewhere else. Her eyes were fixed on her mother, who was pinching the bridge of her nose. It was a gesture Hema was very familiar with. The first time she remembered seeing it was when she'd spilled her milk all over her mother's laptop. The machine had actually sizzled before sparking. The last time was when she'd told her mother that she didn't want to marry Arjun. But this time Hema knew that she wasn't the one in the wrong.

"What were you two just talking about?"

Hema must have misheard or misunderstood.

Her mother looked at Nisha and then Hema. Hema rounded on Nisha. "You tell me."

Nisha looked back and forth between Hema and her mother. "I didn't want you to find out this way. I had really hoped that Aparna aunty would have told you by now."

"Tell me what?" Hema didn't care that her voice sounded hysterical. Her pulse pounded in her ears; her mouth was so sour that she was sure she would throw up at any second.

Nisha pointed to the couch. Hema didn't want to sit. She wanted to shake Nisha and her mother in turn until the truth tumbled out of them, but she pressed her lips and sat, unable to do more than perch on the edge of the couch. Nisha took a seat next to her and grabbed her hand. "Please know this is not the way I wanted you to find out." Hema took a breath, trying not to scream. "Your mother became pregnant with you while she was having an affair with my father. You are my biological half sister."

The room faded from her vision. Her mother's pinched face, the anguish on Nisha's features all melted away. It had to be a mistake. There was no way that she was not her father's daughter. Her mother had done some terrible things, but this was evil. This was beyond anything that even her mother could do to her.

"Can I have a few minutes alone with Hema?"

Nisha looked at Hema, and she nodded. Once they were alone, Aparna took Hema's hand. "I know how upsetting this is. Let me explain."

Aparna took a deep breath. "I was already in love

with Nisha's father when my parents arranged my marriage to your father. I tried really hard to forget him, but he was my first love. Your father is a good man, but all he wanted was a trophy wife. I wanted more out of life. When I saw Mukesh at a social event, all of the old feelings came back. We tried to resist. He was married to Nisha's mother and I to your father. Neither of us could help it. We were both unhappy with our marriages and still in love with each other."

Aparna looked at Hema pleadingly. "I know how close you are to your father, and I never planned any of this. You have to understand that I didn't have a choice in who to marry. I was a schoolgirl. If I didn't marry, there was no place for me to go. Women didn't have choices back then. I was told that my love for Mukesh was infatuation, that I would fall in love with my husband, and I tried, I really did. But I couldn't forget Mukesh, and when I saw him again, we couldn't ignore how we felt about each other. Hema, please understand, I didn't do this to hurt you or Anil."

She went to grab Hema's hand, but Hema pulled away. "Even if I can understand the affair, how could you deceive me and Dad about who my biological father is. How could you do that to Dad?"

Aparna looked pained. "I hadn't planned to do it that way. But Mukesh wasn't in a position where he could claim you as his own. If I told your father the truth, then you and I would be out on the streets. I had to make sure you were taken care of."

"You were ensuring that you had a good life."

"You father knows about the affair."

"But does he know about me?"

Aparna looked away. "I was going to tell him. But it became more and more difficult as the years went on. He loves you so much, and you him. He told me over and over that you were the only bright spot in our marriage. I didn't want to take you away from him too. Why don't you understand that I've secured your future? As the only child, you'll inherit your father's fortune. Your children will never have to be dependent on a man. They will have a different life than we did."

Hema wanted to understand her mother's intentions were good. She too had agreed to an arranged marriage because she hadn't been capable of financially supporting herself. She'd given in to her father's pressure to get married. And here she was, a modern woman, educated and fully capable of advocating for herself. Yet the betrayals were piling up.

"Is this why you couldn't love me?"

"Excuse me?"

"I bound you to Dad. Being a single woman in India is hard enough. Being a single mother was impossible. If I hadn't come along, maybe you could've left Dad. Isn't that right?"

Her mother shook her head, but the way she averted her eyes told Hema that she'd finally understood her mother's apathy towards her. Hema was her mistake. The child that forever bound her to a husband she didn't love, and kept her from the man she did. How could her mother love a man like Mukesh? A man who wouldn't even claim his own daughter?

"How could you see me and Dad together and know what a secret you were keeping?" she asked.

Her mother shook her head. "Tell me something. Now that you know, would you tell your father?"

The question felt like a sucker punch. She couldn't keep something like this from her father. Yet it would shatter him to know the daughter that was his whole world wasn't even his. The one good thing to come out of his marriage was also false. How could she do this to him?

"This is not my betrayal," Hema said. "It's yours. You need to tell him."

Aparna shook her head. "I've kept this secret so long; I don't see a point in telling him."

"How could you still love him?"

"Mukesh?"

Hema nodded. "How could you still love a man who wouldn't take care of his own daughter? What did he give you that was worth giving up Dad?"

Aparna took a long breath. "Mukesh couldn't claim you because it would have ruined his family. Remember, this was thirty years ago. Times were different. You would have been branded as illegitimate. This wouldn't just have affected you but also Nisha. Mukesh did what was best for all of us."

Hema smiled thinly. "He did what was best for him. Just like you did."

"Tell me something, Hema. Have you forgotten that boy, Arun? Your first love?"

Like she could ever forget Arun. And yet, she understood what her mother was implying. At some level, she'd known in her heart that Arun had cheated on her. Yet she'd continued to stay with him, believing that their love would endure. She'd wanted the fairy tale so badly that she'd refused to let anything soil it.

Before Hema could answer, her mother went on. "Because let me tell you something. I tried to love your father. I'm still trying to love him. But I gave my heart to Mukesh, and no matter what I do, I can't get it back."

Hema stood and paced the room. She stopped when she came to a family portrait. It was of Arjun and Rani, their daughter Simrin, Divya and Ethan, Sameer and Nisha, Karishma and Naina. The Singh family. She stared at Divya. Her own heart had never truly belonged to Arun. She knew that now. But Vivek's heart belonged to Divya. Even if Divya didn't return Vivek's feelings, it wouldn't stop him from longing for her, just as her mother had longed for Mukesh, and her father longed for her mother.

Suddenly the knots in her stomach twisted so hard that she ran to the kitchen sink, sure that her dinner was about to come up her throat. Could she really spend her life in love with someone who loved someone else?

# Sixteen

Vivek had been asleep when she arrived home after the talk with her mother. Nothing had been resolved. Her mother asked for time to think. She was still unwilling to tell her father about Hema's parentage. Hema had tried to settle her queasy stomach with ginger chai, and then she'd thrown up. At first, she'd chalked it up to stress. Then it hit her. She was late. Frantically tapping on her phone, she checked her period app and realized that she was at least two weeks late. It had happened before. Sometimes stress caused her to miss a month entirely. She'd gotten her birth control shot when they returned from the wedding. She couldn't be pregnant. Could she?

Her stomach churned. She grabbed her purse. She didn't like leaving the safety of the penthouse suite in the middle of the night, but she hurriedly ordered an Uber to take her to the twenty-four hour pharmacy a mile down the road.

During the thirty minutes it took to go and get the test, her panic level reached a critical stage. If she was pregnant, it would mean the end of her residency. They wouldn't kick her out of the program—that was illegal—but there was no physical way she could keep up with the grueling schedule. Then, once the baby came, she couldn't be absent from her residency, she'd miss too much. Yet, she couldn't go back to work right after having a baby.

When she arrived at the penthouse, Vivek was awake. "Is everything okay? Where did you go so late at night?" He was sitting up in bed, wearing a plain T-shirt and pajama pants Even in her frantic state, she couldn't help but notice how boyishly handsome he looked with hair sticking up as he rubbed his eyes.

She gripped the cheap plastic bag that held the pregnancy test. There was no sense in worrying him until she knew for sure. She needed to go into the bathroom, see what the test said, then decide how to tell Vivek. While she was at it, she could figure out how to tell her father that she was not his biological daughter. It was ten steps to the bathroom, maybe fifteen. Her feet were frozen to the ground, her knees ready to buckle.

He got out of bed, and took the bag from her. "You're pregnant?"

"Maybe."

His face broke into a wide grin, which disappeared just as quickly. "Why aren't you happy?"

Which reason should she start with?

"Hema, what is it? Why are you worried? If you're pregnant, that's wonderful news."

She shook her head. "I need to wait until my residency is over."

He rubbed the back of his neck. "That was the plan, but if it happens now, so be it. We'll figure it out. We can hire nannies, and I'm sure my parents will help."

"Let's see if this is even an issue." Without waiting for a response, she went into the bathroom to take the test. The test took five minutes. She set a timer and sat on the edge of the massive jetted tub.

Vivek knocked. She stared at the door of the bathroom then opened it.

"Can I wait with you?"

She nodded, and they sat on the edge of the tub together.

"I don't want to watch my baby's first steps on a video. I need to be there when he or she goes to nursery school for the first time. And when my son or daughter has a school performance, I want to be there in the front, cheering him or her on. I don't want it to be a nanny." She didn't want to be the type of mother Ma was.

"Maybe you can put your residency off for a few years."

"That's going to hurt me in the long run. While they would let me take maternity leave, my class of residents would move on and I'd be in between my class and the next class. And how long of a break would I take? One year? That's not enough. The baby won't even be walking. Two years? Through primary school, which is five years? They won't hold my residency spot indefinitely, and a long break in my training will hurt my skills. There is no good solution. I will have to choose my child or my career."

Tears stung her eyes. Vivek moved close to her and put his arm around her shoulders. She sank her head into his chest, letting his warmth wrap around her.

He kissed the top of her head. "We will figure out a schedule. Maybe you can do more night shifts when the baby is sleeping."

She pulled back from him. "Right, because I'm a robot who can take care of a baby during the day and work all night. Oh, and maybe I could strap the baby in a sling and go do my lab practices." He didn't deserve the anger and resentment in her voice, but she had no other outlet for it. There were too many things collapsing around her.

"We should've taken more precautions," he said softly.

"You mean *I* should have taken more precautions. You're getting exactly what you need from this deal. I'm the one who's losing out."

Her timer beeped. She sat on the edge of the tub, frozen. Whatever the test said, there was no taking back what she'd just said.

Vivek finally stood and picked up the test.

"Congratulations, your life isn't ruined."

He handed the test to her, and she stared at the Not Pregnant text. She took one more test just to be sure. When she returned to bed, Vivek was gone, a note on her pillow that he was sleeping in a guest room.

Hema couldn't sleep most of the night. She was angry at her mother and had taken it out on Vivek. She hadn't been fair to him last night. Worse yet, the relief she expected when the test showed not pregnant for the second time never came. Instead, she felt empty, left wondering whether she'd gotten the result she wanted. Padding into the kitchen, she found a pot and filled it with a half mixture of water and milk. Neither she nor Vivek ever had time to eat breakfast, so the house staff came in later. Marta set the coffee maker the night before so it brewed first thing in the morning. Hema added cardamom, fresh ginger, a turn of cracked pepper, and cinnamon to the pot along with loose black tea leaves. After letting the mixture boil a few times, she strained the chai into two cups. She'd learned that Vivek loved traditional Indian chai, but Marta could never make it quite right, and he never had the time in the mornings, so he'd gotten used to drinking coffee instead.

She carried the mugs into the guest room. Vivek was still asleep. He lay on his stomach, his arms above his head, and the covers flung off. He only ended up in that position when he tossed and turned all night. She set the mugs on the nightstand and kissed the back of his neck. He stirred and turned, catching her by the arm. She moved with him, rolling on top of him. He wrapped his arms around her to hold her on him. She lifted her head so she could look at him. "I was a little stressed last night, and I took it out on you."

He smiled. "PMS or pregnancy hormones?"

She smacked him playfully. "I'm going to let you get away with that just this once."

He ran his hands up and down her back, and her body responded immediately.

"So, how bad do you feel?" His eyes sparkled mischievously. She felt his arousal through her thin cotton sleep shirt.

"Bad enough to put up with your morning breath," she said, bending down to kiss him. When her lips touched his, her heart threatened to burst from the love she felt for him. They wiggled out of their clothes and made love slowly, taking the time to enjoy being connected with each other. When they were done, he held her for a long time and she snuggled into the warmth of his body, trying to take his strength for what lay ahead for her in the day.

"Do I smell chai?"

"It's probably gone cold."

She got up reluctantly and handed him a cup. He took a sip, then leaned over and kissed her lightly. "I love your tea."

*And I love you.*

# Seventeen

Her stomach was tightly coiled as she knocked on the door of her parents' hotel room.

She and Vivek had made omelets together in the kitchen and breakfasted together. It had been such a perfect morning that she couldn't bring herself to tell him about the drama with her parents. She needed the feeling from that morning to get her through the day. But now she wondered how much longer could they go on living a pretend marriage. Eventually he would realize that he couldn't love one woman and build a life with another.

It was something she wished her mother had recognized early on and saved her, and her father, from the loveless life they'd had. As she lay awake last night, she'd realized that she had traded one fairy tale for another. She'd fallen for Arun because he had laid out a fantasy marriage that she'd always wanted her parents to have. She'd traded the fantasy with Arun for a new one with Vivek, first imagining that her career could be her love, and then, when she fell in love with him, that he would fall in love with her, and they'd live happily ever after.

She was done with fantasies. As much as it pained her, there was another one she had to shatter. The one her father had been living in.

Her father opened the door, his face immediately breaking into a broad smile when he saw her. He waved her into the hotel room. Their suite was tastefully furnished with silver-gray couches, royal-blue carpeting and floor-to-ceiling windows that looked across at another building but had been glazed for privacy. Two bedrooms branched off from each side of the room. Hema took a seat on the couch. A room service trolley stood in the center, and her father poured her a cup of coffee, adding just the right amount of cream and sugar before handing it to her.

He called out to her mother, and Aparna emerged from her bedroom wearing loose linen pants and a blue-and-white blouse. Her face was drawn, her posture caved in. Her father poured another cup of coffee, adding sugar but no milk, and handed it to her mother, who took the cup and sat across from Hema.

"So, your mother says we need to have a family discussion." Her father poured himself a cup and sat across from her mother so they were seated in a triangle.

Hema looked at her mother. Had she told him? Her mother shook her head. "I thought we should tell him together."

Hema waited for her mother to start, but she stayed silent. Her father waited for several beats. "Are you having problems with Vivek?" he finally asked.

Hema sighed. Her father leaned forward and patted her knee. "It's okay. You can tell me. I am realizing that maybe I was too harsh on you. I shouldn't have pushed so hard for you to get married."

"Why were you so sure that I needed to get married" Hema said in a tiny voice. This wasn't the conversation she had come to have, but had her father supported her from the beginning, she'd never have accepted Vivek's deal, she would have never fallen in love with him.

"Call me old-fashioned, my dear, but I feared that if you went off to America without getting married, you would get caught up with your medical career and never marry. You are so passionate about your work but you were hurting after what happened with that boy Arun....I wanted to make sure you had a full life."

"You thought marriage would give me a full life? Is that what it did for you? Did marriage bring you happiness?"

He fixed her with a hard look. "I don't regret marrying your mother. Our marriage is why you exist, why I have you in my life."

Hema laughed mirthlessly. "You are correct, Dad, that your marriage is the reason I'm in your life." She looked at her mother, giving her one last chance to do what she should have done years ago.

"Hema is Mukesh's daughter." Aparna said the words so softly that Hema had to strain to hear.

"Excuse me?" Her father said, his jaw tight.

"She knows," her mother restarted.

Hema couldn't take it anymore. "Dad, I know about Ma's affair. I've known about it for a while. What she'd trying to tell you is that I am not your biological daughter."

Her father's nostrils flared as he took an audible breath. Hema continued on. "But I need you to know that this does not in any way change the fact that you are my father and will be the only father I ever need or want." Her father stayed silent, and Hema's stomach churned.

"Why did you have to tell me?"

Hema's mouth soured. Had she made a mistake? Had her mother been right that she shouldn't have said something?

"It's not right that you don't know. I don't feel any different about you, but you may feel different about me. You have the right to make that decision."

"Aren't you worried that I might cut you off from my wealth? Stop giving money to your foundation?"

Hema frowned. The conversation was not going the way she expected. Was her father in shock?

"I don't care if you cut me off from your wealth. All I want is that you not cut me out of your life. You are the only dad I have, and I love you." Her voice broke, and her father moved to sit beside her. He put an arm around her, and she leaned into his shoulder, sobbing into his shirt.

"My dear daughter, do you think I didn't know?"

She leaned back, staring at her father. He was smiling. Little crinkles of amusement appeared at the corner of his eyes. "I knew from the moment your mother was pregnant that you were not my biological daughter."

Her mother made a sound she couldn't decipher.

"It was written all over her face when she told me. We'd waited so long for a pregnancy, yet there was only fear in her eyes, no happiness. I knew she'd been seeing Mukesh."

Hema opened and closed her mouth several times before finally forming some intelligible words. "Why didn't you...say something or do something?"

"I thought about it. But I loved your mother, and I wanted to give Mukesh time to do the right thing. Your grandparents were dead, and if I turned Aparna out, she wouldn't have fared well. I couldn't live with that on my conscience." He smiled wistfully. "Then I held you in my arms, and I knew without a doubt that I needed you to be my daughter."

New tears streamed down her face. "You stayed with Ma because of me?"

He shook his head. "I loved you both. I still do." He turned towards her mother and Hema turned to see tears in her mother's eyes.

"You asked me yesterday why I stay with your mother." Her father was talking to her, but his eyes were locked onto her mother's. "It's because she is the love of my life. Even if I am not hers. You became my daughter because you were hers."

"Anil. I'm sorry. Hema is right, I should have told you from the beginning." Aparna sniffed. "Maybe if I had..." Her voice cracked.

"Maybe if you had, you would've figured out who the true love of your life was," Hema finished for her.

She looked back and forth between her parents. For the first time in her life, she saw raw honesty between them, and something softer in her mother's eyes. "How could you forgive me and go on with our life?" Her mother's voice was pained.

Her father moved to her mother's side. "I knew I wasn't your first choice, but I hope I'll be your last. We've had a good life, haven't we Aparna? We saw the Eiffel Tower together for the first time. We watched our little girl learn to walk. Then there was that time we got snowed in." Her father began humming a popular old Bollywood song. *"Hum tum, ek kamare mein band ho, aur chabbi koh jaye..."* The song loosely translated to, *You and I are locked in a room, and the key is lost.* Hema's heart lurched at the sly smile his father gave her mother, and the way her eyes widened ever so slightly. It was a romance novel type of moment, one she'd never thought her parents capable of having.

Her mother dabbed at her eyes, then excused herself to go to the bathroom.

"She doesn't like to show her emotions. She needs a few minutes to gather herself."

Hema stared at her father. "You understand and

know her so well. Didn't it get exhausting? Loving her when she didn't return your love?

He grabbed her hand. "Do you know how I knew that you didn't truly love that boy, Arun?"

Hema's breath caught.

"I knew because you were able to live without him. When you truly love someone, you can't live without them. There were many times in our life when I thought about leaving your mother. But then I thought about living my life without her, and I couldn't."

"What if she spends her whole life loving Mukesh?"

He shrugged. "It doesn't matter. Because I get to spend my life loving her."

*How can that be enough for you?*

"Let me go check on Ma."

She knocked and entered her mother's bedroom without being asked in. The bathroom door was open, and Aparna was washing her face. She saw Hema's reflection in the mirror and dried her face.

"What did that get you?"

Hema frowned. Why was her mother angry?

"Your father always knew. All these years I've stayed because of the guilt, now it's all out in the open."

"Isn't that what you want, Ma? Isn't it nice to be free from all the secrets?"

She shook her head. "I didn't want to tell your father about you because I'm leaving him. Mukesh is in New York finalizing his divorce."

The ground opened up beneath her. Hema backed

up until she felt the wall behind her. Suddenly, a lot of things became clear.

"That's where you were last night. You didn't come to dinner with us because you were with Nisha's father. All these years, you didn't tell Dad about my parentage not to spare his feelings but so I would inherit his money." Hema slid down the wall and balled up her legs. "Why, Ma? Why would you do this to Dad? He loves you, more than Mukesh ever will. That man wouldn't even claim his own daughter, and Dad has raised yours."

Her mother knelt down beside her. "Do you think I haven't tried to love your father? Do you think I don't know that he's the better man? I have tried to love him. I've spent more than thirty years trying to make a life with him, to forget Mukesh."

"Then why haven't you? Why haven't you figured out how to be happy with Dad? With me? Why do you need this man?"

Tears welled in her mother's eyes. "Because I can never love anyone else the way I love Mukesh."

Hema's heart dropped to her stomach, and a desperate sadness seeped deep into her soul. She was sad for her mother, who had pined for another man her whole life, for her father, who was about to lose the woman he loved, and for Vivek, who would never get the woman he really wanted.

# Eighteen

Hema desperately wanted to talk to Vivek, but he seemed to have something else on his mind as he dressed for the young entrepreneur awards ceremony.

She entered his dressing room wearing a black gown that left one shoulder bare and cinched at her waist before the asymmetric skirt billowed around her. He looked fabulous in a black tuxedo with a silver cummerbund. He was deftly tying a bow tie.

"You look great. I'll be ready in a minute. Just need to put on the cuff links."

She went to the cabinet in the center of his closet and selected a pair of silver-and-diamond links from a glass drawer. He held out his arms, and she began to put them on.

"Marta said that you're unavailable for dinner with

the Maliks, and with the Reymans. Did your shift schedule change? Marta always checks before booking our social engagements."

Hema stiffened. Of all the things they had to talk about, this was at the bottom of the priority list. "You know that I stay much later than my shift to work in the lab and watch surgeries. I've already taken a lot of time off this week for my parents' visit and this event tonight. I can't afford to fall behind."

He met her eyes in the mirror as she turned and checked her appearance.

"These are important investors. Can't you come to dinner then go back to work in the lab?"

She glared at him. "Why can't you go without me?"

"Because the invitation is not a business one but a social one, to congratulate us on our wedding. This was why it was so important for me to get married. It's the way business works among the New York Indians."

*It's the deal we made.* He didn't have to say the words out loud for her to understand exactly what he meant. The honeymoon was over. Not that they ever had one. Vivek had finally realized that she paled in comparison to Divya, and the love he had for her. He was doing what any businessman would do: he was cutting his losses and getting what he could out of the deal.

"Then reschedule the dinners for my next day off. I can't cut corners on my residency. This is a very competitive program, and if I don't keep up, I'll get kicked out. This residency is why this marriage was so important to me."

"You made that abundantly clear last night."

Her heart squeezed painfully at the harshness of his voice. She shouldn't be having this conversation with him now. Not after the revelation that her mother was going to leave her father. She'd had to spend the day with them, pretending they were a happy family. Her mother had asked for a final day together as a family before she announced her plans. Hema had initially refused, but the smile on her father's face when Aparna suggested it in front of him made her relent. He deserved to be happy for a day. But the farce had broken something in her. She couldn't go on pretending anymore.

He needed to leave. This was not the way to handle things with Hema. Since seeing Divya, he couldn't stop thinking about whether he had rushed Hema into marriage with him. After what happened last night with the pregnancy test, he was sure of it. They had rushed into so much, the marriage, their physical relationship. It could have all come crashing down on them last night. Had she been pregnant, the loss of her residency would've made her resent him for the rest of her life.

He turned to leave before he made things worse, but she reached out and grabbed his arm. "Let's not do this. We've always been able to talk to each other."

His shoulders dropped. She was right. At the very least, she deserved better from him. He gestured to the only chair in the room, and she took a seat. He grabbed a step stool and sat on it. He caught sight of himself in one of the many mirrors in the dressing room and smiled as how comical he looked sitting so low to the ground.

"Are you sure that stool can carry your weight?"

He smirked. "I didn't gain that much weight on the cruise."

She gave him a small smile, and his chest tightened. Over the last week, he'd wished many times over that he'd met Hema before he met Divya, that the experience with Divya hadn't soured him on love. He wanted to go back to being the man who was willing to give everything up for love, but he wasn't.

"You've been distant since we saw Divya last week."

He sighed. How could he explain how he felt to Hema when he didn't understand it himself? It was as if seeing Divya had reopened the stitches on a painful gash. The pain was so intense that he was lashing out, trying desperately to find a way to lessen it.

"It was hard seeing her. It was especially hard watching her so happy and in love with Ethan."

"Do you still love her?"

The question had been burning a hole in his stomach since he'd seen her. Hema looked at him expectantly.

"I want to give his marriage a chance. I want to make it real, just like you do."

"But…"

He swallowed, his throat dry and raw. Hema looked

like she was holding her breath, watching him, waiting. He could lie to her. He could tell her that he loved her. Yet he couldn't. He'd promised her honesty, and that's the least he could give her.

"…but seeing her made me realize that I never want to feel the way I did with her."

The look on her face stabbed him in the chest. He'd never wanted to hurt someone the way Divya had hurt him. Especially not Hema. Hadn't he done everything he could to avoid this very situation?

"What does that mean for us?"

"Nothing has changed for me. I still want this marriage, and I want to make it work." *More than anything, I need you. I need to know that someone can love me, be with me, choose me.*

"But…"

"But I'm afraid that you will leave me just like Divya did."

"That's what this whole dinner with the Maliks and Reymans is about. You're worried that the moment something threatens my residency, I'll walk out on you."

He hung his head. "After last night, I am worried. There's been a lot in my head lately."

"Me too."

"Your parents?" He felt bad about not being able to go to the airport yesterday to receive her parents, but an urgent situation had come up. There was the threat of another hostile takeover, and he had to nip it in the bud. He'd fully intended to make it up to her parents by taking them out to a nice dinner, but she'd hadn't wanted him there.

She nodded. "I found out last night that I'm the love child of my mother and Mukesh Sharma."

Vivek reached out and took her hand. "I am so sorry, Hema! Now I feel like an even bigger shit." He wasn't totally surprised. The private eye he had hired to look into her family noted that the timing of her birth made her parentage suspect, but he hadn't dare bring it up. Not after seeing how close she was to her father.

He squeezed her hand, his heart constricting at the tears that welled in her eyes.

"Hey, you know that he is still your father. Biology is not what makes a parent."

She nodded. "I know. I told my father today, and it turned out he already knew."

Vivek took a breath. "I guess that's a good thing."

"Mukesh Sharma is getting divorced, and my mother is leaving my father for him."

Vivek sucked in a breath. "I'm sorry to hear that. Are you okay? How is your father taking it?"

She buried her head in her hands. "She hasn't told him yet, and I didn't have the heart to either."

"It's not your place." He moved beside her and put an arm around her shoulders, trying not to notice the softness of her bare shoulder.

"Maybe it's a good thing that she's leaving him. If her heart didn't truly belong to him..." He stopped, realizing what he'd just said. She fixed him with such an intense look that an icy cold took hold of him, snaking its way through his veins.

"I've spent my entire life watching my father live in a marriage where he didn't get what he put in. He loves my mother, but she has always loved someone else." Vivek pulled his arm away. Every muscle in his body stiffened.

"I've fallen in love with you, Vivek. But I'm not willing to lead the life my father did. I can't be with you knowing that you can't love me back. I want to have all of you. I deserve to have all of you."

He squeezed his eyes shut and rubbed his temples. "I can't do that right now, Hema. You need to give me more time." He opened his eyes and gave her a pleading look.

"Time isn't going to change things. My mother has tried for thirty years to love my father, and yet she always goes back to her first love."

"It won't be like that."

She shook her head, and his heart dropped to his toes.

"Remember the bet you lost on mehndi night?" She held out her hands. The color of the mehndi had faded to almost nothing. She held out her wrist and pointed to the faint outline of a heart. "Your name was written here, over where my pulse beats."

He found it hard to breathe. *Don't do this.*

"I'm collecting on the bet. You agreed to give me anything I want. I want a divorce."

# Nineteen

"There you are, stranger."

Hema turned to see Divya take a seat beside her. The awards ceremony was about to begin, and Vivek had been asked to go backstage. The Midtown Sheraton hotel ballroom glowed with chic red chandeliers, gold tablecloths, and more than a thousand people seated at tables of ten. It was a big moment for both Vivek and Nisha. Hema was desperately trying to put aside the sickening feeling in her stomach, and to be happy for them.

"Divya!" Hema gave her a hug.

"You've been avoiding me."

She had, but Hema couldn't admit that to her former friend.

"It's been awkward, you know...with Vivek."

Divya nodded. "I know. I hate that it's affecting our friendship. Give it some time. Hopefully Vivek will get over it."

Hema stared at Divya. Did she really not know? "I don't think time will be the balm. You really broke his heart."

"And you mended it."

"I thought I had."

Divya narrowed her eyes. "You don't think he still has feelings for me, do you?" When Hema didn't answer, Divya shook her head vehemently. "You have to know that there is nothing between us. I never would have let my parents set you guys up if there was. He and I never gelled together, and I'm happily married to Ethan."

"I don't think there's anything going on between you two, but I think he'll never get over you."

Divya's eyes widened. "I don't think he has a broken heart. What he has is an ego problem. He's used to getting what he wants, and he hasn't gotten over the fact that he didn't anticipate me leaving him. He's using me as an excuse not to let you get too close to hurt him."

Divya's comments gave Hema pause. Isn't that what he'd said to her? Was he just afraid that if he let Hema close, she'd hurt him the way Divya did? Was that something he could even get over if he hadn't by now?

They chatted some more. Then the awards ceremony began. Once Nisha and Vivek received their awards, Hema made her way to her parents' table.

At soon as she saw her father's face, and the empty seat next to him, she knew that her mother had finally told him.

Her father sat with his shoulders slumped, his face gaunter than she'd ever seen it. "Let's go back to the hotel, Dad." He nodded as if in a daze.

She texted Vivek to let him know that she was leaving with her father. When they returned to the hotel, her mother's room was empty. "I'm sorry, Dad." She hugged her father, willing with all her heart that her mother would come to her senses and realize her mistake. That at any moment, the hotel room door would burst open and her mother would come flying in with tears in her eyes and an apology on her lips.

"All these years. I loved her all these years." For the first time in her life, Hema's saw her father put his head in his hands and sob. Hema's heart shattered into a million pieces, the pain in her chest so intense that she could barely breathe.

It didn't matter whether Vivek wasn't letting her in because he was afraid, or because he still wasn't over Divya. She never wanted to be where her father was right now. At least she knew now that she'd made the right decision asking Vivek for a divorce.

"You know, for a man as smart as you are, you can be a real *gadha*."

Vivek glared at his brother. Being called an ass was not the response he expected in response to the news that his marriage had fallen apart.

Vivek studied the separation agreement that his

lawyer had just delivered to his office. His company rented two floors in the middle of a high-rise building in Midtown Manhattan. Vivek's office was cleanly decorated with a modern white desk, black leather chairs, and artistic drapes to hide the view of the brick building next door.

Vivek had called Vikram hoping to get some moral support, and practical advice on how to break the news to their parents.

"Why are you still stuck on Divya? You two were together for like ten minutes."

"I'm not stuck on her. This is about trust. I thought I could trust Hema. She made promises to me. We've barely been married a month, and she's already bailing."

"Because she thinks you're still not over Divya." Vikram balled a piece of paper and threw it at his brother. "Why didn't you just tell her you love her and move on?"

"Because I promised her honesty. I don't know if I can love her the way I loved Divya."

Vikram leaned forward. "Let me tell you what you love. You love to win, and Divya is the first time in your life where you lost, and spectacularly at that."

Vivek threw the paper ball back at his brother, smacking him squarely in the nose.

"It's not about your feelings for Hema. It's about your ego. You want Hema to love you no matter what. You're testing her to make sure that she'd stick by you no matter what. Her leaving you is a self-fulfilling prophecy."

Vivek glared at him, but Vikram didn't seem to be getting the message. "You're dealing with Hema like you're dealing with James DeSouza. Just because he tried the hostile takeover, you're investigating all of our staff and board members, getting everyone to sign new conflict of interest and confidentiality agreements. You're tightening the company noose to make sure no one can sneeze without you knowing."

"Can you blame me? Someone helped DeSouza. I need to ensure everyone's loyalty."

"Exactly. And that's what you're doing with Hema. Except she's not some board member. She's your wife."

Vivek leaned forward. "And what's wrong with that?"

"Don't you get it? It's too late."

"Because she's already my wife?"

"Because you're already in love with her."

*No. No. No. That isn't true.* He'd been very careful not to fall in love with her. It was just friendship between them, *and incredible sex*. He was never going to fall in love with anyone else. He wasn't going to let anyone else have power over him.

"If I were in love with her, I wouldn't be signing the separation agreement." He made a show of grabbing the Montblanc pen off his desk and signing the papers. He handed them over to Vikram to witness.

"What about her residency?"

"We're required to have at least six months of separation. That gives her time to get an H1 visa, and if she can't, I'll wait to divorce her until she has her status sorted out. I'll still financially support her."

"So let me get this straight. You made a deal with Hema. You're mad that she's not living up to her end of the deal, yet you are going out of your way to take care of her? But you're not in love with your wife, who, by the way, loves you."

"I'm not in love with Hema."

Vikram slapped the table. "I give up. You're not going to get it until you lose her. Give me those damn papers. I'll sign them."

Vivek arrived home to find their bedroom empty. When they returned home last night, he'd slept in the guest room again. He couldn't bear being close to her and unable to touch her. How could she have asked him for a divorce? Every time he replayed the words, his pulse pounded in his head.

He set the separation agreement on her side of the bed. On impulse, he walked into her closet. Evening gowns, Indian dresses, pantsuits, dresses, skirts, pants and blouses hung in neat rows.

He opened one of the dresser drawers, and his pulse jumped. The drawer was empty. Her scrubs were gone, all of them. He checked the shoe shelves, all neatly lined with dozens of pairs of heels. The only empty spot was where she kept her work clogs. All three pairs were gone.

Bile rose in his throat. Where had she gone? He went over the conversation they had in the morning. He told her he would get her the separation papers, but he had never asked her to leave. In fact, he had fully intended to move in with Vikram or into a hotel. She had just gotten comfortable at his place, and it was close to the hospital where she worked.

His knees seemed to betray him, and he sank down into a chair. She'd bolted. Run away. Left him in a place that he'd promised himself he'd never be again.

# Twenty

"I can't let you do this."

Hema was tired of having the same conversation over and over with her father. "You are not stopping me," she said.

"I won't let you onto the jet."

They were having their customary Sunday breakfast together. The hotel restaurant was busy, but they'd managed to wrangle a quiet corner to read the paper together. It had been a month since Hema had moved into the Mahal Hotel with her father. In that month, she hadn't seen Vivek. She had seen the separation papers he had sent, and promptly signed and couriered them back over.

"Then I'll take a commercial flight. I have money from the measly salary I get from the residency."

"You make what a servant in India makes."

"It's enough to pay for a plane ticket."

"The residency is your dream."

"Dreams change." She passed the front page of the paper to her father. "Besides, there are perfectly good programs in India where I can train, and with your money, I can pay one of my current co-residents to come teach me what I miss out on over here."

"It seems you've thought of everything."

*Except how to eject Vivek from my heart.*

She'd put on a good face for her father, hid the fact that her heart felt like someone had ripped it muscle by muscle until it didn't beat anymore. She had gone through the last month in a daze, keeping busy with her residency, trying to push Vivek from her mind and her soul. It hadn't worked. If she stayed in New York, she'd never be able to move on, achieve any of her dreams. She'd think about that pregnancy test, about how much she wished it had been positive. She'd obsess over whether she'd made the right decision to leave him. She'd fail out of her residency for taking too many breaks to walk over to his building just to see if she could catch a glimpse of him coming or going.

The only bright spot in the entire fiasco had been getting closer to Nisha. The connection she'd sensed between her and Nisha had blossomed once the secret of her parentage was in the open. Nisha was her half sister, and regardless of what happened between their parents, they were determined to have a relationship with each other.

Hema's father folded his paper, then grabbed the paper she was holding.

"Hey! I was reading that."

"You need to stay in New York. At least until you talk to Vivek."

"I have talked to him, Dad. He called yesterday and asked if I need any more of my clothes shipped over." What she didn't mention was that she hadn't answered the call but had replayed the voice mail dozens of times, listening to his voice, wondering why she was torturing herself.

"I think you're making a…"

"…mistake. I know."

"Ask me if I'd marry your mother all over again, knowing how the story ends."

She shook her head. "It would be the wrong decision."

"Not for me. I got thirty beautiful years with her, and I got you."

Once again, she thought of that pregnancy test and how that would have bound her to Vivek for life. It wouldn't have let her leave. Except, would she have been happy wondering whether he was thinking of Divya when he made love to her? Stressing about whether he was happy with her? Over-reading his moods and wondering when the day would come that he decided he didn't want to pretend anymore?

"I'm coming with you to India tomorrow. I already talked to my residency director. It's all done."

Vivek threw the papers on his desk. "I don't understand what makes this so difficult. It's a simple contract. Why am I looking at a third draft that still needs work?"

Vikram strode into his brother's office and put his hands up. "Whoa…" He dropped the paper bags of food he'd brought, picked up the papers on the desk, and handed them to the guy whose name Vivek could never remember. The fool who couldn't get his edits right. The man was cowering in fear a few feet from the desk. The guy took the papers with shaky hands and fled.

"Hangry much?" Vikram opened the paper bags and handed his brother a takeout container of lamb sheesh kebab over rice that he'd picked up at the corner food truck.

"The guy will never last in finance with such shoddy work. He needs to learn."

"You're taking out your frustration at losing your wife on your staff."

"Will you stop with that? It's old news."

"If it's old news, why haven't you announced your divorce?"

"I'm giving her time to sort out her immigration."

"She doesn't need to sort out her immigration."

Vivek stared at his brother, who opened his food container and started eating at a leisurely pace. Vivek took several deep breaths. "Out with it."

Vikram chewed the bite in his mouth slowly. "Uncle Anil called Mum and told her that Hema quit her residency and is going back to India."

Vivek jumped out of his chair. "What?"

"That's why Mum sent me here. Uncle wants you

to come over to the hotel like the hero of a Bollywood movie and take his daughter back home."

Vivek paced in his office, his entire body tightly coiled. "Why is she quitting her residency? That was the whole point in marrying me."

"Must I explain it to you like you're a high school teenager?" Vikram turned his chair so he could look at his brother. "The woman is in love with you. But you've convinced her that you aren't in love with her, even though you are, so she's leaving because she can't stand to be around you."

Vivek's head throbbed. This didn't make any sense. *What is she doing? There must be some mistake.* He'd given her a generous monthly allowance, even called the Mahal Hotel and asked that her room charges be billed directly to him after her father left. There was no reason for her to give up her residency. Was it not going well? Had the schedule gotten to her? He'd seen how hard she worked in the first month. She worked twice the number of hours he did. Was she not able to keep up? Somehow, he doubted it. He'd seen her passion and commitment; she'd never let hard work get in her way.

"Bro, you look like a caged animal, pacing around, rattling the bars. Why don't you go talk to her?"

*Because if I see her again, I won't be able to let her go.*

"What is it that you can't give her?"

"She wants my undying love."

"And that's a problem because…"

"I can't."

Vikram shook his head. "You're going to regret your bullheadedness."

"I love the fact that the guy whose longest relationship has been ten minutes is suddenly the expert on my relationship issues."

"I'm not a relationship expert. I'm a Vivek expert. You are a control freak. Remember that time when we were in high school and you were in charge of the junior prom? You had every last detail planned. Then Mr. McClennan overrode all your decisions and you quit the week before the prom."

"Yeah, that was a calculated save on my part. If you remember, the party was a disaster just as I predicted. If I hadn't quit in protest, everyone would have blamed and hated me for ruining it." It had been a difficult decision to give up leading the prom committee. He needed something "fun" on his college application, as his counselor had advised, so leaving the committee meant he had to find another club. But, that was better than being the butt of jokes for the next year at school.

"Exactly. You ran. You protected yourself from the fallout. That's what you're doing now. The whole thing with Divya messed with your head; the fact that you hadn't planned for something and it happened has you scared that it will happen again."

"You have no idea what you're talking about. The fact of the matter is that she left me. I didn't leave her."

Vikram shook his head in disgust, then picked up the rest of his food and threw it in the trash. "She leaves first thing tomorrow morning. You've got to go see her tonight."

Vivek turned towards his computer and began punching the keyboard. "I have a dinner with the board of directors. I've finally got the company and my life back on track. I'm not going chasing after another woman who's decided to leave me."

# Twenty-One

Vivek threw his suit jacket on the bed. He had an hour before he had to leave to meet the board of directors. They'd requested the dinner to celebrate Vivek finally squashing the takeover attempt. It was a major victory, and he should have been happy, but he felt cold. The condo seemed ghostly. Everywhere he turned, he saw her. Sleeping on the bed at the end of a long day, belting her robe as she emerged from the shower, her hair wet and shiny, standing on her tiptoes to kiss him when he returned home.

When he closed his eyes, he could see their life together, her making chai for him in the kitchen, him rubbing her neck after a long day on her feet. Hadn't he been happy?

He walked into Hema's dressing room. When she'd

first left, the room still smelled like her perfume, but now the scent had faded. He stepped to her makeup table. There was a picture of them on the table. It wasn't one of the formal portraits from the wedding but a phone picture that one of the guests had taken of them on the deck of the ship. They were looking at each other. He remembered that moment, could almost feel her silky skin underneath his fingertips, hear her laugh in his ears. His heart squeezed so painfully that he braced himself against the table. When had it happened? When had he fallen in love with her? Why was he in the same place he'd been before, with the woman he loved running away from him?

*I will be there at the mandap.*

He pressed the bridge of his nose.

*I want to have all of you. I deserve to have all of you.*

Had she left him? Was she the one who was doing the running away?

His watch chirped to remind him that it was almost time to leave for the dinner. He took one last look around his bedroom. *This is what I'll come home to tonight.*

"What do you mean, they checked out?" Vivek leaned over the reception counter at the Mahal Hotel, making sure he had heard the front desk clerk correctly.

"I show that they checked out about an hour ago."

"But they weren't supposed to leave until tomorrow. Where did they go? Do you know what airport they're flying out of?" There were five airports in New York with private aviation terminals. While most people preferred to fly in and out of the same one, the airports were so busy that those who could afford to kept two or three options open to make sure they were able to land and take off whenever they pleased.

The clerk shook his head, his blue eyes darting around as if he were ready to press the red alarm button.

Vivek turned away after thanking the clerk. He dialed Hema's number, but it went straight to voice mail. He sent her a text. It said Delivered, but even after waiting an excruciating two minutes, it didn't indicate Read.

Her phone was still on his cell phone plan so he tried the Find my friends function to see if he could geolocate her phone. The system couldn't find her. He looked at his watch. If they left an hour ago and traffic was light, they might already be at the airport and getting on the plane. His own jet was on standby at JFK. He could fly to India, but it would be too late. He'd called her residency director, who had been reluctant to talk to him but finally admitted that he was hoping Hema would change her mind. She was one of the brightest residents he had seen. He hadn't yet replaced her but was going to make an offer tomorrow morning. Vivek begged him to let Hema come back. It hadn't been an easy negotiation, but the guy had agreed to let her resume her residency if she came to her scheduled shift tomorrow.

If she had already flown to India, there was no

way to get her back in time. The flying time to India was seventeen hours one way, and that's if they didn't make a stop in Europe. He had to find out which airport they were flying out of and see if he could stop the plane from taking off. He called his father-in-law, and his phone also went to voice mail. Vivek cursed under his breath.

Several irate text messages flashed across his phone from board members chiding him for canceling on them. It was a spectacularly bad idea to let them get together without him. He didn't fully trust them. But he'd finally gotten his head out of his ass. There was only one thing that was truly important to him, and he had to make sure he got to her in time.

His chest was so tightly wound that it was hard to breathe. How had he messed this up so badly? He eyed his phone. There was only one other person to call. He tapped on his phone and called Sameer.

It only took a few minutes for Sameer to find him in the lobby. The feeling of déjà vu choked Vivek. This is exactly how it had happened before. Vivek standing helplessly in the lobby, begging Sameer for information on where Divya was. His breaths came fast, and his chest tightened even more.

"There's going to be bad weather in Delhi tomorrow, so they left early," Sameer said a little breathlessly as soon as he was in earshot, before Vivek could even ask.

"Which airport did they go out of?"

"Teterboro. It's the only one that had room."

Vivek tapped on his phone. There was no way he

could beat them to Teterboro Airport even if he took the train. They had a one-hour head start. They were probably already boarding the plane.

Sameer grabbed his arm. "I've got a helicopter on the roof. Traffic is bad this time of day. There's no way they made it to Teterboro in an hour. You can probably make it there in ten minutes. Come with me."

Vivek froze for a second, unsure of how to react. The last time he'd been here, the man had been hostile, protective. Now he seemed to share Vivek's desperation. Sameer hustled through the lobby, and Vivek finally figured out how to move his feet and follow him.

Sameer barked instructions into a phone as they rode the elevator. It struck him then. The difference in what he was feeling now, and what he'd experienced then. The last time when he'd been chasing Divya, he felt desperation, his thoughts consumed by how he would look in front of the world if he didn't get her back. But this time his desperation was not for him but for Hema, to stop her from making a mistake. To make sure that she didn't throw her residency away because of him. It was too much to hope for her forgiveness, but he would ask. Even if he had to embarrass himself in front of the whole world.

Soon they were on the rooftop deck. The whip-whip of helicopter blades starting their rotation cut through the noise of the city. Sameer turned to him and held out his hand. Vivek took it automatically. Sameer squeezed his hand, not like the bone-crushing grip of a business rival, but a comforting squeeze. "They said they'll be ready to take off in less than five minutes."

"Thank you, man. I really appreciate this."

Sameer smiled. "Let's call it even, shall we? I kept you from the girl the last time. This time I'm helping you get her."

Vivek returned his grin. "I guess we were destined to be brothers-in-law one way or another."

En route to the airport, Sameer texted Vivek. He'd managed to get hold of the town car driver that the hotel had arranged to take Hema and her father to the airport, and he'd gotten a status on their location. Vivek looked at his watch in dismay.

"Dad, what is it now?" Hema sighed in exasperation. First her father had made them stop five minutes from the airport to find a bathroom, and now he was taking his time getting out of the car.

"You are always in such a rush."

Now Hema knew something was wrong. She was never fast enough to keep up with her father. He was purposefully delaying. "What did you do?"

She slid back into the car and glared at her father.

"I called Vivek's mother and told her we were leaving tomorrow. I was hoping Vivek would have…"

"…would have what?" She didn't keep the anger out of her voice. "Shown up to the hotel with a bouquet of flowers and begged me not to go? Come running out onto the runway waving his hands like Shah

Rukh Khan and standing in front of the plane to make it stop?"

"He loves you, Hema. This morning his mother told me that he has been miserable without you. She's never seen him like this, not even after Divya."

"Well, where is he, Dad? The whole day has gone by. If he wanted to stop me, he would have come by now. Let's go. I don't want us to have to stop in Europe if the weather in Delhi keeps getting bad."

As they walked towards the waiting jet, her father grabbed her arm. "Even knowing how it all turned out, I would marry your mother all over again."

"I know," Hema said wearily.

"It bears repeating," her father said dryly. "Remember that love is worth it."

Hema climbed the stairs of the jet, her heart heavy. She'd left India anxious, nervous and bubbling with excitement. Now she felt empty, gutted, like she was leaving behind all of the important parts of her. She looked back at the tarmac, as if expecting Vivek to come running towards her with that bouquet of flowers, professing his love. Mentally chiding herself, she turned back to the plane. Life was not a Bollywood movie. She was not a helpless heroine; this was a choice she'd made. Time to live with it.

She boarded the plane and stopped in her tracks as she entered the cabin.

"I was going to land a helicopter on the runway as your plane tried to taxi away, but I thought that might be a touch too dramatic."

She blinked, giving her mind a minute to come to

terms with seeing Vivek sitting in the leather seat of the main cabin, his legs casually crossed as he looked devastatingly handsome in a light blue shirt open at the collar and black pants.

"Not to mention the fact that this is New York and you'd likely be shot down before you even tried to land in an unauthorized zone," she said, amazed at how normal her voice sounded.

"Now, see, why must you ruin perfect movie moments?"

"Because they are not real."

He stood and came towards her. She wanted him to sweep her up in his arms, but he stopped just inches from her. "I talked to your residency director; he will let you come back if you show up for your shift tomorrow morning."

It took her a second to process what he'd said. "What? Why did you call my residency director? And why would I go on my shift tomorrow after quitting the program?"

"Because I am not worth giving up your dream for."

Her heart was beating so fast that she could barely hear her own thoughts. He wasn't here to tell her he loved her. He was here to assuage his guilt about her leaving her residency program. He pointed to sheaf of papers on the coffee table. "These are annulment papers."

The words slammed into her, and she reached out to steady herself against a seat. Annulment? That would mean their marriage never existed. With one signature, it was all erased. The separation and up-coming divorce were bad enough, but annulment? Is that why he'd come, to make sure he wasn't legally bound to her? So he could erase her completely from his life?

He stepped towards her. "No deals, no contracts, no understandings. I don't want you to feel like you're stuck with me."

Her throat closed. He wanted her out of his life? Just like that? Even though she was going to move thousands of miles away from him, the thought that it would really be over between them hit her like a cold blast of ice. Her father was right. She had hoped that he would come running after her. That he would realize that what they had was special, that he'd be willing to give her all of himself.

She backed away from him, unable to speak. He stepped closer, so close that his forehead was nearly touching hers. "I want to win you the old-fashioned way. I want to show you how much I love you, and if you deem me worthy, then I'll marry you all over again. I want us to start fresh. To marry each other because we know we're in love."

She stared at him for a long time, not even realiz-ing that she'd started to cry until he brushed his fin-gers lightly over her cheeks. "You're ready to be with me? Love me?" she choked out.

"I've been in love with you since the cruise. I was just too pigheaded to acknowledge it to myself."

She smiled. "When exactly did you fall in love with me?"

"Honestly, I think it was in Stingray City when you leaped on me in the water, screaming like a little girl."

*What is he saying?*

"I love you so much that it scared me. I've been so afraid that you'll leave me that I pretty much made it happen."

He cupped her face. "Even if you never want to see me again, don't give up on your residency. Your director said that you were one of the most promising residents he has ever seen. That's why he was willing to let you come back."

She sniffed, her heart beating a mile a minute. "I don't like the terms of this new arrangement. You don't get to have your way this time."

"What?"

She stepped back so she could look him in the eye. "I'm not signing those annulment papers." She poked him in the chest. "Are you the one who said that once we took those seven circles around the scared fire, we're tied for life?"

She placed her hands on his chest, feeling his breaths as he looked at her with shining eyes.

"Our marriage has always been real to me. Now that you've come to your senses, you're going to spend the rest of your life convincing me of how much you love me. Each and every day."

His eyes widened in disbelief. "Are you really saying what I think you're saying?"

"Yes, she is," boomed her father's voice from behind her. "Do you know how much that wedding cost, young man! You're not getting another one."

They all laughed, and her father put a paternal hand on both their heads. "I'm glad this idiot finally came to his senses, and so did you." He turned to her. "I know I've said this before."

Hema signed. "I know, Dad. If you had to do it all over again…"

"… I would still choose love."

She turned to Vivek, and he bent his head and kissed her. "I love you so much," he said. "I'm going to spend every day showing you just how much."

"Slowly…" she said, smiling. "Very slowly."

\* \* \* \* \*

*USA TODAY* bestselling author **Naima Simone**'s love of romance was first stirred by Harlequin books pilfered from her grandmother. Now she spends her days writing sizzling romances with a touch of humor and snark.

She is wife to her own real-life superhero and mother to two awesome kids. They live in perfect domestically challenged bliss in the southern United States.

### Books by Naima Simone

### Harlequin Desire

*Her Best Kept Secret*

### *Billionaires of Boston*

*Vows in Name Only*
*Secrets of a One Night Stand*
*The Perfect Fake Date*
*Black Sheep Bargain*

### HQN Books

*The Road to Rose Bend*
*Christmas in Rose Bend*
*With Love from Rose Bend*

Visit the Author Profile page
at Harlequin.com for more titles.

You can also find Naima Simone on Facebook,
along with other Harlequin Desire authors,
at Facebook.com/HarlequinDesireAuthors!

Dear Reader,

It's so exciting starting a new series! Exciting and, *fine*, a little scary. There's just something about creating a world, introducing new characters and becoming invested in their happily-ever-afters that's exhilarating. And those very same things are just a wee bit terrifying.

This duet features best friends Nore Daniels and Tatum Haas, who are celebrating Tatum's upcoming wedding with a girls' trip to Vegas. This trip—and finding a beautiful brooch with a legend attached to it—kicks off their journeys to finding love.

Event planner Nore indulges in a one-night stand only to discover the man she surrendered to passion with is her ex-fiancé's estranged brother. Oh yes, things are getting hot and messy. To make them even more complicated—note the aforementioned *messy*—Joaquin Iverson becomes her client in the business she reluctantly runs with her former fiancé. Keeping their night together a secret is a must, yet hiding her desire and not falling back into bed—or on a couch—with him is far more difficult.

Nore and Joaquin are combustible and I hope you fall in love with them even as they take the plunge. Welcome to the girls' trip duet!

*Naima*

# HER BEST KEPT SECRET

## Naima Simone

To Gary. 143.

To Connie Marie Butts.
I'll miss you forever
and love you longer than that.

# One

"A pawnshop? Did you really bring me to a pawn-shop?"

Lenora—or "Nore," as she never answered to anyone if they dared to call her by that godforsaken name—Daniels loosed an evil cackle as Tatum Haas, her best friend and future bride-to-be, stared up at the neon green block letters pronouncing the nature of the store.

Okay, gaped.

Her friend gaped.

"I believe the sign says 'Awn Sho.'" Nore cocked her head, wrinkling her nose in mock confusion. "I'm not exactly sure what kind of performance that entails since I don't know what an 'awn' is but you think Britney Spears will be included?"

"For the love of…" Tatum sighed, the cultured,

proper notes of New England in her voice not concealing her annoyance. At all. "If you insist on bringing me to a pawnshop—and I still don't know why—you can't at least find one that can afford *all* the letters in its name? We're in Las Vegas. Isn't this like the pawnshop capital of the United States?"

"Uh, Houston is actually the pawnshop capital of America," Nore corrected. "As of last count, it has 128 stores."

Tatum snorted and somehow it still sounded elegant. "How do you even know that fact?"

"One does not aim to be a *Jeopardy!* contestant and *not* know those facts." Nore shrugged, swiping at a bead of sweat that rolled down her temple.

She mock-glared at Tatum, who stood under the same vicious, I'm-a-make-you-my-bitch June sun and didn't even *glisten*. They must teach that in the finishing school for Boston belles that Tatum had attended.

"No, really, what are we doing here? I thought we were headed to dinner at the Honey Salt and then Cirque du Soleil," Tatum said, shuffling back on the sidewalk toward the parking lot.

Nore reached out, encircling her wrist and halting her friend's retreat even as her stomach rumbled for the caramelized sea scallops and charred filet mignon at the popular Vegas restaurant.

"Not so fast. We have business here. And you mean *Magic Mike Live*, not Cirque du Soleil." She arched an eyebrow and tugged her friend forward. "This is a girls-trip-slash-pre-bachelorette-party after all. What kind of best friend or maid of honor would

I be if I didn't take you to see hot strippers? But first things first."

With that, Nore grabbed the handle on the pawn-shop front door and pulled. Before Tatum could utter another protest, she entered, hauling her friend behind her.

This wasn't Nore's first pawnshop, but it was definitely her biggest. And her bargain/haggler heart just soared. Cases and cases of glass lined the walls and stood free in the middle of the floor, all containing merchandise from jewelry to electronics to even rarer items like military medals. Larger items such as appliances, luggage and furniture occupied several corners. All for sale.

Lord. She might be drooling.

*Focus, ma'am. Not here to shop for you...although is that a real Louis carry-on...?*

"I see the direction you're staring and unless that Louis Vuitton is paying its share of the Uber ride and dinner check, it stays right where it's at," Tatum drawled.

"Killjoy," Nore muttered, then huffed out a, "Fine."

"Thank God," her friend added, not bothering to utter it under her breath.

But when you'd been friends for as long as they'd been—freshman year of college—and had cleaned up each other's, uh, mess after a night of excessive partying, things like offending each other ceased to be a concern.

"So are you going to tell me why we're here?" Tatum pressed.

"You'll see in just a minute." With determined strides and a pang in her chest that she refused to acknowledge, Nore headed toward the back of the store. A handsome older Black gentleman sporting a well-groomed salt-and-pepper goatee and a dark green short-sleeved shirt bearing the shop's logo stood behind a case.

"Excuse me, hi," she greeted him with a smile.

He returned the smile. "Hello. Can I help you?"

"Yes." As she opened the oversize purse at her side, her lips trembled, echoing the quiver in her belly. And that damn twinge in her chest that she was still refusing to acknowledge. "I want to sell this."

She pulled out a black cloth napkin that she might or might not have swiped from the restaurant they'd dined at the night before and laid it out on the glass counter. Unwrapping it, she revealed a gorgeous two-carat, emerald-cut diamond ring with a white gold band.

Gorgeous…and ugly because of the pain attached to it.

A soft gasp came from next to her.

"Nore," Tatum breathed. "What are you—?"

With her gaze trained on the ring, Nore shook her head. "Getting rid of the trash."

"Nore," Tatum said again, but Nore cut her off with another shake of her head.

"I know what I'm doing, Tate." And for added emphasis she nudged the napkin and the jewelry just a little farther across the glass toward the pawnshop employee. "I'd like to sell this, please."

The older man, whose name tag declared him as Dan, arched both eyebrows.

"Pawn it or—"

"Sell it." She reached into her bag again and emerged with an insurance appraisal. "Here's an appraisal from six months ago."

To Dan's credit, he didn't blink. But working in a pawnshop in Las Vegas, he must see a lot. The least of which was a jilted fiancée wanting to sell her engagement ring. Not that he knew about the jilted fiancée part.

Still…

He picked up the ring and studied the appraisal, flipping through the couple of pages. She knew what he'd see. A bunch of details about clarity, cut, color, measurements, yada, yada, yada. None of it mattered as much as that price in bold font: $16,600.

"You are aware that jewelry depreciates…" Dan started, lifting his gaze from the ring and the report.

"Yes, but not by much given that ring was bought and appraised just six months ago. Not that I care." Nore waved her hand. "Give me your best price, Dan."

He studied the ring for several more moments, then looked at her again, a shrewd gleam in his eyes. Oh, if only he knew that was wasted on her.

"Emerald-cut, two-carat diamond. Good cut. E color and SI2 clarity." He paused. "I can give you six thousand for it."

"Deal."

Dan blinked, but quickly recovered. Probably wanted to jump on the fact that she wasn't haggling and seal the deal as soon as possible. Smart man. Smarter employee. "O—"

"Hold on just a second here," Tatum interjected, throwing a palm up in Dan's direction. She whipped around to face Nore. Grasping Nore's shoulder, she lightly shook it. "Listen, I know the…breakup with James sent you in a tailspin. But you shouldn't do anything out of emotion. How about you just take a beat and think on this for a few days. This is just…rash."

Nore's lips twisted into a smile. By that pause, what her friend really wanted to say was crazy. This was just crazy.

And Tatum might not be wrong.

But she didn't care.

"Tate, I love you like Thanksgiving mac 'n' cheese. Not better, but y'know, in that vicinity. And I get that you're concerned for me, but this isn't a whim. I've been thinking about this since the moment my heart stopped feeling like it was trying to claw its way out of my chest. So about two weeks." She lifted a hand to the one still on her shoulder and squeezed when a soft, strangled sound came from her friend. Needing to soften the words and comfort Tatum, she gave her another smile. "No, it's okay. *I'm* okay—or at least, I will be. But I need to do this, and I didn't want to do it alone. So I waited until this trip when you would be with me. Because I need my girl beside me when I say a final goodbye to this chapter of my life."

"Nore," Tatum whispered, moisture glistening in her eyes.

Oh damn. If her friend started crying—and looking beautiful doing it, too. Who did that?—then she would create a spectacle here in this store. *That* she did not want.

She'd cried enough tears over James Whitehead, dammit.

"Nope." Nore shook her head. "Don't you do it. I spent thirty minutes on these lashes and eye makeup. I'm not about to let you ruin them." Turning back to Dan, she grinned, though yes, it was a bit waterlogged. "Sorry for this episode of Black *Gilmore Girls*. I'm ready to finish up this sale. I'll take the six thousand."

Dan glanced at Tatum, as if waiting for another objection. After a second, he returned his attention to Nore and nodded, smiling.

"Let me go get final approval," he said, gathering up the ring and the appraisal report. "While I'm gone, feel free to look over what we have here just in case you see anything you'd like to buy or trade. And…" His smile widened, flashing a dimple in his right cheek. *Okay.* That quick Dan became a zaddy. "I'm willing to watch a rerun with Lorelei and Rory any day."

With a wink, he strode off toward a closed door several feet behind him.

"Wow. Dan watches *Gilmore Girls*. What time do you think he gets off?" Nore asked, staring after him.

"Oh my God." Tatum groaned, and Nore snickered. "So what are your plans for your sudden windfall? Although James would be choking on his tongue right now knowing you sold it for such a low price."

The corner of Nore's mouth curled even as her chest clutched at just the mention of her ex-fiancé. The man she'd spent the last three years with, planned to spend the rest of her life with... The man who'd broken up with her by fucking email.

Coward.

Dragging in a breath, she deliberately switched her thoughts away from James Whitehead and on to how she could spend her spoils on a ring that, in the end, hadn't been a symbol of commitment and love but disappointment and heartbreak.

Clearing her throat, she perused the case containing glittering rings, necklaces, bracelets and even really beautiful cigarette cases. Still, nothing really caught—

"Oh," she breathed. Her fingers touched the glass as if she could reach through to the piece of jewelry that had caught her eye. A flutter behind her breastbone persisted the longer she stared at the gorgeous brooch nestled between a butterfly-shaped hair comb and a diamond-crusted lapel pin. And she couldn't stop staring. "That's..."

"Stunning," Tatum finished, her shoulder nudging Nore's as she bent down to study the jewelry.

"Would you like to have a closer look?" A woman appeared behind the counter, her dark curls liberally sprinkled with gray and laugh lines fanning out from the corners of her bright brown eyes. More faint lines creased the teak skin around her mouth and forehead, but they only added to her beauty. This appeared to be a woman who enjoyed life to the fullest. She didn't wait for Nore to reply but opened the back panel of the case and carefully removed the brooch. Setting it on the black napkin Dan had left behind, she murmured, "There you go. It's a very unique piece."

Wasn't that an understatement?

Gold and silver fashioned into tiny, fragile-looking flowers—turquoise, pink and dark red—surrounded a lovely portrait. Diamonds and seed pearls studded the flowers and vines, adding to the beauty of the antique piece. The woman, whose back and delicate profile were visible in the painted image, appeared to be Black. A wide-brimmed hat hid most of her features, but the skin of her cheek, mouth, chin and elegant neck was indeed a light brown.

Nore had never seen anything as exquisite.

"The brooch is fifteen-karat gold and silver with diamonds and natural pearls, enamel in the middle. The stone itself is rose cut. The piece is Victorian, dated between 1850 and 1859."

"Victorian?" Tatum touched a fingertip to a pearl. "I've never seen anything like it."

"What she's so delicately trying to not say is I've never seen a Black woman on a Victorian brooch."

Tatum shot Nore a look that clearly called her a mannerless guttersnipe. After so many years of friendship, Nore was fluent in everything Tatum Haas.

The employee whose name badge identified her as Nelle smiled. "Apparently, the painting on the brooch is a depiction of the wife of an English baron. She was the daughter of a Barbadian Parliament member.

They met when her father traveled with the governor general to London and it was love at first sight. It's said they lived many happy years together, and he had the brooch commissioned as one of the many symbols of his love for her."

Nore glanced at Tatum, the fascination bubbling inside her chest reflected on Tatum's face as she stared at the older woman.

"That's a beautiful story," Tatum said. She reached for the brooch, but at the last moment, dropped her arm to her side. "How did it end up here? Uh, no offense." She winced.

"None taken. Here, you can hold it." Nelle lifted it from the napkin and extended it toward Tatum. After a brief hesitation, Tatum accepted it and Nore crowded closer to her friend. Unable to help herself, Nore brushed a fingertip over the painting and the flowers surrounding it. A weird reverence expanded inside her, and underneath it, an inexplicable sense of urgency. "The customer who brought it in said she purchased it at an estate sale. There's more."

The dramatic pause that followed had Nore swiftly transferring her attention from the gorgeous jewelry to Nelle.

The older woman nodded toward the brooch. "It seems a legend is attached to it. Though the baron and baroness loved each other dearly, they didn't have an easy road, as you can imagine. Even the power and wealth of his title couldn't prevent racism and classism. Yet they prevailed and their love and marriage remained strong and true. Therefore, it's said that whoever possesses the brooch will experience that same kind of love. He or she will meet their soulmate, and though the path will be troubled, they will ultimately find a lasting true love."

The cynical part of Nore—the part that had ceased to believe that kind of love existed—scoffed at this "legend." But a smaller, battered part of her yearned to believe. To hope...

Once more she glanced at Tatum, then down at the stunning, elegant solitaire on her left ring finger.

"I'll take it."

The words burst out of Nore before the thought had fully formed. But once they were out there, she didn't negate them. No. She let them stand. Especially when a...rightness settled on her like a soothing balm. That peace calmed the urgency inside her like a cool, refreshing breeze on a sweltering night.

"What?" Tatum frowned at her. "You can't just... Listen, I understand about the ring but this, Nore..." She shook her head. "You don't even know how much it costs."

"Too true." She tilted her head. "How much is it, Nelle?"

"Sixty-two hundred."

"Right." Nore nodded. "I'll take it. Dan just took a diamond ring back there that I'm supposed to receive six thousand for. I'll pay the difference."

"Nore," Tatum hissed. "This is—"

She held up a hand to stop her. "I'm getting it." Then softer, "I'm getting it for you. I didn't find that kind of love but you have, with Mark. And you should have that." She dipped her head toward the jewelry. When Tatum started shaking her head, Nore shook hers right back. "Yes, consider it my bridesmaid gift. It'll be your something old. And something new, too, because well, it's new for you, right?"

"Nore," Tatum whispered, and tears moistened her eyes.

She smiled, and gently took the brooch from Tatum and offered it back to Nelle. "Could you let Dan know?"

Nelle accepted the jewelry, glancing from Nore to Tatum, her lips curved.

"Certainly. Be right back." She turned and headed to the same door Dan had disappeared behind.

"This is crazy," Tatum repeated, just as quietly, but emotion throbbed in her voice.

"So you've said." Nore wrapped an arm around her friend's shoulders and squeezed. "I'm not being impulsive. Okay, maybe a skosh impulsive," she corrected when Tatum gave her another sidelong glance. Chuckling, Nore continued, "But it's almost poetic. Trading what's a symbol of heartbreak for one of love. It's beautiful. And being able to give that to you is beautiful for me." She frowned, mock-glaring. "So don't go ruining the moment by refusing the gift."

Tatum studied her for a long moment. Then she finally nodded.

"Okay. And thank you. I don't think I've ever received a more gorgeous and thoughtful gift."

"Except one." Nore aimed a pointed glance down at her left hand and the ring winking on it.

"Except one." A smile slowly bloomed on her face, and she slid an arm around Nore's waist, squeezing. "I'll accept the brooch on one condition." She paused and her smile expanded into a grin. "You hold it for me until my wedding day. If that legend is really true then maybe in the six months before I get married, you'll find your true love, too."

Nore snorted even as pain tugged at her, twisting. And mingling with it was a terrible longing for something she no longer believed was meant for her. Especially not in the next six months. Hell, she and James had been together for three years, and he hadn't loved her enough to commit. And she was supposed to find the kind of love that crossed cultures, defied society and racism in weeks?

Yes, well, there was also a bridge for sale in Westeros. Dragons, too.

"Sure, I'll keep it until then." She held up a finger, forestalling whatever romance-related nonsense would spill from Tatum's mouth next. "And not because I believe or even want to fall in love again." Court this humiliation, disillusionment and hurt for another go-round? No, thank you. Masochism wasn't on her bingo card for this year. "I want to be the one who pins it on you when you start your new life with Mark."

"Un-huh." Tatum nodded. "We'll see."

"Tate, the brooch is stunning and it has a lovely story attached to it. But you can't possibly believe it's more than that—a story."

A smile that could only be called mischievous curled Tatum's lips. "Like you said, we'll see."

Nore stared at her friend for a long moment, then rolled her eyes, dropping her arm and nudging Tatum's shoulder with her own.

"Whatever. Let's get this taken care of so we can go eat and then scream over hot strippers."

"You mean applaud at Cirque du Soleil."

Nore arched an eyebrow and patted Tatum's arm.

"It's so adorable how you think that's going to happen."

"Oh God," Tatum groaned.

Nore cackled, legends of true love and fated soulmates already forgotten.

# Two

"Nore, you've done a fantastic job. The club is perfect, and the VIP section is just as I imagined. And I don't know where you found the DJ but she's amazing. I'm beginning to believe Joaquin might actually enjoy himself tonight." The beautiful woman in the strapless, curve-hugging black dress praised her with a wide grin.

"Thank you. I'm so glad you're pleased with everything so far." Nore smiled at her client, confusingly named Shorty, as she towered over Nore's own five-foot-six frame by at least five inches.

But then again, nothing about Greer Motorcycles Co. had been expected. Apparently, the high-end motorcycle manufacturer founded by former professional motorcycle racer Joaquin Iverson enjoyed a very laid-back environment. Nore had done her homework. She'd researched the company, which had exploded onto the business and sports scene ten years ago. With the renowned motorcyclist and custom bike builder Bran Holleran at the helm, it'd become a multibillion-dollar company.

The employees she'd come in contact with while planning this surprise birthday party had an easygoing manner, and their colorful ink, piercings and leather and denim seemed more appropriate in a tattoo shop than a wildly successful corporation. Maybe that incongruity explained why she'd enjoyed working with Shorty and her staff so much. As one of the premiere event planners in Seattle, Nore could claim some of the city's wealthiest and poshest citizens as clients. And this hadn't been her first birthday party. But by far, Greer Motorcycles had been her most fun and unique experience. She'd almost miss them after tonight.

Nore shifted, surveying the Capitol Hill nightclub they'd reserved for this Friday night at a hefty fee. Nearly two hundred people mingled, drank and laughed at the two bars on either side of the massive first floor or around the empty dance floor that would be packed later once the guest of honor arrived. The club's DJ—one of the nation's most popular—commandeered the LED booth, and already the guests moved to the music she played. Fifty or so more people congregated in the intimate second floor that possessed its own separate bar and staff. The company's executives and exclusive guests occupied that area.

A carefully curated catering company and waitstaff wound among everyone on both levels offering hors d'oeuvres, the heavier, more filling fare ready to serve once the birthday boy arrived.

"Nore, we have a black Range Rover pulling into the back lot." The voice of Nore's friend and right arm, Bastian Dare, crackled in her earpiece.

Speaking of...

She pressed the mic. "Great. I'll get everything ready in here." Switching her attention to Shorty, she said, "Mr. Iverson has arrived outside. I'm going to tell the DJ to cut the music and you should head to the stage."

"Perfect." She made a beeline toward the booth while Nore told the DJ on the earpiece to cut the music.

In the sudden silence, the chatter swelled, then faded, as all the guests turned toward the stage, giving their attention to Shorty as she climbed the stairs and crossed to the center with a cordless microphone clutched in a hand.

"Hey, everyone. First, thank you so much for coming out tonight to celebrate Joaquin's birthday. You're commended because we all know there's a fifty-fifty chance he'll either stay or duck out the door." Laughter rippled through the crowd. "But know he and all of us appreciate you being here to honor our fearless leader. Who, by the way, is right outside. So, you know the drill." She pushed a hand down, miming silence. "Joaquin will be coming in through the back entrance near the left bar. Let's keep it hush-hush until he steps inside and we all yell 'surprise.' Then," she shrugged, grinning, "let it begin."

A cheer rose, quickly followed by louder shushing.

"He's at the door," Bastien warned in Nore's ear, and she held up a hand, signaling Shorty.

The other woman nodded, and with urgency in her voice, said, "Okay, everyone, this is it. Quiet."

Immediately, silence engulfed the club, and almost as one the partygoers shifted toward the back hall. A hush of anticipation hovered; it even hummed in her chest. For a moment, she forgot she worked the event and almost felt like a guest, included in the festive atmosphere. But with a shake of her head, she shed that temporary slip. No matter how kind or welcoming the clients might be, she could never forget, she was the employee, not one of them.

Hitting the side of her earpiece, she connected with her team once more, this time addressing Caroline, the VIP liaison, she instructed, "Caro, make sure as soon as the lights are back on and the surprise is out the way, a Guinness is in Mr. Iverson's hand and he's guided to the VIP area. Are the hors d'oeuvres set out at his table?"

"Will do and yes," Caro said.

"Perfect." Nore tapped the screen of the tablet she held and checked off those two items. "We'll open the buffet down here thirty minutes sharp after Mr. Iverson arrives and have the staff serve dinner in the VIP lounges at that time. Everyone ready?"

Several voices replied in the affirmative. Satisfied, she clicked the line off.

Show time.

The LED and interior lights shut off, pitching the club in near total darkness, only the exit signs and emergency lighting providing illumination.

The creak of the door opening preceded a deep, rumbling growl that demanded, "The hell is this? I thought you said we were coming here for a drink. This place doesn't look open."

Even disgruntled, the low, rough timbre stroked over the bare skin of her arms, skimmed across the nape of her neck. Grazed the front of her throat. A shiver raced through her, and that was all before the owner of that dirty-sex-in-the-middle-of-the-night voice strode into the main area.

Holy... Had she called him birthday boy?

There was absolutely nothing *boy* about Joaquin Iverson.

Of course, she'd seen a picture of Greer Motorcycles' CEO and cofounder. But good God, comparing the digital image to reality was like equating regular margarine to apple butter. One was fine, but the other was an *experience*.

The muted green of the exit light skimmed over his harsh features, and her breath jammed in her throat. Shadows slashed over one half of his face, and yet she still stared, caught, captured.

*Brutal*.

That's the word her brain pulled free like a magician tugging a rabbit out of his hat.

Brutally sharp. Brutally strong.

Brutally beautiful.

The air lodged in her throat loosened and it whistled out, a balloon with a slow leak. She couldn't decide whether to look away from him or stare until her mind was branded with his image.

She blinked. Tried to look away.

Okay, so she was going with stare.

Fierce angles and bold planes. Dark, thick eyebrows pulled together and nearly met over an arrogant slash of a nose. An obstinate jaw that spoke of an iron will. A thick beard surrounded a wide, ridiculously sinful mouth. Downright blasphemous. The silver hoop piercing the corner of his bottom lip only drew attention to its indecent fullness.

Damn.

If she wasn't careful, she would end up penning a sonnet to his mouth.

The lights crashed on and "Surprise!" erupted in the cavernous room.

She squinted against the sudden illumination but didn't take her gaze away from him. Even if everything inside her screamed to do just that. Like gazing directly at the sun, she should shade her eyes because he emanated danger. To her equilibrium. Her respiratory system.

Her senses.

So she noticed the slight narrowing of his eyes and the minute tightening of his mouth—as she apparently seemed to be a charter member of its fan club—when no one else did. Applause and cheers bounced off the exposed brick of the club walls, and a second later, as if those emotions never passed over his features, he smiled.

And this time, she did glance away.

Not only because Joaquin Iverson's smile should require a warning label.

But also because it was completely fake.

Something shifted in her chest, a fluttering that still felt...hollow. The sight of that forced curve of lips, it didn't hit right. And why she cared that a man, faced with evidence of his esteem by so many people, had to fake a smile, she couldn't explain. And honestly, didn't want to.

This time, she made herself turn away and switch her attention to her tablet. For the next hour and a half, she focused on ensuring dinner was served on time and the rest of the party ran smoothly. Pleased, she finally took a moment to grab a bottle of water from the bartender and stood next to the VIP entrance. From this vantage point, she could view most of the club's lower floor. Bastien covered her and Caro had recently let her know everything was fine above, but until the last person left, she wouldn't truly be off the clock.

Which would only be another two hours, her slightly aching soles informed her...

"Excuse me."

That voice. She knew that voice. And if she hadn't immediately recognized it, the shiver skipping its way down her spine would've notified her of its owner's identity.

Deliberately, she turned away from the partying

guests and met a piercing pair of such light gray eyes they almost appeared silver. The intensity and beauty matched the voice. Hell, they matched everything about Joaquin Iverson.

He shifted an infinitesimal amount forward, but it was enough to nearly dwarf her. Because goddamn, the man was *huge*.

From across the length of the wide room, she couldn't have gauged the breadth of shoulders and chest that any Seahawks linebacker would envy. Couldn't have guessed the looming height that had her suddenly feeling tiny and delicate, a feat that had never occurred before. Couldn't have surmised the power that emanated from his thick, muscled arms and thighs that had a simple white dress shirt and dark dress pants clinging to them like shameless groupies. And at some point, he'd rolled back the sleeves, revealing corded forearms liberally covered in tattoos, and even more creeping up toward the base of his throat.

Once more, her breath did that curious and irritating phenomenon where it evaporated into nothingness. Made it damn hard to speak.

He arched an eyebrow and extended his hand toward her.

"Joaquin Iverson. And you're Lenora Daniels. Shorty says I have you to thank for my party."

As if of its own volition, her arm stretched forward and the moment his long fingers closed around hers in a strong grip, she smothered a groan that clawed to the back of her throat. Like a flue had opened in her belly, flames shot from the depths of her, barreling up her chest, down her arm and to her palm that was clasped against his.

*What the hell?*

She stared at their hands; the blast of desire was incongruous for a simple handshake. If lust lit her up like this with just palm pressing to palm, what would it feel like if he filled her? If that big, naked body covered her as his cock slowly buried inside…

*Okay, I repeat, what. The.* Hell?

Not caring how it appeared, she quickly extricated her hand and just barely managed not to wipe it against her skirt-covered thigh. Self-preservation screamed she reclaim control of herself rather than let him touch her for one more millisecond.

And if there'd been one lesson she'd learned since the breakup with James, it'd been to listen to her instincts. After all, they'd tried to warn her that all hadn't been right with her relationship. But she'd been so focused on making it work, on ending the curse that seemed to haunt every generation of Daniels women, that she hadn't heeded the signs.

Never again would she bury her head in the sand about anything. But especially when it came to men.

"Yes, that's right," she said, forcing a smile and an even tone that mocked the chaotic confusion tumbling inside her chest. The quiet speculation that entered his bright, narrowed eyes only further snarled that confusion. "But please, call me Nore. Only my mother insists on calling me Lenora. And since she birthed me, I can't contradict her. Or at least she doesn't listen when I do."

She smiled wider as she delivered the usual joke about her name when meeting new people, but unlike most others, Joaquin didn't crack a smile. Instead, that unwavering gaze studied her. She'd never fidgeted in her life, yet she had to fight the urge now.

"It's nice to meet you." He dipped his head, and the light from directly above them glinted off the small hoop in his right eyebrow. "Pretty."

For a moment, she blinked, caught between "Say what now?" and "Tell me more about my eyes."

But then he flicked a finger toward the brooch nestled in the folds of the ruffles at her neck. Tatum's brooch. She might've borrowed it for the night because it went perfectly with her outfit. There should still be more than enough of the love magic attached for Tatum's wedding.

"The jewelry," Joaquin clarified. "It's pretty."

"Oh." She lifted a hand to the brooch. "Thank you."

He nodded, scanning the club.

"You've done a great job here, and Shorty can't stop talking about how much she's enjoyed working with you and your staff."

Pleasure bloomed in her chest, almost pushing aside the constriction there.

"That's always wonderful to hear." She paused, then as if some unknown entity possessed her, she added, "Although, why do I get the feeling that you're enduring this party for your staff and guests? That if you had your way, you would've been out of here right after the 'surprise'?"

He studied her for another moment, then the corner of his mouth quirked.

"Am I that obvious?"

"No." *I just happened to be watching you that closely.*

Once more, one of his dark brown eyebrows rose, as if waiting for her explanation. Hell could freeze over, and she wouldn't voice the rest of her truth. Not only would it be inappropriate, but to utter those words would be unlocking a door she might not be able to close.

A door she wasn't quite certain, in this moment, she'd want to close.

"You're right." He slid his hands in the front pockets of his pants. "In my head, I'm counting down how long before I can leave without appearing rude. Or without being missed."

"Good luck with the first one. The second? Impossible." When her words reverberated back to her, she fought back a wince. And prayed the heat streaming up her neck and pouring into her cheeks wasn't visible in the shadows where they stood. "Because you're the guest of honor," she hurriedly blurted out. "And so...big."

And because she needed to be a bit more cringey, she spread her arms the length of his wide shoulders and phantom squeezed the hard muscles.

Just...*fuck*.

Joaquin didn't smirk or laugh at her increasingly

embarrassing awkwardness. No, that already piercing gaze seemed to grow sharper, a scalpel about to slice her open and reveal everything inside.

Her heart thumped against her chest, and for the first time this evening, she tasted a hint of fear on her tongue.

The last time she'd allowed someone access to her vulnerabilities, he'd betrayed her in the most callous, painful way possible. Since then, she'd learned to keep her own counsel. Keep her counsel, hell. Wrap it in chain mail and set sentries around it.

"I get that often."

She blinked, her brain taking a moment to connect Joaquin's words and the dry tone in which they were stated. Seconds later, a smile tugged at her lips, then curved into a grin. And relief poured through her, extinguishing the flames still burning her cheeks.

"I bet." She chuckled, shaking her head. "I apologize, though. That was inappropriate of me to say."

"Why?"

Nore tilted her head, frowned. "Why was it inappropriate? First and foremost, you're my client—"

"It's honest, Nore. Honesty outweighs what you call inappropriate."

"No offense, Mr. Iverson," she said, knowing she was chancing doing just that—offending him, "but you can afford to say that. I can't."

He dipped his chin, his gaze roaming over her face like a physical touch.

"You're right. Again. I'm playing that back in my

head and it was arrogant. And privileged," he said with a nod.

Surprise flashed through her. Here, she'd steeled herself to be dismissed at the very least, but he'd conceded her point, admitted he'd been wrong. She flickered a glance toward his forehead. Nope, no horn. But he damn sure was the first unicorn of a man she'd encountered.

"I've surprised you," he said, practically reading her mind.

"A little." Then, "Yes," she confessed with a soft laugh.

The corner of his mouth lifted again, drawing her gaze there almost against her will. But damn, it was such a pretty mouth.

"Good," he said, blunt, matter-of-fact. "We all need a little of the unexpected in our lives. What's the saying? The enemies of happiness are pain and boredom?"

"Boredom is your imagination calling to you," she countered.

This time his lips didn't quirk. They slowly curved, spreading until a full-fledged smile lit his carved, stern features.

Her breath jammed in her throat. Just in time she prevented herself from taking a step backward, shifting away from the *beauty* of his smile. That wasn't *fair*. One smile had taken Joaquin Iverson from a brutally beautiful man to simply magnificent.

"I like you, Nore Daniels," he murmured.

Another flash of heat swept through her, flushing

her skin and swelling her breasts so even her silk bra and black high-necked blouse seemed to be too many layers against her fevered flesh. Her thighs squeezed together, and she locked down a whimper as a deep, yawning ache bloomed low in her belly, pulsing hot and heavy.

"I need to get back to work," she said, voice as low as his, as soft. Almost as if she were pleading with him to let her go. Or worse...convincing herself to stay.

What the hell was happening with her?

He didn't respond, though. Instead, he cocked his head and for several long moments settled that silver gaze on her face. *What do you see?* The question rebounded against her skull, and she hated that the voice—hers—sounded so damn...desperate.

But dammit, she couldn't lie to herself. As she met that molten stare, curiosity dug into her. Did he see a self-assured, successful, capable woman? Or did she wear her vulnerability, her bruised confidence, like he wore his tattoos? Vivid, unmistakable and visible to the naked eye.

Better question, though... Why did she care what this man, whom she'd barely met, thought about her?

*I don't*, she silently yet fiercely assured herself.

"Why do I make you nervous?" he quietly asked.

"You don't," came her immediate, reflexive reply.

He didn't tsk, but he didn't need to. The disappointment flickering in his eyes was loud and clear.

"Up until this moment, you've been honest and plainspoken with me. And I've enjoyed it more than anything else at this party," he stated, tone blunt. "I don't know why you decided to lie to me now."

He wasn't wrong; she had lied. But never had a man been so frank and direct that it edged on rude. And never would she have believed it could be so damn hot.

Even as wisps of anger curled inside her, desire quivered just under her belly button, pooling in her sex. She didn't do dominant men. After the childhood she'd endured, she avoided men who carried even a whiff of control.

Which meant she should've ducked and dodged Joaquin Iverson from the moment his whiskey-smoke voice echoed in her ear. The moment his earthy scent—redolent of expensive leather, dark chocolate and bad decisions—surrounded her.

"Maybe," she slowly said, meeting his startling gaze, "I'm not lying so much as displaying wisdom and caution."

Oh, fuck that. She was definitely lying. The man made her nerves sing like they were competing for *The Voice*.

"About? We're just talking, so what is there to be cautious about?"

He didn't move toward her but the space between them seemed to shrink, the air evaporating like steam off an Alabama sidewalk after a sudden rainstorm. How was it possible that his already large frame appeared to expand until she couldn't see the VIP entrance behind him, the dark hallway to her left or the stairs to her right?

No, in a matter of seconds, her world contracted to include only...him.

Magic? Some sort of spell he weaved with those silver eyes and big, long-fingered hands?

Or was it just common, old-fashioned lust?

Those eyes briefly dipped to her mouth and a bolt of electricity crackled down her spine like lightning, sizzling in the base of her spine.

Old-fashioned, maybe. But common? She almost snorted. There was nothing common about being lit up like a tuning fork only from a glance. A glance that had stroked over her lips like a physical, sensual caress...or a threat.

"Honesty?" She lowered her tablet to her side, slightly turning and leaning against the doorjamb.

He nodded. "Always."

The way he stated that, so emphatically—hell, almost passionately—she paused. There was *something* behind that. Shaking her head, she filed it away and focused on the conversation in front of her.

Inhaling a deep breath, she deliberately blew it out, then notched up her chin.

"We both know this isn't just 'talking.'"

For the second time that night, she battled the need to fidget. And she barely won this round. He couldn't spy the damn near wild hurtling of her heart against her rib cage. If he could, he'd know what her outward composure cost her.

Thank God for small favors.

"Then what is it, Nore?"

Would it be rude to demand he cease saying her

name? It sounded…indecent, somehow. Illicit. And all too seductive. As if his tongue curling around that one syllable was a precursor to other things he could do with that beautiful, carnal mouth.

"Foreplay."

She'd braced herself for another one of those devastating smiles. Prepared herself for rejection before he stormed off. She hadn't expected that searing flash of heat in his eyes, brightening them so they appeared like liquid steel. Nor had she predicted that his finely honed features could become more stark, more harsh or that his mouth could appear more lush, more… wicked.

She hadn't expected to stare into the face of sex.

The air in her lungs abandoned her.

Maybe total honesty hadn't been the wisest play.

"Honesty?" He drove the word between them like a sword thrust.

She hesitated, but then said, "Yes."

"This isn't foreplay. You wouldn't have any doubts about the difference with me."

He shifted forward, but at the last moment he seemed to catch himself, and that big body stilled, maintaining the distance between them. Had she actually claimed that control didn't appeal to her? Screw that. The obvious power he exhibited over himself, over his reactions, had her sex pulsing. She pressed her spine harder into the doorway.

To insert more space between them or to prop herself up?

She wasn't answering that.

"I don't flirt," he continued with that same unwavering gaze. And dammit, her stomach shouldn't flutter over that admission. "Never saw the point in it. But for you, I'm making an effort. That's what this is."

"And my point still stands," she said, shocked and thankful the words didn't emerge as a trembling whisper. "You're my client, and this—" she waved a hand back and forth "—can't happen. Not only is it unprofessional but highly inappropri—"

Without breaking their visual connection, he pulled a phone free from his pants pocket. His gaze briefly lowered to the screen to press his thumb to it but returned right back to her as he lifted the cell to his ear.

"Shorty." Pause. "I'm still here, calm down. Listen, have you paid the event planner for their services yet?" Another pause. "Good. Send it now." He stared at her, listening to his employee on the other end. "Yeah, now. Thanks." He lowered the phone and shoved it back into his front pocket. "Your final payment will be sent in fifteen minutes. And in—" he glanced down at the chunky black watch on his wrist— "one hour and forty-two minutes I will no longer be your client."

"That's not how that works," she whispered.

"It's exactly how it works," he countered just as softly. "If you want it to. Do you want it, Nore?"

*Do you want it?*

Define "it." Because wasn't that the crux of his loaded question? What, exactly, did she want? More of this banter, this flirtation that went against the grain for him? More time with him? Maybe finding somewhere to sit and talk?

Or...

*Him.*

Did she want him and everything that sinful mouth promised? Did she long to have him wield that sexy—and intimidating—control over her? Have him exert the power his big frame and thick muscles promised? Have him unleash it all on her...inside her?

An answer shivered in her throat, tried to claw its way to her tongue.

But what that answer was, she didn't know.

Her lips parted, ready to shape around the one she *should* give, for any number of reasons.

As a Black woman owning and running a business in a highly competitive field that depended on not just being above reproach, but the *very appearance* of being above reproach, she couldn't afford mistakes. Literally. Where others might have grace, she didn't.

As if she needed another reason, she also didn't know him. More power to the people who could rock a one-night stand, but she wasn't one of them. Or at least, she hadn't been.

And she'd never crossed the line of becoming involved with a client. Just the thought of it... She could be jeopardizing everything she'd worked so hard to obtain.

Yet with every one of these very valid reasons ringing in her head, she couldn't push the only suitable answer out of her mouth.

"Stop overthinking," he ordered, and her stomach contracted at the vein of steel running through it. Lust pumped through her, shocking her with its intensity. Into this astonishment, he continued in a voice that surely was akin to the one that had seduced Eve into her fall from grace. "Give yourself permission to take."

Those words resounded in her head, in her wounded soul.

So easy for him to say. Since she'd been a kid, she couldn't just say "fuck it" and take. God knew she loved her mother, but Margo Daniels had been too busy doing just that—taking—so Nore had to be the responsible, stable one. And years later, when she had thrown caution to the wind, what did she have to show for it? A failed relationship and an unwanted business partner.

So no, "taking" didn't come naturally to her. It fucking terrified her.

And still... Her gaze dropped to his mouth, lowered to his broad shoulders, to his wide chest. When flames ignited, licking at her, she quickly glanced away from him.

"You let me know. The decision is all yours about what happens or what doesn't," he said, and the hard note no longer threaded his tone, but his voice still remained low, cotton-soft and gravel-rough. "I'll wait for you up there." He jerked his chin toward the stairs that led to the VIP area. "If you decide no, you don't even have to show. But if you climb those steps and walk through that door, then I'll know it's a yes." He cocked his head, and his gaze roamed her face again, touching on her cheeks, nose, mouth before returning to her eyes. "No pressure, Nore. And whether you come to me or not, what's between us stays here."

*Come to me.*

A shiver rocked through her. The temptation contained in those three words... She shook her head. No way she could even be considering his sensual invitation. This wasn't her.

*It could be...*

"I need to go." She cleared her throat and nodded at him as she moved back toward the club's main area. "It was nice meeting you, Mr. Iverson," she murmured.

Walking back toward the bar, she tried to put his proposition out of her mind. She had a job to finish, and it required her attention. Because no matter how visceral the attraction or stunning the smile... No matter that even now her body hummed with the residual effects of just being near him and inhaling his intoxicating scent, the answer was no.

It had to be.

# Three

Joaquin Nathan Iverson enjoyed taking risks.

A person couldn't be a former professional motorcycle racer and the founder of his own company manufacturing high-end custom bikes and *not* enjoy taking risks. He'd road-raced in Texas, competed in Spain and finished first in the Superbike World Championship in Malaysia. He'd started a business with a partner and a vision and watched the first motorcycle bearing his company's name roll out on a showroom floor as if birthed.

All of them had been adrenaline rushes, thrilling and life-changing.

And yet, as he sat on a couch in a VIP section of a nightclub, gaze trained on the room's entrance, his pulse pounded in his ears and exhilaration pumped through his veins as if he were back out on a track in Leicestershire, England, vying against the best the sport had to offer.

Had he ever been this wired over a race, over a new custom design? Yes. Over a woman? No.

Not even the one who sometimes haunted his dreams.

He clenched his jaw, mentally shoving the door shut to the memories. For good measure, he slammed a padlock on it. He'd become somewhat of an expert locksmith when it came to his past. It had no place in his present. Especially when the here and now included the sexy-as-fuck event planner who could possibly walk through the door any moment.

God, let her walk through that door.

It was probably blasphemous for him to seek divine intervention in getting Nore Daniels to appear given everything he intended to do to her if she did. But he couldn't bring himself to care. Whatever got her here. Whatever worked so he could satisfy this greedy curiosity about her.

Whatever put him one step closer to satiating this relentless, driving hunger to taste that lush mouth, touch that gorgeous body, hear that husky voice break on his name...

Tension vibrated through him like a steady electric hum. Leaning forward, he propped his elbows on his thighs, clasping his hands between them.

Never had he done...this. Never had he been "this guy."

No conceit but just the truth—as ugly as it might

be. Since the age of thirteen when his voice dropped and his height shot up, female attention hadn't been a hard thing to come by. But when he'd turned eighteen and begun his professional racing career, women flocking to him had taken on a life of its own. And he wasn't naive enough to think it was his face and body that were responsible—damn sure wasn't his personality. No, being an athlete, earning more money and fame than he'd possessed in his life had been the major determining factors. And when he and Bran Holleran, his partner and custom bike builder, had teamed up to open Greer Motorcycles? Yeah, he'd never lacked for companionship. And by companionship, he meant fucking.

He'd never had to chase, to pursue. Not even with Madison—

*Shit.* He scrubbed a hand down his face. Why did his ex, the one woman he'd ever loved...the woman who had betrayed him...keep infiltrating his thoughts?

*You know why*, a low voice rumbled not so much in his head, but in his chest. In that quiet, desolate place he pretended didn't exist.

Today would've been their five-year wedding anniversary.

If she hadn't died a year after they married.

Was that what tonight had been about? Could he chalk up the urgency throbbing in his veins as he talked with Nore, as he savored every detail about her stunning face and ridiculously hot body? Had it all been about the need to forget the fucked-up date he unwillingly kept track of?

An image of Nore Daniels rose in his mind like a mirage—or a warning.

Standing in that doorway, head tilted back, he'd first noticed the warm, rich brown of her wide, thickly lashed eyes. No, not brown. They were too light, too unique for that ordinary description. Tawny. Like the feathers of the owls he used to see while camping with his father years ago. For a moment, he'd lost himself in those eyes and a sense of peace, of comfort he hadn't experienced since those long ago days on the road with his dad, sleeping under the stars at night.

Chest tight with those memories, he'd lowered his gaze to the lovely mass of dark curls that framed boldly cut cheekbones so sharp they could've drawn blood. Lower still to the elegant slope of nose and slightly flared nostrils, to the delicate line of her jaw that he'd bet his own Kawasaki Ninja ZX-10R could turn stubborn in a blink, and on to her chin with its faint cleft. Just as his mind's eye did now, his too-damn-fascinated gaze had zeroed in on the illicit beauty of her mouth. Those wide, plush lips could bring a man to his knees. Literally. And gladly.

That was all before he had a close-up-and-personal view of a body sporting more curves than the most dangerous track. And like when he encountered a challenging racetrack, his body damn near vibrated with the need to ride it.

Full, high breasts pushed against a sleeveless black lace shirt with a high collar that had his fingers itch-ing to cup and mold her flesh in his hands. A tight leather pencil skirt molded to a delicious flare of hips and legs that appeared impossibly long with her black stiletto heels. He hadn't needed to see the ass that deserved its own warning sign. *Caution: One glance may cause instant hard-on.* One glimpse and he'd discovered that fact for himself.

So yeah, maybe this damn near desperate need for the event planner had something to do with the date. But it wasn't the only reason—not even the main one. Nore Daniels, with her soulful eyes, alluring beauty and video vixen body, had that on lock.

And he wanted it. Craved it.

All of it.

Tearing his gaze from the door, he flipped his wrist and peered down at the watch that had once belonged to his father: 1:32 a.m. The party had ended nearly a half hour earlier, and he'd been waiting here since for her to arrive.

Disappointment slid through him, and the power of it should've shaken him. Maybe later it would and he'd be thankful to have dodged a bullet. But right now...

Right now it pressed down on his chest like a heavy weight. He rose and shifted from behind the table—

A movement near the VIP entrance snagged his attention, and he jerked his head in that direction, half expecting to see Shorty standing there, although he'd told her to go home when the party ended.

Lust punched him in the gut, and his abs tightened against the impact.

No. Not Shorty.

He met a pair of golden-brown eyes, and once more that calm invaded him, meshing with the desire and creating a dichotomy that shouldn't cohabitate, shouldn't work. Yet it did.

"Should I be afraid security's going to show up and escort us out?" she asked in lieu of a greeting.

"Taken care of." A conversation with the owner and a large payment on top of what it'd cost to rent the club for the evening had ensured them privacy. Sometimes being wealthy had its perks. "Do you want to be here?" he demanded, and almost winced at the gravel abrading his tone.

If his dick trying to bust past his zipper wasn't a clue to the hunger coursing through him with curled claws, then his voice would be.

"Were you getting ready to leave?" she countered, still standing in the doorway, not having taken a step into the enclosed suite.

"You first." Because her answer outweighed his in terms of importance.

Silence greeted him, and she glanced away. It required every bit of control he'd learned over the years to remain standing in front of the couch instead of striding over to her, pinching that sweet chin and making her meet his eyes.

"Yes," she murmured, turning back to him. "And no." She huffed out a soft chuckle, shaking her head. "I'm here, so yes, I want to be. But should I be here? No."

He nodded; he got that.

"Yes, I was getting ready to leave," he said, answering her question.

Surprise flashed in her golden eyes. "You didn't think I would—" she paused and something else flickered in her gaze—something that had his gut tightening to the point of a dull pain "—come to you," she finished, giving him his earlier words back.

A taut silence pulsated in the enclosed space, and he couldn't remove his gaze from her, from the cascade of emotions that marched across her face. God, he wanted to dive into that beautiful head of hers. The desire equaled the need to bury himself inside her body.

The precedent unsettled him—never had he craved unraveling a woman's secrets as much as fucking her.

That alone should've warned him away with a madly waving red flag. But like a moth lured by the beautiful yet lethal flames, he drew closer. Couldn't resist her.

"No," he admitted. And because he'd demanded honesty from her earlier, he was compelled to give her the same. That, and he despised lies. When you grew up weaned on deceptions like milk, the taste of them became sour on the tongue. "I hoped you'd stay but didn't assume you would. Nothing about you, Nore, is a sure thing." Or a simple one.

Her mouth twisted into a sardonic smile. "Well, at least there's that."

"Meaning?"

"If I'm going to be foolish as hell, at least I went

down fighting." She sighed after delivering that enigmatic statement and thrust her hand through the thick, dark brown curls that framed her face and grazed her shoulders. His fingers and palms itched to tangle themselves in those gorgeous, tight spirals. He fisted his hands as if trapping the imagined sensation, then slowly loosened them. "At the risk of sounding really cliché, this is all new to me. I've never—"

"Fucked in a VIP suite in an abandoned club after your surprise birthday party?" he supplied. "Yeah, me neither."

"Right. That, too." A ghost of a smile flirted with her lips before she sobered, her expression solemn, intent. "I've also never endangered my business, its reputation and my own over a fuck in a VIP suite in an abandoned club after a *client's* surprise birthday party."

The weight of her words, her confession, and what she risked by being there sank into him, settled onto his chest. He understood this, too—and yet he couldn't. The facts stood that if this night were exposed, he wouldn't be penalized for it. He'd weather the storm with mild recriminations. In some circles, he'd even receive winks and metaphorical pats on the back. Nore, though? She would be condemned, branded with a scarlet letter, and she wouldn't recover.

She gambled much, much more showing up here.

"If I were a better man, I'd tell you to turn around and leave. Assure you that this—" he waved a hand back and forth between them "—isn't worth it. But

I'm not that man." She could ask anyone; he'd heard it often enough. So often, he'd stopped trying to be anything but who he was—a bastard, in personality and by birth. "So I'm going to exhibit uncharacteristic selflessness and offer you an out. Last chance, Nore. Turn around and walk out that door."

She studied him for a moment, then softly snorted. "If you had tried to convince me that this wasn't a bad idea, I might've actually left. But you not even trying…" She shook her head again. "I'm not going to analyze what that says about me."

"Why are you risking it?" he demanded.

More than curiosity drove that question. Curiosity didn't describe an almost wild, incessant need to hear her answer. To satisfy a…longing deep inside that was old, familiar and so damn hungry.

A long, silent moment stretched into two, then two more. Finally, she lifted a shoulder in a small shrug. "Honesty?"

"Always," he said, and hated the desperation that tinted his voice, his fucking soul.

That, too, tasted familiar.

"Because I haven't felt this wanted in a long time." On the heels of that admission, she lifted her hands and pressed them toward him, palms out. An impatient sound escaped her as she wrinkled her nose. "No, that's not the whole truth. I haven't felt this *alive*. And God—" she loosed a small, self-deprecating and *sad* chuckle "—I need to feel alive. To feel vital. It's addictive." Another of those heartbreaking soft laughs. "I know I'm not making much sense."

He couldn't speak. Could barely breathe past the stranglehold her words had on his throat. The heat that had been simmering from the moment she appeared in the doorway flared, searing him, blinding him to everything but the need to touch her, taste her. Fucking consume her until nothing remained of either of them but ashes.

She thrust fingers through her hair once more. "I told you it—"

"Close the door."

He heard the blunt, almost cold tone of the order, but with him using every bit of his control to restrain himself—to keep himself from charging across the space and leaping on her like an apex predator—he couldn't help how the words emerged.

Her eyes widened, and even with the distance separating them, he caught her low breath. Saw it with the hitch of her chest. But after the briefest pause, she turned and obeyed, shutting the door. The soft click of the lock sliding into place echoed in the booth like a shot.

Hot, damn near feral satisfaction slid through him.

She sealed her fate with that twisting of the lock.

No, with the *I need to feel alive.* He couldn't possibly let her walk away. Not then. Not now. They were both going down in flames.

"Come here."

She didn't hesitate this time, and another bolt of gratification hit him, sizzled in his veins. Gratification and anticipation. It must have only taken seconds for her to reach him, but the moment stretched, feeling like an eternity. And by the time she stood in front of him, he nearly shook with need. His cock throbbed, echoing the pounding of his heart.

And as soon as she stopped—her head tilted back, those tawny eyes on him, her plush lips parted—he didn't hold back. He lifted his hands and surrendered to the unceasing urge that had been scratching at him from the first time he'd seen her. Tunneling his fingers into her hair, he didn't even attempt to contain his groan. Not with the coarse silk sliding over his skin, tangling in fists.

Until this moment, he hadn't realized he'd been living an existence of sensory deprivation.

And like any man robbed of sustenance, he feasted.

Lowering his head and holding hers captive, he took her mouth. Fuck that. He laid siege to it.

*Don't be a goddamn feral beast and scare her. Gentle.*

The admonishment whispered through his head, and he tried to heed it. Dammit, he did. But as soon as those soft, full lips parted under his, granting him access to the wet, intimate depths of her, he gave up that fight. Angling his head, he thrust his tongue deep, sliding it over and around hers, demanding she meet him, play with him. Fuck him.

And God, she did.

Plunge for plunge. Lick for lick. Suck for suck. The kiss was wild, raw, messy. He didn't hold anything back, but neither did she. If he'd feared frightening her with his intensity, his hunger, all that evaporated under her equally ravenous response. Nore not only gave as good as she got, she ordered him with a frankly erotic lick to the roof of his mouth to give her more.

Using the grip on her hair, he tilted her head farther back, and he drove harder, claiming more and offering it in return. Every slide of his tongue over hers, every greedy suck stroked and tugged on his cock. And when those even white teeth tagged the hoop at the corner of his lip and tugged... Fuck.

Almost painful ecstasy shot to his dick, and with a rumble of impatience, of pleasure, he shifted closer, grinding against the soft give of her belly. But rather than ease the clawing ache, the feel of her cradling him only ratcheted up the need until he fucking shuddered against her.

She tore her mouth from his, her breath hot, moist against his cheek, his jaw. Her hands, which had been fisted in his shirt at his back, loosened their grip and slid down his spine, settling on his waist. Her fingernails bit into his skin there, his clothing no deterrent to the muffled sting.

With a grunt, he buried his head in the crook between her neck and shoulder, relishing the bite. Dragging his teeth up the side of her neck, he nipped the rim of her ear.

"Don't play with it, baby. Harder if you want to mark me."

And to show her just what he meant, he drew the tender, sensitive skin behind her ear between his teeth, pulling, sucking.

Marking.

Her soft, sweet gasp punctuated the air, and he moaned against her flesh. Just as he'd bidden, her nails dug deeper, and the nip of pain flared up his spine, nailing him in the back of the neck before zipping back down to tingle in the base of his spine. With a muffled curse, he bucked against her, grinding, seeking.

Riding on a precarious edge, he sought out and located the zipper at the back of her blouse and jerked it down. In his mind, he apologized for the rough action, but his mouth didn't voice it. The only thing he could vocalize was, "Off."

And to accentuate his order, he balled the material at her waist and tugged the top up, baring the skin of her belly. She lifted her arms, facilitating the removal of her clothing, and as he dropped it to the floor, she reached for him, sliding buttons free. But impatience crawled through him, and he gently but firmly brushed her hands aside. Shunning the buttons, he released his cuffs, yanked his hem free of his pants and pulled the shirt over his head. It joined hers at their feet, and he wasted no time tugging her against him again.

Only then did he allow himself to take her in. And it did nothing to calm the erotic squall whirling inside him. The sight of her—gorgeous, lush breasts cupped in black lace and silk—almost unraveled the tenuous grasp he had on his control. Jesus, she was… Yeah, they hadn't created a word yet to accurately describe the beauty and sensual magnetism of the woman standing in front of him.

"Unless there's something new I haven't heard of where you can stare me into orgasm, I think you should touch me now," she drawled.

She uttered the teasing remark with a smile, but did she know her voice carried the faintest note of uncertainty or that her eyes reflected her discomfort? What the hell had caused this stunning, successful, seemingly bold woman to harbor any doubt about herself? The need to hunt down whatever—or whoever—was responsible for that crime and inflict a punishing lesson rose in him so swift, he gritted his teeth against it.

"I'm having a tough time deciding where to put my hands or mouth on you first." Cocking his head, he lifted a finger to gently trace her eyebrows. "Here, so you'll close these beautiful eyes that tear a hole in me every time you look at me. Or here—" he pressed a thumb to her pouting bottom lip "—because no matter how many times I take this fuck-me mouth, it's not enough. Or here—" he brushed his fingertips over the curve of her breast, just above where the lace ended and then lower to circle the beaded nipple "—because you're so goddamn sexy. And I've been wondering for hours how sensitive you are and what sound you'll make when I get my tongue on you."

Her harsh puffs punched the air, and he wanted those pants to break on his lips, to swallow them.

"Here." She cupped her own breast. "I want your mouth and hands here."

Without looking away from her, he grasped her free hand and lifted it to her other breast.

"Hold them there for me."

A shiver rocked through her as she acquiesced, holding her flesh up to him like an offering. On a groan, he covered her hands with his and, dipping his head, drew her into his mouth, lace and all. Her cry echoed in his ears, another sensory caress, and he rewarded that needy response with a firm pull on the diamond-hard tip.

She arched into his caresses, and with a growl, he yanked the bra cups down and curled his tongue around her nipple, licking and grazing with his teeth before lapping at any sting he caused. Her hands trembled beneath his, but she still presented herself to him, and each quake her of body, each soft whimper enflamed the heat licking at his gut, over his cock. By the time he switched breasts and treated the neglected flesh to the same ministrations, she twisted and undulated against him, a sheen of perspiration dotting her chest.

He sank to his knees, opening his lips wide over her quivering belly, and fingernails scraped over his scalp. He grunted at the pleasure/pain, and a rumble rolled out of him as she gripped his hair, tugging on the strands. Not to push him away, though. On the contrary, she crushed him to her. The demand behind it had a headiness, not unlike a hit of alcohol in his veins.

She was so damn uninhibited in her responses to him, and it was hot as fuck. Addictive. Here, with their hands on each other, his breath bathing her bare skin and her hips jerking forward in a rhyth-

mic, greedy dance, total honesty reigned. Lust, desire—it stripped both of them bare of any artifice.

Locating the zipper at her side, he lowered it and
skimmed the leather down the rounded curve of her
hips, leaving her clothed in her bra, high-cut black
panties and those wickedly sharp stilettos. She was
a dream come to vivid life. A wet one.

"You good?" He checked in with her, glancing up
her torso to meet her eyes.

A gaze, bright with pleasure and lust, stared down
at him, and he had his answer. But he needed to hear
it. Needed her to verify that she was with him.

"Yes." Her low, husky voice stroked over him, and
he nuzzled her belly, sipping at the tender skin just
above the band of her underwear. "Don't you dare
stop."

He chuckled against her, then quickly divested her
of the heels. Then her panties. She stiffened but he
didn't halt, instead cupping her hips, lowering her to
the couch and pressing his mouth to her sex.

Fuck.

Her sharp cry rebounded off the walls, and she
went even more rigid, her fingers gripping his shoulders, her thighs falling open.

*"Oh God."* Her hips jerked upward, bucking into
his lips, his tongue.

With a low hum of pleasure, he cradled her inner
thighs, opening her wider for him. He licked a path
between her swollen, soaked folds, flicking her clit.
Her taste—musky, earthy and so goddamn delicious—filled his mouth. Immediately, she became

his favorite meal, and he feasted. She writhed beneath him, and he tightened his grip, holding her down as he dived into her, sucking, lapping at her flesh. Her cries fell around him, and his purpose was to claim more.

Trailing two fingers through her lips, he gathered the wetness and stroked into her sex, burying his fingers to the base. She shuddered, grinding down on his hand, urging him with each shift and twist to fuck her. And he gladly obliged. Though his cock pounded, jealous of that silken clench around his fingers. He didn't blame it.

Pursing his lips over the engorged button cresting her flesh, he thrust into her over and over. He couldn't get enough. Not of her taste. Not of the flutter of her clit against his tongue. Not of the tight clasp of her sex. He lost himself in her, her pleasure, his. They were so intertwined that when her feminine muscles clamped down on his fingers, milking them, and the bundle of nerves stiffened, he growled. Her cries littered around them, and he didn't let up until she weakly pushed at his head.

"Uncle," she rasped, threading her fingers through his hair. "You win."

He chuckled, and even to his ears, the sound was dark, sexual. Reflecting the lust roaring through him like the wildest storm. Scattering kisses up her belly, on each nipple, her collarbone and, finally, her mouth, he hungrily worshipped her. She tangled her tongue with his, not turned off by the flavor of herself still clinging to his lips.

"I need you inside me." She nipped at the corner of his mouth, his chin. "Please. Now."

Before she'd finished the demand wrapped in a plea, he switched places with her and had her straddling him. Reaching into his back pocket, he pulled his wallet free and removed a condom. Tossing both to the cushion beside him, he reached for his belt buckle, but Nore pushed his hands out of the way similar to what he'd done earlier with his shirt. She attacked his belt, the tab on his pants and his zipper. Within moments, she dipped her hand inside his black boxer briefs, wrapping her fingers around his cock and squeezing, stroking.

His fingers gripped her hips, and tipping his head back, he savored the pumping of his flesh by those pretty fingers. From beneath his lashes, he watched her. Watched pleasure and fascination suffuse her face. It was intoxicating. What man could resist that look on a woman's face while she stroked his dick?

That man might exist, but it wasn't him.

A tautness banded his lower back and he rocked up into her grip. A hot sizzle of electricity hit him, and he lowered a hand, covering both of hers. With his other one, he grabbed the condom, tore the package open and handed it to her. She took it with eager hands and in moments, sheathed him, and he ground his teeth against the caress that should've been perfunctory. It was anything *but* perfunctory.

"On you, Nore." He swept a hand up her back, cupping the back of her neck. "When you're ready."

*Just, please God, don't let her take too long.* He

hovered on a razor edge of control. But to make it good for her, he'd grasp hold to it.

Maybe.

She gripped one of his shoulders and notched him at her entrance with the other. He hissed out a breath at the kiss of her sex to the tip of his cock. Already her liquid heat seared him and he wasn't even inside her yet.

Their gazes connected and slowly, so damn slowly, she sank down over him. Her eyes went hooded, and her teeth sank into her bottom lip. When her lashes started to lower, he shook his head.

"No, baby. Keep those pretty eyes on me." He squeezed her nape, and her lashes rose. "That's it. I want to see everything."

"Everything" being that flare of surprise and consuming heat that darkened her golden eyes. That slight loosening of her features as pleasure claimed both of them. That soft pop as her lip pulled free of her teeth and a low whimper escaped.

Jesus, he was on fire.

He held himself as still as a statue as she branded him with her sex inch by inch. When she paused, her walls fluttering around him, he tried to think of every damn thing to clutch to the shredded remnants of his control. Third-quarter figures. Fried okra. Frolicking damn puppies.

She took another inch.

Yeah, frolicking puppies weren't going to cut it.

Shooting forward, he crushed his mouth to hers, thrusting his tongue deep.

"Get down on me, baby. Take it," he growled against her lips.

With a sound somewhere between a whimper and a sob, she obeyed him. From one moment to the next, he was drowning in liquid fire. A low, deep groan rolled out of him and he buried his face in the base of her neck.

"Fuck," he breathed.

They remained still, her sitting on his lap, him buried high inside her. He wrapped his arms around her back and she wound hers around his neck. He absorbed her shivering into him and gave her his in return.

"I need to move," she whispered.

"Then do it, baby."

She shifted, rising slow, slow, so fucking slow off his cock until only his head remained inside her. Then she retraced the path, her sex swallowing him whole. Again. Again. And again. She rode him, circling her hips, performing a sensual dance that stole his mind and captivated his body. Her every jerk, glide and grind eroded his control and he stroked his hands over her shoulders, curling them, anchoring her as he plunged over and over into her giving, too tight, utterly perfect body.

They were frantic, chaotic, a carnal storm coming together with whispered praises, damp, writhing bodies, dirty passion. It couldn't last; something this unstable that roared toward cataclysmic couldn't survive without a fiery ending. And as her flesh quivered and clasped him, he could tell it closed in on her. Sliding a hand between them, he rubbed her clit, sweeping over it…then pinched it.

Her shattered cry ricocheted off the walls and her sex clamped down on him in a bruising grip, and her slick channel milked him, dragging him toward a release that crackled and sizzled. He pistoned through that fist-tight clasp. One. Two. Three strokes.

And he lost it. Hurtled into an orgasm that seized him, damn near blinded and deafened him. As he sank into an ecstasy that robbed him of his senses and breath, he had one lone thought.

Once wasn't going to be enough.

Not by a fucking long shot.

# Four

"Excuse me? What did you say?" Nore stared at Bastian, resisting the urge to grab her friend and employee by the shoulders and shake answers out of him.

Correction.

Shake the answer out of him she wanted to hear. And that answer *wasn't* that she had a new client consultation in ten minutes with *Greer Motorcycles*.

She pinched the bridge of her nose, willing the panic rising inside her to back off. Having a fit in the offices of the Main Event wouldn't be ideal or a good look for business.

But *damn*. Greer Motorcycles.

Specifically, Joaquin Iverson. Her former client. The man who'd transformed her into an insatiable, reckless and wholly unfamiliar creature for one sizzling-hot night in a VIP suite.

No. She shook her head. No way would Joaquin show up here, in her office, for an event consultation after *that*.

*Especially since you ran out like a guilty thief in the early-morning hours.*

Why yes, she agreed with her know-it-all conscience. There was that.

She pinched her nose harder. Damn, she was screwed. And not in the way that Joaquin Iverson was so good at.

Okay, she had to stop all thoughts like that if she was going to sit across from him in ten—no, eight minutes, now.

"I said, we have a meeting with Greer Motorcycles. They'd like to hire us again for another event." Bastian frowned. "You're going to need to explain this—" he waved a hand toward her face "—reaction to me. This is a Big-and-Carrie-finally-got-married occasion, not a What-the-fuck-Big's-dead moment. We have a huge client who liked us so much they're return business, but you wouldn't know it by your reaction. What's going on?"

Nore loved Bastian. Next to Tatum, he was her closest friend as well as her employee. Yet she hadn't been able to bring herself to tell either one of them about her foolish decision when it came to Joaquin Iverson. Hell, she still couldn't explain it to herself.

"Nothing." She forced a smile but must've failed in the effort because Bastian winced.

"Yeah, don't do that." His eyes narrowed on her, and she wanted to hide. "And I'm a little insulted you'd try to pull this 'nothing' bull with me. Now what's really going on? Is there anything I should know about before we walk into that conference room?" His mouth curled at the corner in a small snarl. "Did the Dickless Wonder do something to you? I noticed he actually showed up in the office today. That's enough to drive anyone to drink."

The Dickless Wonder being James Whitehead, her former fiancé and current business partner. Her stomach pitched and churned, as it did every time she thought of her idiocy when it came to James. Not only had she been stupid enough to fall in love with a man who wouldn't know loyalty if it pissed on his leg, but she'd sold that same man part of the company she'd started with nothing but a dream and a loan. Because she'd allowed her heart to blind her, her business—her baby, the only thing in this world she'd ever been truly able to call *hers*—was paying the price.

"I didn't know James came in this morning," she said, gathering her tablet and laptop for the coming meeting. "Did you tell him about the consultation with Greer Motorcycles?"

"No." Bastian's snarl deepened. "Why would I? Since when has he taken an interest in anything about the Main Event other than using the title of COO—whatever that means—and the check he gets?" He snorted. "Besides, I wouldn't want to disturb his morning Frappuccino."

"That's fair." She injected a teasing note in her

voice when a scream of frustration and rage clawed its way up her throat. Swallowing it like she'd done every day well before her relationship with James ended, she headed toward the door of her office. "Let's go get ready before our clients show up." She paused, but then—*forget it*—she had to know. "Do you happen to know who from Greer we're meeting with?"

"Not sure. Shorty called and set it up so I'm certain she'll be there. I'm not even sure of the exact nature of the event. So we'll find that out together." He waved an arm and gave a slight bow. "After you."

"Manners on a Monday. What's going on? Hitting me up for a raise?"

Bastian laughed. "A raise? Look who has jokes this morning."

"I'm here all week."

Minutes later, the humor and laughter from the teasing and banter faded as Bastien exited the conference room to greet the representatives from Greer Motorcycles. Nerves swirled in, eddying inside her and threatening to tow her under.

She could do this; she was a professional. And besides, *he* might not even be here. He was the CEO. How many executives attended event-planning meetings? The tight band squeezing her chest loosened. *Of course*, what had she been thinking? Joaquin Iverson had more important items on his agenda than a party or whatever event they wanted to plan. He had staff to deal with that.

Exhaling a breath, she moved toward the door, smiling. This wouldn't be so bad after all...

A large, tall frame appeared in the doorway. And the air punched from her lungs.

*Oh God. This was going to be bad. So bad.*

She met a piercing gray gaze, and immediately images from a month ago flooded her mind.

Her, biting and sucking on that indecently full pierced mouth.

Her, fingernails digging into those wide, perspiration-dampened shoulders.

Her, holding on to him as he gripped her hips and slammed up into her.

Her, breasts pressed to the back of the couch, his lips and tongue marking her neck as he took her from behind.

A conflagration of heat bowled through her, and *good God*, she shivered. She actually shivered, and Joaquin Iverson caught it. From the narrowing of his eyes and the slight flare of those arrogant nostrils, she just *knew* he caught the telltale sign betraying her thoughts and her body's reaction to his presence.

Had she said this was going to be bad? Oh no, no. Worse.

Because in a perfectly tailored black suit and white shirt open at the neck, he was just as beautiful, as virile as he'd been that night at his birthday party. And her breasts swelled, nipples hardening, and her sex softened, grew wet in response.

Jerking her gaze away from him, she focused on the two people behind him. She curved her lips in a smile that she prayed was better than her earlier attempt with Bastien. Just to be on the safe side, she avoided looking at her friend.

"Nore, you remember Shorty and Mr. Iverson." Bastian nodded. "Let me introduce you to Bran Holleran, cofounder of Greer Motorcycles. Mr. Holleran, this is Lenora Daniels, owner of the Main Event."

"Nore, please." She moved forward, hand outstretched to the man the same height as Joaquin, and just as large. Gray threaded through his long black hair and his beard though he didn't appear to be that much older than Joaquin. "It's nice to meet you."

"Likewise." Bran accepted her hand with a firm grip before he released it. "And it's Bran."

"It's wonderful to see you again, Shorty and Mr. Iverson," she said, deliberately addressing Joaquin formally. It placed a distance between them—even if it was only in her own head. "Thank you for considering the Main Event again."

"You did such a great job with the birthday party," Shorty said, beaming wide. "But as much as I'd like to take credit, hiring you was actually Joaquin's idea."

"Oh well, thank you, Mr. Iverson." She met his gaze once more and congratulated herself on the steadiness of her voice. "We're delighted to work with Greer Motorcycles again."

"Thank you, Nore." Joaquin nodded, and dammit, he really needed to stop looking at her like that. As if he knew her every secret or was determined to ferret them out.

"Please have a seat." She rounded the conference

table and gestured toward the seats on the other. "Can we get you anything to drink? Coffee, tea, water?"

Minutes later, with cups of freshly brewed coffee in front of everyone, Nore nodded at her future clients. "Please." She spread her hands wide on the table, palms up. "Tell us how we can help you."

"We're about to debut a new model of motorcycle," Joaquin said. His deep voice reverberated through the conference room and stroked over her skin like silk. "It's Greer Motorcycles' first electric motorcycle, a dual sports model. It charges from zero to 100 percent in nine hours and from a standard 110-volt wall outlet. For one charge, the bike travels 175 miles. Of course, it'll have Bluetooth for the owner's cell phone, music, GPS—everything a person would have in a car. And our safety features include antilock braking and slip control systems as well as a cornering-enhanced traction control system. And that's just to name a few features. It's custom built and we're ready to roll it out. Since it's our first model of its kind, we want to do something different. A kind of reveal."

"Wow," Bastien said, a note of awe in his voice. "That's impressive. The latest model I read about charged in eleven hours for 150 miles."

"Bastien is our resident motorcycle enthusiast." Nora smiled. "And he's a superfan, although I promised not to reveal that."

"Good job on that one," her friend muttered.

"No problem." She grinned, shifting her attention from Bastien back to Joaquin, and in that instant her throat tightened around her next words. Because his gaze dropped to her mouth and it touched her like the hot brush of his calloused fingers. She barely stopped from lifting her own hand to her mouth and tracing that phantom caress. A month ago, she'd called this man dangerous. Her opinion hadn't changed. "So," she said, and his stare lifted to meet her eyes. Gut punch. "You'd like us to plan and organize a reveal or launch party."

"Yes," Bran said, drawing her attention to him. And relief sang inside her. "We haven't done one before, parties, all that social shit—sorry." He held up a hand in apology, and when Nore smiled and nodded, he continued. "All that *stuff* really isn't our style. But this is our first electric motorcycle. We've been working on it for years, and while an electric bike isn't new, ours is unique. A lot of hours, sweat and money have gone in to ensure that. So we need to do something different, something big, to launch it onto the market. This event, Nore, will be very important for Greer, for all of us."

"It sounds innovative," Bastian said, pausing from typing on his laptop. "What are the odds of us getting a preview of it?"

"Subtle, Bastian. Real subtle," Nore muttered, and her friend flashed her a grin.

Surprisingly, Bran grinned as well.

"I think that can be arranged. After all, if you're going to be arranging a launch party, you should be familiar with the model you're promoting."

"Exactly. See?" Bastian arched an eyebrow, jabbing a finger at Nore. "He gets me."

Shaking her head, she tapped her tablet open to her notes program.

"Let's talk about guest list size, who must be invited, if we'll be handling that or if you will, venue…"

"I'll cover the guest list and keep you updated on it as people RSVP," Shorty volunteered.

"Perfect," Nore murmured, jotting that down.

For the next hour, she and Bastian gathered enough information to get started, and after discussing a few more details and scheduling a tour of Greer Motorcycles, she prepared to bring the consultation to a close.

"I think we have all the major details down. Except for one thing. What date for the launch?"

"In three months."

Beside her, Bastian stiffened and she blinked.

"Three. Months," she repeated, so stunned she forgot how studiously she'd been avoiding Joaquin's gaze.

His mouth didn't curve into a smile, but his silver eyes momentarily brightened.

"I know it's short notice but we just decided to go forward with this idea, and the model is going into production a month after the launch date. We're willing to pay for the expedience and inconvenience." Joaquin glanced at Bran, who nodded. "How does twice your usual fee work? Plus expenses, of course."

*Holy. Shit.*

The back of her neck tingled and sweat popped on her palms. Her fee for this kind of event wasn't nominal. Doubled? Her heart rapped out a triple-time march, the beat echoing in her head. Yes, the deadline had panic scratching at her, but they'd make it work.

They had to.

*She* had to.

Because with her portion of this fee along with her savings, she just might have enough to buy James out of the Main Event.

Freedom. This job meant total freedom and autonomy again.

Oh yes, come hell or high water, she had to make this job happen.

"We'll make sure your launch is successful," she said past the riotous emotion making a mockery of her self-assured tone.

"I don't doubt it," Joaquin murmured, and that fast the whirl of anxiety, panic and, yes, foolish hope drowned under the flood of lust that swamped her.

That voice. Those eyes. All that combined with his almost harsh beauty and Big Dick Energy had her swimming in heat, and in this moment, she didn't want to save herself.

She needed an intervention before crawling over this conference table into his lap and demanding he give her a repeat of a month ago...

The conference door opened and James stood in the entrance, his toothy showman's smile on full display.

"Excuse me, but Dani said we had a client, and I thought I'd—what the hell is this?" His tone changed like a flipped switch, going from ingratiating to belligerent in seconds.

Shock blasted her, and she gaped at her ex. What. The. Fuck? Was he crazy? Was he through being a lazy parasite and had moved onto saboteur? Could she kill him and get away with it?

All of those questions flew through her mind at warp speed, and by the time the astonishment thawed and red-hot anger crept in, she had settled on the answer to one of those queries.

No, she couldn't kill him. Not only was it illegal but if she did go to jail it wouldn't be over *him*. He wasn't worth her chipping a nail, much less a life sentence.

But still...

"James, excuse me?" she said, trying—and failing—to keep the bite from her voice. "I'm sorry." She shifted her attention back to the silent trio across from her, but one glance at Joaquin's carved-from-stone face, and her heart plummeted toward her ankle boots. "Let me apologize on behalf of my—" *God, I hate saying it* "—partner, James Whitehead. Please—"

"He knows who the hell I am and you don't need to apologize for me," James snapped, shutting the door behind him with a sharp crack and stalking into the room.

Anger suffused his features, tightening his skin over patrician cheekbones and pulling his mouth into a cruel snarl that she'd never glimpsed on his handsome features before. Even his carefully styled dark brown hair seemed to stand on end.

"Watch your mouth and your tone," Joaquin rumbled, his voice not raising.

But it didn't need to. The quiet warning promised enough of a threat that James's lips snapped shut, his mouth flattening and almost disappearing.

Damn. That should not have been hot; she could, and did, take care of herself. But the quickening of her breath and throb in her sex assured her that yes, his response most definitely was hot.

"Fine," James ground out, glaring at Joaquin. "I'll talk to you. What are you doing here?"

"Greer Motorcycles is here for a consultation," Bastian answered, nearly chewing off the words. "If you have an objection, this isn't the professional way to raise it."

"Professional." James sneered, not sparing a look at Bastian but staring at Joaquin, who met his gaze, unflinching. "I think we can forgo that as we're family 'n all."

"Family?" Nore echoed, glancing back and forth between a stone-faced and silent Joaquin and a fuming James. "How... What's going on?"

"Come on, Nore," James said, disbelief and derision coloring his tone. "Are you trying to convince me you didn't know the great Joaquin Iverson was my half brother?"

For the second time in minutes, shock slammed into her like a giant, freezing tidal wave. A roar filled her head just as ice skated through her veins.

Brother?

She tore her stunned gaze away from James's

mocking expression and stared at Joaquin, search-ing... Beautiful silver eyes while James's were a warm brown. Thick, dark blond strands swept back from a bold face of sharp angles and stark planes. That wide, mobile mouth. James's short, dark brown hair emphasized his classical, refined features. Both men were tall, but even sitting in his chair, Joaquin's bulk and muscle seemed to dwarf James's slimmer build. On closer inspection, maybe they shared the same shape of their eyes and possibly the nose, but *brothers*?

"I thought your brother's name was Nathan," she said, acid bubbling in her belly, scalding a path up her chest to the back of her throat.

"It's my middle name," Joaquin explained, matter-of-fact, cold. Except for his eyes. There was nothing cold about those eyes. They burned. "Joaquin Na-than Iverson."

Nathan. Joaquin and the half brother James de-spised were the same person. And from what her ex had told her over the years, the feeling was mutual.

Nausea churned inside her as a sickening thought burrowed itself into her head and refused to be smoked out.

*Is that what the night in the club had been about? Did you approach me because James is my ex? Is that why you're here now?*

The questions rebounded off her skull, gaining speed and volume the longer she stared at him. He couldn't possibly hear the queries, and yet he arched an eyebrow, as if throwing his own question back at her.

Though it was illogical, betrayal clawed at her.

"Whatever you're doing here, forget—"

"James." Nore shot to her feet, interrupting his tirade. "My office. Please." She tacked on the "please" for the sake of the others in the room. Skimming over Joaquin, she nodded at Bran and Shorty. Looking at Joaquin was impossible in this moment. Because if she glimpsed the humiliating truth in his gaze... "I apologize for this...disruption. If you'll excuse me for a moment." Setting a hand on Bastian's rigid shoulder, she squeezed and murmured, "If you'll wrap up the meeting for me?"

She stalked from the conference room and didn't wait or look behind her to see if James followed. Rage propelled her forward, and she didn't stop until she entered her office. Whipping around, she folded her arms as James turned and closed the door, his expression mirroring the fury boiling inside her.

"How could you—" he began from between gritted teeth.

But she slammed up a hand and added a hard shake of her head.

"No, you're done talking. I brought you in here to listen." Lowering her arm, she recrossed it. Either that or yank his perfectly knotted Prada tie so tight it became a noose. "How dare you barge into a meeting with a client and behave so rudely? It's unforgivable."

He gave a derisive snort. "That's no client. That's my asshole bro—"

Again, her hand shot up, halting him mid-pathetic excuse.

"I don't care how he's related to you. This is our office, not a family reunion or barbecue. Once he crossed through that front entrance, he became a client. One who deserves respect since he's also a *paying, return* client. You leave your personal shit at that same door."

"Do you really believe—wait a minute." He scowled, jabbing a finger at her. "What do you mean return client? When was the first time we did business with him and why am I just hearing about it?"

Was he serious?

*Of course he is*, she silently answered her own question. And wasn't that the sad part of it all?

Taking a beat, she studied the man in front of her, wondering where the affectionate, charming, loving man she'd dated for three years had gone. Or had that person been the charade the whole time and she'd been blinded to him? Not that it mattered. Her eyes were wide-open now, and she had an unfiltered view of the selfish, absorbed and lazy man she'd almost tied her life to.

God, he'd done her a favor by dumping her.

Now if she could just get him out of her company as easily as she'd kicked him out of her bed.

Inhaling a deep breath, she deliberately exhaled it then replied to him…without screaming.

"Greer Motorcycles hired us to plan their CEO's birthday party. As for how you weren't aware of it, that I can't answer as we spent months on that account. It wasn't a secret, nor was I keeping anything from you as I had no idea Joaquin Iverson was your brother."

"You sure about that?" His lip curled. "This isn't some childish way to get back at me for breaking up with you and refusing to leave the business?"

Her chin snapped back, and for a long, stunned moment she stared at him. Damn him.

"Get over yourself. If you spent more than five minutes in this office working rather than off 'taking lunch' or 'drumming up business,' then you would've known about the Greer Motorcycle event months ago. And Bastian didn't add today's consultation to the schedule until late yesterday afternoon, so I found out about it this morning along with you. So no one blindsided you in revenge or even gave a thought to you. But the point is, if you cared *at all*, the information would've been available for you to find."

"Yeah, whatever." He looked away, a muscle ticking alongside his clenched jaw.

*Yeah, whatever.*

Irritation flared inside her, and she couldn't have stopped the comparison between him and Joaquin if she'd had a traffic light and a speed bump. No matter how she tried, she couldn't imagine the blunt, nearly brooding giant being so passive-aggressive. So spoiled.

Disgust rose within her, and she couldn't decide who she blamed more for her willful, foolish blindness when it came to James—him or herself.

More specifically, her humiliating, desperate need to be loved and placed as a priority in someone's life.

"Listen, I get you don't get along with your brother—"

"Half brother," he corrected on a snap. "And you *don't* get it. Unless you have an older half sister who treated you like shit growing up, made your mother's life miserable and did everything in his power to break up your parents' marriage. One who's a millionaire and refuses to help your family out, and then shoves his wealth in your face every chance he gets. Since you never mentioned that to me, I'm going to assume you really don't *get it*."

Well, damn. That was a minefield she intended to avoid at all costs. It didn't concern her. Not anymore.

Although the thought of Joaquin, the man with such big hands and an even bigger body, being so careful with her even while powering into her—she couldn't envision him bullying a younger James. Rebellious, yes. Mean, abusive? No.

But hell, what did she know? If the last few months had taught her one valuable lesson, it was that people changed.

Still… Now probably wasn't a good time to tell James about her biblical knowledge of his brother. Correction. *Half* brother. Hell, James had already accused her of using Joaquin to get back at him. Of course, that was bullshit as she hadn't known Joaquin's identity when they'd desecrated that VIP couch. But who she slept with—or didn't sleep with—had ceased being James's business when he'd broken their engagement. And if he did know about her and Joaquin, he would only use that slip as ammo to reject the account.

No, she'd keep this secret to herself.

"Fine." She nodded. "I don't understand your family dynamic."

"You don't. Which is why we're turning down this account." He shifted, as if preparing to leave after dropping that announcement. As if his word was law.

"The hell we are." She didn't shout the objection, but her throat ached as if she had. She fought not to lose her temper all over him and this office like an emotional crime scene. "There is no reason to turn down this client who is paying double for our services."

"I just told you—"

"I heard what you said, but like I said earlier, those issues are personal, and they have no place here."

Besides, if history repeated itself, James wouldn't work on the account anyway. Because he didn't *work*.

"So my concerns don't matter here?" He jabbed a finger toward the floor. "I'm the chief operating officer. I have a say in what happens in this company, including what clients we take on. And I say no to taking this account."

"Yes, you're the chief operating officer," she said even though just stating the words scalded her tongue with bitterness. "But I'm the president, and this isn't a democracy. If you offered up valid, professional reasons why we should turn down Greer Motorcycles, then I would listen and possibly agree. But all you've given me are fucked-up *Brady Bunch* reasons. And I'm not willing to walk away from the money and connections Greer will bring in. You'll need to get over us having your half brother as a client or go with your standard operating procedure—ignore everything. Either one works for me."

"You say this isn't personal, Nore, but it feels that way," he said, accusation coating his voice like condensation on a glass, cold and fairly dripping from it.

She shook her head. A while ago, his disappointment would've had her belly twisting with anxiety, and correcting whatever she'd done to cause that frustration and displeasure would've been her first priority. Making him happy would've superseded everything.

But those days were gone. And she had vowed never to grant another person that much power over her emotions, her actions. Her life.

She would *not* become her mother.

"I can't do anything about the way you feel. And I sense that short of turning down Greer Motorcycles, nothing would change it. As I said, *that* I'm not willing to do. So it seems we've reached a stalemate. Well, not really, since as president, I have the final say. And I say we're taking them on as a client. That is if they still want to hire us after your thoroughly immature and unprofessional display in that conference room."

He scoffed, flicking her complaint off as if it were an annoying fly.

"If you believe Joaquin isn't here just to get a rise out of me, you're deluding yourself. I mean, you're good at what you do, but c'mon, Nore. There are dozens of event planners in the Seattle area. Dozens probably more equipped and experienced to handle a job for a multibillion-dollar company. It's me he's after, not your expertise."

His shot struck her dead center in the chest. Right in the place where all her secret vulnerabilities hid from the harsh light of truth. She wasn't naive enough not to have considered that possibility. Especially given the enmity exhibited between the two brothers in that conference room and now here, in her office.

What if this wasn't about her being good enough to attract a client of his caliber? What if her company was just the rope in a Cain-and-Abel version of tug-of-war?

What if... What if sex with her had been about fucking his brother's ex?

The pain that whipped at her stole her breath, and she stiffened against its lash.

Logic argued, she shouldn't care. It'd been one crazy night that would never be repeated with a man who was as much a stranger to her today as he'd been a month ago.

But apparently, when it came to hurt feelings, logic seemed to be taking a lovely stroll out the door.

She inhaled a low, deep breath and drew her shoulders back. Damn if she'd let James see the bruises his words inflicted. She might not have been enough for him. And might not be enough for his half brother.

But she would damn sure be enough for herself.

"Maybe you don't believe I'm up to the challenge

of this launch, but not only will I prove that I am, but also his guests, who are potential customers, will see it," she said, arching an eyebrow. "So if Joaquin Iverson is using the Main Event for his own reasons, than that's fine. Because I'm using him, too. Now—" she offered James a smile that damn near gave her lips frostbite "—if you'll excuse me. I have a meeting to wrap up with our newest client."

Not waiting for him to reply, she strode past him toward her door. When she reached it, she stood to the side, waiting for him to precede her out. Shutting the door behind her, she continued on to the conference room.

She'd made a decision regarding her company—her stability, her future—once based on emotion. And what a clusterfuck that had turned out to be. She wouldn't make the same mistake twice.

Forget that waiting-on-a-man-to-save-her shit. For years, she'd believed in the fairy tale and that she'd had it.

Now she would be the heroine and save her damn self.

The end.

# Five

Joaquin waited five seconds until the back door of the Cadillac Escalade closed after him, shutting out the cold October wind. Shorty and Bran climbed in the other passenger seats before he loosed the question that had been running laps in his mind for the last forty-five minutes.

"How in the hell did we not know that James-fucking-Whitehead worked at this place?" he asked, locking down his temper with metaphorical tape and glue sticks.

Never had he been the kind of CEO who raised his voice at his employees. Respect. His number one rule. And he wouldn't violate that now. Even though rage rolled through him like thunder. Rage and the

cloying, overwhelming and too-damn-familiar powerlessness that he associated with his family.

With a barely restrained growl, he shrugged out of
his suit jacket and popped the top button on his shirt.
When that didn't provide adequate air flow, he jabbed
at one of the black buttons on the car door, and when
the window slid down, he tipped his head back. He
didn't give a fuck how desperate or out of control he
appeared to the others. Anything to alleviate the sudden sense of suffocation, of slowly strangling.

"I'm so sorry, Joaquin. This is my fault," Shorty
apologized, and the guilt thickening her voice settled
him more than the breeze coming through the lowered glass.

Dammit, he was a thirty-five-year-old man who'd
proved himself in a challenging, dangerous sport he
loved and he was also a successful businessman. He
was not that six-year-old boy who'd once stood, like
someone pressing grubby fingers against a glass, gazing at the family his mother had created. A family
where he hadn't even been the spare so much as the
unwanted—no, *resented*—baggage.

That boy no longer existed.

And he refused to punish Shorty because he'd experienced a momentary regression into his dysfunc-
tional past.

"Stop it. This isn't your fault," he said, rolling the
window up and forcing himself to lean back against
the seat.

"Of course it is," she insisted. "I should've done
my due diligence…"

Splaying his fingers wide on his thighs, he shot her a look, and his senior vice president sighed.

"We've worked together for ten years, Shorty. You wouldn't have chosen a company that you hadn't researched to hell and back. Not to handle a party for me, and definitely not to spearhead the launch of our new motorcycle. There has to be an explanation about how my—" He pressed his lips together, his throat tightening around the word *brother*.

"—about how James came to work for this company."

It was an explanation he might've known if he'd spoken to his mother or brother in the last three and a half years.

"Do you want to call off this launch with them? It's not too late, and under the circumstances—and given your brother's display back there—I doubt it would be much of a shock," Bran said from the front seat. "No offense, man, but your brother's a prick."

"Agreed," Shorty muttered. "I like Nore and Bastian. I have zero complaints and only praises about how they organized your surprise party. But knowing your brother works with them, and witnessing his behavior today, even I have to question their professionalism and decision-making."

For several moments, Joaquin didn't reply. He returned his attention to the window, although he didn't really see the parade of office buildings, local boutiques and array of multicultural restaurants in the vibrant neighborhood.

Instead, he pictured Nore.

For a month, he'd convinced himself to keep away from her after that one sex-soaked night in the VIP lounge. And he'd been successful until the opportunity with this launch dropped into his lap. Entering that conference room this morning, excitement had replaced the blood in his veins. Every breath, heartbeat, neuron focused like a laser on his first glimpse of her.

And damn...

His skin had drawn tight over his bones. Just one look at those gorgeous, lush curves accentuated to perfection in a pin-striped vest and pants with a sheer white long-sleeved shirt, and his cock had woken like goddamn Rip van Winkle. If his body's sudden quickening hadn't been alarming enough, the vise grip on his chest as he met her tawny gaze in that lovely face surrounded by thick dark brown curls would've been a blaring red warning.

It would've been bad form to sweep that long table clean, lay her on it and bring her to a screaming orgasm. Already, the remembered flavor of her sex filled his mouth, his nose. Sitting across from her as if he didn't know the tight clasp of her body, the scent they created together, had been the sweetest torture.

But when James had burst into the room, it'd just been fucking torture.

Because the outrage and betrayal on his younger brother's face as he'd looked at Nore... Anger, he could understand. Hell, it'd coursed through him so hot and consuming he'd needed to grip the chair to keep himself from getting up in James's smug face.

In an instant, he'd remembered why it'd been nearly four years since he'd last been with his family. The toxicity had bubbled within him like acid, and he'd nearly choked on it.

So yeah, he identified with the anger.

But the betrayal? He identified with that, too. Intimately. Had glimpsed it on his own face before when it came to James.

And yeah, they might have been in that conference room on business, but that expression—God, he couldn't get past it—it had been personal.

Bitterness—toward James and, maybe undeservedly, toward Nore—twisted in his gut along with the dregs of an old resentment. And he battled the urge to lower the window once more.

"Joaquin?" Shorty called his name, and from the lilt in her tone, it must not have been the first time.

"We're staying with the Main Event for the launch. For now, we'll trust Nore to keep James in line. At the first sign that he's slipped the reins, we'll pull the event."

"Sounds good," Bran said, and Shorty nodded, but her frown didn't clear.

"It'll be fine, Shorty," Joaquin murmured. "Trust me."

Hours later, those two words echoed in his head when the line from his executive assistant buzzed.

Picking up the phone, he didn't remove his gaze off his computer monitor and the latest report on the KING One, their new electric roadster, detailing its lightweight cast-aluminum frame. Bran's design didn't just enhance agility but gave the rider control whether they rode on urban streets or the open road.

Pride swelled inside him, fierce and hot. Even though the many Sunday school lessons his mother had forced him to sit through assured him pride heralded a big fall, he embraced it. Joaquin had named the bike after his father, and yeah, the OG that he'd been, King Iverson probably would've turned up his nose at an electric bike, preferring his Harley-Davidson over every model ever created. But King would've still been so damn proud of Joaquin, and he would've bragged about his son to anyone who listened.

Joaquin should know.

He'd met his biological father when he was eighteen, and then Joaquin only had King in his life for four short years before he died in a motorcycle accident. And yet, King had been that father.

As he'd done many times over the years, he glanced at the one framed photo on his desk. Raising the receiver to his ear, he swept a gaze over the image of him and his father, standing, arms crossed, in front of his father's Harley-Davidson Heritage Classic.

*This one's for you, Dad.*

"Yes," he said, his voice gravel-rough with memories from the too-short time he'd had with King Iverson.

"Joaquin, a Ms. Nore Daniels is here to see you. She doesn't have an appointment," Magda informed him, tone cool with disapproval.

His executive assistant had two rules: her phone didn't ring more than three times before being answered and no one gained access to him without an appointment. Usually, he abided by her "no appointment rule" but not with that name echoing in his office like a dirty promise.

Or an ominous warning.

Both were reasons to instruct Magda to turn Nore away, and to schedule a time like she did with every other client. But as his hand tightened around the receiver, the hard plastic imprinting against his palm, he knew he wouldn't.

"Send her in. And hold my calls for the next thirty minutes," he said, already standing.

"Yes, sir."

Molten anticipation flowed through him as he shoved his chair back and stalked across the room. When the door opened and Nore stepped in, he waited in the middle of the room, enjoying his front-row seat to Nore Daniels walking into his inner sanctum.

And goddamn, what a show.

She hadn't changed clothes from earlier, and the perfectly tailored, sexy suit emphasized her sensual, confident glide. As inappropriate as it was, he couldn't stop himself from superimposing another, more carnal image over her. Of that form-fitting vest and sheer, billowy-sleeved shirt stripped from her body. Those wide-legged pants that clung to her hips and legs were gone, leaving her bare in front of him, clothed only in the beautiful brown skin she'd been born in.

An itch tingled in his fingertips, tickling with the need to stroke that skin, to follow each curve. His fantasies tormented him with the need, had branded her on his mind so he couldn't forget if he wanted to. And fuck him, but he didn't want to.

Pure self-preservation had him taking a step back... almost. He stopped himself at the last second. Retreat. He'd never retreated from anything in his life—not his mother's hate, not his stepfather's indifference, not his brother's callous little cruelties. Not broken bones in his career and not starting a company at twenty-five when no one believed it had a chance in hell of succeeding.

So no, he didn't do retreating.

But right now, he damn well considered it. Because even though he towered over this woman and outweighed her in muscle mass, if she pressed one of those slender fingers to his chest, she could fell him like a tree.

Only one woman had ever possessed that power over him.

And the reminder of that woman—of how he'd lost her—had ice and steel solidifying in his body.

In appearance, Nore didn't resemble Madison Berry. But the circumstances... They were shaping up to be entirely too familiar. Like a rerun he wanted to turn off.

"I'm surprised to see you here, Nore," he said, crossing his arms. "Did we forget to cover something at the consultation this morning?"

She shook her head. "No, we have everything we need to get started on your launch event. And I apologize for just dropping by here unannounced and without an appointment."

"No worries." He waved an arm toward the sitting area in his office. "Seat?"

"Thank you." She briefly hesitated, then walked over to the black leather sofa and lowered to the corner of it.

He followed her and claimed the matching chair across from her, leaning against the back of the seat and loosely curling his fingers around the arms. Even with the small distance separating them, her earthy, sensual scent teased him. It reminded him of freshly cut wood and rain-soaked wind. Another thing that had haunted him about her. Her unique fragrance that had clung to her damp skin, her wet, tight, perfect sex.

He raised his hand and rubbed a thumb over his bottom lip, inhaling deeply as if he could still taste her. Nore shifted in her seat, and he glanced up, catching her gaze on his mouth. Desire rolled through him, and he inhaled a low, deep breath, forcing his body to relax, muscle by muscle.

"I'm listening," he said.

She cleared her throat. "Thank you for seeing me. I wanted to speak with you about what happened at my office with James. And apol—"

"No." He thrust out his hand. "If you're about to apologize for James's behavior, then you can stop right there. The only person who needs to be accountable for his actions is him."

He'd had too many years of people justifying his brother's conduct, excusing it, covering for him. Damned if he'd sit here and listen to her do the same.

Nore inhaled a breath and briefly looked away

from him. "That's fair," she murmured, returning her gaze to him. "Then I need to apologize for myself. I didn't mean to place you in that position. I didn't know you were James's half brother when we…"

"Fucked?" he supplied with an arched eyebrow.

Crude, yes. But she was regretting him to his damn face so he could be forgiven.

"Met," she said, a faint tightening of her mouth the only sign of irritation. "James has talked about his brother Nathan over the years, not Joaquin, so I had no idea you two were related. Believe me, if I had, I would've…"

She trailed off with a shake of her head and he allowed a grim smile to curve his lips.

"Right. I get it, Nore. You wouldn't have gotten in bed—or on the couch—with the enemy."

Again, she shook her head, harder. "No, that's not what I meant. I'm aware of the strained relationship between you and James. This—" she waved a hand back and forth between them "—would've only inflamed the situation, and I wouldn't want that for you or James."

"There is no *strained relationship* between me and him, because there's no relationship." Unless actively avoiding each other counted. And those seeds of dislike had been sown long before Nore. Long before Madison. "If James has confided in you enough to share who I am, then I have to assume he hasn't held back on why God and Satan get along better than we do."

She hesitated, then admitted, "James has told me

some things about why you don't get along. But I don't feel it's appropriate to share what he expressed to me."

"And I'm not asking you to, although given I've known James much longer than you, I can guess what tales he's spinning." With a rude snort, he launched himself from his chair and stalked across the room, an agitated restlessness prowling through him. He needed to *move*. To burn off the sense of powerlessness that was an inevitable by-product of anything having to do with his "family." And he used that term so loosely, he could drive a fleet of semis through it. "My point is you couldn't deteriorate a relationship that doesn't exist. But that brings me to something else that's been on my mind since leaving your office."

He halted in front of the built-in bar and yanked the stopper of the decanter. Grabbing a thick crystal tumbler, he splashed a healthy amount of scotch into his glass. Belatedly, he glanced over his shoulder and back at Nore.

"Can I get you something?" Turning, he lifted his drink and took a sip, savoring the smooth burn of the alcohol over his tongue and the bloom of it hitting his chest and stomach. "Scotch, wine? Water?"

"No, thank you," she said. Rising to her feet, she traced his path across the room, arms crossed. "There's another reason I needed to speak with you."

He could've made her say it. But a part of him didn't want to hear her relegate him to her closet of dirty secrets. He'd been there before—lived there for most of his childhood.

"Don't worry, Nore." He took another sip, studied her over the rim of the glass. "I am an expert at keeping secrets." *At being one.* "James—or anyone else—won't hear about that night from me. It was a mistake, and it's forgotten."

Damn. When he decided to lie, he didn't fuck around. He went all out.

She blinked, and though she'd already been stationary, her body went even more still. Her long lashes lowered, momentarily concealing her tawny eyes, and the full, sensuous curve of her mouth flattened.

"I'm glad we're in agreement," she said, voice even. "About keeping our former…interaction between us as well as it being a mistake."

That shouldn't hurt. Especially since he'd thrown the first jab. Especially since he stood here trying to convince himself he didn't give a fuck if she regretted him. Her shame over being with him had already been established.

"Satisfy my curiosity." He lifted the scotch to his mouth but when the rim touched his bottom lip, he lowered it. "Is this request more for professional reasons…or personal? I'm just wondering who's asking. The company president or James's lover?"

Her eyes narrowed, and his gut tightened in response. Anticipation crept through him, its sting hot, its bite hard. And he relished it like teeth sinking into his skin. He didn't even have to close his eyes or try hard to remember her teeth marking his shoulder on that couch in the VIP room.

He could even rub the exact spot.

"Does it matter?"

"Humor me."

"The woman asking is the one who built her own company from the ground up, worked damn hard to ensure her business's success and will do anything to protect it." Something flashed in her eyes, and he would give up his Harley-Davidson Fat Boy to decipher that quicksilver flicker of emotion. "And James isn't my lover. He isn't my anything anymore, except a business partner."

"Anymore." The word tasted acrid and foul on his tongue.

"Anymore," she repeated, her chin hiking up. "Not that I need to explain my romantic or sexual history with you. The time for that conversation would've been a month ago. And you didn't seem too concerned with it then."

He tightened his grip on the glass until the ridges bit into palm and fingers. "I deserve an explanation if you were with my half brother at the time. Were you, Nore? Were you still with him when you were fucking me?"

"No," she snapped. "We'd broken up several months earlier."

Knocking the rest of the alcohol back, he set the tumbler on the bar, taking those few seconds to smother the anger, the bitterness attempting to drag him back to a past he'd vowed never to revisit. Sliding his hands into his pockets, hiding his clenched fists from her—from himself. As if he could pretend this conversation didn't eat him alive.

As if her answers didn't sit on his chest like Sisyphus's stone.

"So revenge or rebound?" He nodded, cocking his head. "Which was it? Using me to get over the ex? Or did you know who I was the entire time and decided to get payback by screwing the one man your ex hates?"

"Neither." She shook her head. "Contrary to the charming adage, I don't need to get over one man by getting under another—or on top of him, as the case may be."

Lust shot through him. Her reminder flipped the switch on his memories and images of just how well she did on top of him flickered across his mind like an erotic reel. He ground his teeth against the sizzle racing down his spine, lassoing his lower back and wrapping around his cock.

"And I'll reiterate," she continued, "I had no idea you were James's brother. We did our research on Greer Motorcycles for your birthday party, and nothing in your bio on the site or in your media kits or press releases mentioned a family. Also, like I said in my office, I didn't make the connection because James, your mother and stepfather only referred to you as Nathan. And there weren't any pi—" She abruptly broke off, her lips snapping shut around the rest of her sentence.

But he didn't need her to complete the explanation. And if he hadn't guessed, the pity flashing in her eyes before she lowered her lashes would've tipped him off.

He could've told her to save that pity. Save it for the ostracized boy he'd once been who'd cared, who'd been hurt by his family's emotional neglect. The man he'd become didn't give a fuck.

The acid roiling in his gut belied that thought but another thing he'd learned to master over the years? Ignoring shit.

"Pictures," he finished for her. "There weren't any pictures of me in their house. Don't worry. The truth doesn't hurt my feelings. We're long past that."

Nore sighed, and her eyes briefly closed, lips firming. Moments later, when she looked at him again, the irritation that had darkened her golden-brown gaze had dissipated.

"This isn't going to work, is it?" she murmured. Shaking her head, she raised her hands, palms up. "I had to overrule James on turning down your account because of his personal reasons. But it isn't just James I'm fighting on this."

"I'm not letting you walk away from this event. We have a signed contract." His anger flared like air blown on fresh coals. "You'll have to break it. I won't. But I warn you, Nore, if you do, I will ensure your company's reputation won't survive it."

"You're threatening my business?" she asked, disbelief and outrage not only tightening her features but threading through her voice.

"Yes," he said, bluntly and with zero apology. "I

have three months for this launch of our new bike. It will be a game changer for Greer Motorcycles." And it was the most important design of his career. He didn't just possess a professional and financial investment in its success, but a personal one. His father's name was attached to it. This motorcycle was *his*. "I won't allow any aspect of it to be derailed or compromised. Including how it's introduced to the public and our investors."

A muscle ticked along her jaw, and he studied that small telltale sign of her frustration as she glanced away from him. Her gaze remained somewhere left of his shoulder as she continued to argue with him.

"You don't need to threaten me to do my job," she said. "But I can't when I'm not certain if my client is sabotaging all my work." Finally, she returned her gaze to him, and it resembled tawny chips of ice. "Whether it's intentional or not."

Intentional? What the fuck did that mean?

"Do I insist on being kept in the loop on the decisions regarding the event? Most definitely. But will I hinder you in any way? No. I've just explained what this launch means for the company. As long as you promise to do your job to the best of your ability, you'll have my input but not my interference."

She studied him for long seconds that threatened to stretch to minutes.

"I sincerely hope you mean that," she said. "And, Joaquin?"

"Yes."

"If you ever threaten my business again, I'll quit. Your launch be damned."

Slowly, he smiled.

Anticipation and a hot thrill, not unlike that excitement and pleasure at the start of a race, poured through him.

He didn't trust her. He didn't trust anyone who had even the faintest connection to his half brother. Did he believe her about not knowing who he was that night at the party? Maybe. Her actions pointed toward her telling the truth, but he'd been fooled before. Had his heart torn apart by someone who'd seen his brother as the more advantageous option. Painful lessons from the past hadn't just taught him to question everything—it'd tattooed the lesson on his mind. His soul.

So no, he didn't blindly accept her word about not using him as payback. And he wasn't betting his company on the words falling from her sexy-as-sin mouth.

But fuck if he didn't anticipate finding out over the next three months.

"Understood."

# Six

"So let me get this straight," Tatum said, resettling herself on her couch with a bowl of popcorn tucked between her crossed legs. She lifted a handful and popped it into her mouth. Just a precious few glimpsed this side of her friend. Most were only allowed to see the beautiful and perfectly poised daughter of a media mogul. "A month ago you had a one-night stand in the VIP area of a nightclub, and you're just telling me now?" Tatum glared at Nore from the screen of her laptop set on the coffee table across from her. "Don't quote me but I'm pretty sure that violates a girlfriend code."

"Sorry I didn't make you aware of my sexual exploits, Tate," Nore drawled, shaking her own big bowl of popcorn so the kernels settled at the bottom. "I was too busy contemplating my life choices. Not only that I had given away a portion of my hard-earned company to my asshole, lazy ex, but I'd fucked his brother on a surprisingly sturdy leather couch."

On the screen, Tatum promptly started coughing. Thumping a fist to her chest, she reached for her glass of wine with the other hand. After taking a quick sip, and another…and then another, Tate set her drink back down.

"Excuse me?" she gasped, leaning forward, watery eyes wide as she gaped at Nore. "You did what with who on a sturdy couch?"

Groaning, Nore leaned her head back against the couch and stared up at her living room ceiling. She closed her eyes, but immediately images of Joaquin Iverson bombarded her. A montage of his masculine beauty twisted in lust, of it cold with anger, of it hardened with mistrust and something else. Something altogether too close to…pain.

She lifted her head, shaking it. Joaquin's pain, or lack of it, wasn't her business. Not that she could possibly tell the difference. Her vagina might know him well but *she* didn't. Definitely not enough to decipher what moods and emotions swept through him or how they appeared on his face and body.

Yeah, best not to think of his body at *all*. In any way.

And by "best" she meant safer.

*"Lenora Renae Daniels,"* Tatum nearly roared. "Answer me. What the hell did you do?"

"Oh no. Not the government name." Heaving a

sigh, Nore pinched the bridge of her nose. "I was just getting to the other part of my news. Yesterday, I had a new client consultation with, it turned out, my one-night stand. Who—oh damn, I still can't believe I'm getting ready to utter these words—it seems is James's half brother. The one whose name he's barely able to say without exhaling molar dust from grinding his teeth together. That one. The same brother who gifted me with multiple orgasms that had me glimpsing the other side of wormholes."

Tatum stared at her, lips parted, popcorn forgotten.

"Multiple orgasms? Wormholes?" Tatum rasped. Then louder, *"Wormholes?"*

"Yes." Nore groaned again. "And let me assure you, it is a mysterious, wondrous place."

"I hate you." Tatum nodded. "I love you, sis, but I totally hate you."

"Uh, you know that doesn't make sense, right?"

Tatum tossed several pieces of popcorn at her screen. "You're the one not making any sense. Explain, please. How in the world did you end up having…so much in common with James and this…"

"Joaquin." Nore dug a hand in her bowl, gathering up the snack and stuffing it in her mouth. "And I'm still trying to figure out how this became my life," she said around the puffed corn. "I had no idea I would even see Joaquin again, much less discover he's James's brother. It was horrifying, to say the least. And James didn't help by making a complete ass of himself in front of Joaquin and his people."

"God. James," Tatum's lip curled in disgust, and

she lifted her glass. "Good thing I'm drinking because he drives me to it."

"Oh he was in rare form, Tate." Anger sparked, and she crunched harder on her snack. "First, he embarrassed the hell out of me and Bastien, and then he had the balls to order me to turn down the account. Because of his petty feud I'm supposed to turn away business. I mean, it's not like he's going to be around to do any of the actual *work*."

Tatum shook her head, pouring more wine into her glass.

"You'd think he'd be thankful for every customer since it puts unearned money in his pockets. Even his brother's."

"Half brother's," she corrected with a snort. "They both made sure to correct me on that point. And I agree with you, which is why there's no way in hell I was letting the account go. If I can put up with… discomfort, then James can, too. Besides, he'll get paid, and so will I. Because Joaquin is offering double my fee. With that, along with my savings, I can buy James out of the Main Event. I'll finally be free of him," she whispered.

"Oh, Nore." Even through the screen and the thousands of miles that separated Seattle and Boston, Nore could easily spy the sympathy and love that shone in Tatum's dark eyes. "You loved him. You trusted him. He was going to be your husband, so why wouldn't you have believed he'd be a wonderful partner in life and business? You really have to stop beating yourself up over this and let it go."

"I've been trying." Nore reached for her own glass of wine but didn't sip from it. Instead, she stared down into the ruby depths. "But every time he strolls back into the office from a four-hour lunch, or I hear him brag about being the COO of my company...or I have to look at Bastien with guilt eating me alive because I can't promote him due to the overhead deadweight..." Nore couldn't quite look at Tatum, not when that shame would undoubtedly suffuse her features. "I have no one else to blame. This is all on me."

"You made a mistake. Girl, look at me. Getting on a cross-country flight right now isn't ideal, but I'll make a special trip to kick your ass," Tatum growled. "Last time I checked there was only one perfect person, and you might be able to perform miracles with a seating chart but not with wine and water. Give. Yourself. A. Break. Bastien doesn't blame you. No one at the Main Event does. They love you. If they didn't, they would've left a long time ago. How do I know this? Two words—James Whitehead. Ain't enough pay or benefits in the world to put up with him. Oh, they love and respect you."

"You said 'ain't,'" Nore said, and yes, her voice might be a wee bit thick with tears.

Tatum arched an eyebrow, her shoulders drawing back, and from one moment to the next she transformed into the haughty society princess.

"Darling, the circumstances called for it." A second later, the princess disappeared and her college friend returned. "I understand it's not that easy to accept. But that's why I'm your best friend. I'll be right here to keep repeating all of this until you believe me."

Nore blinked back the sting of tears and covered it by drinking her merlot. Some of the other areas of her life might be shitty, but not the people who loved her.

"Enough about me," she said, clearing her throat. "There are only two months until the wedding. Tell me everything that's happening and if your mother is driving you crazy."

"Well the answer to the latter is God, yes." Tatum groaned, the sound ending on a chuckle. "Did I tell you what she did with the caterer?"

For the next half hour they discussed the wedding plans and Tatum's mother's antics. By the time she wrapped up her tale of her mom almost coming to blows with the florist, Nore was almost on the floor in laughter.

"I lie to you not, Nore," Tatum said, gasping for breath. "Mom held that lily of the valley over her head like a claymore about to strike my florist down. I just knew she was going to have Mom arrested." Shoulders shaking, Tatum wiped a tear from under her eye. "I swear, the only thing she hasn't had an issue with is the dress. Yet."

"How could she? It's gorgeous," Nore protested. But this *was* Regina Haas. She could find issue with orphans and puppies. Tipping her head back, she groaned. "Oh shit. She's probably not going to want you to wear the brooch. 'Dear, it ruins the lines of the dress,'" Nore mimicked Tatum's mom, and the imitation of Regina's proper tone hit the mark, if she said so herself.

"I shouldn't laugh at that," Tatum said. Then did just that. "But that's one battle Mom won't win. You bought that gorgeous piece for me, and I'm wearing it. It's so—" She broke off, her lips pursing as she squinted at Nore.

"What?" Nore squelched the urge to pat her face. Even through the computer screen, the intensity of her friend's stare skimmed over her. "What's wrong?"

"You have the brooch."

"Uh, yeah." Nore tilted her head. "Exactly how much of that wine have you drunk?"

"And according to the legend, whoever possesses it will meet their soulmate. And they'll have a troubled path but they'll find true love."

"I remember," Nore said, twisting the cap off a bottle of water. She had a meeting in the morning, and it wouldn't do to show up with a hangover. "So what?"

"Sooo…" Tatum paused, peering at Nore, and when she shrugged, her friend threw up her hands, huffing out a loud breath. "So have you considered that maybe the brooch's magic or—" she twirled her hand "—or whatever is working on your behalf? Maybe Joaquin, the VIP section and now him being your client isn't a coincidence—"

"Whoa, whoa, pump the fated mates brakes." She barked out a sharp crack of laughter, pushing out her hands toward the screen. "That's…a lot. And I bought that brooch for you, not me."

"So you're saying there's only magic enough for one person? I don't think it works that way."

"Maybe not, but that ship has sailed for me. And I'm okay with it. So let's just focus on your fairy-tale ending and let me…assist."

This whole thing with James had only nailed home what she'd suspected—the Daniels women didn't do long-term relationships. Damn sure didn't do toxic-free ones. How many times had Nore scraped her mother off the floor after another of her boyfriends dumped her, then walked out the door? It'd been a pattern—euphoria, belittling, cheating, abuse, then abandonment.

James hadn't hit Nore, but in hindsight, some of the other characteristics had been there. Including the cheating. Or at least she suspected. And he hadn't been the first guy in her past to mistreat her. Unlike her mother, who even today hovered on the verge of another breakup with an asshole and Nore prepared herself for cleanup duty. She was getting off this fucked-up roller coaster.

"Fine," Tate murmured.

"Tate…"

"What?" Tatum shrugged. "I said, fine."

Nore glared at her friend's too-innocent expression and way-too-agreeable tone.

"I've known you for eleven years and I know you're just humoring me." When she received another shrug in response, Nore slapped a palm to her forehead. "Tate!"

"I'm leaving it alone, I promise." Setting down

her glass on the table, she stretched. "I have to get ready for bed. Meeting with Dad in the morning." Irritation flickered across her face. "I need all the rest possible for that."

"Same. But we're scheduled for a tour at Greer Motorcycles tomorrow." And that was not a tingle of excitement that crackled through her like a live wire.

Nope. Totally wasn't.

A smile curved Tatum's mouth and it spread into a full-fledged grin.

Wary, Nore squinted at her friend.

"What're you thinking?"

"Nothing, just…" Tatum cackled. "You know what this makes you, right?"

"Oh damn." Nore closed her eyes. "What, Tatum? What does this make me?'

"You, Nore Daniels, are a brotherfucker." Tatum snickered.

"Why am I friends with you?" she snapped.

Then her laughter joined Tatum's, and it felt good.

# Seven

"How many motorcycles do you mass-produce each year?" Bastien removed his hard hat, excitement evident in the question he posed to Bran Holleran as they exited Greer Motorcycles' factory.

"That's actually a misconception," Bran corrected, removing his own hat and running a hand through his long salt-and-pepper hair. "We don't mass-produce motorcycles because we custom-build them. Our customer contacts us, tells us specifically what they want in their bike, pays the deposit, and we deliver when it's completed. Because we work closely with the client, we produce about 200 to 300 bikes a year. The KING One is going to change that number drastically."

Nore smiled as Bastien's eyes glazed over, and she

could just imagine the visions of motorcycles dancing through his head. He was a complete gearhead. This tour of the Greer Motorcycles factory had been a treat for him. Belle swishing around in the Beast's library couldn't have been happier. Seriously, she wouldn't have been surprised if Bastien broke out in song.

"If you have time, I can take you on a run on the prototype of the KING One." Bran jerked his chin toward the bay doors. "We have a track out back and they're testing it now."

"I swear, he just shivered, Bran. A full-body shiver," Nore drawled.

"Don't make fun," Bastien said, throwing her side-eye. Then he returned his attention to Greer's co-founder and custom bike builder, "She's not wrong, though. So the answer to that is a resounding yes."

Grinning, Bran held out an arm. "This way. We have extra overalls out back that you can change into."

"That would be incredible." Bastien started to follow, but then halted, glancing at Nore. "Are you good with that?"

"Of course. You're doing research." Nore waved a hand. "Have fun."

"If you want to follow me up to the office, we can have a cup of coffee while we wait on them to finish up. Or we can go watch. Your pick."

That voice. It vibrated through her, strumming over every erogenous zone, known and unknown. Nore sank her teeth into the inside of her bottom lip, briefly closing her eyes before pasting a smile on her face and turning around to face Joaquin.

"I'll choose coffee. Thanks."

Joaquin nodded. "Follow me."

It should've been an easy directive. But when he wore a suit tailored to fit his big body like it had a case of unrequited love, she had problems. Problems focusing on pouring coffee in a roomy break room. Problems concentrating while tailing him up a staircase. Problems drinking said coffee inside the spacious office while keeping a safe distance.

Just…problems.

Sniffing the fragrant brew, she stared out over the vast floor of the busy factory, as awed as she'd been during the tour.

"Joaquin, it's incredible what you've built here. You should be proud."

She didn't glance over, but she felt him move next to her. His leather-and-dark-chocolate scent teased her, and she inhaled it, remembering how redolent it was when emanating from his damp skin.

God. She couldn't escape those memories.

*Do you want to?*

Oh no. She wasn't touching that.

"I am."

She waited, but when nothing else came she loosed a soft puff of laughter.

"Man of few words."

She heard the shrug in his voice.

"No point in lying or pretending a false modesty. I am proud. Admitting that doesn't mean I, Bran, Shorty and a slew of other people didn't bust our asses to make Greer what it is today."

She nodded and finally risked a look over at him. In the two days since she'd seen him, she'd tried to convince herself that the animal magnetism saturating his office and seeping into her skin had been a figment of her imagination. Because that wasn't a... thing. But staring into his hooded silver eyes, with those thick eyebrows arrowed over the arrogant blade of a nose, and that wide mouth with its sexy piercing, so incongruent with the suit and trappings of a businessman...

Oh no, she could no longer deny that animal magnetism was definitely a *thing*.

"That's evident. What's also clear is everyone here's a team, and they respect you. That speaks volumes about you as their CEO." She scanned the almost ruthlessly clean and organized office, the sanitized factory below. "It's amazing what you've done here in ten years. There are a lot of people who can't claim to have accomplished this with their life's work."

He jerked up his chin. "You've done the same. Starting your own business at twenty-three with a small business loan that was paid back within three years of opening its doors. Your event-planning service now considered one of the premiere companies in the state."

Surprise fluttered in her belly, its warmth spreading like butter.

"You've done your homework."

"I always do on those I work with."

A tightness that had taken up residence in her

chest since James had accused Joaquin of acquiring the Main Event's services strictly to screw with his brother loosened. Until this moment, she hadn't even acknowledged that James's assertion still bothered her.

"What is that about?" he murmured, shifting and leaning a shoulder on the window.

"What is what about?"

His gaze flickered over her face, lingering on her mouth for a sizzling moment before returning to her eyes. A weight sank below her belly to settle in a sweet ache between her legs. Only by sheer force of will did she not fidget, squeeze her legs together in a fruitless bid to alleviate it.

"Something just went through your head. And contrary to what you may believe, your face isn't that skilled in concealing it. But your choice. Talk about it or don't."

Blunt. Always so damn blunt. It was a curse…and sometimes a blessing.

"Honesty?" she asked, deliberately throwing them back to the night they'd agreed to forget about.

Deliberately, when it'd been her who'd asked him to leave the past in the past.

God, she had to make up her mind about what she wanted from him.

"Always," he said.

Memories of the last time they'd traded those words whispered through her. What occurred between them afterward. What they'd shared. What she likely wouldn't experience again.

Allowing herself to have this man once more, that kind of pleasure again… That was playing a foolish game of Russian roulette. And she wasn't that capable a gambler.

Switching her gaze away from his intense, molten stare, she peered out the window. Safer that way.

"That you did your research assures me that you came to my company because you have confidence we can do the job you need. And not because…" She trailed off, but finished, "Not because of any affiliation with James."

"You believe I would sabotage my launch, and by extension, my company just to spite James?" The corner of his mouth curled up in a faint half smile, and he slid his hands in his suit pockets. "Or rather, James believes I would do that. Am I correct?"

"He has…strong opinions about why you hired the Main Event," she hedged, regretting opening this door.

His mouth twisted into a harder smile that contained a razor edge and sharp enough to draw blood.

"Let me clear up all misconceptions, Nore. Yes, my team conducted their research into your company. But apparently, James must be a silent partner because if I'd known he was in any way connected with the Main Event, I wouldn't have contracted you. No matter how good you are." He cocked his head. "Which leads to a question I should've asked you in my office. Exactly how involved is James? Because I don't want him anywhere near my project. I can acknowledge that you know a different man than I do.

That you trust him. But I don't, and I won't with this launch. If you can't respect that, you need to tell me now and we can cancel the contract."

"That won't be a problem." The truth backed up in her throat, and for an inexplicable reason it felt like a betrayal not to confess the whole truth to Joaquin about her and his half brother's relationship.

That she'd sold off part of her company for a song. That she didn't trust James as far as a nearsighted mole could see him. That she'd never let him near this account. Never.

But the words remained lodged inside her, because to admit them would mean exposing her for a dupe. A lovesick, blind dupe.

It burned a hole in her gut just to think it. To vocalize it aloud? To spy the pity on Joaquin's face? Or worse? The disgust?

No. She couldn't bear to see it. And yes, that was pride talking, but she didn't care. For the last few months, pride had been her only dependable companion.

"Can I ask you a question?" Out of the corner of her eye, she noticed him nod, and she risked fully looking at him again, but played it safe, steering her gaze to his beard.

And then recalled how the springy soft thickness had abraded her breasts and thighs as he'd sucked and kissed her...

Goddammit. Nothing was harmless when it came to this man.

"Was it difficult giving up racing to start Greer?

I'll be the first to admit, I didn't understand all that I read about your career, but I did get the gist of it. And you were great. It must've been difficult to walk away from that."

"I was great."

She scrunched her nose. "You really must work on that low self-esteem problem."

He didn't smile, but a gleam entered his eyes, making the pewter shine, and her pulse accelerated, throbbing in her temples. If this man ever full-out grinned at her, she might lose her mind and her panties.

Again.

"I told you I don't believe in false modesty," he said, shoving off the window and crossing the room, then tossed his coffee cup in the trash can next to the desk. "I wasn't the usual size or weight of most riders, which should've been a limitation. But it wasn't. I started road racing with the CMRA at seventeen, but I rode bikes long before then. Got on my first one at eleven."

"Good Lord." Nore snorted. "Your mother had to love that."

He studied her for a long moment, a dark eyebrow arched.

"You're right, she didn't. But not for the reason you're assuming. I didn't just inherit my features from my father, but my love of motorcycles, too. And if my mother could've erased both, she would've. Since she met Scott, James's dad, when I was five, she couldn't hide the fact that he wasn't my father. But she could conceal everything else—my history, the other half of my DNA—from me. Including my affinity for bikes. She chalked that up to me hanging around Scott's brother, who owned a garage and worked on them. And yes, it's where I first rode one, but my love for them? My passion for and talent with them? From a father she tried her damnedest to exorcise from my life."

"Where was he?" she murmured, loath to move too swiftly, too suddenly. To move at all.

Because any kind of action might stop him from talking, from revealing Joaquin Iverson to her. She should know more about her client. Any good businesswoman would agree. Understanding her customer meant a more efficient and successful job. It meant...

It meant, she was really reaching and making excuses about why she hungered for intimate information on this enigma of a man.

"My father?" A bright glint entered his eyes, hardening them so they matched the stark, forbidding slashes of his cheekbones, the strong line of his jaw beneath his dark blond beard. "Dead."

Hurt for him, for the little boy he'd been, sank inside her like a weighted stone. "Oh, Joaquin," she breathed.

Her palms itched with the urge to cup his face, smooth over his chest, settle over his heart.

She'd never had her father in her life either; he'd left her mother before Nore had been born. Yet Nore had always felt like something had been missing from her life...missing from her. A small part of her had grieved a man who'd abandoned her, hadn't given a shit about her. So she could just imagine the pain of losing a father to death.

But then the ugly twist of his lips pierced that sympathy, and for the first time she noted the outline of his fists in his pants pockets.

"I should explain. My mother told me my father was dead, but what she really meant was dead to her." That tragic caricature of a smile disappeared, but the shadows darkening his gaze remained. Those clenched fists continued to wreck the crease of his pants. "She lied to me from the time I was old enough to understand. Let me believe my father died in a car accident when I was almost two. The truth was they broke up and she took off, refusing to let him see me."

Her mind blanked, trying to catch up with all that he'd revealed. Attempting to reconcile actions so... cruel and manipulative with the woman she'd met countless times in the three years she'd dated James. Yes, Mona Whitehead could be opinionated and a little controlling, but this? What Joaquin described? She couldn't...

She wasn't even aware of shaking her head until he chuckled, the sound harsh, a little mean.

"What? Hard to believe? Why would the loving, doting Mrs. Scott Whitehead ever do something as callous and heartless as lie to her son about his biological father being alive? I must be lying. Or at the very least, I misunderstood." He shook his head. "'Your father drove drunk, ran a red light and crashed into a road barrier,' is damn hard to misconstrue."

She believed him. Couldn't say why she did so read-ily, so easily. Maybe it was the thin vein of anger...of pain that threaded through his voice that convinced her. Maybe it was that he didn't try hard to convince her...

Either way, she was just that—convinced.

And it sickened her.

"How did you find out?" she quietly asked.

His voice didn't lose its sardonic, cutting tone as he said, "At eighteen, I hired a private investigator to find my father's side of the family, if he had any. My mother said he didn't, but by that time I'd long stopped accepting everything she'd told me as gospel. So I went searching for them. She'd told the truth about one thing. He didn't have any biological family left. But while the investigator hadn't located them, he did find my father."

"Damn." She shook her head, her grip tightening around her forgotten cup of coffee. "That had to be one hell of a shock. For you and him."

He snorted, dipping his head in an abrupt nod. "More so for me since Dad knew I was alive. He and Mom had met and lived in Virginia. When I was about two he'd gotten in some trouble and gone to jail. When he got out three years later, she'd already disappeared with me. By the time he got a job, was back on his feet and had money enough to hire a PI to find us, Mom had married Scott, had James and found an attorney who threatened to bring up every wrongdoing Dad had committed to prove him an unfit father. She wanted him gone from my life as if he never existed."

"And he conceded?" Disbelief and anger trickled through her at his parents, on his behalf. "He did all that to track you down and then bowed under the pressure?"

"While all this was going on, I had no idea. Mom kept it all from me, and at the end of two years of back and forth, I was fourteen. With his money running out, he couldn't fight any longer, and he figured I'd come to him when I was of age. Of course, he didn't know that I believed he was dead." He loosed a short bark of serrated laughter.

"God, this is..."

"Fucked?"

"I was going to say stranger than fiction but 'fucked' works." Nore turned and set her cold coffee on the small table beside her, the thought of a sip curdling her stomach. "You don't have to do this, Joaquin," she belatedly said. Pushing off the window, she stepped closer to him, but drew up short when his eyes narrowed on her. What had been her intention? To touch him? Comfort him? Being intimately acquainted with how he sounded when he came didn't grant her that permission. And he was her client. She dangerously flirted with crossing a clearly drawn line. "This isn't my business, so don't feel obligated..."

Her voice trailed off as his stare intensified.

"Isn't it your business?" he asked, voice low. "We can claim to have a strictly professional relationship, but the truth is we were more than that before we even fucked in that club. Just through association and word of mouth, you were aware of me. Close to being family if things had turned out differently, right?" The pierced corner of his mouth quirked. "So yes, Nore, this is your business."

"This doesn't—" she sank her teeth into her bottom lip, feeling ridiculous even asking this but "—hurt you talking about it? Some things are better left in the past. Dwelling on them grants them a power over your life they shouldn't have. Gives them a place they shouldn't possess."

She should know. God, she should know. All she had to do was trip over the gravestones of her past relationships to see a pattern set by the dysfunction she'd witnessed over and over again growing up. How pathetic that she'd recognized the problem, vowed never to lower herself to be so needy and had ended up handing over half her business just to be loved?

Very. The answer was very.

"If I didn't know better, I would take that question as concern," he murmured, tilting his head and peering at her as if she were a peculiar new species he couldn't figure out.

"And you know better," she replied just as softly. Challenging him. This was what she got for being sentimental.

"You don't need to pretend with me, Nore. Sympathy, kindness, pretending—" he waved a hand, flicking off the emotions he enumerated as if they were annoying gnats "—none of that is necessary for us to get along or work together. I'm not telling you any of this for pity."

"Why *are* you telling me?"

Because right now, she resented him for giving her this glimpse at the wizard behind the curtain, then berating her for taking a peek.

"So you get who I am. So you get why this company *is*. So you understand why this launch can't fail. You said some things are best left in the past. I *am* my past. When you've been deprived of who you are for most of your childhood and young adulthood, you spend the rest of your life discovering just that. This company exists because I couldn't walk away from a sport that bonded me with my father even after injuries had rendered me incapable of riding professionally again. This launch can't fail because this bike is my father's legacy. It's named after him. It's my tribute to him."

"King," she whispered. "His name was King."

He slowly nodded. "His road name was King. His given one was Joaquin, same as mine. Which is why my mother refuses to address me by it. Everyone called him King, though. And it was the only name he answered to."

*Was?*

"Your father..." She swallowed past the thick, terrible emotion lodged in her throat as a looming sense of horror dawned on her. "Your father," she tried again, "he's not... You said you found him at eighteen..."

"I had four years with him before he died in a motorcycle accident. I was twenty-two."

The flint in his tone had her chest constricting and she glanced away from him. Glanced away before he glimpsed the sympathy and concern he'd flat-out told her he didn't want or need from her.

But it would take a stronger woman—a colder woman—than her not to touch him.

Her heart kicked against her ribs, but she didn't allow the deafening rhythm to stop her from approaching him. He watched her, his full, sensual mouth firming into a straight line, but he didn't say anything. Didn't ask her what the hell she was doing. Didn't order her to stop.

So she didn't.

This man's fingers and cock had been inside her, and yet more anxiety worked its way through her now than it had in that VIP area. Somehow, with what he'd revealed, with what he'd shared... This moment seemed more intimate.

She walked up to him, moved past him. Halted next to him. With her gaze fixed on a black-and-white reproduction of the Space Needle at dusk, she reached for him. She couldn't look at him; no, she couldn't look at him and touch him.

Sliding her hand over his palm, she hooked her fingers in his. Tension vibrated from his still frame, and it wrapped around them. Or maybe she just emanated her own. Either way, that tautness filled the room until it possessed its own faint hum, its own spicy flavor.

"I'm sorry, Joaquin," she said, and when his fingers gave a reflexive flinch around hers, her belly spasmed in response. Warmth swirled, pooling, and she closed her eyes, battling back the erotic pull she couldn't deny but, dammit, needed to. "I didn't have a father but there were so many times I wished for a day, an hour, five minutes with him. And you had four years. He must've been a good man if he made such an impact on you. So I'm sorry. I'm sorry you didn't have more time with him. I, more than anyone, understand what an important, priceless gift that would be."

He didn't speak.

And for a moment, his fingers curled around hers, squeezing before he stepped back, releasing her hand.

"Let me take you out back to the track so you can see for yourself how the KING One performs." His shuttered gaze met hers, and if she'd expected to see a softer emotion there, one glance into his steely eyes and his aloof expression disabused that notion. "It might give you ideas for the event."

She nodded, disappointment zigzagging down the middle of her chest. Damn, she hated like hell that it was there. Hated that she allowed it to matter.

Allowed *him* to matter.

Sometimes it truly sucked being her mother's daughter.

Forcing a smile, she waved an arm toward the office door. "After you."

He nodded and stalked across the room. She followed him, suddenly eager to escape the scene of her humiliation. He pulled open the door, but instead of walking through, he stopped short, his big frame blocking the entrance.

"Nore?"

"Yes?" She frowned, staring at the width of his back.

"Thank you."

Then he walked away, leaving her to stare after him.

# Eight

Joaquin pulled into his detached garage, shut off his engine and sat behind the wheel of his Aston Martin for several long moments. For once, he didn't appreciate the meticulously organized shelves and walls with tools and parts or the collection of motorcycles and a couple of cars. For the first time since purchasing his Medina home and arriving here after work, a sense of peace didn't settle over him. It didn't require Sherlock Holmes-level powers of deduction to determine why.

Two words.

Nore Daniels.

Hours had passed since she and her employee left Greer's factory after their tour, but she hadn't evacuated his mind. And he hadn't been able to evict

her. And fuck, he'd tried. But he'd been as successful today as he'd been in the last month. Which was
not at all.

Shit.

He pinched his forehead, then rubbed it, shaking
his head.

The same unease that had wedged between his
throat and sternum this morning remained there now,
and he curled his free hand around the steering wheel,
refusing to massage it. Not that it would do any good.
Nothing would erase the cardinal sin he'd committed.

Never, *never*, did he talk about his father.

The most he'd revealed to anyone was telling Bran
and Shorty the electric model would be named after
him. He hadn't gone into any more detail than that.
But with Nore... He ruthlessly scrubbed a hand down
his face before dragging it through his hair. With
Nore he'd unloaded as if she had a degree and he'd
been laid out on her couch.

Unprecedented and unwanted. As in he wanted
no parts of this shit.

Doubt and caution screamed, *What the fuck are
you doing?* In his small, insular world, trust was a
rare, precious commodity, hard won and not casually
given. Yet in that office, he'd handed over carefully
protected information as if it were Halloween and he
was liberally passing out candy to a trick-or-treater.

He couldn't blame it on that gorgeous face with its
lovely, wide golden eyes, scalpel-sharp cheekbones
and impure mouth. Couldn't fault the body of dangerous curves that he'd mapped with his hands and

tongue so it was imprinted on his mind with startling clarity. No, he'd been with beautiful women before. Had hot sex. Okay, maybe not the mind-blowing, dick-twisting sex he'd experienced with Nore, but still good sex. And none had loosened his tongue so he'd spilled the secrets about his past.

But none had been Nore Daniels.

The ex of his half brother.

How did he get past that? How did he explain being so reckless with her? Not him, who might have made a living out of an adrenaline-driven career, but off the bike? Off it, he guarded every word, every move, every fucking breath just in case it betrayed him. When you grew up in the family he did, it became second nature.

He'd only been able to release that pressure valve with very few people—his father, Bran, Shorty... Not Nore Daniels.

But then she'd held his hand.

Her slender, delicate fingers had hooked around his as her soft, husky voice weighed down with regret *for him*.

A meaty fist squeezed his heart even as its partner pumped his cock.

*That* was why he sat in his car, unsettled and unable to escape her.

She'd held his hand.

The peal of his phone rang in the car, and he blinked at its volume. A tight coil of dread spiraled in his gut as he glanced down at his cell, and he considered not answering it. He didn't believe in premonitions, but he couldn't deny the sense of foreboding warning him who called. And when he picked up the phone and peered down at the screen, that ominous feeling made sense.

His mother.

Goddamn.

Most people got the warm fuzzies when the woman who birthed them called. He just wanted to throw his phone off his dock into Lake Washington. And pray a kraken swallowed it whole.

For a second time, he thought about ignoring it. But he knew Mona Whitehead. She wouldn't give up. Not when she had an agenda and a purpose. His mother would eventually show up on his doorstep, and God knew Joaquin didn't want her tainting the sanctuary of his home. This call was the lesser of two evils.

Teeth clenched so hard a dull ache bloomed along his jaw, he hit the answer button and brought the phone to his ear before he could change his mind.

"Mom," he said, the greeting flat.

"Nathan."

His middle name scraped over his nerves, like fire-tipped nails. He hated it. He'd always hated it. Because whenever she called him that it was a vivid, stark reminder that she resented a part of him.

"What can I do for you?" he asked. No niceties because that wasn't their relationship. She didn't pretend to care how he was doing, and he gave her the same courtesy.

"You can explain to me why you're going to your

brother's place of business and bothering him," she snapped.

"Is that how he's telling it?" A hard smile curved his mouth, and bitterness trickled through him. "Interesting."

"How else is he supposed to tell it?" she demanded, voice rising to a shrill, offended note. "It's the truth. Did you or did you not show up at his office? Did you or did you not approach his partner for a meeting? It's beneath you, Nathan. It's not enough to have your own company and refuse to support or even hire your brother, but now you want to sabotage him? Where did I go wrong with you?"

He waited for her diatribe to peter out, this tirade nothing new. At some point the toxic nature of it shouldn't burn like acid—he should've developed protective scar tissue over the years. But it still scalded; he still forced himself not to flinch.

He still asked himself what he had done—other than be his father's son—to draw her enmity.

In thirty-five years, he hadn't discovered the answer to that mystery.

"Yes, his partner is organizing an event for my company. James neglected to tell you an important piece of information—that I didn't know he worked for the Main Event when I contracted them. They planned another party for Greer a month earlier and he had no part of it nor did he attend, so I don't know why or how I would've been expected to know he worked for them."

"James said this so-called event you've hired them

for can be handled by anyone. Now that you *know*—"
he could easily imagine her curling her fingers in air
quotes "—your brother is an owner of the Main Event,
you can easily back out."

"Once again, you've been misinformed," he said,
breathing deep to force a calm into his voice that the
anger in his chest belied. Leave it to James to run to
their mother to fight his battles. He would forever be
a mama's boy. Especially when he knew Mona would
take his side without fail. "This isn't a simple party,
and we're on a tight timeline. His partner is skilled
and talented at what she does and I need the best.
So I won't be switching to another event planner on
such short notice because James is uncomfortable."

"You never have cared about anyone but yourself. Just like your father." She delivered the knock-
out blow.

And again, not the first time it'd been thrown or
that it'd landed. But it could be the first or the thou-
sandth, it hurt. Because she meant it as an insult, as
a slur against King and Joaquin.

"I'm sorry you think so negatively of me, although
I'm proud to be my father's son. Is there anything
else?" He needed to get her off the phone before he
started pounding the steering wheel. His only victo-
ries with his mother were that he hadn't allowed her
to see how her words affected him. He refused to give
her that. "I have some work to finish."

"Just because you have a name for yourself and
a big house in Medina doesn't mean I'm going to
stand by and let you bully your younger brother. All

that money and you're still jealous of him. It's sad, Nathan."

The connection ended and he closed his eyes, the phone still pressed to his ear for several long seconds. Even though she no longer tore him down, her voice echoed in his head, and his grip tightened around the cell. Only when pain throbbed in his palm did he loosen his hold and deliberately lower his arm, dropping the phone to the passenger seat.

Part of him acknowledged that he used to answer her calls out of punishment, like a form of self-flagellation. A dysfunction he couldn't understand but also couldn't deny. Somehow, he felt like he deserved her neglect. Her abuse.

And the other part of him—the weaker part—accepted that he'd taken her calls because he wanted her love.

Yes, he was a walking clusterfuck of emotions.

"Dammit," he muttered. Shoving open his door, he exited his car.

The heaviness from his conversation weighed him down as he crossed the drive and climbed the steps to his home. Towering old trees surrounded the two-story house, sheltering it and lending the place an otherworldly feel. With brick patios, decorative French doors, a wide deck where the morning sun greeted him, a dock that sat on Lake Washington, his home was his shelter from the storm of life. But even as he stepped into the high-beamed foyer and his footsteps echoed over the wide-plank hardwood floor, his chest remained tight with anger, his shoulders stiff with tension.

Without slowing his stride, he stalked through the living room, the dining area, the kitchen, through the French doors and out onto the deck. He circumvented the firepit and strode down the steps to the dock, stripping out of his suit jacket and yanking on his shirt. Pausing long enough on the edge to toe off his shoes, he jumped, the frigid water of Lake Washington swallowing him in its dark depths. For long seconds, he didn't swim for the surface, just let the darkness surround him until his lungs burned, threatened to explode. Only then did he push for the top.

When his head broke the surface, he gasped deep, painful lungfuls of air. Tipping his head back, he treaded water, staring at the sky, and let...go.

# Nine

Nore glanced down at her cell, checking the time. 1:32 p.m.

Okay, he was only two minutes late. She stepped back and frowned up at the brick building sitting on the waterfront. In the daylight, the tall, nondescript three-story structure didn't seem like anything special. But she'd been inside, and... She peered down at the phone again, impatience and anxiety ricocheting through her.

In the two weeks since their consultation with Joaquin, Bran and Shorty, she had set up tours of three different venues. And Joaquin had vetoed every one of them. Too small. Too big. Too ugly. Too pretty. Yes. Too. Fucking. Pretty. She still didn't get that one. Shaking her head, she pulled her jacket tighter around her. But this place? This was perfect. Or at least she believed so.

She just hoped Joaquin did.

"Nore."

Nore turned around, facing Joaquin.

Damn him. CEOs shouldn't look so hot with beards and pierced mouths and linebacker shoulders filling out peacoats. It wasn't fair.

"Joaquin, you're late."

He arched an eyebrow. "A meeting ran over. I apologize for the three minutes."

"Sarcasm duly noted. And not appreciated." Turning back to the building and dragging her too-fascinated gaze from his mouth, she said, "If you're ready, they're waiting for us inside."

"Lead the way."

Inhaling a deep breath—and instantly realizing what a mistake it was when leather and chocolate invaded her nostrils and settled on her tongue—she pulled open the smoked-glass front door and entered. And decided breathing wasn't really a necessity.

She stepped into a dim, large, octagon-shaped foyer from which a gorgeous crystal chandelier hung from the cathedral ceiling. Mirrors and ornately framed 1920s-themed photographs were mounted on the padded olive-green walls that resembled cushions. Sconces with rose-colored bulbs cast their light across the vast area, leaving halos along the concrete floor. It was an eclectic space, and just as cool as Nore remembered it.

"What is this place?" Joaquin asked from just behind her, his voice a rumble in her ear.

She battled back the shiver that tried to work its way up her spine.

"A speakeasy," she said, not glancing over her shoulder at him. It was enough pretending his closeness didn't affect her. "Here's the manager now."

An older Black woman entered the foyer out of another entryway, a smile wreathing her lovely face. With her dark hair cut close to her head and clothed in a white long-sleeved shirt and gray pin-striped pants with suspenders, she could've stepped right out of the roaring '20s.

"Welcome. You must be Nore Daniels and Joaquin Iverson." She extended her hand toward Nore. "I'm Helen Moore, the manager of Holt's." Helen shook Nore's and then Joaquin's hands. "Thank you for considering Holt's for your event. Mr. Iverson, when Ms. Daniels explained the kind of space you desired, I think we have what you need. But let me give you a tour and you can decide for yourself."

For the next twenty minutes, Helen guided them through the vast space that included a large gathering room with two beautifully appointed bars, high tables and chairs, couches and a stage complete with spotlights above and below it. A mural covered one wall and a floor-to-ceiling window looking out over a private courtyard the other. Off the main gathering room branched several smaller ones, each boasting smaller versions of a stage, art, couches and tables.

"The bars would be full service, of course, and

you are permitted to bring in your own caterer if you'd rather not use ours. The waitstaff would serve throughout the entire space, not just the main room. We would also open the bars in the adjacent rooms. The same goes for those stages in case you would like to showcase other products. You can use as much or as little of our building as you need." Helen led them back into the main area, turning to face them with a smile. "I'll give you a few minutes to talk, and then we can discuss your decision."

With a nod and smile, Helen walked away, but first stopped by the bar and instructed the bartender to provide them with drinks.

"So." Nore slid onto a barstool and smiled at the young man with the slicked-back hair as he set her red wine in front of her. "Thoughts?"

Joaquin didn't immediately reply. He picked up his tumbler of whiskey and sipped from it, his silver gaze scanning the room. Nore ordered herself to stop staring at that mobile mouth curved around the lip of the glass and the up-and-down motion of his Adam's apple. Her fingertips tingled with the urge to caress both.

*He's a client. Which means he and his Adam's apple are off-limits.*

"Don't leave me in suspense," she said, covering her nerves with a soft laugh.

"Tell me what you're envisioning," he ordered, and his voice betrayed none of his thoughts.

"Well, in this would be the main gathering area. I received your guest list so we're talking two hundred guests, which will fit easily in here. Still, I suggest bringing in your own caterer because we're thinking about a themed menu along with special themed drinks. On the stage, we would showcase the KING One. And we could use screens and projectors to run videos of the KING One in action. Its test runs, close-ups. On the various stages in the other alcoves and rooms we can display either different Greer motorcycle models or even specific parts of the KING One that make it unique." She paused, studied his closed expression. He gave her nothing. "Of course, if these ideas don't work for you, we can go back to the—"

"It's perfect."

She blinked, momentarily stunned into silence.

"Excuse me?" When the corner of his mouth quirked, she snapped out of her stupor, remembering she was a professional, dammit. "Sorry, I was just preparing my argument about why this would work for all your needs and you cut me off at the knees. But you did indeed say this place was perfect. Your words."

"I did say that."

"Perfect. You said—"

"Nore," Joaquin muttered.

She held up her hands, palms out, letting loose a short, low chuckle. "Sorry, sorry. It's just after three other places I was beginning to doubt I'd ever hear that word." She smiled, satisfaction radiating through her, warming her. "I'm so glad you like it, though. I do, too. The outside is deceiving, which for me, is part of its charm."

"I agree. I didn't know where you were bringing me at first. But stepping inside?" He shook his head. "It's like entering another era. And I love your ideas. Every one of them. Including displaying the different parts of the KING One on the smaller stages. We can even install boxes that will tell people about those parts and what makes them unique."

"Or, hear me out," Nore contradicted, "we can have members of your team, who know the bike inside and out, stationed at the stages to talk to your guests about those parts. It's more intimate, engaging, and if people have questions, your team can answer them whereas a box cannot."

Joaquin rubbed a finger over his bottom lip, his steady gaze locked on her.

Nodding, he said, "You're right. That's a much better idea." A smile touched his lips, and the constriction in her chest resonated in her sex. *Don't you dare fidget on this seat.* "You are really good at what you do."

The compliment slid under her emerald sheath dress, stroking over suddenly sensitive skin, leaving pebbled flesh behind. She didn't need his affirmation, but... Fine. It was nice to hear. Especially since James hadn't given that to her. He'd only told her how much better she would be with him, not how good she was just as herself. That should've been a huge red flag. One she'd willfully missed.

"Thank you," she murmured. "It's a group effort."

"And you are the head of that group. Take the compliment."

Waving off his words again hovered on the tip of her tongue but instead, she stared into those intense, beautiful eyes. How did he do it? How did he so easily twist a person into knots and make them want more than they should? Reach for more than was wise…?

"Would either of you like another drink?" the bartender asked, interrupting and thankfully shattering whatever spell Joaquin so effortlessly weaved around her.

She jerked her gaze from his, switching it to the young man behind the bar, and granting him a smile that was undoubtedly a little too wide and too grateful.

"No, but thank you."

He nodded. "Let me know if you do."

Joaquin also turned down a refill, and she couldn't put off looking at him any longer. But now she'd had a couple of minutes to collect herself and she inhaled a silent breath, the mantra, *He's a client. He's a client*, chanting through her head on repeat.

"Once you're finished—" she dipped her head toward his half-filled tumbler "—I'll call Helen back in and we can start getting the contracts signed." Nore snorted. "It will be nice to nail down a venue. Bastien was about to pull out the big guns. And by that, I mean his Disneyland pamphlets."

"I don't know." Joaquin shrugged a wide shoulder, taking another sip of whiskey. "You should've put it on the table. Especially since I've never been. It could've been fun."

A record scratched in Nore's head and she frowned at him.

"That's not true."

A dark eyebrow arched and he stared at her over the rim of his glass.

"I think I would be in a more expert position of saying I've never been to Disneyland, thank you."

She waved his sarcasm away with a flick of her fingers. Although it must be noted that it was *excellent* sarcasm.

"Maybe you forgot since the trip occurred a long time ago, but I saw the picture on your mom's mantel. A family shot with the castle in the background. I remember it because I was a little jealous since I've never had the chance to go."

Joaquin tipped his head back, finishing of the rest of his drink and setting his empty glass on the bar. He didn't glance at her but stared at the tumbler, twirling it between his fingers. The motion might've seemed casual but the tendons standing out in taut relief in his neck belied that impression, as did the tightening of his jaw visible even beneath his beard.

Unease curdled in her belly. Dammit. Why had she brought up this topic? Like ghosts in an attic, some things were better left undisturbed. Because when troubled, they didn't go back to sleep.

"You're right. There's a family picture on the mantel. But I'm not in it."

Her confusion deepened, and she leaned forward, flattening her palm on the bar.

"So you were somewhere else in the park—"

"No, Nore," he said, voice as flinty as the gaze he lifted to her. "I wasn't somewhere in the park. I wasn't in the park at all. My *family* didn't include me on the trip."

Shock barreled through her. She stared at him, unbelieving. Because no. *No*. Her mother could get wrapped up in a man and be forgetful, even neglectful when it came to Nore. But never *cruel*. And what he just described—even the abridged version—was flat-out *cruelty*.

Pain seeped through the shock. Pain for the boy he'd been and the man who sat across from her today. Both still bore the scars of rejection.

"The trip was a gift from Scott's parents. Mom took that to mean they planned and paid for it for their only grandchild. So she arranged for me to stay with friends while all of them went. Later, I found out she told Scott's parents I didn't want to go. She'd lied to them and me. The truth was she just didn't want me there."

Until this moment, Mona Whitehead had been a slightly too overprotective but otherwise nice woman and mother. But now... Now, if she stood in front of Nore, she would do a little less respecting her elders and a lot more of treating people how they deserved.

Fury rose swift and hot, searing her. Children were gifts, given to parents to be protected and loved. And as a child who'd been one but not so much the other, she understood the ache, the confusion, the shame of feeling unworthy.

"You do know it's not your fault that your mother couldn't give you what she didn't have."

Joaquin didn't reply for such a long moment, she started to believe he wouldn't. And she cursed herself for overstepping. For forgetting that, yes, she'd dated his useless half brother, but other than sharing orgasms, the only connection she and Joaquin shared was event planner and client.

She sighed. "I'm sor—"

"And what doesn't she have?" he asked.

"A fucking heart."

The truth burst out of her, uncensored and raw, and in that moment she didn't give a damn if it offended. But in the next second, with the words echoing between them, she almost flinched. She was talking about his *mother*, after all.

More seconds of silence passed between them, and once more she prepared to apologize but then his lips twitched. Once. Twice. Then slowly curved into a smile. And it was the closest thing to a grin that she'd witnessed on him. Not full-fledged but near enough to set her heart on a hundred-yard dash.

*Holy shit.*

She changed her mind. Before, when she'd been naive and ignorant, she'd wanted to see a no-holds-barred smile spread across his face. God forgive her, for she'd known not what she asked. She hadn't even received her wish and she might fall out.

Reserved Joaquin was brutal beauty.

Teasing Joaquin was effervescent and stunning.

Glancing away, she peered at her empty glass,

longing for more wine. Anything to occupy her hands and mouth before she did something incredibly stupid and career-murdering.

"Part of me wants to admonish you for not admonishing me," she said, still not looking at him.

"Part of me thinks I should. But I'm not a hypocrite, so I won't."

She should leave it at that. Let it go. But...

"I'm really glad you had those four years with your father. You deserved those."

Long, thick fingers pinched her chin, gently but firmly turned her head and forced her to meet his gaze. This was the first time he'd voluntarily touched her since their night together and it rippled through her, a current of pure electricity straight to her sex. She tried to stifle the shiver but she couldn't. There was no containing it, and when those silver eyes dipped to her thighs, she knew he hadn't missed it. Humiliation should've scalded her alive. And later, after she climbed back in her car, maybe it would. But now, with her clit pulsing and an ache yawning deep within her, she couldn't care.

She just wished they were back in that VIP lounge where he could satisfy the hunger.

"Thanking you could become a bad habit for me," he murmured. His thumb swept over the skin under the corner of her mouth, grazing the curve of her bottom lip. She swallowed down a groan. "Thank you, Nore."

"You're welcome," she whispered.

He didn't release her, and she didn't turn her head

or remove his hand. No, instead she leaned into his hold, and his thumb pressed harder into her lip, the pressure a firmer touch. A decadent reminder of how his mouth had once possessed hers.

"Excuse me."

Nore startled at the sound of Helen's voice, but Joaquin didn't snatch his grip away. He squeezed her chin, his stare capturing hers for several seconds longer before leaving her skin branded with his touch.

He was the first to turn to Helen. Nore closed her eyes and ordered her hands to remain on her thighs. To not raise them to her face or her mouth to trace the phantom caress she could still feel.

Oh damn, she was in so much trouble.

*He's just my client. He's just my client.*

But as she watched him stand and approach Helen, his taut muscles flexing in a seductive dance beneath his suit jacket, that mantra rang hollow and false.

Oh yes. So much trouble.

# Ten

"**P**ermission to speak freely, sir."

Joaquin glanced up from his computer screen to see Shorty smiling down at him, her hand raised in a mock salute. Snorting, he leaned back in his office chair, raising an eyebrow.

"Seriously?" He smirked and jerked his chin to the chair in front of the desk. "Sit down before you hurt yourself with that."

Chuckling, his friend and senior vice president lowered into the visitor's seat with a sigh.

"It's almost seven o'clock. When are you going home?"

"I could ask you the same question."

She gasped, the sound loud and exaggerated. "Leave before the boss? What kind of slacker do you take me for?" She held up a hand. "Don't answer that."

He snickered. "Now how about the truth. What're you still doing here?"

Her smile ebbed and she crossed her legs. He frowned. Shorty didn't fidget.

"What's wrong?" he pressed.

"Your mom came by earlier," she softly said.

He stiffened. Since the phone call three weeks before, he hadn't heard from his mother. Which wasn't unusual. Her contacting him at all had been the odd occurrence. Yet now, she'd not only phoned him but had also shown up at his office? He shook his head. This was too much.

"Let me guess, it wasn't for my birthday," he drawled. When she narrowed her eyes, he quietly asked, "Why didn't you tell me?"

She pursed her lips, meeting his gaze without glancing away. That's one thing he'd always admired about Shorty. She didn't intimidate easily. And honesty was her default.

"Because you were in a meeting, and I wasn't going to interrupt a professional matter for a personal one. It was a call I made and I stand behind it. Also—" she paused, then inhaled a deep breath "—she didn't come here for a nice mother-son chat. She was here to start some shit about that fuckup brother of yours, and I refused to give her our space and our time to do it. Not on my watch."

Hurt battled it out with love and gratitude for this woman. Shorty had been with him and Bran from Greer's genesis. They'd known each other, had worked together, been friends, damn near family, for ten short years, and she sought to protect him. Meanwhile, the woman who'd birthed him ignored him, at best. At worst, begrudged every breath he took.

Not that this was new to him. He'd figured that out at six years old when she'd replaced him with a new family and made him feel like an interloper in her husband's home.

And yet... Yet, every ignored birthday...every personal and professional milestone they neglected... every call for money... Didn't matter that he should be immune to their behavior by now, it tore another piece of his soul away.

As it did now.

"She had to love that," he murmured.

"Yeah, she did," Shorty teased, but her gaze was watchful, attentive as it roamed his face. "And yes, she was mad. But she was also mad on the sidewalk. Out of respect for you, I didn't match her energy, but Joaquin..." She shook her head. "What the hell? I almost lost it all over your mother. And I was raised to respect my elders. But she almost made me forget my morals and Christianity."

Despite the topic and the black hole burrowing deep in his chest, he huffed out a short laugh.

"The Christianity is always the first thing to go." He rocked back in his chair and curled his fingers over the arms. "Thank you, Shorty. I appreciate you having my back. But I don't want you to worry, okay? I'll handle Mom. And James. You were right not to interrupt my meeting, because that's personal shit and all of our focus needs to be on this launch."

"I sense she's not going to give up," Shorty warned.

"Probably not." Definitely not. "But that's not the only thing on your mind. You've never been afraid to talk about my mother before. What else?" he asked, switching the subject. He had to take Mona in small doses.

Sighing, she propped her elbow on her knee and leaned forward. "Feel free to tell me to mind my business, okay?"

"Okay."

She snorted. "Don't know why I asked. Listen, we're close enough that I can get in your business and you can forgive me. And that I can warn you about what I see and you'll respect my opinion because I am your friend."

"Shorty," he rumbled. "I don't need a disclaimer. Just say what you need to."

"Fine." But again, she paused, and exhaling a long, low breath, finally said, "I know that you and Nore Daniels have more than a platonic relationship. Or you've had."

He slowly straightened, tension and surprise vibrating through him.

"What are you talking about?"

She grimaced. "Believe me, talking about your sex life is not my idea of a great way to pass my evening. It's actually traumatizing and I will be flushing my ears out with bleach after this. But a month ago, after your birthday party, the owner of the club called and asked if he should include the extra hours you spent there with the Main Event's invoice or send it directly to you. Considering you couldn't take your eyes off Nore and I saw you talking to her earlier that night, I put two and two together. I haven't mentioned it because it's none of my business. But now that we've rehired her, you've started spending time with her again *and* James is her ex—not to mention your mother showing up here is no coincidence—I feel like I have to say something."

Shit.

He hadn't seen this coming. His fingers curled into a fist and concern wound a path through him, twisting in and out of his ribs like a snake. But that concern wasn't for him; it was for Nore. He could imagine her embarrassment if she discovered Shorty knew about them having sex. Her first worry would be that Shorty didn't respect her or believed that Nore made a habit of sleeping with clients. He and Nore's association might not have been that long, but Joaquin had come to know her well enough to be sure that's the path her mind would travel. In the next instant, he made the decision that this discussion would stay here. Nore wouldn't find out.

He could save her from that.

"One, I will be the only person you say anything to. This conversation won't go past this office. We clear on that?" he asked…ordered.

"Of course." Shorty nodded. "I wouldn't say anything to Nore just as I haven't brought it up to you until now."

"Good. And Shorty, as my friend and the vice president of Greer, you have the right to be concerned and to come to me. And I'm not going to lie to you. We were intimate one time, and it was the night of my birthday, but since then, it has only been professional."

Memories of that smaller, delicate hand squeezing his. Thoughts of him sharing his past with her. The sensation of her skin branding his fingers. *Professional*, he silently scoffed. Not the truth. But dammit, not necessarily a lie either. He hadn't put his dick in her.

*Yet.*

He ground his teeth together, hating his subconscious in this moment. Hating his cock more for pounding in approval.

"People have started out with the best of intentions when it comes to keeping things strictly business, and then let their, uh, feelings become involved," Shorty pressed. "But this launch is the next big thing for Greer. I don't have to tell you that—you know it better than any of us. When we're so close to rolling out the KING One, we can't allow anything to derail us. Not distractions. Not negative publicity. Definitely not your half brother. And unintentionally—or intentionally—Nore could be James's way to screw with you...or worse." She stared at him. "It's only been a year since he last called begging you for a loan and cursing you out, demanding shares in Greer. A too-quiet year."

"And you think Nore might be inclined to help

him with a little payback. Or corporate intrigue?" He arched an eyebrow. "Sorry, Shorty. But James doesn't have the mental bandwidth for a conspiracy, and Nore…" A frown creased his forehead. "I don't have the details to the circumstances behind their breakup or to how he ended up in her company. Last I'd heard he was working at some retail store in Bellevue. Still, with that…tension between them at our initial consultation? I don't think there's any love lost. And I doubt she would help him cross the damn street, much less come for me."

"You willing to bet your launch's success on it? On her?"

*Yes* leaped to his tongue, but at the last second he couldn't release it. Because a tiny seed of doubt lingered deep in a place he was ashamed to admit even existed. The place where he yearned for acceptance and love from a family that had never made a place for him.

Did he believe Nore plotted against him with James? No.

Did a part of him believe Nore had chosen James first and just by comparison, Joaquin was destined to fail, to be a distant second in her eyes? As he'd always been when it came to his brother? It'd happened with his mother, with Madison…

That *yes* died a slow, agonizing death on his tongue. He tried not to lie to himself. After being deceived about something as basic as the existence of his parent, he abhorred lies. So he didn't answer Shorty's question, but instead skirted it.

"I don't trust anyone with my company but you and Bran."

"Joaquin," she murmured. "I don't mean to offend—"

"You didn't." He softened his voice. "I promise, you didn't. I appreciate your concern and that you came to me with it. But there's no need to worry. I'm good, and we're good. Okay?"

She sat quietly, studying him. Then she nodded.

"Okay." Rising from the chair, she smiled at him. "My job here is done so I'm going to head out. And you should, too."

"I'll be right behind you."

With a wave, she left, closing the door behind her. He continued sitting in his chair, staring at the door but not really seeing it, his thoughts on the conversation.

He wanted to dismiss it, put it out of his mind.

But his heart, the one that had been broken far too many times by the people he loved and wanted to be loved by?

Well, that was a different story.

# Eleven

"My company jet?" Joaquin stepped into the cabin of Greer's Cessna Citation Latitude, scanning it as if the answer for why Nore had brought him there would emerge from one of the six executive seats.

He turned to face her as she moved in behind him.

"Patience," she said, and with a smile that struck him as a little nervous, she skirted him and sank into one of the chairs.

"What's going on, Nore?"

"I know we agreed on the speakeasy, but I have one more venue to show you. Before I wasted your time, I ran the idea by Bran and he's not opposed to a destination location. We want to make sure we cover every base to ensure we pull off the best event possible." She buckled in.

"Excuse me, Mr. Iverson." A smiling flight attendant appeared next to him and extended an arm toward the cabin. "If you'll have a seat, the captain is ready to take off now."

He didn't move, instead frowned at Nore.

"I don't like this. No one mentioned anything about leaving the state for this meeting. And for damn sure no one ran by me a destination launch. I should've had input on this idea. Because I would've nixed it. So this isn't necessary..."

He couldn't explain the vise that constricted his ribs, the talons that clawed at his chest. For anyone else, he'd label it panic, but he didn't have panic attacks. Yes, he liked to be in control; he freely admitted that. With a past like his, where he might have had food, clothes and a home but his emotional stability had been as precarious as taking a stroll on a tightrope while drunk, he needed to be in charge of his world. Especially the company that was his. Because no one had begrudgingly handed it down to him, he hadn't had to beg for it or feel shame for having it. No, he'd earned it.

And maybe his protectiveness of Greer veered toward over-the-top, but it was all he had in a world that had only taken from him.

"Joaquin."

Nore's low, husky voice penetrated the suffocating stranglehold pinning him in place. He met her soft golden-brown gaze and the band around his chest loosened just a fraction.

"You're right. I should've given you more details

about today's destination and meeting. But I guess I also had a little anxiety about your reaction to it considering all the noes in the past. Not that it's an excuse, because this is your launch and your right to reject any space that doesn't fit your vision. I'm hoping this does, though." She stretched a hand toward the seat next toward her. "I apologize for not being completely transparent with you. We haven't known each other long, but I hope you can believe that I won't betray the trust you've placed in me."

*You willing to bet your launch's success on it? On her?*

Shorty's question whispered through his mind, returning to haunt him.

He stared at Nore, at her lovely face, those beautiful, bright eyes.

Hell.

He glanced at the flight attendant, nodded and moved down the short aisle to the cream-colored leather chair next to Nore and lowered into it. Her lips curved into a smile that lit her gaze like liquid sunshine. And it glowed inside him, warming his veins, as if the sight of that smile on her lips and in her eyes was the source of his pleasure.

He looked away from both.

This was a business relationship. She'd made that more than clear. That was all she wanted when she'd visited his office.

A mistake.

He'd thrown that word out there to describe what he'd been to her, what had happened between them, but she'd jumped all over it. A mistake she had no intention of repeating. He'd better keep that forefront in his mind. No matter how soft or kind those eyes appeared or how pretty and tempting that mouth seemed, he would abide by her request.

"Disneyland?"

The word raked his raw throat as he turned from the wondrous, sparkling view of Sleeping Beauty's castle to look at the woman beside him. Though the unmistakable landmark castle declared where he stood...though the iconic statue of Walt Disney and Mickey Mouse removed any thought of dreaming... though he'd even suspected this was his destination as soon as they'd landed at John Wayne Airport and driven the thirty minutes to Anaheim... He still couldn't believe he was here. And that Nore was behind it.

"I know this is extremely unorthodox and I am undoubtedly overstepping and being incredibly inappropriate. I mean, I hijacked the company jet for personal reasons." She huffed out a breath, twisting her hands in front of her. "But you've never been to *Disneyland*. And that seemed like such a crime. Especially *why* you've never been. And well, we're a little under three hours away by plane..." She trailed off, and if she twisted her fingers any harder, she might break them.

He still couldn't speak. Could barely push air past his throat that had swollen to three times its size. He should be angry. And yes, embers of that all-too-familiar emotion kindled in his belly along with a sticky morass of others—wonder, a child's joy, grief, embarrassment. He stood here, like one breathing exposed nerve, feeling *fucking everything*, and worse, she and anyone willing to really look could see it. See him covering these cheery streets like an emotional oil spill.

Blinking, he tore his stinging gaze from her and back to the happiest place on earth, taking in the Halloween-themed park with its massive pumpkins with mouse ears, towering jack o' lanterns on stilts and huge ghosts and witches. Kids of all ages walked and ran around laughing and screaming, enjoying themselves, eating, talking, heading toward Downtown Disney or the rides.

And oh fuck, did he want to lose himself in it all.

"Say something," she whispered.

Shifting his attention back to her, he took in the concern darkening her whiskey-bright eyes. Concern for *him*. After she'd done all this—flew from one state to another to create a stolen memory—her first consideration was *for him*.

Oh fuck.

Every reminder that this was a business relationship, and he was a mistake she had no intention of repeating, escaped him and he jerked her into his arms.

"Thank you," he muttered into her dark curls. Inhaling her fresh, earthy scent into his lungs, he closed his eyes, held her tighter. He cupped the nape of her neck with one hand and threaded his fingers through her curls with the other, tangling and fisting them.

Tilting her head back, he pressed his lips to her forehead, her elegantly arched brows, the delicate bridge of her nose. "No one has ever done anything like this for me before. Ever thought to do anything like this for me before. Thank you, Nore."

*Thank you for looking at me and seeing someone special enough to give this to.*

He brushed his mouth over hers, intending it to be gentle, a symbol of his gratitude only, not sexual. But even as he lifted his head, lips burning just from that barely-there contact, a soft sound escaped Nore and her hand cradled the back of his neck. She shot to the balls of her feet and crushed her lips to his. For a moment, he froze, but only for a moment. That's how long it took for her sweet, earthy taste to penetrate and he groaned, his good will and restraint turned to dust.

His mouth parted and he took swift control of the kiss, his tongue driving forward, sweeping into hers, tangling with her in a dirty duet that he could never grow tired of. Her nails bit into his skin while the other hand fisted his coat at his back. Like a starving man, he luxuriated in every lick, desperate for the next suck. And she opened wide for him, surrendering to him even as she countered him.

Jesus, how had he gone without this for months? How had he so arrogantly believed he could resist having this, *her* again?

Only a giggle and a subtle cough penetrated the fog of lust that enshrouded him, and he tore himself out of it with a physical force that was damn near painful.

"So I'm guessing—" she cleared her throat, shifting her hand from his neck to his shoulder before stepping back "—you're okay with my surprise?"

The corner of his still-tingling mouth quirked. He brushed his fingers against the back of her cheek before lowering his arm to his side.

"Yeah, I'm okay with it."

"Good." She clapped her hands together and grinned. "So what are we hitting first? Downtown Disney or Space Mountain? And you're not leaving here without Mickey ears. Just sayin'."

"I wouldn't dream of it," he said. Shaking his head, he returned her smile and held out his hand. She stared down at it, and after a brief hesitation, accepted it, entwining her fingers with his. "Let's go."

The rest of the day passed in a colorful, screaming, beautiful blur of amusement park rides, food that only teenagers should eat, games, shopping on Nore's part, shows... He tried to pack a childhood into one day. And as he and Nore sat at a table at the Jolly Holiday Café patio after the fireworks, waiting for the thick crowds on Main Street to thin out before they headed for the exit, he could say they'd given it their best try.

He glanced at the woman sitting next to him, her curls shielding part of her lovely profile, and he stretched his arms along the table, his fingers curling into the wood. Either that or stroke those dark strands away from her face, caress that smooth, beautiful brown skin. And he'd taken enough liberties today. Hell, his mouth still burned from their earlier kiss, and though it was hours later, he swore her taste lingered on his tongue.

Inhaling a breath, which contained the scents of treats from the café's now-closed bakery, he scanned Main Street's buildings and the Matterhorn in the distance. That kiss, her unique flavor, this day—they would all be intertwined in his memories, unable to be separated.

"Holy…" A low, exaggerated gasp came from his right. "I do believe that's a smile on your face."

He scoffed. "It's too dark to see. You're imagining things."

"Oh I'm sorry," Nore drawled. "My mistake. Must've been gas."

He snorted. Then, a moment later, "Thank you for today. It's been…" The proper words failed him, probably because they became trapped in his too-tight throat.

Her hand gently squeezed his thigh. "You're welcome." She tilted her head back, staring up at the trees and dark sky. "Although this wasn't an altogether altruistic field trip. I did kind of enjoy myself. Just a little bit, mind you." She held up a finger and thumb, holding them about an inch apart.

"Just a little bit? So that wasn't you screaming on Guardians of the Galaxy? Got it." He nodded, smirking.

"Pretty rude of you to mention it," she grumbled. "But seriously." She smiled at him. "Thank you for letting me share this day with you. It's been one of the best days I've had in a long time."

"When was the last one? The last really good

day?" he asked, finding himself insatiable for details about her.

Other than her being a business owner and James's ex, he didn't know much, and he craved more. What was her favorite color? Movies? Was she a Seattle native or born somewhere else? From today, he'd discovered she loved hot dogs with mustard and relish and disliked ketchup, but what else? What other foods? What made her sad? Happy? Angry?

The questions and the urge to crawl inside Nore's head and mine this information for himself bombarded him and he unconsciously shifted closer, turning toward her. Eager for whatever she would give him. This…need should've warned him, scared him.

But he didn't heed it.

Or maybe, in this moment, in this place, he didn't care.

"My last good day?" she murmured, and he caught the flash of her smile in the shadows. It struck him as wistful, and nothing could've prevented him from sliding a hand under her tight curls and cupping the back of her neck. "That's easy. Several months back I took my best friend Tatum to Vegas. It was a combination girls' trip and bachelorette party before her wedding."

"You two are close?"

"You know how you have Bran and Shorty?" When he nodded, she did as well and said, "That's how I am with Tatum. We've been friends since college. Me and my mother…" She sighed. "Well, I've just accepted we are what we are. Sometimes you just have to meet and love people where they are, because wishing they'd change, wishing your relationship with them would be different, only leads to more pain. For you, not them. Because they're not changing no matter how hard you plead, cry or rage. That's where Tatum comes in. When I met her, she became my family, my sister in every way except blood."

"You're lucky to have that, have her." Because he couldn't help himself—and because it fascinated him, her seeming acceptance of her relationship, or lack of it, with her mother, he asked, "Do you talk to your mom?"

"Sure. I make a point of calling her at least once a month, and if she hasn't fallen in love—" she huffed a small chuckle "—she'll even call me before I reach out. That's our dynamic. That's us. I could accept it or be bitter about it. I decided to accept it so I could have her in my life. She loves me in her own way."

He nodded, letting that settle in his soul. He couldn't help comparing it to his own relationship with his mother. Deciding to put it aside for now, he refocused on her.

"Besides the obvious reasons—I mean, Vegas." He cocked his head toward her, and she shrugged, grinning. "What made the trip so memorable?"

She peered into the darkness for several seconds, her hand still resting on his thigh, and her fingers contracted on his leg, then relaxed.

"Sorry, I—" She jerked her hand off his leg, cradling it against her chest. "I didn't mean…"

"Shh." He reclaimed her hand, gently but firmly

lowering it back to his thigh, their fingers entangled. "Go ahead. Finish."

Nore stared at him, and he returned the stare, not offering an explanation for why he held her hand. Because he didn't have one.

"One reason is I got to spend time with my best friend who I hadn't been able to see for a while other than through FaceTime and Zoom calls because she lives in Boston. And then..." She bowed her head. "There was another reason we were in Las Vegas. It hadn't been that long since my breakup with James, and Tatum wanted to get me out of Seattle. More specifically away from him. He'd...broken my heart. I can't even lie about that. Even knowing what I do now about who he is, that doesn't change how I felt about him, and I needed space and time away. She knew that. But instead of this gloomy 'woe is me' trip, we had the best time. And I'd decided to move on from James, to let go."

*He'd broken my heart.*

*...that doesn't change how I felt about him.*

Pain flared in him like a hot poker. For her. For the echo of hurt and insecurity that crept inside him like a crafty thief.

"It would be easy for me to be bitter about love. Especially given my recent and past history with it. But I look at Tatum and Mark, her fiancé, and I can't doubt that it exists. They are so in love with each other. It practically emanates from them, and to be with them... It's enough to want to smack 'em." She laughed. "I found this pawnshop, and my plan was just to sell my engagement ring."

He loosed a loud bark of laughter. "Holy shit. You didn't."

"I damn sure did, and for way less than he paid for it, too." She smiled. "So I planned to just get rid of this final symbol of my failed engagement, but then I saw this beautiful brooch."

"The one you wore the night of my birthday party?"

Nore nodded, absurdly pleased he remembered something so small about her. Especially since she recalled every single detail about him.

"The same one. The saleswoman told us about this incredibly romantic legend attached to it—about the owner of it finding their soulmate. On a whim, I decided to lay out the whole six grand for it so my friend could have it on her wedding day when she's marrying her destined other half."

He quietly studied her, searching her golden eyes, touching on every detail of her face.

"You really believe in that? Soulmates? Destiny?"

Nose scrunched, she tilted her head. "We're seconds away from Sleeping Beauty's castle where happily-ever-afters are the norm rather than the exception, right?"

"That's rumor."

"Well, in that case…" She shrugged. "I want to believe. That's all I got." She laughed. "What about you?" She squeezed his fingers. "Do you believe?"

He thought of finding his father. Losing him. Falling in love with Madison. Discovering the truth about her and James, having his heart broken only to find her again…and lose her again.

No, he didn't buy into happily-ever-afters. They belonged in places like Disneyland where magic lived and the doors closed on it at eleven.

Standing, he guided her to her feet and started following the thinning crowd toward the exit.

"Let's head home."

# Twelve

Nore closed out her calendar for tomorrow, taking note of her early-morning calls and meeting. She opened up an email, jotted down a quick message to Bastien about the conference call with a particularly...exacting client and hit Send. Stretching her arms above her head, she groaned and...smiled as her gaze hit the Cinderella snow globe sitting on the corner of her desk.

Hard to believe just yesterday evening she'd been in California with Joaquin as fireworks lit up a dark sky over Sleeping Beauty's castle. It'd been magical. And that beauty had been in the wonder and quiet joy that had lit his silver eyes.

She'd taken a huge risk with that trip. Persuading Bran had been surprisingly easier than she'd expected, and then getting Joaquin on the plane without betraying where they were headed...? That'd all taken a minor miracle. But his reaction, the expression on his face, the joy, that hug, that kiss... It'd all been worth it. More than worth it. So had spending the day with him as he enjoyed Disneyland for the first time. Maybe, technically, she had given him the gift of going to the amusement park, but he'd really given it to her. Experiencing his delight, it'd been...incomparable.

But it'd been that little half smile and the soft glint of happiness in his gaze as he stared up at those multicolored fireworks that had clued her in that she'd gone too far. That she could no longer lie to herself about him being just a client. Or that their night in that VIP lounge was just a one-off. No. He still set her on fire. Still made her forget her damn name with just a touch of his lips to hers.

She'd been so damn careless.

She'd guarded herself against his physical pull, but had been completely unprepared for and cavalier with the emotional draw. And now it was too late. Her gaze fell on the snow globe again. Stupid to buy the thing, much less set it on her desk.

Yet she didn't remove it.

Dammit, she'd been careless.

"Where were you yesterday?"

Shit. This was what she got for staying late.

Who was she kidding? This was what she got for letting love blind her into prostituting her dream. And it seemed there would be no end to how long she would pay the price for it.

Smothering a sigh and the anger that sparked to life inside her, Nore leaned back in her chair and gave her ex a narrowed stare.

"A closed door obviously doesn't mean what it used to," she said, voice flat.

"It's not like you were in a meeting." James waved off her objection and dropped down into the chair in front of her desk.

"And it's not like I invited you into my office either," she ground out, powering down her computer. "As it is, I'm getting ready to leave. So whatever you want is going to have to wait until tomorrow."

"Is a trip to Disneyland considered a business expense now?" he asked as if she hadn't spoken. "I'm all for creative financing but I don't think even I could twist that around."

She stared at him, struck speechless. An ugly shock, like being doused with frigid ice water, crashed over her and she froze, unable to move.

James nodded, a sneer riding his mouth. "That's what I thought. Not sure how the happiest place on earth figures into a motorcycle launch."

"I don't have to explain myself to you," she said, finally locating her voice, and dammit, that response sounded so damn lame and *guilty.* And the deepening curl of his lips confirmed it. "The Greer Motorcycles account is not yours and you have no association with it, so I don't have to justify any decision to you."

"When it's company money you do. And since

Bastien was here and he didn't know where you were yesterday, I'm assuming that trip was more personal than professional. If that's the case, then you're wrong. It's absolutely my business."

"Hold up, James." That anger flamed into roaring life, and she had to pause, inhale a deep, calming breath. Okay, no, that didn't work. She had to settle for sounding somewhat calm. "You might work here, but no one here has the right to second-guess my actions."

"I don't just work here. I'm part owner—"

"And that means dick," she snapped. "Don't drop that on me like it's supposed to *mean* something. It might sound impressive to your little friends and the people you wine and dine out there on company funds, but you and I both know you haven't done shit to earn that title except pass a check to me and dole out empty promises."

"Don't make this about us. Relationships don't work out all the time, and you need to let that go. This is about our company and how you're being foolish and blind with a client," he spat the word *client* as if it tasted like shit on his tongue.

"Oh, believe me, I've completely let go of our relationship and am so thankful for that. What I'd like to know is how you discovered where I was yesterday, since I did tell Bastien but he most definitely would not have relayed that information to you."

For the first time since he'd waltzed into her office, his arrogant facade showed cracks.

"Does it matter?"

"Why yes, James, it does matter," she said, an acidic sugar coating her tone. "You came into *my* office uninvited and self-righteously demanding answers, so you can give me that one."

"Fine." His mouth thinned until it almost disappeared and his eyes narrowed. "I read your emails."

For the second time in minutes, shock blasted her.

"You did what?" she rasped.

"I read your emails. The flight and amusement park ticket information were in there," he said, louder, almost defiantly, his chin notched high. "I couldn't get any answers from Bastien, and it wasn't like you to be out of the office all day without anyone knowing your location. And since you took on Nathan's event you've been secretive. So I decided to find out what was going on. You haven't changed your password since we were together so…" He shrugged a shoulder.

"How. Fucking. Dare. You." She slowly rose from her chair, flattening her palms on her desk. If she could leap across this desk and go for his throat, she would. This self-entitled, spoiled prick. Had he really…? How had she ever…? God, she couldn't even finish a whole sentence in her head she was that *furious*. "You invaded my privacy, read my private emails, and then you have the *fucking balls* to march in here and demand an explanation from me? *Are you kidding me?*"

"There's no need for all that, Nore, God." James winced, standing, too, and thrusting his fingers through his hair. He glanced toward the door, maybe judging the distance and how quick he could get to it. At least he wasn't as dumb as a box of hair. Just a bag. "I wouldn't have had to go to those extremes if you had just shared with me—"

"No." She jabbed a finger at him. "No," she repeated. "You don't get to blame me or try to defend your indefensible actions. And FYI, I haven't been secretive, James. You've just suddenly taken an interest in this business. And that your interest comes on the heels of acquiring your brother's account doesn't strike me as a coincidence."

James threw his hands up and barked a hard, ugly laugh.

"So what if it is? What? Am I supposed to feel guilty about not wanting anything related to Nathan near me or what's mine? For years he's had his career in racing, had all that fame, the endorsements and the money that came with it. Did he share any of that with us? Hell no. He helped his deadbeat father out, though. Set him up real nice before he died. Same thing after he started Greer. Wouldn't even give me a job when I asked." He slashed a hand through the air. "I didn't want a handout, just a job. But he wouldn't do that for his family. He acts like we don't exist. And now suddenly, out of the blue, he shows up, needing the services of the company that I partly own? No, something's not right. Now that I have success on my own, he wants to take that away from me, humiliate me. And he'll use anything or anyone he can to do it. Especially if that 'anyone' is my gullible ex-fiancée."

*Maybe if you didn't always expect someone to give you something and earned your own way—hold up, wait.*

"What did you just say to me?" she asked, "gullible ex-fiancée" breaking through her internal diatribe.

"You heard me," he said, mouth twisted, a spiteful glint in his eyes. Why did she have the feeling he was enjoying this? "Like I told you before, you're good at what you do, Nore. But so are a lot of other companies. What makes you special to my half brother, the millionaire who could've gone to any of those more well-known, more established companies, is *me*. It's always been about me, for as long as I can remember, and you're just stepping in the middle of it."

"You sure do have an important opinion of yourself," she said, and hated that the words emerged not as strong, as steady as she'd wanted.

And that James heard it.

His smile was faintly pitying.

And she hated him for it.

"Tell me something, during that flight to California, did Nathan mention Madison?" Nore didn't bother answering, but James didn't grant her time. He settled back in his chair, fingers linked over his flat belly, and smiled up at her. She didn't take her seat again, though from that self-satisfied smile, she probably should. It meant nothing good. "I was twenty-one and Nathan was twenty-seven. I'd been dating this girl named Madison for about six months. We'd met at a party and had been spending a lot of time together. Come to find out, she'd also been spending a lot of time with Nathan. When he found out, he made her choose—and she chose me. He's never forgiven me for that. So what do you think is the best way to get back at me for winning the woman he loved? Getting the one who loved me, maybe? Even if it's seconds?"

"Why didn't you just add 'sloppy' in there? You damn sure implied it," she whispered.

"I don't think that way, but Nathan?" He shrugged. "I tried to warn you when you took him on as a client but you wouldn't listen. Everything about him coming here, hiring you, is personal. Whatever you plan on getting out of him—connections, money, references—it's all going to be for nothing. Believe me, I know. When it comes to him, it's always for nothing." He paused. "But it doesn't have to be."

Nausea churned and tossed in her belly, and her fingertips pressed into the desktop until a dull ache throbbed in her fingertips.

*So what do you think is the best way to get back at me for winning the woman he loved? Getting the one who loved me, maybe? Even if it's seconds?*

His words bounced off the walls of her head, over and over, growing louder and louder. Striking right at the heart of her every insecurity. Her mother loved her, but Nore had never been a priority. The men parading in and out of her mother's life had; Nore had been second.

In relationships, her mother had always placed the men first, but they hadn't given her the same respect.

Or maybe she didn't demand it.

Pain and soul-deep sadness pulsed inside Nore, and she couldn't speak past it.

James must've mistaken her silence as encouragement because he continued.

"You've been to his factory, right? I saw that on your calendar and in your emails that you and Bastien went on a tour a few weeks back. So you saw this new motorcycle that he's about to launch." James scooted forward on his chair, his eyes gleaming with an eagerness that had nausea rising. "If you could—"

"No."

"C'mon, Nore. Do you understand the money we could get for any kind of information on Greer Motorcycles' latest model? I'll gladly sell you back my part of the Main Event—"

"Shut up, James. Stop talking. I'm not hearing this. And I can't believe you would even think about..." She shook her head, hard, and shot up a hand. "You know what? I can no longer say that. I can believe you would consider betraying your own blood like that and thinking I would sink so low to help you—for what? Petty revenge for an imagined slight that hasn't even been committed against me? And money you somehow feel entitled to just because you're related?"

She laughed, and it scratched her throat.

"Get out of my office, James. And I'm going to say this once, so make sure you pay attention. I have a professional relationship with Joaquin." Lies. That bridge hadn't just been crossed yesterday but torched and the ashes tossed to the wind after that kiss. But damn if she'd let James know that. "Yesterday was business-related and I had no obligation to explain myself to you then, and I'm just giving you a courtesy now. One you won't get again. And you're going to stay away from anything having to do with the Greer

Motorcycles account. If I find out you've interfered with it again, directly or indirectly, I'll tell Joaquin myself and I don't care how it makes this company look. And if you ever violate my privacy again, I will make you regret it."

His face tightened, red pouring into it. He shot to his feet, his tall body fairly vibrating.

"You can't—"

"I just did," she interrupted him with a chin jerk toward the door. "I might have to share this business with you, but not this office. Get out. And don't come back in unless you're invited."

James glared at her one last time, but wisely he didn't utter another word before he spun on his heel and exited the room. Good of him since he'd just proposed corporate espionage.

As soon as he disappeared, the door closing behind him, she sank down into her chair, the anger deflating from her.

Staring at the door, she just felt…nothing.

Nore stood at her front door, eyes closed.

She didn't need to peek through the peephole to see who graced the other side. A glimpse through her living room window at the black Aston Martin sitting at her curb declared the identity of her evening caller.

Pressing her forehead against the wood, she silently cursed. Part of her wanted to turn around and walk right back down the hall, ignoring Joaquin's presence on her porch. But the other half of her… Well, that hungrier, more foolish half longed to throw open the door and burrow her face against his wide chest.

In the end, she did neither.

She compromised by opening the door but standing safely on the other side of the entryway. Not touching him.

His wide shoulders nearly blocked out the porch light, and hurling herself against his big frame became a close call again.

"Joaquin, what're you doing here?" She narrowed her eyes. "And do I want to know how you ended up here on my doorstep since I didn't give you my home address?"

He arched an eyebrow. "Probably not."

Anger spiked inside her and she shook her head. "Great. Two invasions of privacy in one evening. Must be a record."

He went still, his shoulders tensing under his black peacoat, his expression carefully blank.

"I don't know about the first invasion of privacy, but the copy of the venue contract included not just your company's address but your home one. I came here tonight because I didn't get a chance to talk to you today and all my calls were going to voice mail. I got a little worried. I apologize for misusing the information, though, and if you want me to leave, I will."

*Shit.*

She pinched her forehead then rubbed it.

"No, it's fine. I'm fine." Stepping back, she waved an arm. "I'm sorry. Come in."

His gaze bored into hers, but then he moved forward, his leather-and-chocolate scent teasing her like a decadent caress. Closing the door behind him, she mouthed a curse once more. This had "bad idea" written all over it in '80s style graffiti. Her emotions were bubbling too close to the surface, too volatile. And yet she walked past him, leading the way into her sunken living room. Her tall bay windows allowed the artificial glow from the streetlights into the room, and scattered lamps provided more illumination.

She surveyed the room, attempting to see it through his eyes. Overstuffed couch and love seat with a couple of comfortable armchairs that she loved to curl up in with her favorite books on rainy days. Coffee and side tables with bookshelves, a cushioned alcove, and a large fireplace. It was a cozy room, and her favorite in the house besides her bedroom.

It also revealed a lot about her, and she crossed her arms over her chest as Joaquin silently scanned it. What did he see? Her love of comfort? As a child who'd grown up lacking comfort, she didn't deprive herself; she refused to. Did he perceive her love of books, of art? It'd been a close call in college between business and a literature degree.

Anxiety rose inside her. Anxiety and longing. The push and pull between wanting to be seen and fear of being exposed.

"So what did you need to talk to me about that was so important?" she asked, dragging his attention away from her home. Or trying to.

He turned, but when that pewter gaze settled on her, more specifically on her face, her throat and lower to her crossed arms, she had the urge to order him to examine the living room again.

"What do *you* need to talk to me about?" he countered.

She started to frown, to object, but at the last second she turned and walked to the dormant fireplace. Would've been a nice night for a fire, actually. But she'd just thrown on a sweater and leggings when she'd gotten home along with a couple more blankets on her bed.

And yes, she was mentally stalling and avoiding his question.

With a sigh, she didn't face him but asked, "How did you know?"

"One, you're a businesswoman, and you would've called me back just to make sure I wasn't trying to reach you about the launch. That you didn't clued me in something might be wrong. Second, Bastien left me a voice mail. On his way out for the night, he noticed James going in your office and got a little worried. He, too, tried to call you but no answer. Since he knew we were…together yesterday, he wondered if I would check on you."

"Well that, along with this visit, is highly inappropriate."

"Inappropriate?" She didn't sense him move, but his scent enveloped her, his heat reached out to her. No, she didn't need that fire. Not with his big body behind her. "We passed inappropriate a long time ago. But definitely last night. Don't try to close the door now because it's convenient. Because you're scared."

"Who's Madison?" She lobbed the name at him like a bomb set to detonate. It was self-preservation, and desperate.

"Look at me."

She stiffened. For the first time since she'd met him, a little fear of *him* trickled inside her. That ominous, dark tone had a shiver tripping down her spine.

"Turn around and look at me, Nore."

Closing her eyes, she obeyed the underlying steel in his voice, and tipped her head back, meeting his hooded gaze.

"Say that again. When you throw a jab like that at me, at least have the courtesy to look me in the face."

She should be quaking at that hard voice, at the harder eyes. And yes, she was. But not in fear. That trickle had morphed into another form of anxiety. A sexual anxiety twisted with anticipation and excitement. What did he intend for her and would he make it hurt…good?

Holy hell, who had she become in the last twenty seconds?

"Will you tell me about Madison?" she murmured.

"She was my wife."

The blow to her chest nearly brought her to her knees. Air whistled in her lungs, and her pulse pounded in her ears.

*His wife?* That didn't… James hadn't… She shook her head.

*His wife?*

"Joaquin…"

"The night of the party, the night we had sex. It would've been our fifth wedding anniversary."

She briefly closed her eyes, then opened them, meeting his steady, piercing gaze.

"You used me? Is that what the night was about?"

"I needed you. I wanted you. And yes, I wanted to forget and lose myself in you. So yes, I used you."

"Did it work?"

He stared at her. "Yes."

"Then good," she said, voice fierce. "You need to use me again?"

His nostrils flared, his eyes gleamed.

"Yes."

She fisted the lapel of his coat with one hand, balled her fingers in his hair with the other and surged to the balls of her feet. With zero hesitation, she opened her mouth over his, her tongue thrusting between his lips, tangling and sucking, daring him to meet her, dance with her.

Use her.

Unlike in the amusement park yesterday, there was no hesitation on his part. As if her mouth lit a fuse, he exploded all over her. Both of his hands buried in her hair, his nails grazed her scalp, and she groaned, tipping her head back into those big palms. Quick as lightning, he seized control of the kiss, and she surrendered it. Willingly, with delight and an eagerness that would probably embarrass her later. But now? Now she just wanted his lips, tongue and teeth on her with no mercy.

Those big, hard hands abandoned her hair and slid

down her back all the way to her ass, palming her, molding her. He bent at the knees and cupped the back of her thighs, hiking her in the air so she wound her legs around his waist.

Her breath expelled from her lungs into his mouth, and he swallowed it. The thick ridge of his cock rode the flesh between her legs, nudging her clit. Heat flashed through her, at both his show of strength and the hard length that stirred her pleasure, stroking against her over and over.

"Where are we going?" he growled against her lips, keeping up that insane rhythm against her sex.

Good God, how did he expect her to think, much less speak?

"Bedroom." She gasped as his cock head hit the sensitive bundle at the top of her folds. His pants and her leggings might as well as have been air, that's how insubstantial they were when it came to her pleasure. "That way. Second door. Right." She jerked her head in the direction of the hallway.

He strode toward the hall, his long strides eating up the hardwood floor. In just seconds, he entered her room and set her down on the bed. But quick as a flash she shot off the bed and set a palm to the middle of his chest. The chest that had zero give. A shiver rocked through her. Damn, the man could've been chiseled from marble.

She met his gaze, and the smoke there, the lust...

He might've used her that night to forget his anniversary, but she harbored no doubts that he desired her. Not with how he looked at her. Like he could break and remake her with the fire in those eyes.

And she'd let him.

She'd let him do every devastating, wondrous thing he wanted. Hell, she'd probably beg for it.

Not breaking their visual connection, she pushed him to the bed, and yes, she acknowledged that she only managed that because he allowed it. Still…he allowed it. And she intended to take full advantage of it. With slightly trembling hands, she shoved his coat from his shoulders. Then stripped his sweater from him, leaving him powerful and half-naked in front of her. Dropping both garments to the floor, she smoothed her hands over his shoulders and arms with a hum of appreciation, of pleasure. He was just so damn beautiful.

"What're you doing, baby?" he asked, his fingers threading through her hair again, fisting the strands.

She didn't answer, but continued rubbing her cheek over his pectoral muscle, over the flat nub of his nipple, the washboard ladder of his abs. Retracing the path with her lips, she tasted him, his unique flavor like a delicacy. Impatient, she attacked his slim belt and the closure on his pants, as well as his zipper. Moments later, she dipped her hand into his dark gray boxer briefs and wrapped her fingers around his thick, long cock.

Both of them moaned, their twin sounds of need saturating the air.

He throbbed in her hand, and she squeezed, stroking him from base to tip. A hiss escaped him, his hips

surging up to meet the pump of her hand, and that—
the twist and grind of his giant body at her machina-
tion—had a thrill spiraling through her. Had power
crackling over her like a lightning strike.

It was an aphrodisiac.

And yet…it wasn't nearly enough.

Bowing her head, she swept her tongue over the
flared head, the musky and delicious and addictive
flavor of him an immediate hit to her senses. She was
hooked. And there was no way she wasn't returning
for more of him.

A rumble like thunder rolled above her, and powerful thighs spread, made space for her even as he
held her in place with one hand in her hair and the
other cradling her jaw.

"Goddamn, look at you," he muttered, voice gut-
tural, raw, hungry. "So fucking beautiful, taking me."

His praise was a caress, and she bloomed under
it. Raising higher on her knees, she took more of
him, sliding him along her tongue until he nudged
the back of her throat. Deliberately breathing through
her nose, she relaxed her throat muscles and allowed
the tip of him to penetrate her. After a moment, she
pulled back, breathing hard, peppering kisses along
his length.

"Fuck," Joaquin rasped, harsh blasts of air punching the room as if he'd run a dash. "Again, baby.
Again. Please."

She obliged. He would never need to beg her.
Swirling her tongue around his bulbous tip, and
sucking on him, she sank down on him once more.

And his groan stroked over her ears, her nipples, the swollen, wet folds of her sex. One hand fisting the fat bottom half of him, she slid the other beneath her leggings, touching her slick flesh. She whimpered, and his fingers tightened in her hair, dragging her off his cock.

"Damn that." He tugged her head back, leaning over her and crushing his mouth to hers for a hard, brief and hot-as-hell kiss. "If you're going to get off, it's going to be on my dick, not your fingers."

With that proclamation, he lifted her off the floor and deposited her on the bed. Unlike in the VIP lounge, he stripped them both naked. Having his gorgeous, bare, big body pressing her down into her mattress, covering her from head to toe... Tears burned her eyes and she closed them, squeezed them tight. Wrapping her arms and legs around him, she clung to him and buried her face into his neck, this moment almost too much to contain.

His hand cupped the side of her face, tipping it back, giving her no choice but to meet his gaze.

"Ready, Nore? You with me?"

"Yes." She arched her back, rubbing her breasts against his chest, gasping at the bright, electric sensations pulsing through her at the contact. Twisting her hips, she ground her sex against his cock, pleading with her body for what she was starting to suspect only he could give her. "Inside me, Joaquin. Now."

He didn't make her wait. She'd barely finished the sentence before he surged forward, driving himself inside her to the hilt.

Full. So full.

She shifted beneath him, a fine edge of pain mixing deliciously with so much pleasure. They blended seamlessly, heightening each other until she couldn't stay still, couldn't stop…wanting.

"Please…" She twisted, bucked, whimpered. "Move, Joaquin. Please, move."

"Yeah." He grunted, slid his hands underneath her, palmed her ass and lifted her up, serving her to him. "God, yeah."

And he fucked her. Took her. Claimed her.

Broke her.

Remade her.

She wasn't coming out on the other side of this the same. It was more than his cock pistoning into her, dragging over nerve endings and setting them singing. More than him hitting a spot so high and deep inside her that it had her caught between crawling away from him and clinging to him. More than his fingers all over her sex, rubbing, circling, teasing, making her wetter, hotter. More than those raw, sexy sounds rumbling out of his throat as he pounded into her in a damn near primal rhythm.

It was more.

It was all of that.

With a desperate, needy cry, she reached down between them, and together they caressed her clit in tight, concise circles. And she snapped. In half. In pieces. She exploded so hard, it hurt. Oh God, it hurt. And she embraced that sweet, beautiful pain.

Above her, Joaquin thrust into her, his giant body

jerking, then stiffening over her. He grunted into her neck, and he pulsed deep inside her, filling the condom. The last thing she held on to before she tumbled into oblivion was the brush of his lips over her throat and the hoarse call of her name.

And how it sounded like a prayer.

# Thirteen

"Tell me about her?"

Joaquin blinked into the darkness, his arm around Nore's waist, his face pressed to her chest. Beneath the covers of her bed, their legs tangled, and the musky scent of sex hung thick in the air of her bedroom.

Their sex.

It should've felt wrong to talk about the one woman he'd loved and lost while wrapped around another woman, their damp skin pressed together, her heart beating under his ear. Should've. But it didn't. Madison had been his past. And this woman. Well… He didn't know what she was to him.

She was damn sure here in his present. But the thought of a future with her? It fucking terrified him.

Not when *her* past could so easily rip anything away from them. He'd had too much taken from him by his family. Too much. He'd vowed never to let them have that power over him again.

"You don't have to, Joaquin," Nore murmured, her fingers whispering through his hair, brushing over his temple. "Only if you want to."

"I want to," he said, his voice echoing back to him.

Shifting, he propped his shoulders on the mound of pillows, and before he could gather her close, Nore curled against his side, pressing her breasts to his chest and sliding her arm across his abdomen. She hooked her leg over his hip, her sex a damp, somehow comforting warmth on his thigh. He burrowed his fingers in her hair and slid his other arm under his head.

Staring at the ceiling, he continued, "I was twenty-seven when I met Madison at a fundraiser event. She was a beautiful woman—inside and out. For me, it was love at first sight." He laughed, and it was rough, ragged against his throat. "Sounds pretty pathetic for a man my age. Especially when she was twenty-three. But I fell. Hard. I knew, after just five months with her, that she was the woman I wanted to spend the rest of my life with."

"It doesn't sound pathetic. Not at all."

He let loose another chuckle, and closed his eyes, an echo of his humiliation burning in his throat, his chest, even after all these years.

"Oh, you weren't there. You didn't see me. I was an athlete. Not to sound like an asshole, but I was used to women throwing themselves at me. Used to them wanting things from me. I wasn't a fucking amateur with milk on his breath, and yet I didn't *see*. Not with Madison. I might as well as have been a teenager again. I did everything for her, bought her everything. Paid her bills. Just handed over cash. No questions asked. All because I loved her. What I didn't know was that she was playing me the whole time. Her and James."

A small, tight, pained sound escaped Nore, and her arm tightened around him. He tried to relax his body—he did. But he couldn't breathe past the tension. Couldn't talk himself through it. And with Nore naked in this bed with him, her scent drying on him, after just being inside her, he hated himself a little for it.

"You know this, though, right? That's how you know about Madison? James told you this part?"

"No." Her curls tickled his chin as she shook her head. "He didn't tell me much. Just hinted that you two were involved with the same woman, she chose him and you never forgave him for it. And he's been paying for it ever since."

"Right." His mouth curled in a bitter smile. "He has the victim role down to a science."

She pressed a kiss to his pec, settling her hand over his heart.

"Tell me."

"We were together for five months when I returned home early from a business trip and decided to surprise her. I went by her apartment but I was shocked when I walked up on her and James and overheard them arguing. About me. He wanted her to get more money from me because he had his eye on a Camaro. Since she'd just asked me for rent money, she couldn't hit me up again so soon, but James told her to get me to buy her a necklace or earrings so she could conveniently *lose* them and he could buy his car."

"Joaquin," she breathed.

Nore propped her elbow on his abdomen and stared down at him, her tawny eyes bright with anger for him but also so soft with hurt. Also for him. It warmed that chill lodged right under his ribs.

"God, I'm so sorry." She cupped his jaw, swept her thumb under his bottom lip. "No one deserves to be treated like that. Least of all you. You gave all of yourself and you should've received all of her in return. Not lies. Not betrayal. And definitely not from the people who are supposed to love you." Fire flashed in her eyes. "I *really*, really wish I knew you back then. I would've woken up every day and chosen violence on your behalf."

He wouldn't have thought himself capable of laughing with true amusement in this moment, but here he was. Laughing,

"What did you do? Did you confront them?"

"No, not right there." An image of Madison and James on that sidewalk in front of her apartment complex, haggling over him as if he were an item up for bid, rolled across his mind's eye like a film. Vivid, in color and in stark detail. "I left without either one of them noticing. Days later, when she expected my return, I invited her to my home for dinner, gifted her with a necklace and told her it would be the last one from me. She could decide to keep it or give it to James for his car."

"Damn," Nore breathed.

"Yeah, damn. At least she didn't try to pretend not to know what I meant. She admitted to first dating James and how he'd convinced her to *meet* me and con money out of me. James just wanted the cash, but her? Apparently, Madison's mother had stage three breast cancer and piss-poor insurance. It didn't cover all the medical bills, surgery and prescriptions. So she let him convince her to use me."

"She had a choice," Nore snapped, her fist thumping him on the chest. He tipped his gaze down from the ceiling to her again and her narrowed eyes spit fire at him. "Yes, her situation is sad and tragic, and this is coming from someone who lost her grandmother to cancer. But that doesn't give her an excuse or a free pass to use someone else and abuse their trust for her own ends. Her choices may have sucked, yes, but she had them. She could've come clean to you. How about that one? She had the option of coming to you and telling you the truth, and knowing you and your heart, you would've helped her. But she didn't. She continued to lie, and worse, squeeze money out of you to give to James. So not all of it was for altruistic, selfless purposes. No, she doesn't get a pass."

"Calm, baby." He lowered his arm and stroked a hand up and down her back.

She hiked up higher, shoving her face into his.

"You. Deserve. Better," she ground out.

He lifted his head up, pressing his mouth to hers, sliding his tongue over hers and tasting not just her unique flavor but the gift of unconditional kindness and support.

"Thank you for thinking that," he murmured against her lips.

"I don't want your thanks," she said. "I want you to believe it." She touched her forehead to his. "This isn't the end of your story, though. How did Madison end up your wife?"

A heaviness crawled into his body, infiltrated his chest and squatted.

"Three years later, we were visiting one of the local hospitals and dropping gifts off in the pediatric wing. On the way out, I saw Madison. She was waiting at one of the elevators that led to the towers for the oncology units. I thought it was for her mother, but it wasn't—it…"

"It was her," Nore breathed when Joaquin trailed off. "She had cancer."

"Stage four breast cancer." His throat constricted around the words. "The doctors had given her six months. I had her for a year."

"Did you marry her to give her medical care or because you still loved her or…?" Nore whispered.

"Yes," Joaquin said, the answer rushing out of him. "All of it. I saw her and the love hadn't diminished but neither had the hurt, the pain. But knowing her time on this earth could be counted in months, in fucking hours, I didn't care about that anymore. None of it mattered. And I didn't want her to worry about anything—not money, not bills, not anything—but taking care of herself and being happy and pain-free for however long she had. She'd already lost her mom, and she didn't have anyone else. But for a year, we had each other."

"You, Joaquin Nathan Iverson, are a real-life hero."

He jolted, and he stared at her, speechless. No one had ever, *ever* called him that. Not even at the height of his racing career.

"How can you say that? You heard the first part of my story where I was a fucking patsy, right? I willingly wore blinders and let myself be played by my brother? And it isn't heroic to take care of a dying woman who I happened to love. That's just being human."

She smiled, and it struck him as wistful, sad.

"You just proved my point. Not everyone would do what you did, Joaquin. Most people wouldn't marry a person they would lose in months. A person who, sad but true, they would see as a debt, a burden. And that's not even considering what Madison had done to you in the past. So excuse me if I still see you as one hell of a person. And I think if Madison was alive, she would agree with me." Given her fierce tone, Joaquin decided against arguing with her. That and the emotion piling into his throat wouldn't allow him. "And as for being played, well..." She sighed, falling to the pillows beside him, her shoulder bumping his. "Ask me how James became my business partner."

"How did James become your business partner?"

When she didn't immediately answer, he turned his head and looked at her. She now stared at the ceiling.

"I fell in love. Short and not so sweet. You want to talk about being willfully blind? That was me." She shrugged a shoulder, the movement restless. Maybe embarrassed. "I met him at an event I threw for a client, and he was a guest there. Sound familiar?" She slid a glance at him.

"Please don't compare what happened between us to you and him," he growled.

"That's fair." She frowned. "It didn't happen like that with him and me anyway. It wasn't...combustible. More gradual. He pursued me, and I admit it, I was flattered." She chuckled but it was dry, brittle. "Flattered and enthralled that someone as handsome and charming as James chased me. And when he caught me, he didn't let up. At least not at first. But there were other signs that he wasn't all that he seemed. I just didn't want to see, so I missed them."

She turned her head, met his stare. And they looked at each like that for several long moments. It should've been uncomfortable, awkward. But instead, he could've remained like that, gazing at her, into those beautiful golden eyes, for hours.

"The first time he suggested that he invest in my company, I laughed it off. He worked at one of those clothing retail companies at the time, and he said he wasn't happy. I could understand that, but what did he

know about event planning? And the Main Event...
it's mine. I built it, was the sole proprietor, and after
a lifetime of hand-me-downs and secondhand everything, it was the first thing that was *only* mine and
earned from my own hard work. So no, I didn't want
to share it. Not even with the man I'd fallen in love
with. But James is persuasive. And by the third time
he asked, we'd been together for a little over two years
and I said yes. Because he'd proposed, we were going
to be married. And if I'd share the rest of my life with
this man, why wouldn't I share my business? At least
that's the argument he made, and it was a good one."

She scoffed and rubbed her palm over her chest,
right over her heart. As if a pain pulsed under the
spot.

"As soon as he gave me that check for twenty thousand dollars and I gave him the title of chief operating
officer, he changed. Gone was the attentive, charming, loving man I became engaged to, who made me
feel like a priority. Who I'd been in a relationship
with for two years. He'd been replaced with a selfish,
spoiled, lazy critical boy with a God complex. And
he now owned part of my company."

"Baby," he murmured.

Sitting up and propping his shoulders against the
headboard, he drew her into his arms. He brushed a
kiss across her forehead, and her hand curled around
his neck as if grounding herself. And he hoped he
could be that anchor for her.

"Has he harmed your business?"

Her small puff of breath caressed his clavicle.

"Depends on your definition of harm. Has he actively sought to destroy it? No. But he's deadweight. A suck on our resources, man power and finances. He spends, but brings nothing in. I've paid back his investment three times over in the year since he's given it to me, and still he refuses to let me buy him out. James likes having the title of COO too much, but likes none of the work. And then he decided he'd rather have the company and not the fiancée." She fell quiet, and when she spoke again, her voice was barely audible. "I sold a part of my company away for love. And every day I have to stare the consequences of my decisions in the face."

Joaquin flipped Nore over, pulling her under him and sliding inside her. Then, when the silken, hot clasp of her felt too damn wet, too damn good, he withdrew, reached for his wallet and a condom, and sheathed himself. In seconds, he wedged himself back between her thighs and thrust deep in her sex again, her sigh of pleasure echoing in his ear.

"No consoling words? No pep talk?" she gasped, arching tight against him.

"Fuck him." He slid free until only his tip remained inside her, then slowly pushed back in, twisting his hips and rubbing the base of his cock against her clit. Her throaty laughter ended on a whimper. "Fuck him for not seeing who he had in front of him."

Another thrust.

"Fuck him for taking your love and not treasuring it as the gift it was."

Thrust and twist.

She cried out.

"And fuck him for fucking up. None of it was, or is, on you. You, Nore Daniels, are fucking perfect."

Then he proceeded to show her just how perfect.

# Fourteen

At the knock on her office door, Nore smothered a groan.

Dammit.

And her morning had been going so well. The caterer for Greer Motorcycles' launch had come up with a great themed menu and a tasting. The speakeasy had sent over the drinks menu as well. Shorty had sent over the guest list and only a few people hadn't RSVP'd. Also, Nore had a new client consultation scheduled in a couple of hours with a Fortune 500 company.

But now James stood in her doorway like a harbinger of doom.

And Mona Whitehead stood right beside him.

Just…dammit.

Had it been only four nights ago that she'd curled next to Joaquin, exhausted from a night of maki—sex.

Sex.

Pump the brakes on that.

Her heart thudded against her sternum. Last time she'd moved so fast, it'd ended in disaster and that disaster strolled into her office, uninvited, once again. That disaster ended in her selling away a part of her dream.

*The fantasy always felt good when it started out, but when the gloss faded...*

But this felt different. Joaquin was different.

*They all feel different.*

God, and here she sat, arguing with herself. She sighed. All signs pointed to "not good."

"James," she said, rising from her chair and rounding the desk. She held her hand out to his mother. "Mona, this is a surprise."

"A pleasant one, I hope." Mona smiled and pulled Nora in for a hug, the older woman's light lilac scent familiar and yes, comforting.

For three years, Mona had been a mother figure to Nore, and even with the tales of how horrible she'd treated Joaquin ringing in her head, Nore's own memories warred against those tales. How could the doting, at times funny, woman she'd known wear the same cruel, harmful face Joaquin had experienced?

"Of course. It's good to see you," Nore murmured, hurt and confusion swirling inside her. "How're you doing?"

"Fine, fine. But I don't like not seeing you as much as I used to. Just because you and James are no longer dating doesn't mean you should be a stranger. I still see you as the daughter I was never blessed with." She patted Nore's arm. "And it's not like you and James are no longer connected since you continue to run a business together."

"This is true." Nore slid a glance at James, who leaned a shoulder against her window. This wasn't the first time Mona had shown up at the office. In the past, she'd visited to take Nore out to lunch or to see James. But a kernel of unease rooted in her belly, twisting. This wasn't an impromptu, innocent visit. She just knew it. "What brings you by today? Just wanted to see James?"

"Always, but I wanted to talk to you as well."

The sense of foreboding deepened, but she forced a smile and waved toward an empty chair, taking the other one.

"Please, sit. What can I do for you?" Although she had a suspicion *exactly* what this visit entailed.

"Well, I have to tell you, Nore, I've been talking to my son, and what I've been hearing saddens and worries me. He's told me that my other son has been sowing strife here at work between you two. And I hate that for you." Mona covered Nore's hand, squeezing it. "James and you aren't together, but you have a company to run and it's been going so well. It's been so successful. I don't want to see Nathan come in and ruin that for you."

Anger stirred, and she deliberately fought the urge

to snatch her hand from under the older woman's. Did she hear herself? Or did she just not care?

Yes, that was most likely the case. She didn't give a damn. Not about what she said and not about her older son.

"Like I told James, taking the Greer Motorcycles account is great for the Main Event. Not just financially but for the connections it will bring. Now, let me apologize that your son brought confidential company business to you when that is not only unethical but also illegal. He shouldn't have burdened you with that," she said, voice so sweet she hoped they both ended up with dentist appointments after this conversation.

Mona's lips firmed before she smiled, but the corners were pulled taut. With narrowed eyes, she tilted her head.

"He just had so much on his mind that he wanted to talk to his mother since Nathan is his brother."

"About the Main Event's business. And if there is strife, then James has it within himself. I don't have a problem with Greer Motorcycles. And since James isn't working on the account *at all* in *any way whatsoever*, he shouldn't either. Unless this has nothing to do with the account after all, and this visit and this conversation have everything to do with his brother and your son. Which would make it personal. Which would mean it has no place here. At my company. In my office."

"You mean, *our* company," James interjected for the first time.

"Oh, welcome to the conversation," she drawled. "I was wondering if you were going to participate or just let your mother be your mouthpiece. And don't fool yourself. Thirty-five percent doesn't make this our company. I still run it. I still own it. I still have the power. You're just a glorified employee. And even if you never sell that thirty-five percent back to me you will never be what you desperately want—Joaquin."

Mona gasped as crimson poured into James's face. He shoved off the wall, and Nore notched up her chin. And smiled.

"Excuse me," Mona snapped, shooting up from her chair.

Nore stood as well, the anger that had been embers combusting into a five-alarm fire.

"Now, I don't want to disrespect you, so I'm going to ask you to leave my office before I lose my restraint. I refuse to discuss company business with you. I'm not your son. I will say this, though. You have two sons. And the oldest's given name is Joaquin. Not Nathan. And he's worth two of the one standing over there. Now, if you'll excuse me…"

She turned and strode to the door—and drew up short.

Because Joaquin stood in the doorway.

Damn.

He stared at her, his expression carved out of stone, gray eyes hooded, unreadable. After a moment, they left her and shifted to his mother and James.

"Nore." Pause. "Mom. James."

"Isn't this convenient?" James sneered, glancing

from James to Nore. "We were talking about you, Nathan. I'm sorry, *Joaquin.*"

*You can't leap across this room and put your hands on him. You implemented the no-tolerance policy yourself. And you can't even handle an episode of* 60 Days In *without cringing.*

The reminders did only a little to calm her. She still wanted to lay James out.

Joaquin arched an eyebrow. "Is that so?"

"No," Nore ground out from between gritted teeth. "James was getting ready to escort your mother out because we have nothing further to discuss. Nice to see you again, Mona. Bye, James."

"Not so fast." James crossed his arms, and the corner of his mouth curled.

The devil probably wore the same smile. Possessed the same glint in his—or her—eye. Mean. Vindictive.

"I'm glad you arrived when you did," James said to Joaquin, though he continued to look at her. "We were having a conversation about strife in the company, and frankly, I think it's time to clear the air. Nath— I mean, *Joaquin,*" he stressed again, and Joaquin's eyes narrowed on his brother, "I've had a problem with Nore taking on your account, but that shouldn't be a shock to you considering our...relationship. And at first, Nore was adamant about keeping Greer as a client. But after I explained how much this affected and hurt me, she agreed to have my back as a loyal girlfriend and coworker would."

Icy dread spread through her like a virus, impossible to root out. It froze her voice box, paralyzing her, and she could only stare in horror as James spun his lies like a malicious spider.

"When she went on that tour at your factory, I asked her to gather details and take notes of that new model of yours. See what we could do with it. Things like that could be valuable for your competitors. Bring some good money in our pockets." His smile widened into a grin that he turned on Joaquin. "Sounds familiar, doesn't it? Worked once, I figured it could again."

Joaquin's face hardened, but he didn't say a word. Hell, she couldn't tell if he even breathed.

Fine. She had more than enough words for both of them.

"Get out." The order emerged as a ragged whisper. "Get. Out. Now," Nore repeated, and this time it was louder. Strained and hoarse, but louder and firmer. "You are beyond mean and petty. You're pathetic, jealous and small. You're such a horrible little boy because you're damn sure not a man." She switched her attention to Mona. "This is all your fault. If you hadn't raised him—and I use the term very loosely—pitted against his older brother, making him think the sun rose and set out of his rotten ass, he wouldn't be so worthless and corrupt. Now you are responsible not just for the piece of crap he is, but for every life he damages. That's on you. I hope you can live with it. But honestly, I don't give a damn if you can or if you can't. Both of you, out of my office. Now. Or, my elder or not, part owner or not, I'll call security and have them escort you out."

James, for once, used common sense—or his sense

of self-preservation—and guided his mother out. She sputtered the whole way, but never did she say a word to Joaquin. And that sent Nore's temper skyrocketing several more degrees. Only Joaquin's still-stony visage kept her rooted. Because James's lies echoed in that office like a death knell.

Madison had betrayed him with James, with lies.

And now James, knowing just where to drive the knife, had thrust and twisted it, using Nore as the weapon.

"Joaquin." She moved forward, her hands stretched toward him. But then she drew up short, lowering her arms. "James lied. I never planned to betray you."

He arched an eyebrow. "All of that? He made it up?"

She splayed her hands wide, palms up. "Yes, no." She briefly closed her eyes, then opened them, met his. "No, he didn't make up the part about approaching me with the plan to take notes about the KING One to your competitors. But I turned that down flat. I would never do that to you. And I told him that."

"But you also didn't tell me about what he proposed. Why?" he asked in that same cold, flat voice.

"I forgot about it, Joaquin," she whispered, risking taking a step forward, her hands stretched toward him. "I honestly forgot because it was so ridiculous that I didn't give it a second thought. I'm sorry I didn't mention it to you. But tell me you believe me."

"I do."

Relief coursed through her. But as fast as it swelled, it disappeared. Evaporated. Because he didn't move toward her. Didn't clasp her hands in his. His expression didn't soften. Those eyes didn't gentle.

"You do?" she asked.

"Yes," he said. "James has never told the truth and I don't know why he would suddenly start today."

She huffed out a breath. "So it's not so much that you believe me as you're aware your brother is a snake. I'm not sure if I should be offended or grateful." She studied him for several long moments, and that seed of dread that had taken root in her belly earlier bloomed. Her breath whistled in her ears and it was all she heard. "Maybe I should hold off on that gratefulness," she murmured. "Say it."

"Nore," he said.

"No." She shook her head. Shook it hard. "Say it. Or wait." She shot up a hand. "Let me say it for you. We're done. Whatever we had or started to have. Or were on our way to having. It's over. There. Am I right? Did I say it okay?"

His lashes lowered, but then they lifted and he pinned her with a piercing stare that stole her breath. Propelled it right from her body and left a red-hot pain in its wake.

This was what she got for daring to open up again. For sharing her body.

For giving her heart.

When would she learn?

"What I walked in on, Nore... I distance myself from it. By choice. I had to grow up with that shit and I damn sure don't want it around my company. I thought it would stay separate, but I walk in with my mother and brother discussing it. And James even going so far as threatening everything I've worked for. I can't risk it. I *won't* risk it. I fooled myself by thinking I could keep you separate from your past with him. It's not possible. And I won't put everything on the line. Again."

"Because this—" she waved a hand back and forth between them "—isn't worth it. I'm," she whispered, the desperate, god-awful truth of it hitting her even as she said it, "not worth it."

"Baby," he murmured, stepping forward, but she shuffled backward.

"No. You don't get to call me that, and you definitely don't get to touch me. Not now. Not ever. You know, I'm so tired of being second, third or not even a consideration in people's lives. Of being good enough for the 'meantime' but never the 'forever.' Of not being worthy of the fight. Well, today has shown me something. Has revealed something. I've always shown up for everyone else, but not for myself. It's time I place myself number one. Time I fight for myself. Because I am worthy. And I'm more than worth the risk. But you can't stop being Mona and James's victim long enough to see what's right in front of your face."

She took another step back.

And then another.

"If you decide that you no longer want us to plan Greer's launch, I understand. If that's the case, please let us know in writing. Until then, we don't have a scheduled meeting, and I have a busy day, so if you could see yourself to the door?"

She turned and headed to her desk, not sinking to her chair until she heard the office door quietly close. And even then, she didn't sit. She reached for her cell, pulled up her Favorites list and selected the top name. It rang once before the call connected.

"Hey, woman," Tatum warmly greeted.

"Tate, I need you," Nore rasped.

"I got you."

# Fifteen

"I figured I'd find you here."

Joaquin didn't glance up from cleaning the handlebar on his Kawasaki KZ900. Not even when Bran set a case of beer on the workstation of his garage.

"You can try to ignore me, but I'm not going away. I will drink all of your beer, though," Bran threatened. Although it was more of a promise than threat. His friend would follow through.

Heaving a sigh, Joaquin tossed down his rag in the pail next to his motorcycle—one of several bikes in the collection he housed in his garage—and rose to his feet. Crossing over to his friend, he grabbed one of the beers, twisted the cap off and tipped it to his mouth.

"Thanks," he said, wiping his lips with the back of

his hand. Because he had manners like that. "You've checked on me. You can tell Shorty I'm still breathing. Mission accomplished. There's the door but I'm keeping the beer. Bring an IPA next time."

"You're an ungrateful lil' shit," Bran said. And jumped up on the station, doing the *exact opposite* of leaving. "In the ten years of Greer Motorcycles' existence, you've been out of the office one time outside of business trips. And that's because you had pneumonia. Even then we had to force you to stay in bed and ban you from the building."

"I remember since I was there. Or rather, not there," Joaquin drawled.

"But you haven't been to the office in the last four days. Excuse us if we're a little concerned and want to make sure you haven't gone for one of your little dips and decided not to swim back for the shore this time."

Joaquin slowly lowered his beer bottle and set it down on the counter with a dull thud, his gaze not leaving his partner and friend.

"Didn't think I knew about that, did you?" Bran murmured. "Yeah, I do."

"I've never considered not swimming back," Joaquin quietly said.

Bran's gaze roamed his face, and after several moments, his friend nodded.

"We all need to silence the noise every once in a while. I get it, brother, I really do." He moved forward, clapped him on the shoulder. "But when do you stop using a jump in the water as a stopgap? You've let your past dictate your present and your future for too long. When do you stop running and start living? I knew your dad. Family and freedom. Those two things are what he valued above all else. And he wanted them for you. He would've hated knowing you were tied to your past—a past that included him."

His chin jerked back as if struck.

"What're you talking about? Dad—finding him, my time with him—was the happiest part of my life…"

"And yet you wear it like chains. Yeah, in some ways, you let him and your time with him motivate you, propel you forward. Like with Greer and the KING One. But in other ways, you let it hold you back, keep you bound. Keep you afraid to love. Afraid to lose. He would be the first to tell you, yeah, shit went to hell with your mother, but he got you out of it, so he would deal with her all over again just to have you. And again, yeah, he only had a few short years with you. But they were the best of his life, and so worth it. You were worth it. Family and love are worth it. Are worth risking everything."

*I'm so tired of being second, third or not even a consideration in people's lives. Of being good enough for a "meantime" but never the "forever." Of not being worthy of the fight.*

Joaquin closed his eyes, pinched the bridge of his nose. What had he done? Had he actually walked out of that office letting her think she wasn't worth the fight? Not just first in his life, but *his life*? When the truth was he was fucking terrified. He was scared to lose. Scared she would find him unworthy. Scared she would walk away from him like others had before.

Just…scared.

But he couldn't live like that anymore. Couldn't live alone, a terrified boy in a man's body.

Couldn't live without…her.

Somewhere between spying her across a crowded club and Main Street Disney, he'd fallen in love with her. And now he'd probably lost her for good. But he couldn't go down without trying to get her back.

Worthy of a fight? He'd show her a hell of one.

"Is our come-to-Jesus moment over? Because I have a case of beer to finish off." Bran held up another beer.

"Bring it up to the house." Joaquin smiled, and it was his first real one in days. "We have work to do."

"It's about damn time," Bran grumbled.

Yeah, it was.

# Sixteen

"I still can't believe you're here so close to your wedding. You shouldn't be, you know," Nore admonished Tatum, sliding an arm around her best friend's waist and squeezing.

A part of her still couldn't believe Tatum stood there with her. A week ago, she'd called Tatum, crying after Joaquin had left her office, and the very next day, her friend had shown up on her doorstep, luggage in hand. And she hadn't left her since. Even though Nore had assured her she could.

Still, Nore was secretly delighted Tatum had stayed. Damn, it felt good to have her here. When dealing with a broken heart, a girl needed her best friend. But she couldn't be selfish too much longer. Tatum had a wedding to attend in three more weeks, after all. If she had to stuff the woman in her own Louis Vuitton suitcase, Tatum was returning to Boston tomorrow.

"Listen, when my best friend needs me, I'm there. Mark understands. It's girl code," Tatum assured her as they entered the Main Event's lobby. She'd shown up to take Nore to lunch, and damn, had she mentioned how much she was going to miss her? "Besides, I'm going to see you soon when you come to Boston before the wedding to help me stay sane. And by that I mean run interference with Mark's mother." Tatum rolled her eyes. "Lord, I love her but she's driving me *crazy.*"

Laughing, Nore held up a hand, pinkie extended. "I solemnly swear to cockblock your mother-in-law."

*"Oh God."* Tatum slapped her hand down. "Please promise to not say cockblock around my mother-in-law. Promise on your Backstreet Boys poster."

Nore gasped, splaying her fingers wide over her chest. "You go too far. I'll swear on the NSYNC poster but not Backstreet Boys."

"Bitch," Tatum muttered.

They eyed each other, snickered. Then dissolved into cackles.

"I love you, woman," Nore whispered. "Thank you for…everything. For being here."

"Always."

They moved at the same time, hugging each other tight.

"Uh, excuse me. I hate to interrupt this beautiful Hallmark moment," Bastien said from behind them.

"And yet you did." Nore turned around, giving him side-eye.

He grinned, completely unrepentant. "This is true. But I have a question." He lifted his chin toward the hall leading to the main offices. "I'm just wondering why James's office is completely cleaned out. And if you were aware of it."

Nore blinked. And blinked again because surely she hadn't heard him correctly.

It'd been several days since she'd seen James, but she'd assumed he had been smart for once in his life and was avoiding her. His office door had been closed, and she hadn't gone knocking. But apparently there seemed to be another reason behind that closed door.

She glanced from Bastien to Tatum, who looked at her. And Nore wondered if the hope she spied in Tatum's eyes reflected in her own.

"You don't think…?" Tatum whispered.

Hope lifted her head, and for a moment, Nore let her rise. But only for a moment. Then she pushed her back down. She was through playing with that heffa. In the past few days, she'd given hope too much credit, and she was done with her antics. First, with love, and now with James?

Nope. Not going there.

"No." Nore shook her head. "James willingly walk away from a free paycheck? Not happening."

Tatum scrunched her nose. "Point taken." She tugged on her elbow. "But we have to check out this empty office. Make sure it's not a figment of our imagination. What could it mean then?"

"That he's moved into mine?" Nore muttered, only half joking. Because she would *not* put it past him.

The three of them headed down the hall and paused in front of James's closed office door. Bastien swung it open and she slowly exhaled, staring at the vacant room, where only a desk, a couple of chairs and a file cabinet remained. Nothing personal of him lingered, and once more, hope tried to rise inside her, more persistent. It stayed longer this time before she snuffed it out. Before she could be bitterly disappointed.

Because she knew James Whitehead. And he simply would not walk away. Not when she'd damn near begged with words, tears and money to get him to do it.

Yet this...didn't make sense either.

"Where did he go?" Bastien whispered as if they stood on the doorstep of a church instead of an empty room.

"To hell, hopefully," Tatum grumbled.

Nore snorted. "You've been hanging around me way too long. Your mother would be perfectly mortified to hear that come out of your mouth."

Tatum acknowledged that with a smile and shrug.

"James isn't here and he's not coming back."

*Holy shit, that voice.*

Tatum and Bastien whipped around, but Nore didn't.

That voice. The cotton-and-gravel texture of it

had resonated within her from the first moment she'd heard it months ago, and it did now. She smothered the shiver it elicited, refusing to give him that reaction, because those silver eyes would see it; they missed nothing. They never had.

Slowly, she turned around and met Joaquin's gaze.

"Joaquin," she said, proud her voice remained calm, even, when everything inside her screamed. "What are you doing here?"

"Two reasons. To break the news about James leaving the Main Event, effective immediately. Well, as of nine last night."

He had to be lying. And as soon as her heart found its way from her throat and back to her chest, she would demand he tell her the truth.

"How would you know that information?" Tatum asked, her tone slightly belligerent. To be expected since Nore had spent the last week eating ice cream, crying and watching Netflix over this man.

Still, thank God she could ask him because Nore continued to struggle with her breathing.

Joaquin glanced at Tatum but his attention switched back to Nore and held. And that stare touched her to her soul. Maybe deeper. It wasn't fair. He'd rejected her.

He'd hurt her.

She didn't want him to touch her.

"I know because he signed a contract last night returning his thirty-five percent ownership to Nore for a one-time payment of five hundred thousand dollars."

She was going to faint. A dull roar filled her head.

*Five hundred thou—*

She didn't have that kind of money. Her company did well but… *Oh God.*

"You?" she rasped.

Joaquin nodded, his intense gaze never leaving hers.

"I'm surprised the asshole didn't try to hold out for more," Tatum bit out.

"You said it," Bastien muttered.

"He did." Joaquin smiled, and the warmth in it penetrated Nore's shock. "But I told him he would take the five hundred or I would sue him for breach of contract since he had shared confidential information about my launch with our mother. And since my attorney advised me I could sue either the Main Event or him personally—and I assured James I would choose him—he accepted the proposal on the table."

"You have never offered him money before. You've never given him money before. Not even a job. Why now?" Nore whispered.

And hope, dammit, that insistent wench wouldn't leave her alone. Unlike before, Nore didn't push her away. She let her stay.

Joaquin studied her, his gaze a physical touch that she shook under. And this time, she didn't try to hide it.

"Because you—your happiness, your security, your peace, your dreams—are more important to me than my past with him. I want to wake up to you every morning. Watch a sunrise with you. Take you for your first motorcycle ride. Stand by your side while you continue to pursue and succeed in your career. I want it all. And I want it free of pain and resentment and bitterness. I can't love you as you deserve and still hold on to the past. So that's another reason I paid James off. I was letting go. For both of us."

"You said there were two reasons," she said, her voice almost nonexistent.

Tears stung her eyes, and she blinked them back. Beside her, Tatum clasped her hand, squeezing.

Joaquin shrugged a wide shoulder.

"You. That big and that simple. You. I love you, Nore."

The first tear escaped and she wiped it away. Joaquin took a step toward her, but she held up a hand, forestalling him.

"No." She shook her head. "You hurt me."

"I know, baby. And I'm so sorry."

"And I'm not one of those fairy-tale damsels that need to be rescued."

"I know that, too. It's a privilege to be by your side and watch you battle for yourself."

She nodded.

Then practically leaped across the few feet separating them and threw herself into his arms and crushing her mouth to his. His groan was a balm to her battered soul as his lips parted and kissed her with a passion that left her breathless and hungry for an hour and an empty office. Thank God they now had one right behind them.

"I love you," she murmured, peppering his chin and jaw with kisses. "I'm so in love with you."

He laughed, and his arms locked tight around her, lifting her clean off the floor.

"Baby, I didn't think I would hear those words from you. I love you more."

He took her mouth again, and she gave in to the sweetest, hottest kiss.

Tipping her head back, she grinned up at Joaquin, trailing her fingertips through his beard.

"Ask me again if I believe in soulmates and destiny," she said, reminding him of the question he'd put to her during their Disneyland outing.

He smiled and pressed his lips to her forehead, her nose and finally, her lips.

"Do you believe in that? Soulmates and destiny?"

"I'm looking at you, so yes. Yes, I do."

# Epilogue

"So I actually get to hold the famous brooch."

Nore peered over her shoulder at Joaquin as he cradled the brooch, and the beautiful piece appeared even more delicate in his big hand.

A hand he'd just used to gift her with an orgasm that answered the question that yes, indeed, life did exist on Saturn, thank you very much.

God, she loved that hand.

And him.

"Yes, and here." She passed him several sheets of white tissue paper and a silver-and-white gift box. "Would you wrap that for me? I need to finish packing if I'm going to make it to the airport on time."

Still studying the jewelry, Joaquin accepted the paper and box, and she returned to folding up the clothes she needed for her trip to Boston. Tatum's wedding wasn't for another week, but they'd planned for her to come out ahead of time to help with last-minute details. Such as Plan Mother-in-Law. That would be in full effect as soon as Nore landed at Logan.

"Do you really believe in the legend?"

Nore glanced up from placing the stilettos that would go with her maid of honor's dress into her suitcase to look at Joaquin. He still held the brooch, his head cocked to the side, and he seemed fascinated by it.

Stepping away from her bed and luggage, she walked over and paused in front of him, staring down at the jewelry as well. Unable to not touch him when so close, she encircled his wrist, feeling his strong pulse under her fingers.

God, she loved him.

It'd been only weeks since he'd shown up at her office declaring his love for her in something out of a straight-to-streaming romance movie, and she'd fallen deeper in love with him every day. She suspected it would always be like that, and considering she planned on spending a lot of years with him, that was a long plunge.

She was okay with that, too.

Especially since she knew she wouldn't be taking the plunge alone.

"I don't know," she said, answering his question. "I mean, it brought me to you. And our path damn sure wasn't easy." She chuckled. "But I believe more than anything, our love is true and lasting." With a shrug, she leaned her head back and smiled up at him. "So yes, I guess I do believe in the legend."

His solemn, quiet gaze moved from the brooch to her face, and it roamed over her for several seconds before meeting her eyes.

"I do, too, baby. I do, too."

\* \* \* \* \*

*Don't miss these other sizzling stories from Naima Simone!*

Vows in Name Only
Secrets of a One Night Stand
The Perfect Fake Date
Black Sheep Bargain

## SECOND CHANCE RANCHER & FAKE DATING, TWIN STYLE

### SECOND CHANCE RANCHER

*Heirs of Hardwell Ranch* • by J. Margot Critch

After a Vegas wedding, billionaire black sheep Wes Hardwell returns to Texas intent on divorce. But his brief "honeymoon" to get Daisy Thorne out of his system makes him question if Texas *and* Daisy are the happily-ever-after he's been yearning for.

### FAKE DATING, TWIN STYLE

*The Hartmann Heirs* • by Katie Frey

After her latest fender bender, serial bad driver Amelia Hartmann needs a solution—fast. Pretending to be her celebrity twin is the best solution. Except the other driver is former NFL star Antone Williams. And he's determined to find—and seduce—the Hartmann sister who crashed into his life!

## JUST A LITTLE JILTED & THEIR TEMPORARY ARRANGEMENT

### JUST A LITTLE JILTED

*Dynasties: Calcott Manor* • by Joss Wood

Jilted by her boss *and* her famous, superficial fiancé, model Eliot Gamble needs a life reset. But an unexpected, steamy weekend in Soren Grantham's bed works, too! The competitive swimmer is stunned by Eliot's depth and passion. Is love the next step they've both yearned for?

### THEIR TEMPORARY ARRANGEMENT

*Dynasties: Calcott Manor* • by Joss Wood

Personal assistant Ru Osman is tired of people trying to control her—including her new boss! But the notoriously difficult Fox Grantham is more consumed with seducing her than replacing her. Will passion and purpose collide for these professional opposites?

## BLUE BLOOD MEETS BLUE COLLAR & ONE STORMY NIGHT

### BLUE BLOOD MEETS BLUE COLLAR

*The Renaud Brothers* • by Cynthia St. Aubin

Single dad Remy Renaud doesn't remember his one night with television producer Cosima Lowell. Which is fine by Cosima, because filming his family for a reality show is the professional break she needs...if the embers of their connection don't set both their worlds ablaze.

### ONE STORMY NIGHT

*Business and Babies* • by Jules Bennett

When a storm strands Mila Hale with her potential new boss, she plans to keep things all business. But playboy Cruz Westbrook is too reckless, too wild and too damn sexy—and determined to indulge in unbridled passion until he finds the one...

You can find more information on upcoming Harlequin titles,
free excerpts and more at Harlequin.com.

HD2in | CNM0323

# Get 4 FREE REWARDS!

**We'll send you 2 FREE Books <u>plus</u> 2 FREE Mystery Gifts.**

**FREE** Value Over **$20**

Both the **Harlequin® Desire** and **Harlequin Presents®** series feature compelling novels filled with passion, sensuality and intriguing scandals.

---

**YES!** Please send me 2 FREE novels from the Harlequin Desire or Harlequin Presents series and my 2 FREE gifts (gifts are worth about $10 retail). After receiving them, if I don't wish to receive any more books, I can return the shipping statement marked "cancel." If I don't cancel, I will receive 6 brand-new Harlequin Presents Larger-Print books every month and be billed just $6.30 each in the U.S. or $6.49 each in Canada, a savings of at least 10% off the cover price, or 6 Harlequin Desire books every month and be billed just $5.05 each in the U.S. or $5.74 each in Canada, a savings of at least 12% off the cover price. It's quite a bargain! Shipping and handling is just 50¢ per book in the U.S. and $1.25 per book in Canada.* I understand that accepting the 2 free books and gifts places me under no obligation to buy anything. I can always return a shipment and cancel at any time by calling the number below. The free books and gifts are mine to keep no matter what I decide.

Choose one: ☐ **Harlequin Desire**
(225/326 HDN GRJ7)

☐ **Harlequin Presents Larger-Print**
(176/376 HDN GRJ7)

Name (please print)

Address                                                                                                      Apt. #

City                                        State/Province                              Zip/Postal Code

**Email:** Please check this box ☐ if you would like to receive newsletters and promotional emails from Harlequin Enterprises ULC and its affiliates. You can unsubscribe anytime.

---

Mail to the **Harlequin Reader Service:**
**IN U.S.A.:** P.O. Box 1341, Buffalo, NY 14240-8531
**IN CANADA:** P.O. Box 603, Fort Erie, Ontario L2A 5X3

**Want to try 2 free books from another series!** Call 1-800-873-8635 or visit www.ReaderService.com.

---

*Terms and prices subject to change without notice. Prices do not include sales taxes, which will be charged (if applicable) based on your state or country of residence. Canadian residents will be charged applicable taxes. Offer not valid in Quebec. This offer is limited to one order per household. Books received may not be as shown. Not valid for current subscribers to the Harlequin Presents or Harlequin Desire series. All orders subject to approval. Credit or debit balances in a customer's account(s) may be offset by any other outstanding balance owed by or to the customer. Please allow 4 to 6 weeks for delivery. Offer available while quantities last.

**Your Privacy**—Your information is being collected by Harlequin Enterprises ULC, operating as Harlequin Reader Service. For a complete summary of the information we collect, how we use this information and to whom it is disclosed, please visit our privacy notice located at corporate.harlequin.com/privacy-notice. From time to time we may also exchange your personal information with reputable third parties. If you wish to opt out of this sharing of your personal information, please visit readerservice.com/consumerschoice or call 1-800-873-8635. **Notice to California Residents**—Under California law, you have specific rights to control and access your data. For more information on these rights and how to exercise them, visit corporate.harlequin.com/california-privacy.

HDHP22R3

# HARLEQUIN
## PLUS

Try the best multimedia subscription service for romance readers like you!

---

## Read, Watch and Play.

Experience the easiest way to get the romance content you crave.

Start your **FREE TRIAL** at
www.harlequinplus.com/freetrial.